Everlasting Rain

Siobhán O'Connor

Copyright © 2023 Siobhan O'Connor

All rights reserved.

ISBN: 9781399962179

Purple Anchor Press

DEDICATION

When I started writing this story ten years ago, I had no idea it would become such a big part of my life. It's an odd feeling now being able to invite everyone into a world that has only ever existed inside my head.

I am grateful to my editors (of Spanish and English languages), proofreaders (especially my mother), and everyone who has shown an interest over the years. Mostly, I am grateful that I never gave up, and I have now accomplished a lifelong dream of seeing my work in print.

In the year 2501, sorcery emerged in some humans as a genetic disorder. By 2523, Earth's tectonic plates had been disrupted by Elemental sorcerers, destroying the Ancestor world. Magic was outlawed. Countries split into tiny islands over the next few millennia, forgetting their origins, and a new world power emerged called The Tripartite: a trio of Sovereigns, Scours, and Swashbucklers ruthlessly competing for rulership of the Islands of Na'Revas.

A hastily drawn map of the Islands of Na'Revas by Ximo Palomino, Year 4119

PROLOGUE: CRYING SKY

September, Year 4111
Ortivana Island

It rained for the first time in a millennium; that was the first sign I should have run.

I yanked free from Father's grip and lost him in the crowd for a split second, wondering if this was my chance. He pulled me close again, and we continued our midnight seance, merging with the nobility gathered by the gallows in *An Caisleán* Courtyard in the centre of the capital, Ortiva City.

I huddled into him, my face pressed against Father's shabby trench coat, getting more soaked by the second. Ortivana's heat was overwhelming, but the high-born smelt fresh, doused in their expensive perfumes. I was surprised they couldn't smell Father's sweat, for I could, despite his best attempts to mask it. If they discovered his identity, we would be forced up onto the gallows to join the other rebels lined up in chains, waiting for death.

"Skin them all!"

"Flay them!"

"Traitorous bastards!"

The crowd pulsed in disgust, surging towards the wooden scaffolding, almost knocking me flat into the cobblestones. As the town crier condemned the convicted, I tried to escape again, but Father scooped me into his arms for a better view.

"You can't make me watch," I said, facing the opposite direction. Staring over his shoulder was worse, seeing hundreds of bloodthirsty faces.

"You have to."

"Why?"

"You're witnessing history," he whispered, brushing my russet hair to the side, saving it from plastering my face.

It was raining harder than I ever imagined it could, as if the Goddess was trying her best to drown us. Beyond the prisoners, the shadowy silhouette of the triple-spired cathedral, *An Caisleán*, was engulfed in an unnatural funnel of clouds that smothered its trident, along with the last glimpse of amethyst sky. With an unexpected craving for Mother, I refocused on the prisoners, counting six men and one woman linked to individual posts on the podium. Some of them were bleeding. Some badly bruised. Most were struggling to stay upright at all.

The female prisoner sank to her knees. Her platinum hair penetrated the night like only the moon could. She was sobbing openly, the way one cried when all hope was lost. A tear streamed down my own face to match. I could spare one for the woman who cried so many.

Her sobs became hysterical as the last of her fellows were tied to the remaining pillars by the silver-armoured soldiers with purple hoods. *Scours. Hunters of sorcery.* As I listened to the raindrops bouncing off their metallic armour, I wondered again why Father insisted I come with him. Eleven years of life hadn't prepared me.

"A day will come when sorcerers rise up against those who oppress them!" the woman announced to the crowd. She stared at me. I shivered. "*Tar Amach.*"

Father had uttered those same words to his comrades, but no one ever explained what it meant.

The woman's proclamation changed to whispers which echoed in the courtyard, creeping up on me like a fly buzzing between either ear. A raindrop trickled down my spine. I hugged Father tighter; his stubble prickled my cheek like sandpaper. I winced as a spark shot from the woman's body, burning a deep hole in the podium.

The crowd fell silent.

The town crier cowered behind the executioner, and those at the front backed away as more sparks forced their way out, causing cracks along the woman's forehead and neck. I gasped as I glimpsed her insides. *Hollow. Like a rotted tree trunk.* The next spark of sorcery struck the low-hanging clouds, and a colossal bolt illuminated the sky. People screamed. The rain fell harder, and I wondered if she was manipulating the weather. The Scours wielded their strange weapons – silver staffs with crystals that burned with peculiar light – and I immediately feared for the woman. I wanted to yell at her to stop.

I must warn her!

I shook Father's shoulders, expecting him to save her, like I had watched him save so many sorcerers in the war, but he glared with the same disgust as the nobles. Wiping my tears, I stared back at the gallows and screamed as the crying woman caught alight.

HOPE

December, Year 4128

Defining moments of a rebellion stand the test of time, signalling where the war was won and lost.

Lana Hale strutted through Ortiva City's gates, past the golden armoured Sovereign soldiers. It was a welcome change of pace to climbing over the sandstone walls in the dark, but infiltration required a different kind of nerve. Her identity papers were in order; her invitation to the Sovereign social flawlessly duplicated by an artistic homeless man down by the docks. Two mason jars of clean drinking water was a high price for his services, but she was one of the few brave enough to steal them from military caravans, and the old critter sensed her desperation.

His artistic speciality was caricatures. Tonight, Hale resembled one of herself despite considerable experience in conning nobility. It was usually easy for her to slip into another's shoes, to carry herself like the high-born, playing the traditional role of wife-cum-stand-in-mother for every ungrateful male fat cat of royal blood. This time, she succumbed to the worries of an actual mother, wondering which of her flock would misbehave.

"Go home," she'd told her youngest brother, Lucian, for the millionth time that day. She had shooed him away from the city gates prior to using her fake invitation to pass the Sovereign guards.

"But I want to come," Lucian complained, batting his hazel eyes up at her and holding his ceremonial dagger she had bought him from Milagros last year. He had been pestering her for weeks to let him help the Freebooter rebels, convinced he would become some kind of folk hero. But this war had no heroes. There were criminals on both sides, killing out of spite. Tonight, Goddess-willing, that would end.

The Ortivanian nobility had come out in force this evening, hoping to curry favour with the regime. *An Caisleán* Cathedral loomed in the distance, with hundreds of people hoping to gain entrance, if only to get out of the Everlasting Rain that had been falling for fourteen years. Hale was relieved her papers and accent had been solid enough to permit her inside. The ballroom, once a place of ancient worship, was filled with people in their finest attire, stinking up the palace with their colognes.

Hale sipped wine she snatched from a passing tray, taking in her surroundings. Her heart rate settled. All was calm for now. Lucian might have finally heeded her orders, but there would surely be more rebel infiltrators who required telling off before the night was through. Dressing dockworkers and farmers in fancy suits did not a noble make, but lookouts were essential should things go tits up, and in Hale's experience they often did.

Beneath the elegantly carved arches and intricate mosaics, she became distracted by the living embodiment of the noblewomen she was imitating. They swung from the arms of their men, upholding Ancestor traditions. Women and men were equal in this age, but some stench of the ancients still lingered where Sovereign wealth was concerned. Hale suppressed her disdain as a mousy young woman was scolded for leaving her man's side by an older lady who wore so much jewellery it was surprising her knees hadn't buckled under the weight.

Turning a blind eye to the public berating, Hale glanced up at the musicians playing on the dais in front of the Sovereign generals, enjoying a rare moment of entertainment seldom found in her world. When the song finished, she searched the rest of the ballroom for her accomplice, who was supposed to have met her at the city gates. Showing up to an event uncoupled was uncommon and she was already attracting disdainful looks from the rich and powerful. *I need to find him soon or my cover is blown.*

Finishing her first goblet of red, she snatched another from a passing tailored waiter. Wine in Ortivana had no equal. It was one of the few things every native could be proud of and something worth fighting for if you asked any peasant outside the city walls. If you asked Hale, freedom was a more powerful motivator. Ortivana had been the piece of meat in a game of political tug of war for longer than she had been alive. On one hand, the nobles preferred the golden-armoured Sovereign dictatorship, which gifted clean water and bountiful parties. On the other hand, some preferred the overthrown Scours: sorcerer-hunters that sucked the life out of every man, woman and child who dared be born with a magical abnormality. The Scours had forced the sorcerers into hiding in a manner akin to the Ancestor's witch-hunts. Loyalty to Sovereigns and Scours was split down the middle in noble circles. The only thing they could all agree on was that they never wanted Ortivana to fall under Swashbuckler rule. Pirates were the last thing this island needed.

Spotting whom she had been searching for, Hale necked the rest of her drink. Scooping the end of her burgundy, floor-length silk dress, she slid through the lively dance floor, cursing her high-heeled shoes. They were stolen like the rest of her attire. She couldn't have afforded something so sleek in her wildest dreams, but they had been necessary for this particular intrigue. As had bringing Felix Legat.

"Goddess, can you at least pretend to be enjoying yourself?" she said, sidling up beside him.

"Let go of my arm, Lana," Felix said.

"We're pretending to be married," she reminded him, casting anxious glances to ensure they weren't drawing attention. The old lady who had reprimanded the young woman was throwing them daggers.

"You're my sister."

"Adopted sister," Hale corrected.

She didn't often remind him of this. He had been like a real brother to her once, but they had become estranged since their father, Milak, was murdered, making it difficult for them to lead the rebellion in his place. Gone was the mischievous blond-haired boy she had once idolised, replaced by a sour twenty-six-year-old man with a silver topknot and goatee who gave the impression he would sooner shank someone than save them. They clashed often, with Felix preferring the brutality of war over Hale's heists and strategic attacks. She aimed to minimise losses while inflicting damage on their oppressors. There was no point in winning a war where everyone had died for that freedom. She had worked for months to put this final plan in motion, but part of her sensed that Felix didn't want the civil war to end. It would make his particular brand of cruelty obsolete.

She tightened her grip on his arm, feeling his bicep flex beneath the black suede jacket he had sported for the occasion. His violent outbursts had never been aimed at her, but she often sensed he disliked taking orders.

"It's nearly time," she whispered, as Felix continued to fiddle with the bottles of alcohol displayed on the open bar. "What is your problem?"

"Problem?" He scoffed. "Since when have you ever listened to anything I have to say?"

"You want to do this now? Here? We are *so* close."

He unscrewed a bottle of whiskey and took a sniff before downing a few gulps. "Mm. Not bad."

"Stop it," Hale said, taking the bottle. "People are staring. Felix!" she hissed, snatching another from him, placing it back on the counter. "I swear on the Goddess' backside, if you mess this up, I'll—"

"You'll what?"

He shook out of her grip, meeting her gaze. For the first time in her life, she was frightened of him. She straightened up, staring into his grey eyes, unwilling to reveal how much he had shaken her. There was only a year between them, but she often acted like the older sibling. He was akin to throwing fits when he didn't get his way.

"That's it. You're done," she said, snatching the last bottle out of his clutches. "I knew it was a mistake bringing you tonight. I don't understand why you insisted on it."

With a snide grin, Felix walked away.

"Felix!" She stared after him, shaking her head. "Dick."

As the pendulum overlooking the dais chimed eleven, she made her way towards the left side doors leading out of the ballroom. Recalling the blueprints she had stolen and memorised, these doors, guarded by two golden-clad soldiers, led to where she wanted to go. Without Felix to distract them, she would have to form another plan fast. As she quickly racked her brains, screams erupted from the other end of the hall.

The musicians' instruments grinded to a stop, and the guards left their post to investigate purple smoke that was rising over the nobility. Hale caught a brief glimpse of a familiar head of jet-black hair and cursed, then seized the opportunity to dart through the unguarded exit. As fast as her heels would take her, she jogged down the marble corridor and slipped behind a stone plinth upholding an ancient statue as a small platoon of Sovereigns raced to the ballroom. She waited several minutes until she heard lighter footsteps come from the other direction. Reaching from her hiding place, she smothered a small boy and dragged him out of sight.

"Stop struggling. It's me." He froze, staring up at her. Sensing it was safe to do so, Hale removed her hand from his mouth. "What are you doing here? And what are you *wearing*?"

Lucian swivelled onto his bottom, readjusting his multicoloured outfit and flattening his hair. He had soot on his cheeks. "Felix smuggled me in as one of the kitchen staff. He said I could help."

Hale refrained from cursing in front of him. How was her thirteen-year-old brother supposed to be more helpful than experienced Felix? It made no sense why he would allow his little brother to take his place in history.

Hale sighed. "Go home, Luce."

"Oh, come on!" Lucian begged, getting onto his knees. "I haven't been training with you all summer for nothing. The war is almost over, and I want to make a difference. You saw how good I was in there."

"It was reckless, not good. What was that purple stuff?"

Lucian didn't answer, and Hale guessed it was something illegal that Felix had given him.

"I'll behave," Lucian said. "I understand how important this is. It's my future too. Ortivana's future. I won't mess it up, sister, I promise."

Precious time was ticking. She silenced Lucian again as more soldiers raced past their hiding place. Knowing they couldn't linger any longer, she gestured for him to return to the ballroom.

"You want to help? Go back in there and tell Felix to meet me at the vault. Tell him to stop pissing away this opportunity. Then you get out the same way you came in and don't ever let me catch you hanging around this city again."

Lucian hung his head. Without another word, he checked the coast was clear and trudged back to the party. Hale resisted the urge to laugh as she watched him go. He reminded her so much of herself at that age. She had gate-crashed her father's heists on more than one occasion, and he'd been even less pleased to see her. Children understood war in different ways. In some manner, they were more equipped to deal with it, but they never understood that this was the exact reason adults wanted to keep them far away from it. That innocence and optimism was worth protecting. That beautiful, untainted view of the world before politics and patriotism sullied all.

Hoping Lucian would heed her, she crept out from behind the plinth and made her way down the hallway, towards what she hoped was the Sovereign vault. She had been dreaming of this moment for months, since word reached her ears of a secret weapon named Viperidae the Sovereigns had apparently hidden there. She had no idea what Viperidae was, and her investigations had drawn a blank, but if the Sovereigns possessed something this powerful, they couldn't be allowed to keep it. Using their own weapon against them was Felix's idea; Hale wanted to keep it as a deterrent, a bargaining chip for them to broker Ortivana's independence. They could argue when they had it in their possession. *For now, I'd settle for finding the damn thing.*

After several minutes jogging, Hale had turned too many corners to count. *An Caisleán* was larger than anticipated. This was the first time she'd been inside, having grown up beneath the cathedral's trident her whole life. It had been repurposed by each new government. Some said the Sovereigns had even built a prison high up in the smallest tower, but with any luck she and Felix would find Viperidae and escape without finding out if that was true. Prisoners rumoured to have been sent there had never been seen again. Occasionally the Sovereigns would hold public hangings in *An Caisleán's* courtyard in the town square, but they were mostly political executions for noble entertainment. The Scours had been the real executioners, burning sorcerers alive. She could still recall the smell of burning flesh. Whatever happened tonight, she couldn't fail.

Each corridor twisted into another, presenting her with endless challenges. Hiding places grew more limited as Sovereigns left the surrounding barracks. Lucian's distraction was doing its job, emptying this side of the cathedral, but she hoped he made it out before someone noticed he didn't belong. She'd have marched him back to the city gates herself if she'd had the time.

Twice she was almost caught by passing guards and hid in a small nook that presented itself in time. Having grown up without much food, she was lithe enough to slip behind a marble column or duck beneath a stained glass window. Sitting beneath the sill as the latest platoon passed, she decided she could lose her high heels. Their muffled footfalls along the faded purple carpet that lined the cavernous corridors could be enough to attract unwanted attention.

Finally, she arrived at her destination, a nondescript locked door. Felix was waiting for her.

"What took you?" he asked.

"Got turned around. How did you get here first?"

"I followed the route you were supposed to."

"Ha ha." She rolled her eyes.

Felix straightened up off the wall. "Let's get this over with."

"Yeah, I don't like your company much either."

She withdrew a leather pouch from the garter strapped to her right thigh beneath her dress and chose the appropriate picks, jiggling them in the lock. It popped open easily but she wasn't as pleased as she ought to have been. *Wouldn't the Sovereigns better protect something this important?* Again, she sensed she was falling into a trap, but retreat wasn't an option. They would endure, regardless of the outcome; such was the nature of this war.

She prised open the metallic door to avoid it squeaking, and she and Felix stared into immediate darkness.

"After you," Felix said, gesturing inside.

He scowled at her as she struck a match behind his ear and lit the lantern on the inner wall. It did little to penetrate the thick blackness, but it did illuminate the top of the lone staircase that awaited them a metre ahead. She took point, beckoning him to follow. Felix pulled the door closed behind them, casting them into further darkness. With each step Hale took down the staircase, a voice in her head screamed for her to run. The stone was cold against her bare feet, and the air became cooler as they descended. Felix brushed against her; she flinched, regretting the wine she had consumed.

When the staircase finally ended, she paused. Felix collided with her.

"Shit."

"Shh," she said, straining to get a sense of their surroundings.

The lantern's flame licked along the off-white silhouettes of nearby statues. *No, not statues. Tombs.* Sweat streaked down her temple. She was glad Felix was here. If not for his sunny personality, then for his muscle. Nothing about this place screamed 'vault', and she wondered if she had remembered the map wrong. *Why would the Sovereigns hide a dangerous weapon this far underground with no protection?* Ignoring the desire to flee, she prowled deeper into the necropolis, keeping Felix within touching distance.

The silence was unnerving; not even the scurrying of a rat to keep them company. There was no breeze, but something was breathing on her face. She closed her mouth to stop whatever was attempting to invade her, but even inhaling through her nostrils was unpleasant. Trying not to picture supernatural entities, she kept the lantern steady.

As they approached the opposite wall, she stretched out, praying to the Goddess they would find something to make this all worthwhile. Her fingertips grazed the crumbling corners of a dusty grave, and she traced the unevenness of where the stone used to be inscribed. Dates that were still legible stretched back as far as ancestral priests in the 2000s, footnotes in history after the passing of two millennia.

The lantern flickered as the door they had entered through reopened.

She and Felix spun around. They froze, listening as someone descended the staircase. Hale concealed the lantern behind a statue, casting them into shadow before their pursuer could touch the bottom. She grabbed Felix's arm. He tensed but didn't shake her off this time. The heaviness of the footsteps told her their pursuer was a man.

"I know you are in here," the assailant called.

She couldn't place the origins of his accent to any island she was familiar with.

Felix's silvery-blond hair was the only thing that stood out in the darkness, enough for her to notice him scarper. *Felix!* She called internally, losing sight of which direction he went. Shivering, she hugged her body, colder than she had been all night. The footsteps of the assailant came closer, and she hunkered, pressing back against the damp stone. She held her breath, sensing he was about a foot away, on the other side of the gravestone concealing her, his panting giving away his location. To her relief, he took off in another direction, leaving her with a decision to make.

Seizing her chance, she tiptoed back towards the staircase, feeling her way there. It was only a matter of time until the man found their lantern, leaving nowhere for them to hide. A weapon would have been useful, but she would have never gotten one past the guards, and she hated using them regardless. Feeling around in the darkness, she closed her fingers around a piece of rock. It would have to suffice.

Using the training her father had instilled in her from an early age, she listened, waiting for the moment that would dictate her next move. A scuffle broke out behind her, and she heard Felix cursing.

"Felix!" she called aloud. There was no use being quiet now.

The two men grunted as their blind fight collided with nearby ornaments, knocking things over as they wrestled. She ducked as she was showered with debris and dust, unable to tell where it was falling from. *Is the crypt caving in?* Felix sounded in pain, but she couldn't get to him. She listened as the fight led back towards the stairs. Following the sound, Hale did her best to stay calm, but her palm was sweating on the rock, and her legs were on the verge of giving up. This entire plan now seemed foolhardy. Was it desperation to win the war that had sent them on this wild goose chase, or had she actually been that naive?

When she found the foot of the stairs, both Felix and the attacker had gone. Unnerving silence fell over the crypt again, but the spirits had retreated in the chaos. Hale stared up the staircase, noticing light streaming in through the open doorway. There was no sign of any Sovereign soldiers yet. Readjusting her grip on the rock, she started her ascent, taking each stair two at a time. About halfway up, her foot slid on something warm, and she spotted a dark puddle in the faint light. This mission had gone horribly wrong.

He's ok. He's fine. We'll be ok.

She reassured herself until she got to the summit. As soon

as she was able to peer over the top of the staircase, she slowed, taking each remaining step one at a time. There was movement in the corridor. Stifling a cough as the dust caught the back of her throat, she paused, sensing someone was waiting for her, ready to attack as soon as she entered the light. Pressing herself against the wall, she slid along it towards the open doorway.

She held her breath, listening for the assailant's respirations to better pinpoint their location. *They're on my left. How am I getting out of here?* She couldn't stay forever, and there was surely no back exit. No. This was the only way she could leave. Whoever had planned for this had made it so.

Counting the seconds in her head, she took a deep breath and darted into the corridor. Her attacker reacted simultaneously. Momentarily blinded by the bright light, Hale took a swipe with the rock, clocking him round the head. He fell away, landing on his back, and she stood over him, panting as her vision refocused, readying herself for another attack. When he didn't get up, she lowered her weapon-wielding arm, watching blood stain the purple carpet beneath his head. She spotted a small sword hanging from his waistband.

The rock slipped between her fingers, bouncing across the carpet.

It wasn't the assailant.

It was Lucian.

INTERROGATION INTERRUPTUS

Three Years Later

"Why don't you tell me about your brother?"

Hale examined the reflection of her eye in the depths of her mug of water – green like her father's had been. The liquid was so clear she could make out ripples flickering across the surface, and she swirled the cup again, creating more. *Crazy that we would fight to the death over corundum and sorcery, yet this is the purest form of treasure.* The Sovereigns were buttering her up today. She had refused everything they offered so far, but she was debating whether to break that rule. *One tiny sip won't hurt.*

The Sovereign interrogator facing her stretched across the table. He moved the cup aside. "Ms Hale, are you still with us?"

She stared over his head at the stained glass mosaic on the far wall. For all its variety of colours, it failed to block out the amethyst tint of sunlight behind it. Each glass shard was arranged in a deliberate pattern, created with so much care that had it been on the wall itself, it would have been a fresco to behold. Tiny frames held together by grooved strips of leading created the image of a woman cradling a little boy. Both their cheeks streamed with tears as the Everlasting Rain hammered against *An Caisleán*'s upper tower.

A fist collided with her face when she didn't answer. Her head lolled to the side. Stunned, she wiped away a trickle of blood running from her nostril into her mouth. Knowing the beatings were coming didn't make them hurt any less.

The interrogator glared at the man behind Hale; the one

who had thrown the punch, silently admonishing him. "Ms Hale. Your brother," the interrogator prompted again, refocusing his attention on her. His thick Stonawal accent told her he wasn't local like the other soldiers, meaning his hatred wasn't personal and he was willing to talk. "Aren't you getting tired of playing these games?"

Her chapped lips split as she sneered. "N-Not like I have anything better to do."

"She'll never break," the other guard interjected, pacing behind her, cracking his knuckles.

"Not if you keep rearranging her face," the interrogator replied. "You have already blinded her in one eye. This violence is getting us nowhere." He was an older man, unlike the others, and sounded like he had grown tired of such brutality. Still, Hale knew he was no friend to her.

If he wears that golden uniform, he's never giving me a fair trial.

The interrogator twirled his handlebar moustache and observed her from across the table. "Time is running out. Your execution date grows closer, and you still haven't told us anything that might prolong your life."

Forming even the simplest of words was becoming more difficult the longer she spent in this wretched place.

"I understand how you might see it," he continued, filling the silence when she didn't reply. "That this isn't a life worth living, but it is the only life available to you now. Most rebels don't get that honour. What I offer is a chance to have your stay here become more pleasant. Fresh water." He gestured to the cup. "No more beatings. No more starvation. No more torture." She still didn't bite. "No more being labelled 'The Child-Killer'."

At this, Hale met his eyes. "That's" – she coughed, swallowing blood-tinged phlegm – "t-that's what people are calling me?"

"That's what you are."

She leaned towards him, resting her heavy shackles on the table. "Fuck you," she said with as much venom as she could.

The other guard dragged her back, and she was wrestled to

the ground by two more as the interrogator watched on. What little air she had was knocked out of her, until finally they linked her under the arms, picking her up. She slumped forwards, dribbling blood across the ground. Rough fingers touched her chin, tilting her face upwards to inspect her. Her eye rolled, and she could barely make out the interrogator's face.

"Get her back to her cell. We'll continue this line of questioning tomorrow once she's had time to think of some answers."

He let her head fall, and she watched the stone floor change from concrete to marble as they dragged her from the interrogation room. The corridor flashed beneath her until she dozed off.

When she came to, she was back in her cell, lying face down on the damp concrete. Water was dripping somewhere nearby, and the familiar scent of sweat and faeces welcomed her home. Every bout of torture always ended the same. *I told them nothing. I told them nothing,* she reassured herself, reliving every question they'd asked to make sure she hadn't given anything up.

Her bruises pulsed as she dragged herself on top of what little straw remained of the makeshift bed along the bars. Purple sunlight streamed into the dim cell through a crack in the ceiling, but she had no way of telling if it was the same day. Time had no place in prison. Everything blended into one. A soft moan passed through her quivering lips as insufferable life came rushing back, the affliction settling deep into every orifice. Death hadn't come for her as soon as she'd hoped. Survival was an involuntary reaction, and she defied the desire to die despite how much she craved it.

"How you holding up today, lovey?"

Her good eye flickered open. In the cell next to hers was a gaunt old woman with wiry hair and leathery skin that hadn't seen daylight in decades. She was leaning against the rusted iron bars, staring into Hale's cell as she had done from the first day Hale was thrown in prison.

"N-Not now, Merta," Hale said.

They were the only two prisoners in this wing, and Merta was an endless chatterer. On occasion, Hale welcomed the distraction. Merta's questions followed every torture session. It was like an unspoken agreement between them, one the old woman felt obliged to carry out.

"You know the drill, kiddo. Beat me at a game, and I'll leave you alone."

She placed a battered deck of cards through the bars and Hale reluctantly reopened her eye, the other having been swollen shut. "Three-card Monty," she murmured, half asleep.

"Fine." Clearly, she had wanted a longer game, but she laid out three cards, nonetheless, holding up the middle one to show her the queen. "Ready?" She shuffled them, criss-crossing each card over the other. Finally, she settled the deck, and stared at Hale expectantly. "Where's the queen?"

"M-Middle."

Merta flipped it over. Hale already knew she'd picked right, but hearing Merta curse gave her a small amount of satisfaction. Three-card Monty was old hat for a con artist. It wasn't Merta's fault she didn't understand how to perform the sleight of hand necessary to deceive the guesser. Revelling in her meagre victory, Hale drifted off into a fitful sleep.

It wasn't until something cold pressed against her back that she jolted awake.

Thinking she must have fallen asleep against the bars separating her and Merta's cells, she sat up, only to find Merta's back against hers through the gap. "Merta?" She touched the old woman's shoulder and recoiled. "Shit!"

Hale scrambled to the other side of her cell and backed against the mossy wall. Her stomach heaved, and she vomited, bringing up the foamy lining of her stomach. The retching was painful and never-ending. By the time she'd finished, she had curled into a ball beside her own vomit, unable to get up. Was this what her life had become, waiting for the perfect moment to die like Merta?

"I can't." She clutched fistfuls of her hair. "I can't!"

"Can't what?" a voice replied.

Hale lifted her head. "M-Merta?!"

Someone laughed. "The dead do not talk, sweetness. Not to us, anyway."

Realising the sound was coming from outside her cell, Hale stared through the bars. A strange woman stood in the shadows, leaning against the wall with her arms folded, one leg crossed over the other.

"Are you …" Hale tried to sound brave. "One of them?"

"One of them?" The woman snorted. "Do not insult me, *por favor*."

As she neared the bars, her olive skin was illuminated by the dying embers of sunset shining through a crack in the ceiling. She smirked at Hale, who was caught off guard. Hale pushed herself off the floor, but instead of approaching the stranger, retreated to the furthest wall.

"S-Swashbuckler," she whispered, spotting the folded scarlet bandana that held her long stygian hair in place. The woman had golden piercings, one in her nostril, the other below the centre of her bottom lip. Despite her pirate affiliations, however, it was her eyes that terrified Hale the most. They were a piercing amber ringed with smoky liner, intense in their beauty. Hale hugged her starved body as if one gaze from this woman would deem her upcoming execution unnecessary. Her prison rags barely concealed her dignity, not that she had much left to protect. "Stay back! I mean it!"

The woman chuckled; there was a hint of amusement amidst the hostility. "You have nothing to fear from me," she replied, rolling her 'r' sounds in an accent that Hale couldn't place. She had heard it once before, back when the assailant was stalking her in *An Caisleán's* crypt.

Don't think about that.

"What do you want, Swashbuckler? To sell me?"

"To rescue you, in fact," she said. "My name is Admiral Esmeralda Rivera." She bowed her head. "*Encantada*."

There was a jiggling sound, and Hale presumed Esmeralda was picking the lock of her cell. Stories of Swashbuckler slavery were told to children from an early age, normally to scare them into obedience. Her mother's voice echoed in her head. *'Don't go running away on me again in the market, or those wretched pirates will get you.'* There was truth behind the threat, but like most scary stories, the real versions had been forgotten over time.

Hale's legs shook so much that she slid down the wall, unable to stand any longer. A second later, the cell door popped open, and Esmeralda entered. As Hale tensed, the pirate held up her hands.

"Relax. I am not here to hurt you," she said, as Hale curled into a tight ball, hugging her legs, hyperventilating. Esmeralda's features softened, and she hunkered in front of her. She brushed a strand of Hale's scraggly hair from her face. Hale recoiled, swatting her away.

"Don't touch me!"

She couldn't stand it. Everyone that had touched her recently was either violent or dead. She couldn't recall gentleness. She glanced over at Merta's corpse and resisted another urge to vomit, reliving the coldness. *How long had she been pressed up against me?*

Esmeralda rested her hands on her black suede slacks, observing Hale as if wondering how best to lure her out of her protective shell. Admiralty must have been good to her once, but up close Esmeralda's dark camisole was frayed and ripped, suggesting she had come upon tough times. The bronze daggers strapped to each of her thighs looked ludicrously out of time and place, as if they had been stolen from a much wealthier patron; much like the golden necklace she wore, its anchor pendant resting in her cleavage. Her arms were thin but toned, with numerous scars spoiling the otherwise flawless tan skin. Hale wondered how she got them. She glared into Esmeralda's eyes, which appeared softer up close but no less intense.

"How did you get in here?" As far as Hale was aware, no one had ever broken into Sovereign prison, much less been so relaxed upon doing so. "T-The guards will be back any moment." She hadn't said the words as a warning, but as a threat.

"They will have a hard time doing that, considering they are dead."

It was then that Hale noticed the droplets of blood pooled on either side of Esmeralda's leather boots, having dripped from her daggers. "Is that supposed to r-reassure me?"

"Shouldn't it? It means you are free." She held out her hand, inviting Hale to take it. "Come. I am sure you don't want to stay in this hovel, uh? To die a slow death like that old witch." She jerked her head at Merta's corpse in the adjacent cell.

"S-She was my friend."

"Oh." Esmeralda straightened up. She walked towards Merta, stretching through the bars to check her pockets.

"Don't touch her!" Hale cried, repulsed. To her surprise, Esmeralda withdrew something and brought it to her.

"A memento?" she said kindly, offering Hale the battered pack of cards. "We cannot take her with us, I'm afraid. But it's something to remember her by." She waited, watching as Hale glanced from the pack of cards to her and back again, sensing it was a trap.

Hale unravelled her limbs. She considered accepting the gift, but her arms wouldn't obey. Instead, she stared at the cards until Esmeralda withdrew them, shoving them into her back pocket.

"Fine," Esmeralda said. "Then we do this the hard way."

Before Hale could object, Esmeralda bent down and scooped her into her arms like she weighed nothing. Hale fought as best she could to no avail, the anxiety of being carried sending her into a spiral. Her skin was prickling with hot needles. Each step Esmeralda took vibrated painfully through her bones, and she sensed the pirate's urgency had finally taken place of any tact.

Dazed, Hale sensed the scenery changing as Esmeralda ran, with smells she had associated with prison soon replaced by the scent of burning lanterns. The pirate's footsteps echoed differently now, the corridor flickering from light to dark as they passed each lantern, finally reaching a set of stairs. Hale guessed it was stairs because of the change in Esmeralda's gait, for she could see nothing beyond the nausea.

It was as though Esmeralda could read *An Caisleán* inside out. Soon, they were descending another staircase on the far side of the complex, having not encountered a single Sovereign guard. Splashing roused Hale from her semi-conscious state; she realised Esmeralda was sprinting through sewer ducts that led beneath and beyond the cathedral's perimeter.

A breeze caught her hair, and the first droplets of Everlasting Rain tickled her face. Delirious, she opened her mouth to drink it, but quickly closed it, remembering the Rain was a toxic blight upon the land, ensuring no life would thrive. She was unsure how much time had passed. Despite her discomfort, she nuzzled into Esmeralda as the stranger carried her beneath the amethyst sky, darting across the courtyard in front of the cathedral, the would-be location of her upcoming execution.

By now, the sun had set, and evening had taken hold. Still, Ortivana's stifling heat remained. Hale could smell Esmeralda sweating, and her pace finally slowed. Her honeyed perfume, mixed with perspiration, soon gave way to the odours of Ortivana's marketplace, something Hale had not been privy to since her arrest. She caught a glimpse of the skeletal stalls that had closed up shop for the night.

A solitary bell rang in the distance, and Esmeralda cursed in a foreign language, quickening her pace again. Soon, the night was chiming with multiple alarms and men's cries as the Sovereigns rallied. Hale wondered if they had found Esmeralda's victims, or if they had already discovered she had escaped. They would never make it out of the city alive. At this point, it would be a miracle if they got as far as the walls.

She groaned as Esmeralda readjusted her grip. Three times they darted into alleyways to avoid Sovereign platoons charging down the street. As they waited in silence, Hale listened to Esmeralda's heartbeat, counting each one until the danger had passed. She didn't much like being carried. Against all odds, they eventually reached the sandstone city walls.

"What now?" Hale mumbled, barely able to speak.

She recalled from memory that the walls were around twenty-feet high and four bricks wide, with lookout-points stretched every quarter mile. Esmeralda wasn't interested in the summit, however. She placed Hale on the ground, resting her against the stone. Wiping her wet hair away from her face, Esmeralda began gouging out loose bricks at the bottom, stacking the debris to one side. When there was enough space to slide through, she withdrew her daggers, posting them to the other side of the wall. Hale watched her squeeze through, and Esmeralda's legs disappeared, leaving only a trail in the sand.

Hale peeked through the gap. *How did she make this?* The escape had obviously been pre-planned, but finding enough time to distract the soldiers and dig should have been a death sentence for anyone who tried. The walls were supposed to be impenetrable, susceptible only to sorcery.

Esmeralda reached through from the other side. "This is going to hurt."

Hale shook her head. "I c-can't."

"You must."

Hale scanned her surroundings, wondering how the guards hadn't already found them. The alleyways were devoid of golden soldiers, but it wouldn't be long until they came this direction. She stared up into the Rain. *Goddess, help me!*

"Hale!" Esmeralda hissed. "Take my hand. Hurry!"

How does she know my name?

The sound of approaching troops echoed in the streets behind her. Reluctantly, she allowed Esmeralda to drag her through. The jagged stone tore what was left of her clothes, and, with it, her skin. Her cracked rib poked her lungs, hampering her scream. When she reached the other side, Esmeralda stifled her wheezing, but the noise had already attracted their pursuers.

"Here!" a soldier called. "I found something."

"They're through the walls," another shouted. "Go

around!"

Before they could spot them through the hole, Esmeralda picked Hale up again and ran into the surrounding desert, without so much as a light to follow. It was only when they were over the first sand dune surrounding Ortiva City, that Hale realised she was finally free.

ORTIVANA

Once they found cover amidst the dunes, Esmeralda put Hale down like a mother placing a newborn into a crib. The Sovereigns would have miles of pitch-black desert to search, gifting them a brief reprieve. She produced a wooden lantern from her satchel, sprinkled it with what smelled like rum, and stuck it into the desert floor, lighting it. The flame was enough for them to see each other, but small enough for the smoke rising over the dune not to attract attention. She flopped down on her back beside Hale, catching her breath, clutching her rum bottle like a lifeline.

Hale stole a glance at her. It was impossible not to stare. Esmeralda was as soaked to the skin as she was, her camisole clinging to her torso. Hale wondered how this woman had risen to the rank of admiral when she looked barely over thirty. *Why is this a lifestyle such a beautiful woman would choose for herself? She could claim the attention of anyone rich enough to give her luxury.* Hale had seen it before as beautiful women were poached from the docks for Scours in the previous regime to wed. A few years later, that same woman would 'forget' where she came from and be amongst the crowds in Ortiva City, calling for the heads of sorcerers and Freebooter rebels. Most in this age craved such status, protecting them from the rife poverty, toxic Everlasting Rain, and constant fighting.

Esmeralda sat up, and Hale averted her gaze, wary of being caught gawking. She offered Hale the half-drunk bottle of rum.

"Water," Hale requested.

"Suit yourself." Esmeralda rustled in her satchel again and tossed a metal canteen at her. Hale tried to catch it, but it slipped through her broken fingers. "Sorry," Esmeralda apologised, unstoppering it for her.

Hale tilted her head back and allowed Esmeralda to pour some down her throat. She choked on it immediately, and Esmeralda put the lid back on, placing it on the sand beside her.

"Small sips, uh? Don't waste it." She whacked Hale's back until she had stopped coughing.

"What date is it?" Hale asked. She winced as the hardened scar down her left eye stung.

"We are almost in December. Year 4131."

Hale blanched. A tear leaked down her face, and she covered it in the crook of her elbow. *Almost three years to the day.* She couldn't believe the nightmare was finally over. Esmeralda said nothing more, tactfully giving her time to resurface. Something scuttling along Hale's body made her jump, but before she could yell, Esmeralda had pinched the bark scorpion's sting with her quick reflexes. She lifted it off her and twisted it to death, flinging the chitin away.

"Did it get you?" Esmeralda asked. Hale shook her head. "*Bueno.* We shouldn't linger much longer."

"Where are we going?" Hale asked, unwilling to be picked up again.

"Anferan. An island east of Ortivana. You know it?"

"The Scour homeworld? It's not safe there."

"And that is exactly why we must go." Esmeralda searched in her bag, this time producing a letter. She held it out to Hale who read:

Lana,
I don't know if this letter will find you, but you are my only hope.
I will be blunt; your sister has disappeared. I fear she has been abducted by Scours, discovered because we were forced to flee to Anferan. Her magic has always been unstable, and it was foolish bringing her here, but the Sovereigns were rounding up anyone with Freebooter affiliations. We couldn't risk your father's old enchantments protecting our cottage any longer.
It pains me to write you since you tore our family apart, but finding Cecerie is my top priority. She's the only child I have left. If it means

hiring Swashbucklers to break you out of a prison I have long felt you deserved, then I will pay that price.

Come to Anferan. I'm staying at The Smuggler's Cottage under the protection of a woman named Maven. All will be explained when you get here.

Aveline.

There was no denying her mother's penmanship, but the words were cold. She had always thought her mother or sister would come to visit her in prison, to give her a chance to explain, but when no one did, she concluded that they would never forgive her for Lucian's death. Still, reading it in her mother's own writing was a fresh kick to the gut. She folded the letter and gave it back to Esmeralda, who was watching her.

"So, you're the hireling?" Hale guessed.

Esmeralda shook her head. "She's not paying me. She is paying Maven, a woman who I am unfortunately indebted."

"How did you even find out I was in that cell?"

"I have my ways."

"K-Killing people for information?" Hale couldn't hide her disgust.

"That is some accusation from a convicted murderer," Esmeralda snapped. "What? No 'thank you for helping me'?"

Hale looked away. "You're doing this for yourself, n-not for me."

The admiral got to her feet. "This is not the right place for this conversation. You can hate me when we are on the ship." She tried to pick her up again, but Hale recoiled. "What is wrong?"

"I d-don't like being touched." Hale panted. "Please. Don't." She turtled up again, trying to stop herself from shuddering. Esmeralda might as well have been asking her to jump headfirst into the fire.

Esmeralda hunkered beside her, the Rain running down her face. "Sweetness," she said, softening her tone, "we have several miles to travel to the docks and we have an army on our ass. I either carry you, or I leave you here."

"I want to try walking for a bit. If I'm to die, I'd rather do it on my feet than in your arms."

Esmeralda grumbled but to Hale's surprise, obliged. Hale allowed her to help her up and followed as Esmeralda led her over the hill. The gentle breeze when they got to the top of the dune was soft against her beaten face. It had been so long since she'd been outside. Warm, mushy sand granules soothed her bare, rat-bitten feet, and things that she had once taken for granted were now a gift. The wailing coyotes in the wild. The arid air, untainted by the Rain. Ortivana was still a desert, despite the unnatural downpour, its sky as purple as the day a sorcerer had scorched it. She lost her balance staring up at it and landed on her bottom.

Esmeralda scooped her up without further discussion, and Hale didn't have enough energy to object. She had barely made it over the hill.

"You're going the wrong way," she mumbled instead, recalling these dunes like they were old friends.

"I am not."

"The Hundred-Wide Road is further east."

Esmeralda chuckled. "You're not half as dead as you look, are you?"

Hale counted Esmeralda's breaths; anything to distract from her pain. She nuzzled into her warmth, burying her face from the downpour. "If you keep h-heading south before east, you're g-going to walk into a Sovereign checkpoint," she persisted.

"That checkpoint no longer exists."

Such news would have pleased Hale once, but she couldn't help wondering what else about Ortivana had changed since she had been imprisoned. "What happened when the war ended?"

"It isn't over," Esmeralda said. "Some still resist, but at this point, it is futile. Villagers are being rounded up as we speak. The Ortivana of your memories is long gone."

"As long as the vineyards survived."

It soon became clear they did not. Hale choked on the thick smoke as they travelled past the ruins of each one. She dreaded to think what had happened to the vintners and their families, noting the collapsed ruins of their cottages. Thinking of her own cottage, she asked, "How did my mother and sister make it out alive?"

"The magical forest that surrounded your home was burnt to the ground, but I got your family out before they were captured and brought them to Anferan aboard The Eider's Cry. It is the only non-magical ship in Na'Revas. Completely untraceable."

"You have a loyal crew. M-Most would never smuggle a sorcerer without payment."

"Who said I didn't pay them, *hijo de puta?*"

"You did," Hale said, coughing again. "Th-The way you dress. The holes in your clothes. I doubt you have enough corundum to fund a crew."

"Precious stones are not the only form of payment," Esmeralda snapped. "That came out wrong. What I meant is they are loyal to me. The ones that remained, anyhow."

Hale detected a note of sorrow in her words. "S-Sorry, I didn't mean to offend you."

"How could you offend me, Ortivanian? Your own crew is in tatters, look around you! Between the two of us, who is carrying who?"

Now it was Hale's turn to lament. She wished she had the strength to fight her off, but even holding up this conversation was exhausting. "You wouldn't say that if you k-knew what I've dragged my people through. We won some famous victories over the years. Though, I suppose it hasn't all been glamourous."

"War never is. I can hear it in your voice; and that scar of yours isn't exactly hard to miss."

Hale touched it. The thin slice stretched from the middle of her left eyebrow to halfway down her cheek. "If you know, then why do you insult me?"

"You think that's an insult?" Esmeralda laughed. "You

won't last two minutes at sea."

It took over an hour for them to reach the coastline, or that's what it felt like to Hale. The saltiness on the air told her they were getting closer to the ocean, even though it was too dark to be sure. The civil war hadn't yet touched the docks, whose buildings remained largely intact. It was suspiciously devoid of guards, and Hale wondered how many Esmeralda had killed. She couldn't recall their arrival at the harbour, nor Esmeralda's whispered words of encouragement. All she remembered before blacking out, was a glimpse of the most majestic ship she had ever seen.

THE EIDER'S CRY

Indiscernible weight stamped on Hale's chest, and she gasped, waking from her nightmare. She scowled at the unfamiliar ceiling through blurred vision and sprang upright. Gentle hands directed her back onto the threadbare pillow as she tried to get out of bed.

"You have a fever," Esmeralda said. "Try to relax."

She placed a damp cloth on Hale's forehead, not unlike ones the Sovereigns used to suffocate her with as she struggled for relief, sucking water into her lungs. A brief chill followed by the sound of a trapdoor slamming against the wind startled her. She scanned the ship's cabin, spotting an old man descending a ladder. He was carrying an obsidian pot under his arm, along with a bowl of utensils.

"Wh-Who are you?" Hale asked, trying not to sound scared.

"Name's Walter," he said, placing the lidded pot on the nightstand beside Esmeralda. "Brought ya some grub, kid." He wheeled an over-bed table to her like she was his patient, and she watched him ladle a spoonful of what appeared to be soup into a delph bowl. He stared at her expectantly. When Hale didn't eat, he laughed, taking the first spoonful himself. "Happy? It ain't poisoned, ya know."

"N-Not poisonous to you if you have the antidote."

He snorted. "Ya're a live one, I'll give ya that." His accent wasn't as attractive as Esmeralda's. "But ask yarself this. Why would I waste good poison on ya when one swift wind could blow ya overboard?"

He's got me there.

Hale scanned her skeletal arms and the baggy rags she was smothered in. Reluctantly, she lifted the spoon. It slipped between her fingers into the bowl, spattering her with broth. Esmeralda filled her a spoonful instead, bringing it to her lips. Their eyes met, and Hale reluctantly accepted. As soon as she swallowed the first mouthful, frenzy took over, distracting her from Esmeralda's allure. The broth was thick and rich. She doubted even the Sovereigns ate this well, at least not those stationed in Ortivana. Swashbucklers were traders, however. *Seems only right they have the best rations of the Tripartite.* As she wolfed down every bite Esmeralda fed her, she surveyed the dark cabin, deciding the ship must be a major trader. *If not in slavery, then in goods.*

When she'd finished half the bowl, Walter poured her a smoking potion. "Here. Get this down yar neck. It'll have ya up and about quicker than any natural healing means."

"I d-don't abuse sorcery," Hale said.

Walter laughed. "Neither do we, kid. This is brewed willingly, I promise. I haven't been draining any mages."

He filled her a glass of water from a pitcher, placing it into her lap. Hale was barely aware of what she was holding, still dazed at the luxury of the meal. She allowed Walter to tip the potion into her mouth and washed down the acidic taste with some water. Her stomach squirmed.

"We will leave you be until the food settles," Esmeralda said, getting to her feet.

She put Hale's water on the nightstand and shook a blanket out, throwing it around her, tucking it beneath her chin. Hale panicked as Walter began cleaning away her leftovers. Seeming to understand, he moved the bowl back into her sightline, as if used to this overreaction from starved prisoners.

"Don't worry, kid. I'll leave it here for ya to finish. If ya want some more, I'm making the crew dinner in the scullery later. Ya're more than welcome to join."

They turned to leave.

"Don't go!" Hale pled, fighting the overwhelming urge to drift off again, having no desire to relive her nightmares.

"Please. D-Don't leave me here."

Walter exchanged a glance with Esmeralda.

"I … will stay for a bit," Esmeralda relented. She re-seated herself on the stool beside Hale's bed. Walter filled her a goblet of wine then cleared away the utensils and disappeared down a circular corridor.

Hale unclenched, remembering how to breathe. She gazed through the ship's scum-covered porthole, watching the remains of daylight disappear. The sky was an odd colour. She had no concept of what was real anymore. She sensed Esmeralda watching her, but she'd lost the ability to speak. Esmeralda took an audible sip of wine. Three gulps later, she spoke.

"Don't worry, uh? You will get used to it."

Hale met her eyes. "I grew up beside the ocean. The s-sea doesn't scare me."

"Then what does?"

You.

"I don't know," Hale said instead, staring back at the ceiling. "Am I afraid of everything, all the time? Or am I afraid of nothing anymore? I don't know what's worse."

The admiral snorted softly. She took another sip, watching Hale over the rim of the glass. "How is your stomach? Do you have any pain since eating?"

"What accent is that? You're not from O-Ortivana."

"Neither are you. Not anymore, anyway."

Hale straightened up, resting back against the headboard. "What do you mean?"

The amber in Esmeralda's eyes became enhanced in the candlelight as she leaned closer. "Sovereigns do not recapture escaped prisoners. You can never go back, Hale. Do you understand me?"

"Why are you s-so concerned with my safety?"

"You don't think you are worth saving, sweetness?"

"Don't call me that," Hale said. She took a shaky sip of water, almost dropping it when she placed it back on the nightstand. "What am I, Esmeralda? Your guest or your prisoner?"

"Well, do you see any shackles?"

Hale took a surreptitious glance at her wrists, bearing bruises of her previous chains. "P-Prison is not so easily defined. I am on your ship. I am in your bed. You don't need shackles to contain me."

"But wouldn't that make it more fun?"

Hale faltered. *Is she …? No. She couldn't be.*

A smirk played at the corner of Esmeralda's lips. There was an edge to her; wildness that kept Hale off-balance. But when Esmeralda spoke again, it was with that same smoothness, warming her like the first beam of dawn touching her skin.

"I have something for you," Esmeralda said, withdrawing an eyepatch from the top drawer. "Here. Let me." She leaned over to put it on her, but Hale cowered. "Ey. I won't hurt you." When Hale didn't unravel, she sighed, placing the patch beside the cup of water. "I'll leave it here, but you might want to cover that eye before it gets infected. You can put it on yourself when you are ready." She cleared her throat and got up. "I'm needed up on deck. We should be approaching calmer waters in the next few hours. By morning, it will be safe for you to get up if you feel like walking."

"Oh. Ok. I'll try."

Esmeralda tucked the covers back around her as Hale's teeth started chattering. "We will be in Anferan in a month or so. Plenty of time for you to process this whole," she gestured, searching for the right word, "*calvario.*"

Hale frowned. "Hm?"

Esmeralda waved it off. Hale watched her ascend the ladder to the upper deck, letting the wind slam the trapdoor shut behind her. She cuddled the blanket, wishing her head would stop spinning, and drifted off into another fitful sleep.

*

Glimpsing her ridiculous attire in the mirror on the nightstand, Hale froze. When she had woken this morning, she'd put on the eyepatch as Esmeralda suggested. One emerald eye now stared back at her, inspecting numerous scars across her neck and face. For a peasant, her skin had been remarkably flawless. Now it looked like someone's favourite whetstone. She pinched her nose, stifling the oncoming sneeze, but it still managed to reopen some blood vessels.

"Ow!" She snatched the washcloth from the basin and stemmed the flow, preventing it from staining her new clothes.

Sliding her rat-bitten feet into a pair of faded, black leather boots that someone had left for her, she tucked in the laces instead of tying them. They were wide enough for her to conceal a steak knife from the late lunch Walter had left by her bedside. She stretched as she stood, and her legs cracked. The second dose of his potion had accelerated the healing process, but she was still unsteady like a toddler. She strode towards the ladder, grabbing it before she fell, and climbed, using all her strength to push the trapdoor open at the top.

Her dishevelled hair rippled in the breeze at the first glimpse of daylight, and her baggy shirt clung to her bony frame. She clambered up on deck, rather ungracefully for someone who used to be able to con her way into upper class socials. The scenery stopped her in her tracks. *A blue sky?* The lack of Everlasting Rain surprised her even more. *Being this dry outside is—*

Brine sprayed up against the side of the ship, soaking her.
Well, that didn't last long.

Shielding from the peculiar sun and shaking out the water, she cast her view towards the exquisite ocean; cerulean, reflecting off the sky. This wasn't the ocean she had grown up alongside. She had learned from studying as a child that the Neverending Ocean was a capacious ecosystem – it had smothered many ships over the centuries. The only ship in the immediate vicinity was theirs, gliding with delicate ease, timber planks groaning as the rush of the waves licked along the bow.

It was several minutes before she'd had her fill of the stunning view, and she withdrew, guilt-ridden, like she was cheating on her homeland. She missed Ortivana already. How she would love to go back; to go to the markets like the old days, to take Cecerie shopping on one of her sister's monthly furloughs from the protection of their cottage. The bazaars sold and swapped goods with what little foreign trade reached Ortivana's shores. Never again would she place another bet on the cockfights, or watch the sword-swallowers ply their trade, or listen to the musician playing a broken lute that was out of tune. She was an exile. *What an odd notion.* What good was it fighting for Ortivana's independence when it stole her own freedom in return?

She took in her more immediate surroundings, spotting the ship's helm upon the raised aft. Esmeralda was there, donned in a black woollen tailcoat with golden trim, the lapels quivering in the wind. Her crew worked under her close attention – thirty burly men, tanked up on Goddess knew what, with arms so muscled they rendered a weapon obsolete. There wasn't a single Swashbuckler who wasn't tattooed or pierced. Some had missing limbs, replaced with archaic, magical prosthetics. Hale could tell they were made by a sorcerer, and a cheap one at that, judging by their ludicrous transparency. Each leg or arm had a bright silver outline depicting their shape, and they were fully functional, unlike ancient prosthetics. *Shading them obviously costs extra though.*

"You c-certainly attract the most intimidating sorts," she greeted Esmeralda, grabbing hold of the binnacle to steady herself as the waves became choppy. "Are there any giants left in the wilds?"

Esmeralda chuckled. She passed the helm to the imposing man beside her and gave Hale a once over. "Good to see you up and about. The eyepatch suits you." Hale wasn't sure she liked the idea of 'suiting' anything Swashbuckler related. "This is Jakson, my first mate." Esmeralda gestured to the muscled man over half her width and height. His skin was so dark the whites of his eyes seemed intensified. *Or maybe they are magically enhanced.*

Hale wondered how Esmeralda claimed such respect. *What must she have done to earn it?* Jakson nodded at Hale in greeting, unlike the others, and obeyed his admiral's request to take over the helm.

"*Vamos*," Esmeralda said, gesturing for Hale to follow. "I will give you a quick tour of The Eider's Cry." She pocketed what Hale recognised to be an antique sextant – a delicate instrument used for navigation – and guided her past the hardworking crew, strutting towards the front of the ship.

The Eider's Cry possessed a royal quality Hale instantly adored. Its deck was more regal than the hold, panelled with polished mahogany. Intricately carved taffrails formed a barrier around the ship's edges, and she leaned over at Esmeralda's instruction, noting a wooden dinghy and four cannons poking through portholes on the starboard side. She glanced up at the mainsail protruding vertically from the ship's centre, awed by the red, yellow, black, and green, fluttering beautifully in the wind.

"*Somateria mollissima*," Esmeralda said, following her gaze. "The Common Eider. It's what my enemies fear me as."

"An eider? Isn't that a duck?"

"A sea-duck," she confirmed, smirking. "You can't choose your nickname. I know it's not intimidating, but that's the point. Gives me the element of surprise. And gives people who cross me something to remember."

"I'd prefer not to be remembered." The words escaped Hale before she could stop them. Something flickered behind Esmeralda's eyes. *Sympathy, perhaps?* Her embarrassment deepened.

They stood together, staring out at the sea. Hale cast discreet glances at the admiral as she began rolling up her sleeves, noting numerous scars trekking up her swarthy forearms. *From battles? Torture? Self-inflicted?* She paid particular attention to Esmeralda's golden wrist cuffs, trying to judge if they were as heavy as they appeared. *No one without Sovereign affiliation would bother with gold nowadays.* She was glad when Esmeralda distracted her, but her joy didn't last when Esmeralda bent down and withdrew the knife she had hidden in her boot.

"What are you planning to do with that, uh?"

Hale hung her head and noticed they were wearing the

same style of boots. The clothes she was wearing must have come from the admiral's own wardrobe. She was slightly taller than Esmeralda, which is why the slacks didn't quite reach her ankles to hide the knife's hilt. Touched by this stranger's unexpected kindness, she couldn't justify the knife's necessity.

"You don't have to steal the silverware, Hale. No one here is a threat to you. Not under my watch."

"It's *your* watch that worries me," Hale said. The ship swayed and she collided with Esmeralda, who steadied her. She straightened up, her face flushed. "S-Sorry."

"I should be apologising to you, no?"

"Why?" Hale asked, squinting out at the ocean.

"Because your sister is missing," Esmeralda said, as if this was obvious. "You have my condolences."

"She's not dead," Hale snapped. "I mean, I hope she isn't." She cursed her momentary lapse. "Will you help me find her when we get there?"

"I am already helping, am I not?"

"Sure, but …" She struggled to find words. "As much as I know my sister, I'm not familiar with Anferan, or its people. Do you have any leads I can follow?"

"Your mother was the last person Cecerie had contact with. I am taking you to her when we dock." Something told her Esmeralda wasn't being completely upfront. "Anferan is ruled by the Scours and their Commandant Trevus. He conspires with a man named Escudero, who makes his living by kidnapping sorcerers and selling them."

"So, h-he's a Swashbuckler too?"

"Your mother will know more."

Hale clutched the ship's rail. Since Father's murder, she'd helped Aveline raise Cecerie and Lucian. *But what happened to Lucian. What I did.* She stifled the memories, realising Esmeralda was staring. "What?"

"Why do I get the impression that you would rather get sent back to the gallows than speak with your mother?"

"Goddess, am I that obvious?"

"As subtle as a brick." She grinned.

"Oh? And what of your family?"

"It's getting rough out here, sweetness. Head back downstairs. Walter could use your help in the scullery."

Hale limped to catch up with her as she walked away. "You seem to know a lot about me, *Admiral*. What? I can't ask personal questions?" Esmeralda pretended she hadn't heard her. "Hey! I'm talking to you."

Hale gave up pursuit. *Come on, Lana. You're better than that.* As she descended into the hold, she cursed her rusty persuasion techniques. Once, she could have charmed someone out of the deeds to their house. Now, she could barely pass a background check.

Dodging the swinging hammocks, she hobbled past the sleeping quarters, wondering where Esmeralda's cabin was. That was surely the place to find out more about her. *I must figure out how to get in.* She balanced against the curved wall as The Eider's Cry hit rougher waters. A rich aroma of simmering gravy swept up her nose, coaxing her into the scullery despite her growing nausea. Walter's humming triggered a memory.

"I know that song," she said.

He glanced over his shoulder, continuing to stir the huge pot on the stove. "Heard some idiot playing it in that disgusting tavern ya have back home." He sprinkled black seasoning and mixed it in.

"Skrigg's Sewer?"

"That's the one. Ya go often?"

"I can put away my drink, if that's what you're asking."

Walter wheezed a laugh. He slid the silver lid back over the steaming pot and retreated to the workbench behind him. Hale watched him pour a goblet of wine. He offered it to her. "It's my last bottle. Keep it on the down-low, ya hear? Just toilet wine left when this goes."

"You s-sure you want to waste it on me?"

"Just don't puke it up, or I'll be mortally offended."

She played it safe, taking a small sip. *Goddess, now we're talking.* Her stomach danced. Ortivanian wine had no equal. The vineyards were about the only good thing the island was famous for, besides its purple sky, Everlasting Rain, and civil war. It was the first drink she'd had in three years. *I hope my rotten gut won't spoil the ambiance.*

"So," Walter said, resting his backside against the counter. "What's the story between you and Es?"

"Shouldn't I be asking you that?"

"What *I* wanna know is why the most self-serving Swashbuckler I've ever met is saving some infamous rebel, when she could be stealing some much-needed corundum?"

"Maybe you should ask her."

"Maybe *you* should, if ya know what's good for ya, kid." He shuffled back to the pot.

Hale tried to subdue her hunger as Walter took a taste. He scooped up another, holding it out for her. "Tell me what ya think. More pepper?"

She allowed him to feed her. The stew scorched the tip of her tongue, and she exhaled steam. The taste was even better than the smell, and she swallowed, wincing as the scalding meat and potato combo slipped down her gullet, warming her insides.

"Goddess, that's amazing. What is it?"

"Cow. Ever seen one up close?"

Hale shook her head. "Only addaxes roam Ortivana. Them and the coyotes. A-And the scorpions. Not exactly good stew material."

"I suppose the desert isn't the terrain for them. Quite common in Anferan though. Live on nothing but grass and water."

"We don't get much water back home. D-Drinkable water, I mean," she added when Walter arched a brow at her, presuming he was referring to the Everlasting Rain. Realising he was distracting her, she brought them back on topic. "You aren't a Swashbuckler, are you?"

"No pulling the wool over you, is there? I'm a cartographer if you must know. Took over for Esmeralda's old friend, Ximo, when he decided Swashbuckler life wasn't for him anymore. Been sailing with Esmeralda ever since."

"Doesn't she have any family?"

He stared. "Now ain't that a loaded question? Thought we were having a casual chat."

"N-No such thing where I'm from."

He pointed to a cupboard under the counter. "Grab the bowls and cups, will ya? Set the table. This is near ready." Hale did as she was told, but she hadn't given up her quest for information. Seeming to sense this, Walter continued. "Look, kid. Ya sound like ya're doing recon, but ya have the wrong source. All I can tell ya about Esmeralda is what has happened since I met her. Hell, I don't even know the whole story, and I ain't stupid enough to ask."

"So, what do you know?" She hooked the cup handles, scooping them up in one go, and separated them around the table.

"We were exiled from Anferan a few years back by an underground leader we used to work for named Maven." He watched her pick up the stacked bowls next. "That's how we ended up in Ortivana. Trading you to Maven is probably the only reason we're allowed back."

"So, I was right! You are selling me?"

Walter caught the stack of bowls before it slipped through her fingers. He laughed, balancing them in her arms again. "We ain't slave traders, kid. Esmeralda doesn't dabble in all that. She hates anything to do with sorcery, tell ya the truth. This ship is the most outdated one in the Swashbuckler fleet, because she refuses to use magically enhanced helpers."

Hale continued setting the table as he carried the huge pot from the stove and placed it on a trivet in the centre. Hale took the second ladle he gave her and together, they filled the bowls with stew. It seemed odd that Esmeralda was helping her find Cecerie, if what he was saying was true. He was a better source than he realised, and he wasn't finished.

"Only piece of personal info I can tell ya about her is that she'll be thirty-one in March and she's from Xevería."

"Never heard of it," Hale said.

"Well, ya wouldn't. It's an island far off most maps. Weird

place. Full of religious nuts that worship the old machines. Artificial Intelligence from the ADA. Advanced Digital Age," he explained when she appeared confused. "As soon as sorcery emerged in human children in the 2500s, technology stopped working. Xeveríans are under the impression that worshipping old chunks of metal will bring back the golden years." He laughed. "Idiots. When has praying ever helped anyone?"

"And Esmeralda is one of them? These religious nuts?"

"Ya think I'd be working for her if she was?" He snorted. "Esmeralda is unlike any woman I've met, Hale. Ya wonder why all those men up there follow her instead of overthrowing her? That's not something ya're going to discover by grilling me with stupid questions. None of us have made it this far as Swashbucklers without scars, but I'd trust her with my life and that's the truth. Anyone ya can say the same for?"

Hale was silent. There had been a time when she and Felix had been inseparable.

"Take that as a 'no'," Walter said.

"T-Take it whatever way you want."

She slapped the last spoonful of stew into the bowl a little too hard, and Walter sensed not to push the issue. Thinking about Felix made her sick. It had been a long time since she'd dwelled on him.

Walter pointed to her wine. "Make sure ya finish that before the others get here. I don't want any of them catching wind I have it."

She sank the remainder, drowning the memories, as Walter disappeared to call the crew.

RULES

The Swashbucklers packed into the scullery that evening, causing chaos lasting well into the night. After eating, Hale sat at the furthest end of the dining table, mulling over the latest cup of toilet wine, ruing that Walter had run out of Ortivanian. Over the top of her glass, she observed Esmeralda, winning numerous rounds of the six-person poker game at that end of the table, while the rest of the Eiders chatted around the scullery.

Hale had spotted a few irregularities in the game that she was sure the men were too inebriated to catch. Occasionally, Esmeralda would meet her gaze as if aware Hale was watching. If she was, it certainly hadn't deterred her from cheating her way through every game thus far.

As the pot of corundum grew bigger, Hale limped towards that end of the table, taking her empty goblet with her. She squeezed between the surrounding Eiders, leaning between Esmeralda and Walter for one of the many gallons of wine.

Esmeralda tugged the hem of her shirttail hanging out the back of her breeches. "You're quiet tonight, Ortivanian. Don't you usually have forty questions?"

"You mean you'll answer them this time?"

Esmeralda toasted her. "Touché." She took a sip. "You play poker?"

Hale felt the others watching. "No, but I understand the rules. Unlike some."

"Let's play then, if you've got the stones."

"I-I don't bet corundum. In Ortivana we played for favours, not fortune."

"And how does that work?" Walter asked from Esmeralda's other side, sounding sceptical about something he couldn't spend.

"Um, r-relatively the same. We wager one favour at first. Throughout the game, you can raise or call the number of favours you want to bet."

Some of the Eiders grumbled in disapproval.

"Well, colour me intrigued," Walter said. "Clear the table, boys. I wanna see what the kid's got."

They moved aside the traditional game, and Hale took up the seat Walter vacated for her, placing her refilled goblet on the table. She swept up the scattered cards, recognising Merta's deck, and shuffled them higgledy-piggledy, passing them to Walter. Despite a few of the Eiders laughing at her expense, the scullery was quieter than it had been all night as every Swashbuckler closed in around them.

Esmeralda struck a match behind Hale's ear to light her tobacco-stuffed pipe, blowing the resulting smoke in her face. Hale hadn't been expecting sporting behaviour and wondered if Esmeralda knew she had once been a heavy smoker. Even simple interactions with her triggered Hale's last nerve, as quickly as the green smoke had reignited her addiction. She longed for a drag, staring at the pipe as Walter dealt two cards, face down, to both players.

"I'm in," Hale said, checking them. He had given her duds. *Of course.*

"In," Esmeralda said, exhaling fresh smoke. She hadn't even glanced at her cards.

Walter dealt the flop, placing three cards facing upwards, and everyone leaned in for a look.

Jack of spades. Queen of hearts. Ten of spades.

With a gesture from both women to call, he dealt the turn card.

Two of diamonds.

Hale's heart quickened. Beneath her open cuff, she was busy sliding out the cards she'd palmed during her feigned shuffle. She nodded again to continue, spotting a flicker of doubt behind Esmeralda's eyes as Walter flipped over the river.

Queen of spades.

"Time for show and tell, ladies." he said. Esmeralda flipped over her cards and her men whistled. "Eight of diamonds. Nine of spades. She's got a straight. Hale?"

Everyone stared. She thumbed the dog-eared corners of her cards, trying to flatten them beneath her open lapel. Discreetly taking the duds into her sleeve, she relinquished her new cards, leaving them face down on the table.

"Well?" Walter said. "What are you waiting for?"

Hale didn't show them. She sat with her hands in her lap, staring at Esmeralda, fumbling the dud cards further up her sleeve, and buttoning the cuff closed. As the Eiders protested, Esmeralda's impatience got the better of her. She flipped over the face down cards herself.

Walter read: "King of spades. Ace of spades. Son of a bitch."

The Eiders muttered, some of them shifting their weight. Esmeralda's jaw jutted as she stared down at Hale's improbable hand. Thinking she was going to attack her, Hale braced herself, as Esmeralda processed her first defeat of the night. The admiral's stool scraped along the floor as she got to her feet, and she left the scullery without a word.

As soon as the trapdoor slammed, the Eiders erupted. They hammered the table, slopping their overflowing drinks across the already sticky floor. Hale was bombarded with fist bumps and hair ruffles from people oblivious to the fact she was uncomfortable being touched. Flashbacks from prison tormented her as Swashbucklers, who had been wary of the outsider, were now hugging her as though they were old friends.

"A royal flush!" Walter's voice pulled her out of the abyss. Sensing she was spiralling, he passed a cup of water into her trembling hands. "We'll be talking about this one for years. When Es is out of earshot 'course."

The men laughed.

"Think she'll ever forgive me?" Hale asked. Cheating at poker was child's play, even with an audience watching. With a drunken audience, she barely broke a sweat. She still had to dispose of the evidence up her sleeve though, impossible now the attention on her had increased.

First mate Jakson squeezed her shoulder as she tried to leave. "You smoke, Hale? Here, I'll roll you a cig."

Oh, you beautiful human.

She watched him make it, and put it between her lips, lighting it off the end of his burning match. It was such an outdated tradition, but as the nicotine rushed over, both sickness and euphoria overcame her. He forced her to pound three shots of grog, and she was thankful for the heavy stew lining her stomach. Seeing no opportunity to get rid of her cards, she waited until it was acceptable to leave.

A half hour later, the sweat-infused scullery had her clawing for the trapdoor to escape. Inhaling the night air, she twirled another of Jakson's cigs as she limped along the starboard side of the ship, staring up at the stars, thinking of home. The wicked figurehead of the eider carrying a lantern in its beak guided the ship through the ocean. She stopped behind it, leaning over where the railings met to watch the parting sea. Every so often a white ripple of waves would disturb the black. Swashbuckler life was growing on her. *Or it's the wine.* Whatever it was, she was beginning to understand the appeal of leaving a war-torn country behind.

She massaged her temples, fighting off prickling flashbacks, desperate to be rid of them. They were embedded deep, stabbing every chance they got. She placed the cig in her mouth and patted her pockets, searching for the box of matches she'd swiped.

"How did you do it?"

Hale turned. Esmeralda hadn't gone to bed early as presumed.

She gave Hale cover so that she could light another match, but rather than help, it distracted her. Hale had to strike the match more than once. With the third try, the cigarette caught alight, and she inhaled, offering a draw to Esmeralda. Together, they leaned on the ship's wooden rail, unable to see much on the horizon but staring out at it anyway.

"Do what?" Hale asked. She rubbed her hands together to stop them trembling.

"*Ay, por favor.*" Esmeralda made a face as she passed back the cig. "A royal flush the first time we play? What do you take me for?"

Hale smirked. "Beginner's luck."

"Or a stacked deck."

"Whatever do you mean? Walter shuffled the cards after I did. Didn't he set them up the way you wanted?"

She waited for denial, but Esmeralda laughed. Hale's own amusement was fleeting as another wave of panic surged through her. She could no longer contain her distress.

"Are you ok?" Esmeralda asked.

"Don't." Hale took a swipe at her. She clutched her hair, cowering as the soldiers continued to hit her. "Stop. Please."

Esmeralda restrained her, pinning her arms to her sides. "*Tranquila.* You're ok," she repeated in Hale's ear, giving her something in the present to focus on, to remind her where she was.

The Eider's Cry had disappeared. The sound of the ocean rushed, but in Hale's mind, it was a stream of water. An endless stream that filled her lungs …

She gagged as she stared up at the face of the Sovereign soldier. He knelt on her chest, pinning her to the floor. She smelled stale smoke off his uniform. Her screams were muffled. She squirmed to avoid the stream of water, but the other soldiers kicked her. She clambered for air, choking on the roughness of the damp cloth suctioning down her throat. The soldiers were laughing. Her lungs were filling. She was drowning. It was over. She was dead.

Wind rustled her hair as she came to, lying on the deck. Esmeralda was sitting nearby, resting against the taffrail, brow furrowed. "Flashbacks?"

Hale answered with a nod. When she was able to move, she pushed herself up, resting against the railings beside Esmeralda. She dried her clammy forehead on her sleeve. The only thing worse than reliving trauma, was having a stranger witness it take hold. She flinched as Esmeralda patted her leg.

"Just breathe," Esmeralda said. "It will pass."

"H-How do you know?" Hale asked, her voice barely audible.

As usual, Esmeralda didn't respond. She continued rubbing Hale's thigh, unaware it was making things worse. Hale shook her off. Realising Esmeralda was still holding the cigarette, she snatched it off her, helping herself to another draw, desiring something much stronger than tobacco.

"Tell me something," Hale said, eager to take the focus off herself. "What has you wandering out here a-after everyone else has gone to bed?" She exhaled smoke with each word. "Don't you sleep?"

This question, like all, caused Esmeralda to feign ignorance. Every conversation they had teetered on a knife-edge, with Esmeralda distancing herself, giving nothing away. Hale wished for her sake that staying distant was an option, predicting that her only way off this ship was likely through the woman sitting next to her, but something about Esmeralda kept drawing her in. All the answers to her questions were sitting here in front of her, if only she had the correct cipher.

"Of course I sleep," Esmeralda answered after a long pause. "During the day."

Something about that was off. Hale got the sense Esmeralda chose this shift pattern for a reason. *Either that, or I'm paranoid.* That could well be true. Maybe Esmeralda was normal. Maybe she was the weird one. Staring down at her trembling body, she was inclined to agree with the latter. The Sovereigns had destroyed her humanity.

"Are you cold?" Esmeralda asked, watching her jitter.

"Why? You about to o-offer me your coat?"

"Haven't I given you enough of my clothes?" She moved closer, nonetheless. "Put your head on me." When Hale didn't, she cupped her cheek, directing her to rest on her shoulder. "You're ok."

"You s-say that a lot."

"Because you don't believe me."

Hale tried to snuggle in, but it was agony. Something told

her Esmeralda understood, but it never stopped her from initiating contact. Just as Hale considered retreat, the clouds erupted, bringing more pleasant memories of home. She calmed as she watched puddles form across the deck, enjoying the thick droplets bouncing off the surface, sending ripples throughout the little pools. The lids of the water barrels stacked beneath the mainsail were overflowing within minutes, and the cigarette between her fingers grew damp. She flicked it away in disappointment.

"Do you mind?" Esmeralda said, her chin resting against Hale's wet hair.

"S-Sorry." Hale clenched her jaw to make her teeth stop chattering.

Esmeralda seemed to sense she was apologising for something other than littering. "We can sit here for longer if you like. You probably won't remember it anyway."

At this, Hale raised her head. "I won't?" She massaged her temple. *Is this real?* It was a vivid dream if it wasn't. She struggled to her feet, and Esmeralda got up too. Hale pushed her off. Her touch was disorienting now. "Am I dreaming?"

Her voice resounded, out of sync with her lips. Esmeralda guided her by the arm, unwilling to trust her unsteady legs to descend the stairs into the hold. Hale had no strength left to push her away.

The rainfall became muffled as the trapdoor closed above her, replaced with the drilling snores of thirty men. She lost all sense of direction. Someone was helping her out of her wet clothes, peeling them away from her burning skin. They sat her down, sliding off her boots, whispering comforts she couldn't understand. When her face hit the pillow, the world stopped spinning, and she gradually remembered how to breathe.

Listening to the chorus of snoring reminded her of Felix. It used to drive her insane when they were teenagers. He'd slept in the bed above hers, while Cecerie and Lucian shared the other in their tiny L-shaped family cottage. She remembered when Felix had been sent to bed early once, for stealing from the market stalls. When their parents beggared off to bed, he leaned over to present her with a small, battered pocket watch.

"Father won't be happy," she said, inspecting the onyx artefact when he dropped it onto her bed.

"Who cares? It was worth it," Felix whispered. "Happy birthday, sister. You're always late for everything. Now you have no excuses."

The memories faded. The place where Esmeralda had held her still burned even though she was sure she was alone. She pushed away the blanket, allowing the chill in the air to soothe her skin. Her head was spiralling. Desolate, she stared up at the low-hanging ceiling, unable to understand why no one could touch her.

LA FE CIEGA

Diosa, ayúdame. No puedo seguir así. No puedo.

The next morning, Esmeralda leaned over the edge of The Eider's Cry and retched as quietly as she could into the sea. She hadn't been this sick in ages. She wiped her mouth on the sleeve of her coat and rested her chin on her forearm, wishing she was on solid ground. She should have been sleeping by now, but the strange way Hale had collapsed last night had worried her enough to make rest impossible. Working half the morning shift had seemed like a good way to keep an eye on her, but as the exhaustion set in, so too did Esmeralda's regret. Her stomach heaved again, and she clamped her mouth, wrestling the bile back down her throat.

Someone squeezed her shoulder.

"*Almirante,*" Walter greeted her with horrible pronunciation. "*¿Cómo estás?*"

"Stick to the Sovereign tongue," she joked. "Has anyone else noticed me vomiting?"

Walter chuckled. He leaned on the rail beside her, staring out at their surroundings, bathing in the sunshine. "Far as they're concerned, ya hungover. Don't worry 'bout it."

She accepted the canteen he passed her and swigged some water, spitting it over the side. Swallowing a few sips, she let the liquid settle in her stomach, hoping it would stay there.

"It's been a while since we've shared a ship together, uh?" she said. Walter nodded. "What made you come along in the end? You were keen on staying in Ortivana."

"I couldn't let ya go back to Anferan alone."

She scoffed. "It's my fault you were exiled in the first place, *amigo*. You should have ditched my ass the moment we docked."

"True. But like I told ya then, Es, ya'd have to do some dark shit to keep the crew together. Ya'd never have survived it without me."

Still, Esmeralda struggled with decisions she'd made which had set them all on this wretched path. She wondered, again, if she had bitten off more than she could chew accepting the contract to break Hale out of prison. In her coat pocket, she fiddled with two wrinkled playing cards she had found after undressing Hale to put her to bed. Such skilful trickery that even *she* had missed it, and while it didn't prove Hale was dangerous, it said something about her abilities. Swindling a room full of scammers was impressive. What they knew about their prisoner was a drop in the ocean and would remain as such until they offered Hale more rope, to either hang herself with, or hang them.

"Do you think she will be ready for Anferan?" Esmeralda asked.

They stared over at the centre of the ship where Hale was training with Jakson. The silver dagger the ship's quartermaster had given her this morning was too heavy for her weakened frame. Esmeralda recognised talent beneath the rust and wasted muscle, but it was hard to watch someone so thin being put through their paces by such a menacing buccaneer. It might have been too soon to give her a weapon, but she had a strange urge to protect her, even if Hale's fragility was temporary. The Ortivanian was recovering from the worst of her ordeal ahead of schedule, despite being partially blind and saddled with a limp. It was the scars on the inside that Esmeralda feared, though. She hoped she hadn't pushed Hale too far.

"Ya think it was a good idea to give her that?" Walter asked, clearly thinking the same thing.

Esmeralda had met the same resistance from the crew. Jakson agreed to some light training with Hale at his admiral's request, but he was only humouring her. Still, she was thankful that he had acknowledged the benefit of having a willing ally rather than a reluctant recruit.

"She must train," Esmeralda said. "Anferan will eat her alive, and that's if Maven doesn't."

"That's not what I meant."

"I know what you meant, Walter, but it is far better than her carrying around a steak knife in her boot. How did you miss that one, *ciego?*"

He snorted. "She's sneakier than we give her credit. I'm worried what she'll do when she finds out who ya've been dealing with. She already senses something ain't right."

Esmeralda swallowed the rising bile again. "*Ay, coño.*" She took a moment to compose herself, swallowing her saliva. "Look, I'm not here to be friends, but I have to show her some kind of faith."

"*La fe se puede matar.* Isn't that what ya told me when we first met?"

"Walt—" She gagged on her words.

"Relax. I ain't gonna screw ya, but ya must admit, this is pretty fucked. Ain't she been through enough already? There's no redemption in this for ya, I hope ya realise, before it's too late, and ya drag all our asses down with ya. Again."

Esmeralda squinted up at him. "She needs an arm around her, not one holding her back because you're all afraid of what she can do."

"Tsk, I ain't afraid of nobody. 'Specially not some washed up rebel."

They watched as Jakson tripped Hale onto her back. Her new dagger clattered across the filthy deck. He offered to help her up, but she ignored him, retrieving her sword and dusting herself down. The next attack Jakson threw, Hale dodged, winning the duel with surprising agility, poising her dagger at his throat. For someone who claimed she didn't like to fight, Hale certainly had the talent for it. The Eiders watching the sparring session cheered, and Esmeralda stared at Walter pointedly.

"I guess she does have potential," he relented. Esmeralda leaned back overboard as fresh bile exploded from her. Walter massaged her back. "Ya need to get over this."

"I've tried," she groaned. She watched the streak of vomit drip down the side of her beloved ship until it was swept away in the waves. "*Madre mía*, my bed is calling. *Ayúdame, por favor.*"

Walter steadied her as she got up, traipsing along the deck towards her cabin at the ship's rear. Hale's distrustful gaze followed her, as if she feared Esmeralda would utter the commands to sentence her to death at any moment. Massaging her stomach, Esmeralda nudged open the circular wooden door to her private quarters beneath the raised aft, where a steep staircase led to the private deck. She descended, closing the door behind her to block out the persistent rush of the ocean. Her headache cleared. At the foot of the stairs, she opened another door, lit the lantern on the wall and stared around the dim cabin.

The four-poster bed in the centre took up the most space, adorned with a bear-hide blanket that beckoned her aching muscles. In the right corner stood an ornate armoire which she flung her coat into, along with the clothes she removed, too exhausted to hang them on hangers. Beside it was a petite, round table with two stools tucked underneath. A crystal decanter sat in the table's centre, half full of whiskey. She poured a glass and knocked it back, bringing a refill to her nightstand.

Getting into bed, she considered the other side of the cabin, where a three-metre-long tree-trunk table was covered with maps and piles of unopened scrolls. She contemplated doing some research, but a perfectly timed yawn told her she was too far gone. Exhaling, she relaxed against the headboard. After a few minutes, she glanced at the magical clock as she picked up her drink. It read 13:35, blinking purple sorcery. Walter had given it to her during one of their first raids together. She remembered how wary she'd been of it at the time. The Ancestors had used machinery like this in the old ages, but sorcery hadn't powered it back then.

Nadie debería tener tanto poder.

You don't think anyone should have this power? Not even me?

The second voice in her head wasn't her own. She never

once thought in the Sovereign tongue, but it had been speaking to her for years, on and off. She recognised it, of course, but stranger or not, it never failed to make her shiver when her brain was invaded.

Desperate for a cure, she knocked back the rest of the whiskey, slamming the empty glass on the nightstand. It wasn't the best thing for a raw stomach, but it was the only remedy she had to combat insomnia and that torturous voice of her past. She lay down, willing herself to fall asleep before the next shift was upon her.

*

The point of a cool blade rested along her throat, and Esmeralda woke with a start.

"I thought I owed you the favour," she whispered.

The cabin was dark. Her attacker's breaths warmed her face. She stared up into the shadowy torment of Hale, whose un-patched eye was wide and fearful. She was straddling her, pinning her to the bed, but Esmeralda didn't fight her off, having expected nothing less the moment she'd given her a weapon. Her only surprise was that it had happened so soon.

"Why? *Why* are you doing this?" Hale said, showering her in saliva. Her voice was weak despite the venom behind it. Her weapon shook as she balanced the edge of the blade against Esmeralda's neck.

"For Cecerie." Esmeralda coughed, as the pressure on her windpipe increased. "*¡Ay!*" She winced, swallowing against the sharpness.

"Why? What is she to you?"

"Everything."

Her reply gave Hale pause. She leaned even more weight on the blade, and Esmeralda hissed as it split her skin. "Tell the truth. I'll k-kill you!"

For a second, Esmeralda feared she would. She watched her contemplate the consequences. To her relief, Hale finally withdrew.

Esmeralda coughed as air swept back into her lungs. She sat up, touching the small, stinging cut on her throat where the blade had drawn blood. Reaching for the lantern on the nightstand, she twisted it to life. The clock read *19:02*. Hale had timed her break-in with the crew's shift change.

Despite her exhaustion, Esmeralda was wide awake, but there no longer appeared to be much threat. The Ortivanian had frozen. She eased the dagger from Hale's grip, unwilling to tempt fate further, and placed it on the nightstand. When her heart had settled, Esmeralda spoke.

"What was your plan, uh? To slit my throat and swim back to shore?" She slipped her legs out from beneath the blanket, swivelling to sit on the edge of the bed beside her.

Hale's pained expression deepened as the light illuminated her misery. "I d-didn't break in to kill you. I just wanted information."

Esmeralda glanced towards her desk. It had been tossed. In fact, most of her quarters had. "No. Killing isn't your style, is it?" Ruing the mess, she subdued her anger, facing the would-be thief. "What were you searching for? Slave papers? I told you already, I'm not selling you."

"I don't know." Hale's voice was barely audible, like she had used all her energy in the assault. "What did you mean about Ceci? W-Why would s-she mean everything to you?"

Suddenly aware that she was in her underwear, Esmeralda leaned around her for a purple kimono she'd stolen from a Coutoreál heir; a fleeting dalliance that had ended with her being forced to climb out the window to escape the woman's livid Queen. She searched for an excuse to give Hale.

"I meant I want to help her. To help you both." She slipped her arms into the kimono, belting the lapels. "I didn't want to worry you until you've recovered fully, but I do, in fact, have a lead." Hale perked up. Esmeralda ruffled out hair that had stuck to the nape of her sweaty neck beneath her collar. "Escudero is a Fleet Admiral I once worked for. He makes a living from stealing magical children and selling them to Scours."

"So?"

You should tell her about me.

Esmeralda ignored the voice in her head and continued. "I have been tracking him for years, which is why I know he is connected. I got word from one of my associates that he is in Anferan." She gripped the side of the bed. "You want the truth? This is what made me accept the contract to break you out of prison. *You* are my ticket out of exile, a way to bargain with Maven to let me dock in Anferan again. And when I do, I'm going to find Escudero and do what needs to be done for us both."

Giving Hale a portion of the truth pacified her. Taking advantage of the silence, Esmeralda got up and poured them a whiskey. She sat back down beside her, placing a glass into Hale's lap. Hale gazed into the glass but didn't drink.

"How do we find him?" she asked, swirling the contents

Esmeralda sank her own in one gulp to dull the age-old fury inside her. "If I knew that, I …" She trailed off, not wanting to open the door showing how much hatred she held for that man. The glass shook as she set it on the nightstand. She got to her feet, distancing herself from Hale, who was no doubt brewing another question. "That's all I have for you right now."

"I don't believe you."

Esmeralda spun, wearing her meanest sneer. "You've got some nerve, Lana Hale."

"Spare me." Hale slid her glass across the nightstand, untouched, and got up. "I may be broken, Admiral, but I'm not an idiot. If you don't tell me, I'll—"

"You dare threaten me on my own ship!" Esmeralda closed the space between them. "After what you've done? If it had been anyone else breaking in here …" She unclenched her fists, wrestling fury. Hale lunged for the dagger again, but Esmeralda slammed it down. "Don't be stupid, *amiga*. You are in pain, but that doesn't give you the right to make demands of me. Your corpse would be feeding the fucking crows, had I not saved you."

Hale's eye sparkled. "Maybe you should have left me to rot."

She relinquished the dagger and limped towards the door. Esmeralda intercepted her, grabbing her arm. Hale recoiled and Esmeralda held up her hands so as not to startle her further. "Look, I know this is hard, but—"

"You know nothing!" Hale snapped. Her glare evolved into her staring at anything but Esmeralda, darting around the cabin. She wobbled as the ship lurched and hugged her body against some unknown breeze, but Esmeralda knew at this point that coldness had nothing to do with it. "I ... I didn't used to be like this."

Esmeralda suffered an unexpected pang of empathy. "That makes two of us, sweetness."

Hale snorted. "Yeah, right," she said, smirking as she gestured around the elegant suite. "You're doing horribly for yourself, what with a ship, a loyal crew, and a source of income."

Esmeralda snorted. *Esta mujer.* Her cheekiness had no bounds. "Well, you should know better than anyone that appearances can be deceiving."

As the ship creaked against the waves, their argument finally ran out of steam. Silence was the only thing they could agree on. Esmeralda stared around the room herself, unsure how to continue. She bypassed Hale, stretching over the mess to get to the desk, scooping a few of the scrolls off the floor.

"In truth, I am circling the drain, Hale." She leaned on the desk's corner, ironing out the strain in her neck. "That is how you say it, no?"

"Depends," Hale replied. "On why you would be. And what any of it has to do with me."

Esmeralda nibbled her lip, wondering if she should tell her. Keeping it inside was killing her. The longer she spent in Hale's company, the heavier the truth weighed, but she couldn't come clean. Lies and deceit were more her speed. Before she could utter another lie, the door slammed, and Hale was gone.

Esmeralda waited, hoping for her to return, but the woman's footsteps continued their retreat to the upper deck.

The solace Esmeralda normally enjoyed now felt tainted, for the longer she spent in the Ortivanian's company, the more overrated solitude seemed. She didn't want to fight this problem alone anymore. She didn't want Hale to feel alone. They had both lost more than the other would ever know, but she had learned enough of Hale by now to sense that telling her the truth wasn't an option. Esmeralda had stopped trusting the truth a long time ago.

Ruing their exchange, she tidied up the rest of her scattered research, thankful Hale hadn't found anything of value. Thankful her secrets were still intact.

*

Later that evening, Esmeralda made her way up on deck for her next shift, taking over the helm from Jakson. Most of the crew had gone to bed, meaning she was, once again, alone. She hooked her arms around the ship's wheel, keeping it steady as she packed her pipe and sparked up. She would miss Ortivana's wide selection of weed. As she guided The Eider's Cry through the night, she hoofed the first draw and sang in her mother tongue.

"En este mundo maldito
Bajo las luces del cielo
He conseguido tesoros
Aún tengo muchos de ellos.

Una botella de ron
Y veinticinco mujeres
Les pago con una gema
No necesito dinero.

Y a pesar de las risas
Siento en mí esta deshonra
Y todo lo que hay en mí
Son vacíos sentimientos

Solo quiero a esa persona

Que quiera reírse conmigo
Pero este maldito mundo
Solo da resentimiento."

"Ain't heard ya sing that one in a while."

She jumped. "*Diosa, Walter.* You scared me shitless."

He chuckled, shuffling towards the nearest barrel with his cane and took a seat, grunting at the effort of bending. "Jakson said ya were awake. Just came to check ya were alright."

"Why wouldn't I be?"

"I spoke with Hale."

Esmeralda tensed. She took another puff. "You here to tell me 'I told you so,' *viejo*?"

"Nah, that cut on ya neck does it for me." He waited, but she didn't laugh. "Besides, the more I considered what ya said, about having a bit of faith in her, the more I realised ya were right. Eventually, Maven will sink her claws in her. Hale has to know we're on her side."

"Are we?" She silently begged for a different answer than what she was thinking.

Walter grasped her meaning. "Why don't ya tell her already? I'm sure both of ya could come to some arrangement."

Esmeralda shook her head. "I tried."

"But she's the reason ya're—"

"No!" Her anger wasn't with him, but he was the closest thing to her besides herself, and she was tired of picking on herself. "*Diosa mía,* give it a rest, ok? I've had a hell of a day."

Leaning his weight on his cane, Walter got back to his feet. She ignored him as he breathed down her neck. "Ya can't undo the past, Esmeralda. I won't be a part of this. What ya're planning to do with that kid is—"

She jerked the helm, causing the ship to waver. Walter grabbed the water barrel as he lost his balance, holding onto it for support. As soon as the ship levelled out, he stormed back to the hold without another word. She would pay for that tomorrow, but he hadn't left her much choice.

He's right, Esme. This is wrong.

"¡Cállate!"

Screaming at the voice in her head was a sure sign of madness. She took another hit of weed, letting the effects wash over her, sensing the night would be a long one.

EVERGREEN

January, Year 4132

In the weeks that followed, Hale found her sea legs. Each time she remembered breaking into Esmeralda's cabin, the foolhardier it seemed. She sat on the deck one morning, perched against a hogshead, hoping to clear her mind. Open on her lap was an old, tattered manuscript; the only one Walter had. It wasn't overly interesting – about a small boy taking care of a flock of sheep, but something about the boy reminded her of Lucian.

Walter was holystoning the deck nearby, content to do the menial jobs others weren't. He and Jakson were the only crewmembers who spoke to her. The rest of the men ranged in age; the oldest, a grump named Fidel who had an ear-horn and permanent grog blossom. Esmeralda occasionally threatened Fidel with 'keelhauling' whenever he got abusive. Hale had no idea what that meant but it sounded painful. She caught a few names of the others here and there, but she kept forgetting them, and it was now beyond the point where she could reintroduce herself.

The calendar on her bedside that morning had informed her it was mid-January and she realised with a pang that she'd missed her twenty-ninth birthday on the 11th. She closed her book and got up to stretch her legs, beginning to feel her age. She squeezed past Walter who was kneeling at the foot of the stairs leading from the aft to the lower deck.

"Oh, sure! Just let the old man scrub it all."

"What?" He stared up at her expectantly. "Oh! S-Sorry. Would you like some help?"

"My back would."

She bent down and continued cleaning while he sat on the bottom stair to rest.

"Where's Esmeralda?" Hale asked. Cleaning the dirt from the deck was oddly satisfying. "I haven't s-s-seen her recently." *You know, since I tried to kill her.*

"Sleeping," Walter said, unstoppering his canteen, taking a sip.

"Why does she always work nightshifts?"

"No idea, kid."

He focused too much on placing the lid back on, and Hale wasn't fooled. So many things about Esmeralda were off. *Or maybe I'm paranoid.* Going by how things ended in Ortivana, she had every right to be cautious. Had Felix continued the war without her? Had he used her murder conviction as an excuse to usurp her? If the civil war was ending, was he even still alive?

A shout from the crow's nest distracted her.

"Come about!" the Eider on watch yelled.

Jakson wheeled the ship towards where the watchman was pointing, and the crew rallied.

"What's happening?" Hale asked, as the men darted past her.

Walter pointed to a ship looming in the distance and her stomach dropped. It became more difficult to balance as The Eider's Cry sped up, and she watched the other ship edge closer, despite its best attempts to evade. The Eiders cheered, some of them withdrawing their swords and dread filled Hale as they pulled parallel with the other vessel. She withdrew her sword, unsure what to do.

Jakson raced past her and scaled the railing with the others, landing upon the deck of the other ship. Hale glanced at the helm. The quartermaster was now keeping it steady. Noticing how the pirates were using dangling ropes to pick up momentum, she caught one that had just cast Fidel into the air. Grasping the frayed rope, she backtracked, giving herself enough runway, and, hobbled as fast as she could, leaping into the air.

For a second, she thought it had worked. She soared like the others for a glorious moment, taking off like a bird in flight, but her ascension peaked too early. Before she knew it, she was falling, slamming hard onto the deck of the very ship she'd hoped to vacate. She heard soft laughter above her.

"You have a lot to learn before you go swinging off into the abyss," Esmeralda said.

You're telling me.

Hale scrambled back to her feet, pretending she wasn't hurt. In truth, her arse was throbbing. She massaged it, embarrassed by the quartermaster's laughter.

"*¡Cállate!*" Esmeralda snarled at him.

He fell silent.

The admiral ruffled her hair in the wind and tied it back with her bandana. Dark rings around her eyes confirmed Hale's suspicions that she had just woken up. A faint waft of sweat indicated she hadn't yet bathed. *Or shaved.* Hale noted a dark shadow under her armpits, but Esmeralda didn't seem to care. Hale couldn't blame her. She wished she looked half as good first thing in the morning.

She listened to Esmeralda giving orders to the crew as they reappeared from the merchant ship's hold, tossing crates of loot onto The Eider's Cry, into the arms of those aboard. Hale glimpsed the emblem on the sides, the same one on the ship's flag.

"A bird?" she asked.

"The White Dove Merchant Guild," Esmeralda said. "They operate out of Floresta and Anferan, and formerly out of The Cuatro Isles when Ortivana was run by Scours."

When I was a child.

She observed the merchant ship's crew. Six merchant men and one woman dressed like a cook, untroubled at having their possessions stolen by force. They lined up on the deck at Fidel's instruction, none of them putting up a fight.

"Don't they care?" Hale had witnessed her people fight to the death over flatbreads and a few grapes, yet these people were unperturbed.

"I'm sure they do, sweetness. But most Swashbucklers beat merchants to death. Mine simply hold them until we get what we came for and release them."

"And that's somehow better?" Hale asked. "I mean, you're s-still robbing them blind, are you not?"

Esmeralda saved her reply as one of her men shoved a crate into her arms. She passed it to Hale, who almost keeled over. "Toss that to the man behind you."

Hale swung the crate as best as she could at the pirate waiting a few metres away by the trapdoor. She repeated the action until all the booty had been stored in the hold. The ten Eiders aboard the merchant's ship jumped back aboard and Esmeralda waved away the pillaged vessel, signalling they were free.

"You hungry?" She yawned, stretching. "Let's check if we found anything interesting. If I eat Walt's stew one more time …"

Hale followed her through the trapdoor.

The lower deck was full. Grumblings from the crew made her wonder what type of booty they were used to if this was classed as a meagre lot. For her, it was paradise.

Esmeralda cracked open the lids of a few of the boxes and Hale's jaw dropped as she rustled through numerous trinkets, some of which she guessed were worth a small fortune.

"C-Can I have this?" she asked, holding up a battered silver pocket watch. It reminded her of the one Felix had given her, the original having been stolen by the Sovereigns.

Esmeralda 'mm'd' in response. When Hale didn't thank her, she looked up. "You ok?" Some residual frown Hale wore as she stared at the watch gave her away.

She exhaled. "Reminds me of my older brother."

"I thought you only had a younger brother."

"Felix was adopted. He came to live with us when I was eleven." She remembered the night before his arrival; the night the Everlasting Rain first fell. Meeting Felix the next day had helped her forget.

Yells from above distracted them. Hale followed Esmeralda

back up on deck, worried there was another raid. The commotion taking place beyond the mainsail became apparent the closer they got. A small group of Eiders amassed around an ongoing brawl between Fidel and another crewmember.

"Give it!" Fidel growled, trying to pry something from the other man's grip.

"I found it first!" He hit Fidel with his prosthetic arm, which Hale was surprised to discover shot electricity. The onlookers cowered as lightening bounced off every surface before darting into the sky.

"Ey, break it up!" Esmeralda ordered, pushing her way into the clearing where the two of them were thrashing on the floor. "There's to be no sorcery on this ship, artificial or otherwise. What's going on?"

Fidel let go before the other man could bite him. He scowled up at Esmeralda. "This greasy bastard has claims on loot that isn't his."

"Figaro, show me the loot," Esmeralda demanded. Figaro did as he was told. "That's it? A measly emerald?" She stared from one man to the other. "*Estáis de coña, ¿no?* Get up, both of you."

Fidel pushed Figaro a final time and hauled himself to his feet first. Figaro scowled as they straightened to attention, wary of making eye contact with Esmeralda.

"Admiral," Figaro began. "It's not what—"

She held up her hand, stopping him. He reluctantly placed the egg-sized emerald into her palm. "The loot on this ship is mine, until I tell you otherwise. You want it that much? You can fight for it once we get to Anferan. *¿Os queda claro?*"

"*Sí, Almirante,*" both men mumbled, like children being told off by their mother despite the fact they had at least twenty years on her.

They departed in opposite directions, and Esmeralda cleared away the audience, ushering them back to their posts. She addressed Hale, the only person remaining. "Sorry you had to see that. Those guys should know better."

"A-Anferan has a market for organised fights?" Hale asked.

She had seen Swashbuckler brawls in Skrigg's Sewer back home but had always assumed it was drunken scuffles, not something fit for an arena.

"It's the most common way to solve disagreements amongst our people. Half of our culture is fighting each other. Probably why we're the most divided of the Tripartite." Esmeralda inspected the stone in the light of a nearby lantern. "It's flawed. You'd think those mongrels hadn't seen one. Take care of this for me, will you?"

She tossed it to Hale who almost dropped it.

"Me?" Hale had never seen corundum that big in her life. It weighed more than a pebble but not as much as a boulder. She could have whittled it down and lived off it for a year.

"Just until we reach Anferan. Then these *tontos* can duel for the blasted thing."

Hale was sure she was being tested in some way, but she pocketed the emerald all the same. If Esmeralda was toying with her, she'd toy back, and hopefully make some profit in return.

*

16*th* January, Year 4132

"Ok, Hale, here are the rules. Don't accept a bet from anyone," Esmeralda said. "Don't talk to any captains or admirals without my express permission. Don't, and I cannot stress this enough, *steal* anything from anyone, under any circumstances, until you have a contract from Maven to do so."

Hale sighed. "Aren't I allowed to have *any* fun?"

Esmeralda stifled a laugh. After all Hale had suffered, there was a glint of mischief in her, more apparent the longer they travelled. She had an inkling Hale was about to break every rule she had set her, but that didn't mean she would let her. An admiral's job was to keep her crew in check, even if she might break those rules herself. The first time Esmeralda had set foot in Anferan, she had inadvertently caused a turf war between the Saristca Armada who ruled the Northern Seas, and the

Souzas, whose Lord High Admiral, Luan De Abreu, ran successful businesses in Anferan and hosted disputes in the arena in Puerto Libre. He was an overweight sack of shit, but an amenable one at least. The leader of the Saristca, unfortunately, was not. The trio of scars on her back tingled as she remembered previous encounters with Fleet Admiral Escudero.

Stop thinking about that.

For the first time, the voice in her head shared her sentiment. *Lo siento,* Esmeralda apologised.

Anferan's mass erupted from the sea ahead of them, curving upwards like a volcano. She ushered Jakson to help the men wind in the larger sails to avoid them getting caught in the island's hairline. Esmeralda recalled hotspots of extinct volcanoes scattered a few miles north along the equator. It was uncertain if Anferan itself was still active, or if sorcery prevented it from being a danger. Only the Goddess knew what the Scours did with stolen magic in Oblivion Tower, on the highest peak of the island, visible to all. The sight of it couldn't sink Esmeralda's spirits. After three years of exile, three years of feeling like she'd lost her way, she finally had Anferan in her sights.

She inhaled the damp as the ship sailed through dangling branches which dipped backwards into the ocean from the coastline, like hundreds of abandoned fishing rods waiting for a nibble. The Eider's Cry trickled along, rustling the leaves and gossamer as it brushed against Anferan's hip. The island whispered to her visitors, inviting them in only to swallow them in the dense shrubbery. Esmeralda knew the island's beauty was an illusion.

She watched Hale catch the overhang as the ship drifted by, ripping leaves from one of the branches. The verdant collection settled in a pool of moisture in her palm, and it was the first real smile Esmeralda had seen her wear.

"Ey, boss," Fidel yelled up at Esmeralda, loud enough for everyone to hear. "Ain't this broad of yours ever seen a bush before?"

The others laughed.

Hale quickly threw the leaves away, years of sadness shadowing her face.

"Shut it, Fidel," Esmeralda snarled. The crew were stung into silence. She wasn't sure why it had angered her this much, but she wasn't alone with the sentiment.

Walter shuffled towards Hale. "Bet ya didn't have a view like this back home, huh, kiddo?" He bent down to pick up the leaves she'd tossed, offering them back.

Hale recoiled and they blew overboard. She turned away, clutching the taffrail. Esmeralda wondered how often she'd fathomed jumping over since coming aboard. Walter gave her an understanding smile that she was oblivious to and left her be, and Esmeralda stared back out at the horizon, wary some of the crew had noticed her concern.

The Eider's Cry gave the illusion it was drifting back into open waters as the coastline of Anferan curved inward, and a dock five times the size of Ortivana's came into view. She could barely see through the criss-crossing masts of a hundred ships, some of which dwarfed hers in comparison. The harbour was littered with people trading their wares, unpacking loot, or setting up stalls to sell their catch of the day. Esmeralda barked orders, directing the ship through the mass of maritime traffic until they had eased The Eider's Cry into a free space by one of the chipped concrete piers. It stretched out an arm, scooping them into a section of harbour between another ship and what could only be described as a floating house.

Two anchors hanging from either side of The Eider's Cry's bow were dropped, with ropes running from the cathead into the sea. The crew stretched a long cable in deliberate loops across the deck, enabling it to unravel without entanglement. Jackson and Fidel fed the other end of the rope through the unplugged hawser hole in the side of the hull, and everything was tied with the tightest of knots. Once the ship had settled along the pier, Esmeralda's stomach settled too. She was keen to get on dry land. Hale echoed that sentiment, making sure she was first to depart. Eager as she appeared, she faltered at the end of the plank.

"Get a move on," Fidel growled behind her. He shoved her face-first onto Anferan soil, lugging a crate of ladies' frocks over her.

Esmeralda cursed as she watched each of the Eiders bypass Hale, one by one; caring only about the loot they were offloading. The Admiral left the ship last, as was customary. By this time, Hale had picked herself up and was watching the bustle in the marketplace.

As Esmeralda stepped onto the pier her balance wavered. Adjusting to a surface that didn't sway always gave her a sense of vertigo, one that she preferred to succumb to away from witnesses. She stood at the end of the pier, far from Hale, and began silent meditation, trying to block out the sea's rush.

Uno, dos, tres, cuatro ...

By the time she got to ten, her head had cleared. Leaving the ocean behind her, she headed towards the mainland, scooping Hale along with her. "You ok, sweetness?"

Hale didn't answer.

The initial stench of body odour in the coastal marketplace soon gave way to damp and mould. Although the sun was shining, there had been a recent downpour, causing the gravel to mush beneath their feet. The pong of raw meat and fish circled Esmeralda's nostrils and she watched the fishwife by the nearest stall beckon Hale to view her catch. Heaving, Hale rushed away. Between the persistent aromas and crazed marketgoers, Esmeralda managed to catch up with her in the crowds. She tugged her tunic to stop her running.

"Slow down, *amiga*, you are causing a panic."

Glares from citizens Hale had pushed past made her falter. "I've n-never s-seen so many people in my life," she said. "And it's all so *green!*"

"*Perenne*," Esmeralda said. "Evergreen. You and I both come from desert worlds. We are not used to lush forests and humidity."

Hale was careful not to brush up against more customers as

she fought for a better view of the mountain overlooking the docks. Esmeralda followed her gaze, hoping she wouldn't ask about the black tower of Oblivion at the summit. She had hoped Hale would be able to settle in before she learned about the horrors of that place.

With Hale momentarily distracted, it gave Esmeralda an excuse to get closer to her. Her hair smelled of peaches; the long, flowing side of her undercut rippling in the breeze. Walter must have given her some fancy soap this morning to go with the new trim. It tickled Esmeralda's nose. Coming back to her senses, Esmeralda watched her scanning the market stalls, flexing her itchy fingers. Hale slipped them into the pockets of her breeches, but Esmeralda could sense her sizing risks versus rewards, scouring for something to steal.

The crowds thinned and she continued observing Hale surreptitiously checking out jackets and robes with bulging pockets and Swashbucklers with dangling purses. Swashbucklers were easily recognisable by their luminous prosthetics, and Hale wisely avoided them. They dressed light, in shorts or three-quarter lengths, with various types of rapiers swinging from hip holsters. Most were patched into crews, and Esmeralda was familiar with the various emblems emblazoned on leather vests.

"Skull and bones," Hale muttered, as if she also knew something about it.

"The Saristca Armada. Escudero's men. They have more members here than Ortivana. You see that one?" Esmeralda jerked her head in the direction of another man. "Emblem of the Blue Shield Souzas, sworn enemies of the Saristca."

Members of each crew were glowering across the docks. It was odd that so many were competing in one place, with Swashbuckler presence more profound in Anferan than usual. Esmeralda might have been out of the loop since her exile, but the crews were flexing more than usual. She had little insight into this particular game despite once being a key player, so decided it was best to get Hale out of harm's way.

The rest of Anferan's people were difficult to place.

Esmeralda had almost forgotten the fair-skinned flamers that spent their days begging along the docks. Hale had clearly never seen such a collection of humans either, with skin so pale it seemed transparent. She stared too long at a frizzy-haired, middle-aged woman with three messing toddlers, and the mother ushered her chattering flock away from the dishevelled foreigner. The children screamed at her wild appearance, and Hale looked up at the sky as if asking the Goddess what she had done. Her gaze didn't return, the blueness still seeming surreal.

"Do I look strange to you?" Hale asked.

"You look ..." Esmeralda scanned her body, lingering where her breasts should have been. Hale folded her arms over her baggy, half-buttoned tunic, as if wishing she hadn't asked. She glanced at Esmeralda's figure, no doubt suffering a pang of envy at the healthy curves and tan skin. Sensing her discomfort, Esmeralda replied with the only lie that would suffice. "You look fine, sweetness."

"I look like a torture victim."

"*Isn't* that what you are?"

"No." She answered too quickly. "I-I mean, I don't want to be. I've never been this skinny before."

"It's nothing a few meals and more training won't fix. You're lucky to still be alive."

"Am I?"

It saddened Esmeralda that she had to ask. She moved closer to Hale so that no one could overhear them, meeting her naked eye; so green it could rival Anferan. "Someday, you alone will be able to answer that. I freed you from that prison once but won't do it every time you send yourself back there."

Hale stared back to where The Eider's Cry was docked, as if silently wishing she was back on board.

"Hale." Esmeralda touched her arm and she stiffened but didn't push her off like usual. "You are doing well. This is all just going to take some getting used to."

"What if I can't get used to it?"

Years of turmoil were etched across her ghostly face. She

was kind of beautiful, even in pain, but there was no way Esmeralda could convince her.

"We have a saying in Xeverían," Esmeralda said instead. "'*Como echar agua al mar*': 'Like throwing water into the sea'. I can give you all the advice in the world, but if you don't heed it, then my words are pointless. The best advice I can give you is to help yourself get better. Small victories. Everything will fall into place once you stop seeing yourself as a victim and start living like a survivor. This world is full of survivors."

The tension left Hale's body as Esmeralda released her. Noticing mismatched buttons on her tunic, Esmeralda redid them for her, ignoring Hale's gasp. When she eventually exhaled, Esmeralda felt Hale's breath tickle her face. It was hard to ignore the warmth of her skin through the cotton. Failing to hook the last button, Esmeralda wondered what had made her redo them. She fumbled. Hale's staring was distracting her. Finally, she managed to close it. Hale became rigid as Esmeralda withdrew a dagger next, sliding the confiscated blade into her empty weapons belt.

"You will need that back."

"I don't want it," Hale whispered.

"This island isn't safe without one," Esmeralda said. She unhooked the belt, which had sagged with the dagger's weight. "Tuck your shirt in."

Hale did as she was told, pulling the drawstring of her breeches tighter, and Esmeralda caught a glimpse of her protruding pelvis. Weeks of eating Walter's stew had fattened her up a little, but she still had a long way to go.

When Hale had fixed herself, Esmeralda hooked the belt back around her waist, pulling it to the tightest loop. Her fingers lingered on the clasp. She paused, knowing that if she looked up, she would meet Hale's gaze. True enough, their eyes met, and for a moment they were the only two people on the island. The noisy surroundings faded into the background. Blood pounded in Esmeralda's ears. A lock of Hale's hair caught in the breeze and Esmeralda made to tuck it behind her ear. Hale pulled away, having reached the end of her tolerance, and the illusion was shattered. Before Esmeralda could apologise, they were interrupted by a fight breaking out in the market.

Shoppers were screaming, fleeing the scene. Esmeralda caught a brief glimpse of the receding hairline on Figaro's head before he was tackled through a fish stall, ripping the canopy. Fidel had the speed and stamina of a younger man when the occasion called for it. He bashed Figaro's face as Esmeralda ushered Hale to the front of the circling audience. Hale was offered a wager by the man to her left, and an impish grin crossed her lips. She accepted a slip from the bookie, tossing something into his tin bucket.

"I told you not to do that," Esmeralda said in her ear, as Fidel and Figaro's tussle became a roll on the ground exercise with each man trying to strangle the other. "What did you bet?"

"Figaro to win." Hale showed Esmeralda her betting slip.

"No. What did you bet *with*?"

Esmeralda checked the odds on Hale's slip and Hale's facade cracked enough for her to understand. From there, Esmeralda's amusement was short-lived. She shoved the slip back at her and watched the rest of the fight with folded arms. If Fidel won, there would be no prize to speak of.

After another five minutes of pathetic clawing, Figaro knocked Fidel out, leaving the old drunkard unconscious in the mud. As the crowds thinned, Hale collected seventeen emeralds from the bookie and passed the one she'd been keeping safe to Figaro, pocketing her winnings. He tipped his battered tricorne at her, bathing in the accolades of the crew, who were eager to discuss the fight's finer details.

The crew headed up the hill towards the tavern on the cliffs overlooking the docks. Once they were a safe distance from where the bookie could overhear, Esmeralda intercepted Hale.

"Admiral?" Walter called back, concerned.

"You go on," Esmeralda said, blocking Hale's path. "Tell Maven we're coming. I won't be long." He ushered the crew on without an explanation. Once they were alone, Esmeralda rounded on Hale. "Give it to me," she said.

Hale shoved both hands into her pockets. "I won it."

"And what would you have done if you had lost it, uh?"

"I'd have duelled Fidel or Figaro myself."

"And you would lose. I asked you to keep that emerald safe, I did not give it to you. You are in my crew? You listen to orders. I may have saved your life, but I will not accept your insubordination. Now give it to me. *Ahora.*"

Hale flicked up her eyepatch. If Esmeralda were any lesser being, she'd be repulsed by the scar tissue beneath. It was raw, but the lid had reopened, showing bloodshot white around a corneal scar that spoiled half of the formerly green iris.

"You see this?" Hale said. "You know where I've come from. W-What I've been through. Do I look like I'm afraid of you, *Admiral?*"

"You look like you're afraid of something, *Lana.* Now give it to me. I won't ask you again."

A moment passed, each reluctant to flinch. Finally, Hale gave in. She dug into her pockets for the corundum pouch, shoving it at Esmeralda.

"Bet with my possessions again, *estúpida,* and it will be the last thing you do, understand?"

Hale didn't reply. She followed the others who were a quarter-mile up ahead.

Esmeralda deflated, watching her go. She'd been reckless, overstepping the mark, betting with corundum that didn't belong to her. It was easy to forget who Hale was beneath her injuries. The legends of fleeing refugees often spoke of her strategic planning. They spoke of her ability to end a battle without picking up a sword; of sending men and women into impossible odds and ensuring they came out the other side. What they didn't speak of was her sneakiness, which told Esmeralda she was talented enough not to get caught. Keeping a careful watch on her, Esmeralda followed the trail towards Maven's tavern.

When she arrived at the door of the thatched, two-storey cottage, Hale and the crew were already inside. Esmeralda paused, listening to the muffled chaos. In the years she had been exiled, little about the establishment had changed. Located on the outskirts of Anferan's slums, it attracted all sorts of clientele, most of whom familiar to her. Some, she still owed a great deal of corundum. She braced herself for the unpredictable welcome, entering The Smuggler's Cottage for the first time in three long years.

The tavern's pebble-dash interior and low-hanging ceiling made her claustrophobic. She scanned the crowds for Hale, knowing the mass of sweating patrons would be sending her into meltdown. True enough, she spotted her at the furthest corner of the bar, shoulders tensed as if ready to punch the next person who brushed against her. Esmeralda contorted her body through the drunkards and took up the vacant stool beside her.

"Relax," she told her.

Hale clenched her fists to stop them shaking. "The hell is that?" she asked the bartender, staring into the dusty glass of red wine he'd served her.

"Wine," he replied, offended.

Hale made a face. "C-Come to Ortivana and I'll sh-show you wine. That looks like piss-flavoured prune juice."

Esmeralda sniggered. "Get her an ale, Foric. And me as well while you're at it. Assuming I still have a tab here."

Foric glanced at her, then did a double take. "Admiral? Admiral Rivera? Goddess' backside! It is you!"

Esmeralda leaned towards Hale, eager to get her out of harm's way. "Why don't you go find us a—" Her suggestion was drowned out as a posse of Swashbucklers dived on her, swallowing her in a sweaty huddle.

"Admiral, you're back!"

"Where the hell have you been?"

"… said you were dead!"

She was soon paid respects by half the tavern, and lost Hale in the sea of admirers and old acquaintances, both male and female. They peppered her with questions, none of which she answered truthfully. As the rowdy fan club finally cleared off, she scanned the tavern, finding Hale in a private booth in the corner. Her relief was short-lived as she locked eyes with the woman Hale was sitting next to.

REBEL REUNIONS

"Well, well. Queen Eider returns."

"Maven," Esmeralda replied icily, sliding into the opposite side of the booth.

Hale glanced from one woman to the other. *Esmeralda uneasy? An uncommon occurrence.*

Maven gave the impression of a rotund, overgrown child in a fancy purple waistcoat and breeches. Her ginger ringlets were ridiculously unkempt, adding to her particular brand of wildness. Her hands could have crushed a baby's skull, and a faint hint of sandalwood wafted under Hale's nose as Esmeralda disturbed the air around her, taking a seat at the table.

"Good to have you back," Maven said. Her accent reminded Hale of the nobles' in Ortiva City.

I wonder if she's from there.

Esmeralda pursed her lips. "You could try being a little more convincing."

"And you could try being more gracious. After what you did, you're lucky I didn't have you clasped in irons the moment you docked."

Wary of getting involved, Hale searched nearby for some warmth to combat Anferan's chill. She focused on the open fire beside her, a solitary form of comfort amongst the unfamiliar. The majestic stone mantelpiece wouldn't have been out of place in a noble's estate, and she stretched towards it, beckoned by the heat. As her sodden, pre-owned clothes dried, she scraped muck from her boots from the trek here. By the time she zoned back into the conversation, Esmeralda had drunk half her pint.

"What?" She shrugged at Hale's scowl. "I bought it."

"Well, you owe me another," Hale said, folding her arms. She hadn't been in a tavern in years and would have liked to enjoy a proper pint if she was bereft of real wine.

"So, this is the one you rescued?" Maven asked Esmeralda, as if Hale didn't speak for herself.

"No, no, I only own her for the night. Figured I earned a good frolic between the sheets after the long trip. You know how it is." Esmeralda winked at Hale and leaned back in her chair, eyeing Maven. "Actually, you probably don't, uh?"

Maven's lip curled. "Watch it, Es. You're only back a minute and you've already slipped into old ways."

"If that were true, she'd have a woman on each arm," Walter joked, appearing at their table. He was carrying two steins; one for himself and one for Esmeralda, who bounced out of her seat to snatch it, sinking her face into its froth. "Don't mind if I steal her away, do ya, Boss?"

"Take her," Maven said, waving them off. "I often wonder why I bother recruiting Swashbucklers. Dirty hallions, the lot of you."

Walter tried to remove Esmeralda from the situation, but intent on furthering Maven's irk, she leaned over the table towards her. "We are partners, Maven. *No eres la jefa.*" With a cheeky tilt of her head, she then poured some of her ale into Hale's glass. "There you go, sweetness. Drink up. She'll bore you half to death if you don't."

Hale rescued the pint as Maven slammed her meaty fist on the table, knocking the empty tankards onto the floor. Savouring the first taste, she watched over the rim of the glass as Esmeralda was ushered away. Walter nodded to Hale in reassurance and disappeared into another crowd of Esmeralda's fan club.

Anger was radiating off Maven, and Hale was unsure how to make conversation with her. Her stomach squirmed, but Maven wasn't nearly as intimidating as Esmeralda. Still, she stared at the floor. She followed one stain the whole way to the tavern's centre, where patrons were doing jigs over the top. The melody of an attractive bard and her harp reminded her of Ortivana's marketplace. She'd never heard such an instrument being played in tune, or with such skill.

As another woman beat a solitary drum beside the harpist, Hale laid her head back. She gazed up at the roof as the music cajoled her headache. Old monetary notes from centuries previous papered the entire ceiling. She wondered how the Ancestors could have ever considered them worth something. Faded faces of formerly significant others stared down at her, full of self-importance with their tens and twenties.

Maven had also become distracted too, watching Esmeralda arm-wrestling Fidel. "She's normally not friendly to anyone outside her crew," she said to Hale. "But you and she seem rather close considering."

"As close as a mouse and trap it gets stuck in." Hale watched Esmeralda kick out Fidel's stool leg. His elbow slipped off the round table, giving her the win and plaudits.

Maven revelled in her reply. She got up, flattening her waistcoat. "Come. Let's leave the filth out here, shall we? You and I have much to discuss."

She shimmied her huge girth from behind the table. Opening a door next to the booth, she waited for Hale, who bypassed her, entering a cramped office floating in thick smoke. Maven pointed to a simple wooden chair, facing her cluttered desk. Hale obliged, happy to take the weight off.

The office was fancier than she'd expected. It was stifling and lavishly decorated, but the mountains of clutter made it appear small at first glance. Facing the doorway was a life-sized, golden-framed portrait of a woman modelling herself around a scarlet curtain. Behind Maven's desk was a bookcase that covered the wall from ceiling to floor. The books were hardbacks mostly, damaged and varying in colour beneath years of settled grime. Hale couldn't conceal her interest.

"You read?" Maven asked, gauging her expression.

"The Scours burned all books in Ortivana before I was born. My father t-taught me to read with what little pages survived."

"Well, feel free to borrow them whenever you like." Maven sank onto the brown leather chair on the opposite side of the desk. "I can only imagine what Admiral Rivera has told you about me. She may hold clout on this island, but Anferan is mine, and you would do well to remember that." Hale stared. Maven forced herself to smile. "But let's not get off on the wrong foot, mind." She opened a drawer, producing a box of cigars. "I had them imported from Coutoreál."

Hale picked one up, inhaling the rich scent of a real tobacco brand. Maven was trying to impress her. "What do you want with me?"

Maven came to her side of the desk to light her up with the candle she was holding. Hale sensed she was about to interrogate her, much like her former captors. The woman inspected her visible injuries up close like she was a prized ox at the market. Arching the candle for better vision, she flicked up Hale's patch without permission, and Hale beat her away.

"I d-don't like people touching me!" *Why must everyone insist on it?*

Maven snorted. "Maybe you're not like Esmeralda." She gestured to the patch Hale was flattening. "Can you even see out of that? I can't say I have much use for the blind."

"The infection is gone," she said, like that made a pick of difference to her sight. "And I'm not interested in whatever deals you and Esmeralda have struck, s-so whatever you want to use me for, the answer is no."

Maven paced, linking her arms behind her back. "I'd like to know who she has talked me into buying."

"Buying?"

"Well, you are something of a bargaining chip. Rivera owes me a great deal. If I accept you into my service, she has agreed to work for me too, in lieu of exile."

"Work *with* you, don't you mean?"

Maven's nostrils flared. "Of course," she answered through gritted teeth. "Just a figure of speech."

Hale could see the obvious flaw in this plan. "Why would

you go to all this trouble to acquire my services?"

Maven withdrew one of the books from the shelf behind her and flicked through it in a way that suggested she hadn't much interest in reading herself. She slammed it closed, casting a plume of dust, and slid it back in between its sisters. "I've heard what you can do."

"Oh, you have? Well, shit, I didn't know you were a fan."

"You might want to watch your tongue, considering I hold the key to any future you have worth living."

Hale snorted. "Right. Well, sorry to disappoint you, but these days I can't do much more than throw up and fall over. So unless you want me to join that brothel you have in the basement, then I'm afraid you're shit out of luck."

"Stories of your exploits from Ortivana are repeated by fleeing refugees; every one of them in awe of 'Hale', the leader of the Freebooters."

"That was my father. Not me."

Whatever doubts she had about her father had been sent to the funeral pyre along with him. From the night he had taken her to her first execution in Ortiva City as a child, she had kept reservations. She had watched him closer than ever since that day, as he rose to the leadership of the Freebooters, surrounding himself with loyal followers, all of whom doted on her, his eldest daughter, as well as his adopted son, Felix. They were the prodigal children, groomed to take over the rebellion should he perish. Cecerie and Lucian had been born later but hadn't received quite the same parading.

Maven re-seated herself at her desk. "Would it help if I tell you a few of my favourites? Perhaps you could clarify which have been mistaken identities. I wasn't aware legends of your father and your own were intertwined."

Hale picked residual shavings of cigar from the tip of her tongue. "I don't usually admit to committing crimes. H-Helps keep my head off the block."

"And how did that work out for you in *An Caisleán*?"

Hale was stung. "That was different."

"Was it?" Maven leaned across the desk. "They say you

murdered your kid brother. Cracked his little skull in cold blood." She waited for effect. "Lucian. That was his name, wasn't it?"

Hearing his name was like a whip to Hale's ears. She flung her lit cigar across the desk and the dried paper stacks caught fire. Maven yelled and sprang to her feet, scrambling to put them out.

"What is the matter with you! Where are you going?"

"To find my fucking sister. You can't help me."

Maven rushed to the door and slammed it shut before she could open it fully. "I'm not finished yet."

Hale didn't like competing with her beefy hand for the doorknob. Reluctantly, she followed Maven back to the messy desk and they both sat back in their respective chairs.

"Let's keep things civilised," Maven panted. Taking a moment, she tidied a portion of the mess. "It wasn't your youngest brother I wanted to speak of anyway. I'm more interested in the eldest. Felix Legat. Tell me of your relationship with the Swashbuckler."

"Swashbuckler?" Hale couldn't contain her surprise. "He isn't affiliated with them, or any of the Tripartite." That was a lie, but Maven didn't need to know how he had sold her out to the Sovereigns. She defended him on instinct now, more than loyalty. *He's proven he isn't worth the latter.*

Maven trapped a ginger ringlet behind her ear. "Either you're protecting him, or he's been playing you too."

"How do you even know him?"

"He was important to me, once. He is no longer."

"He never mentioned you," Hale said. *Not that I can remember, but Felix had more secrets than I realised.*

Maven stroked her double chin, a single grey hair protruding from it. "Let's get to the reason why *you're* here." She picked up Hale's discarded cigar and stubbed it out in the ashtray. "I don't want another hireling. If I thought you were just a simple thug, you wouldn't be sitting there." She flung a brown envelope across the desk. "You'll find our goals are aligned. A sorcerer like your sister running loose on this island is bad for business. It will attract unwanted attention from the Scours, so I want her found as much as you do."

"My sister isn't a sorcerer." She was reluctant to let this woman use her, even if she was eager to set off on Cecerie's trail. "You have your facts wrong."

Maven sneered. "I have no time for whatever game you want to prolong, Hale. Just find her and get her off my island. You'll have all the resources you need. See Foric at the bar for your room key."

They got up. She held out her hand. Hale glanced down and shuddered. "L-Like I said, I don't like touching people."

"Might I suggest a decent pair of gloves?" For the second time, Maven rifled in her top drawer and withdrew a black pair, giving them to her. Hale took them, knowing they wouldn't work. Haphephobia was as much mental as it was physical.

She slipped the envelope into her pocket and put the gloves on, not wishing to appear ungrateful. Again, without permission, Maven touched her, shaking hard. *All that so she could squeeze my damn fingers?*

"We've set your mother up with a self-catering suite upstairs," Maven said, walking her to the door. "We're at full capacity for the next few months, otherwise I would give you separate quarters, but I've had a bunk moved in for you to share. How does that sound?"

Worse than prison. "And the privy?"

"At the end of the hallway. You'll find the washroom facing it. We only have one bathtub, I'm afraid."

Hale recalled the bogging patrons and decided she'd rather not put her naked flesh into a shared tub. "Is that it?"

"For now. You'll have to earn your keep while you're here by fulfilling a few of my contracts, so try not to stray. I have eyes everywhere."

"Can I borrow one?"

Maven scowled, having exhausted her supply of fake niceties. Swallowing a few choice words for her, Hale departed the office, back into the sweat-infused pub.

She spotted Esmeralda sitting alone by the bar, and ordered

another drink from Foric, straddling the empty stool beside her.

"Abusing my tab?" Esmeralda teased. When Hale didn't laugh, she became serious. "How did it go?" Hale snatched the pint and sank it until the halfway mark. Esmeralda helped herself to the rest without invitation. "Pretty gloves," she said, staring at her new attire. "Real suede."

Hale pulled them off and stacked them on the counter. "All yours." She took the mug back, careful not to graze Esmeralda, and sank the remains. "You knew, didn't you?" she asked, stifling a burp.

"Knew what, sweetness?"

"That I'd be trapped here the moment we docked. 'I have eyes everywhere'." She imitated Maven's accent.

Esmeralda shifted her weight. "It's not as bad as it sounds. There are opportunities here. You don't always have to fight the regime, Hale, you can choose to manipulate it instead. I mean, isn't that what you did in Ortivana?"

"And what makes you think I want to do it again?"

There was a *clunk* on the table. "Take it," Esmeralda said, gesturing to the sack of emeralds she'd confiscated earlier.

"What?"

"Consider it a hiring fee." She smiled. "I meant it when I said I'm not into slave trading. Just don't bet with my loot again or you're off my crew."

Hale was speechless. It was more corundum than she had owned in her life.

Esmeralda took something else from her pocket. "Here. Walter drew you a map of Anferan, and Foric gave me your room key. You're in 103 upstairs. Your mother is expecting you." When Hale hesitated, she added, "Maybe a purse full of corundum will sweeten her up. I'd lead with that, were I you."

Hale smirked. "I'd be better off s-spending it downstairs." She nodded towards the sign for the brothel. Esmeralda's laughter cut through the tension.

"Get out of here, you. I'll see you in a few days when you get settled." She did something she'd never done before and placed a gentle kiss on both of Hale's cheeks.

By the time Hale unclenched, she was gone. The places her lips had touched tingled. Hale wiped her cheek, pulling herself together, confused as ever by the enigma that was Admiral Rivera. She pocketed the map and key and searched for the staircase through the crowd. Her legs became heavy as she climbed the rickety stairs, eyeing room 103 at the summit. When she reached the top, she scanned the short corridor leading to the left, counting ten more numbered suites. Her hand trembled as she slid the tiny skeleton key into the lock. As soon as she opened the varnished door, she was transported back to her childhood by the intoxicating aroma of her mother's cooking.

NEW LIFE

She slipped into the L-shaped suite and was reminded of their cottage in Ortivana. An old bunk bed was the first thing she spotted straight ahead, beside a huge, mirrored vanity table. To the right was a small living area consisting of a faded, red two-seater, and a snug armchair and coffee table in front of an open fire. Aveline was cooking on the stove by the far wall.

Hale unbuckled her weapons belt, relieved to discard the weight. She dropped it onto the two-seater along with Maven's envelope and exhaled. The dining table was set for one. She welled up as she stared at the back of her mother's blue knit cardigan. *Can't believe she's still wearing that thing.*

"M-Mother?"

Aveline froze. "So. You're still alive."

There was a roughness to her Hale didn't remember. The years had obviously not been kind. Her hair was grey and brittle, with only a hint of brown remaining. The tone of voice she used had been reserved for Hale many times, although there was a newer, more venomous undertone.

"Sorry to disappoint you," Hale replied.

Aveline resumed what she had been doing. She scooped a ladle of peppered potatoes and fried steak onto the nearest plate. Hale recognised the smell as coyote. Aveline sat at the table, tucking in as Hale stood awkwardly in the middle of the room. She watched her jab the steak, sawing it with a blunted knife.

Bet she's imagining that's my neck.

"You know," Hale continued, eager to break the silence. "A s-small part of me thought you might be happy to see me."

"After what you've done? The gall."

"You don't want to hear my side?" The last thing she wanted to do was talk about Lucian, but to be shut out without so much as a *question* of her innocence ... She buried her bubbling fury.

Aveline took a bite of steak. "The Sovereigns told me what happened," she said, mid-chew.

Hale gave an exasperated laugh. "Yeah. I bet they did."

The knife was put under strain again as Aveline cut another piece. "I don't want to hear it, Lana. You're only here because of Cecerie. Because I can't bear to lose another child. Just find your sister, and then crawl back into whatever hovel you crawled out of."

"But—"

"No!" She slammed the knife down and Hale flinched. Aveline interlocked her shaking hands as if in prayer and bowed her head. "Goddess! I wish you'd just d ..."

"Died?" Hale sank onto the arm of the two-seater, suddenly unable to stand.

Aveline's chair scraped across the floor as she sprang to her feet, flinging her uneaten plate into the sink. It smashed, and a moment passed where no one spoke. She stood with her back to Hale, leaning against the sink's edge.

"For three years, child, I wondered what I would say if we ever met each other again."

"Well, I think you've said it all. But I didn't—"

"I don't want to hear it!" Aveline exploded, turning to face her. Witnessing the loathing her mother held for her was far worse than anything the Sovereigns had done. "Tell me how it happened that day! How you killed your little brother, my *son*, in cold blood."

Hale shrivelled as Aveline encroached on her personal space. "S-Stop!" She shielded as her mother started slapping every inch of her she could find. Suddenly, Aveline grabbed her by the collar.

"Tell me how you cut his life short. How you cracked his skull and watched him die!"

Hale slunk backwards onto the seat to get away from her.

She swivelled her feet onto the ground and sat grabbing her hair, rocking back and forth as the memories consumed her. "It wasn't ..." Tears threatened to spill. "W-Wasn't how it happened. I didn't mean it."

"Then tell me," Aveline begged, kneeling in front of her, trying to peel Hale's hands away from her face. "You took my boy. My Lucian! Tell me your side so I can string you up and do what the Sovereigns could not."

Hale never replied. The reunion was worse than she had imagined.

Aveline eventually quit badgering her. Shaking, Hale listened to her retreat, and only when the coast was clear did she surface. She glanced over her shoulder at the bed. Aveline's hair was visible beneath a thick blanket on the top bunk. Relieved, Hale allowed herself to breathe.

Eager for something else to focus on, she picked up Maven's letter, sliding out the piece of parchment inside which bore thin, slanted handwriting. It contained possibilities linking Cecerie to Escudero, his last known location, a beautifully painted portrait of Cecerie that used to sit on the mantle in their cottage, a list of her family members, and Escudero's known associates. Even details on what type of sorcerer she was, and how powerful on a scale of one to ten.

A four? Well at least she's kept some things secret.

Worried as she was for her sister's safety, Hale couldn't subdue the excitement that came with having a plan. Her life had been devoid of purpose since her arrest. Every day she'd curled into a ball in her dank cell, telling herself that if she ever escaped, she would live a normal life. Buy a small house with a vineyard, far away from society; a tranquil place where she could read, untouched by politics and war, making a simple living as a vintner. That was in the beginning, before the years passed by and she realised the world didn't miss her. That no one was coming to save her. In Ortivana, she had fought for a cause. For liberty. Pride. Nationality. When she finished reading Maven's instructions, she guessed hunting Escudero would be anything but.

*

July, Year 4132
Six Months Later

A light breeze lifted Hale's red wig, and she caught it before it blew away. She still couldn't adjust to Anferan's bluster. Even the rain wasn't the constant, ever-present downpour she was used to, practically ice by the time it landed.

She lifted her foot out of a puddle, choosing a flatter pavestone for her expensive burgundy heels. Shivering, she tightened the lapels of her silk shawl around her shoulders. Wearing a shawl was the style, but her black dress was already damp, and it offered little against the Anferan weather.

They moved up in the queue.

"Stop fidgeting," she snapped as Esmeralda readjusted her wig for the millionth time. "Did you remember the papers?" The admiral patted her bra, signalling the new identity papers were stuffed there. "C-Couldn't think of a better place to put them?"

"I can think of somewhere *else* to shove them."

"Yeah, y-you and me both."

They moved up another place, buffeted forwards by High District's nobility behind them, waiting to enter the Council of Commissioners with the rest of the politicians. It was surreal, the long line of redheads, varying in shade and style. Natural red was lauded in Anferan, with those unfortunate enough to be born otherwise sporting wigs in keeping with the times.

"Here's the plan," Hale muttered in Esmeralda's ear. "We sit up on the balcony at the front. Don't speak. L-Let me do the talking."

"*Can* you talk? That stutter of yours has no fucking quit."

Hale glanced at the heavens. *Goddess, why didn't I bring Walter?*

They finally entered cover beneath the green canopy that was shielding the front of the queue from the downpour. Esmeralda withdrew the papers Hale had forged a month earlier and passed them to the concierge who inspected them.

She sensed Esmeralda's nerves and prayed she wouldn't give them away.

"Ms Ryland," the concierge said, giving them back with a bow. "We were expecting your arrival from Coutoreál. Please accept my condolences upon the death of your father, and of the loss of your eye in defending him."

Hale gave a downcast smile. "Thank you." *And thanks to a local fisherman for spreading that little rumour.*

He addressed Esmeralda. "Ms Leál? I'm afraid I do not have your name on our guest list."

"What?" Esmeralda glanced at Hale. "That cannot be right. Check again."

As the man checked the guest list a second time, Hale got close enough to whisper. "Good sir, I do not wish to cause a scene. I confess this is, er, r-rather unorthodox, but Señora Leál is my," she paused for effect, "mobility assistant. I agreed to take her with me under the insistence of my mother. In my haste, I may have forgotten to register her."

The man stared into her solemn expression and softened. "Of course. I'll, er, give you a pass this time. Just make sure your entry papers are in better order in future."

Hale slipped him an emerald; one of the few she had left. "My thanks."

The concierge moved aside, allowing them to enter the elegant Hall of Commissioners. Hale stared up at the huge rotunda in the centre, aghast. Before she could comprehend the tapestry on the ceiling, Esmeralda dragged her behind a stone pillar out of sight.

"What was that?" she hissed at Hale. "These identities were supposed to be foolproof. Isn't that why I am wearing this flaming bonnet?" She tore off the wig.

Hale twisted free, becoming lightheaded. "I got us in, didn't I?"

"By pretending to be blind?"

"I *am* blind, dickhead. Calm down."

"Well ..." Esmeralda searched for something else to complain about. "A *señora* is a married woman, sweetness, and

I left all my rings at home."

Hale cursed improvising with a language she didn't speak. Little things like this often foiled the best laid plans. She took off one of her two rings, tossing it to Esmeralda to put on.

"Ooo! A ruby!" Esmeralda admired it.

"I want it back when this is over."

"Pft! Don't act like you bought it." She fixed her wig and, as they slid out from behind the pillar, linked Hale's arm.

Hale beat her away. "What are you doing?"

"Aren't you pretending to be my wife?"

"No, you idiot. Just …" She realised Esmeralda was messing with her. "J-Just …"

"Yes?"

"Oh, shut up," Hale finished, blushing.

Chuckling, Esmeralda snatched them both some canapes from a passing waiter, as Hale ironed out a kink in her neck. They scanned the hall. The leader of the Scours, Commandant Trevus, was supposed to be here. Getting him out of Oblivion was said to be a rarity, but they had laid some bait, and this would be their only chance to question him on Cecerie's whereabouts. Hale slipped her disgusting half-eaten canape into a passing nobleman's pocket and took a moment to compose herself. Infiltration was the easy bit. It was what happened inside that usually got people caught. Esmeralda's nervousness wasn't helping.

"What do we do next, *genia*?"

"Calm down," Hale said, irritated by her constant snark.

She snatched them both drinks, hoping it would subdue her. Months of preparation had led them here, with Hale sneaking into high-born events on a weekly basis, detailing who did what. Anferanian politics were more complicated than Ortivana's, but she had become accustomed to masquerading as nobility and understood how to play the game. Esmeralda, however, continued to fiddle with her wig, and had sloshed wine down the front of her dress.

Goddess, save me.

Trying to teach a Swashbuckler decorum was like trying to

teach a scorpion to somersault; Esmeralda was pricklier than ever, and somebody was going to get stung. The reason Maven had wanted to recruit Hale was becoming more apparent the longer she stayed. Esmeralda was one of the few Swashbucklers with a brain, but a lifetime of raiding hadn't prepared her for mingling with lords and ladies. Some of the ladies were ogling them with disdain as she removed her shawl, revealing the remnant of a huge scar above her strapless dress.

"Put it back on," Hale said. "People are staring."

"So?"

A loud bell rang in the hall, saving Hale a retort. Esmeralda linked her arm but got a slap on the wrist. Esmeralda slapped her back and linked her again, and Hale stifled a whimper. *Mobility assistant. Ugh.*

They entered the Council of Commissioners with the other couples, taking their seats on the upper level. By the time they sat down, Hale was sweating. She sank into her chair, sliding her sweaty arm from Esmeralda's as the ceiling started closing in. Sound came back in waves, and her skin throbbed. She fought to stay conscious, sipping her wine for something to do. When she was able, she leaned her arms on the balcony like Esmeralda, and they stared down at the council meeting, which had already begun.

Anferan City Hall's high-ceilinged chamber was packed with around eighty politicians in each theatre-style gallery, pointed towards a central pulpit on ground level where a woman was addressing the court. Although she spoke through a slim microphone, her voice wasn't magnified, as would have been the case generations previous. The microphone was merely for show, with no power in existence to spark it into use beyond that which was magical and forbidden.

"... a consistent string of burglaries in the High District." The woman paused to sip the glass of water beside her notes. Her monocle dislodged, and she caught it at the last second. "The Ortivanian rebel, an escaped convict, known only as 'Hale', has been rumoured to be on our shores in recent months. Although there are many who doubt the retellings of chaos that have followed her, it is with great regret that I inform the Council of Commissioners that this fabled legend is indeed running amok."

She paused. "After murdering her brother, she was incarcerated and sentenced to the gallows, however, that execution was disrupted by Swashbuckler activity and never took place. There have been rumours that the missing convict resides within the lower regions of Anferanian society; that is to say, the slums and southern docks of our island."

The politicians grumbled at the mention of Anferan's underworld, even though their own places of business were equally as corrupt. A purple-robed faction in the forefront were ludicrously out of place and time, the main focus of the event, despite the keynote speaker. Almost every noble in the room was watching the black-robed leader seated closest to the front.

That must be Trevus. He was watching the speaker with beady eyes that peered right through her. *I wonder if that's why she's nervous.*

She continued. "In the interest of public safety, all citizens of High District should, therefore, be indoors for a ten o'clock curfew until this murderer is apprehended – no exceptions. All valuables should be locked away in home safes. The head of each household is the only family member permitted to carry weapons. This includes, but is not limited to, functioning guns; blades; bows and bats. Any use of sorcery, as with all Na'Revas Territory Law, is prohibited under punishment of death."

Her voice carried further this time, as though to reinforce her point. "Any and all association with Hale will be punishable in the name of both Scour and Sovereign law. We have contacted Sovereign representatives in Ortivana regarding her immediate arrest and retrieval. They will be arriving on our shores within the next week or so, and I expect you all to treat them cordially. I will keep you informed of resulting correspondence. Good day, commissioners."

A smattering of applause followed, and it became clear that parliament was adjourned. Flattening her salmon-coloured crocheted cardigan and grey pencil skirt, the woman stepped away from the pulpit, bypassing Commandant Trevus who made to catch up with her. Her low-heeled shoes clicked across the marble, which bore the emblem of Anferan under the overhead rotunda: a white palm with a red leaf behind it. Hearing Trevus' voice echo in the corridor behind her, the woman hurried to lose herself in the political traffic spilling out of nearby offices.

"Mrs Fontaine! Mrs Fontaine, please, wait a moment."

She slithered between another gentleman in a navy suit and a woman wearing a canary yellow dress. Together, they wandered into the sunlight streaming through the open double doors of the Hall of Commissioners.

Hale and Esmeralda kept their heads low as they passed silver-armoured security and rushed down the fifty-set staircase leading to High District Plaza, tailing Mrs Fontaine and her company. At the foot of the stairs, they squeezed between elegantly dressed shoppers flocking down Market Way. They passed the central slate-grey fountain of a rearing horse, its rider stretching upwards in victory. Hale and Esmeralda finally managed to get within earshot. By this point, Trevus had caught up with his quarry.

"... read the guard reports," he said. "How is that possible?"

"You told me he was in your pocket," Mrs Fontaine replied. "By the Goddess, Trevus, if you've led that lowlife to my door, so help me—"

"So help *you*?" Trevus grabbed Mrs Fontaine but was beaten off by the suited man on her arm.

"I wouldn't do that, Commandant," he warned.

"Stay out of this, Pontfedil. You may be funding this little project, but I won't hesitate to have you arrested."

Pontfedil's jaw twitched. Hale pretended to be inspecting the local produce, as she strained her ears to pick up more.

"... my family business is wrapped up in this," Mr Pontfedil was saying. "I wish Escudero had never introduced me to him. You told me you would arrest him."

"We have no evidence."

"There are letters in *my* safe in *his* writing, so don't give me that, Trevus. And now the sister is here? Find that bitch and give her back to the Sovereigns, then you and I deal with him as planned." He snatched Mrs Fontaine's arm, leading her away.

Hale made to follow, but Esmeralda stopped her. "Trevus is this way. Hale!"

Hale shook her off and rushed after her new targets, filled with a familiar rage.

TRACES OF THE PAST

The crowds thinned as Mrs Fontaine descended the cavernous Steps of Segregation, with Hale in pursuit. Hale removed her heels to tiptoe, hooking them around her fingers. The muscles in her legs burned by the time she reached the filthy floor of the slums, behind Mrs Fontaine who had landed moments before. The man named Pontfedil was gone.

The sun didn't shine down here. Dirty faces of playing children peered up at Hale as she walked the cobblestones of the tight, criss-crossing streets. Sewage had trickled down from High District, pooling in surrounding alleyways. The lines of terraced houses were smothered in moss, making it difficult to distinguish between windows and doors. Neighbours loitered outside their homes smoking and gossiping. They eyed Mrs Fontaine's fancy clothes and fell silent until she passed, mocking her when she was out of earshot. Hale smirked at the comments, nodding to a few locals. She tossed her fancy shoes to a young girl, whose face lit up.

At the end of the street, Mrs Fontaine toe-poked a loose bladder ball back to another little girl. The child scooped it up and ran towards her mother. By now, the feet of Hale's tights were soaked and torn. She continued behind Mrs Fontaine who was impervious to the poverty. At long last they came to Slum Square, littered with the usual druggies and drunks. A thatched two-storey tavern came into view overlooking the steep hill leading down to the docks. Hale decided to act. She picked up a loose stone and chucked it at the woman, darting behind The Smuggler's Cottage.

"What the …" Mrs Fontaine's gravelling footsteps stopped.

Hale darted around the back alley of The Smuggler's Cottage until she came out at the front entrance, overtaking

Mrs Fontaine to cut her off. She glanced out from the corner of the building. Mrs Fontaine was scratching the back of her head where the pebble had hit her. Seeing a solitary boy playing in the square, Mrs Fontaine marched towards him. Hale stalked her, rushing to catch up. As soon as she was close enough, she grabbed Mrs Fontaine in a choke hold, squeezing until the woman fell limp.

The boy watched, appearing more impressed than scared. Hale laid Mrs Fontaine's unconscious form on the ground. She searched her back pocket and threw him one of her smaller emeralds – enough to get him some dinner for a week. The kid caught it and beamed, no stranger to being paid for his silence.

"Impressive," Esmeralda said, coming up behind her.

Hale jumped. "Where did you come from? Any luck tailing Trevus?"

She scanned the square. "No, he must not travel by foot. I'm a good tracker, but he left nothing behind."

"Maybe he's using sorcery to get around?"

Esmeralda shrugged. "Makes sense, I suppose, considering no one ever sees him."

Hale wiped her sweaty forehead, then focused on Mrs Fontaine. "Can you help me with this?"

Esmeralda scooped Mrs Fontaine into her arms and Hale got the door as they entered the candlelit tavern. They greeted the usual drunk woman nursing a pint in the corner booth and entered the back office next to the fireplace.

"You're back," Maven greeted them, breaking off her conversation with Walter. "How did the council …" She stopped, spotting the woman in Esmeralda's arms. "You abducted the commissioner? Hale, what the—"

Esmeralda bypassed Maven, who had pulled back a life-sized, golden-framed portrait, showing the cubbyhole it concealed. She placed Mrs Fontaine inside, hooking her wrists onto one of the iron shackles attached to the wall. Maven tapped her face a few times to bring her round and Mrs Fontaine awoke.

"What are you doing? Release me at once!" She scrambled

to the furthest corner.

"Recognise me?" Hale asked, sliding into view.

Mrs Fontaine glanced at them all and rested on Hale. "Eyepatch," she whispered. "The Child Killer?"

"Aw, Hale, you're famous." Esmeralda sniggered.

Hale ignored her. "T-Tell me who the man following you was."

When Mrs Fontaine didn't answer, Maven shoved Hale aside and bent down, grabbing Mrs Fontaine's cheeks in a vice-like grip. "Fontaine? Of whom does Hale speak?"

Hearing Maven's fist connect repeatedly with the woman's face forced Hale to wait in the office. She sank onto the chair facing the desk.

"¿Estás bien?"

Hale waved away Esmeralda's concern. She winced as each of Maven's digs connected with Fontaine's face, until finally, the woman answered.

"Trevus of Oblivion!" Mrs Fontaine gushed through her tears. "I got him a seat on the council years ago, but he never comes. Ever. Not until today. I was as surprised to see him as anyone. I think he's taken an interest in her." She pointed at Hale. "I was supposed to meet him in Oblivion to give information I had on you, but when he discovered I invited the Sovereigns to Anferan ..." She shuddered.

Maven glanced at Hale, who confirmed with a nod.

"Shit," Maven said. "I hadn't anticipated this."

"It was only a matter of time before they came for her," Walter said.

Hale zoned out as the others argued. Her stomach twisted at the image of Sovereigns docking in Anferan. Only when the argument got more heated did she tune back in.

"... must calm down." Maven's voice came back in waves. The portrait hole had been closed, with Mrs Fontaine locked inside. "If Trevus is interested in Hale, it means we're on the right track. He must know where Cecerie is, or at the very least be hunting her himself."

"Do you know a Mr Pontfedil?" Hale interrupted.

Maven nodded. "Nobleman. Lives in High District. His family is in the mining trade. Why?"

"He also buys sorcery," Walter interjected. "Nobles are famous for using magic to fuel their estates in secret. I tell ya, Cecerie never realised how much danger she was in when she set foot on these shores."

They had now kidnapped a high-ranking commissioner in their quest to find her. *Yet another crime to add to my tally.* "I ... I can't do this, I'm sorry."

"Hale, wait," Maven said as she got to her feet. She tried to slip her a tiny piece of parchment, but Esmeralda snatched it. "Fine, you can go as well! Meet my contact tonight to offload some stolen goods at this location. Come back here when it's done for a debriefing."

Esmeralda chuckled. "Debriefing, uh? Nobody wants to see your ginger hoo-haa."

Maven flipped her the bird, and they left her office before Esmeralda's filthy mind could derail the conversation. The three of them sat at their usual booth, as Maven left the tavern.

"Ya sure you're up for working tonight?" Walter asked, as Hale rested back against the chair, haunted by Sovereigns. "Es and I can manage a simple burglary if ya aren't."

She rubbed her forehead. "Can you f-find out where this Pontfedil lives? If we're to rob an estate, then let it be his."

"Sure. Leave it with me, kid."

"Thanks. Then I'll go get changed and we can leave. Goddess, I hate wearing dresses."

"I don't mind," Esmeralda teased, checking her out.

Walter slapped her across the back of the head. "Come on you. Let's grab some food." He led her over to the bar as Hale headed for the stairs.

Entering the suite she had come to call home, Hale collided with her mother on her way out. Aveline slipped past her like she wasn't there, and Hale slammed the door behind her. Six months of not speaking hadn't been easy.

She made her way to the vanity table beside their bunk and slipped out of her soaking tights, kicking them into a ball in the corner. Sliding open a drawer, she withdrew a black long-sleeve top and stone-washed denims with frayed ends. She sat on the edge of the bottom bunk, inspecting her lean muscles. Regular meals had her close to full health, but a good night's sleep had been impossible to come by. Lying awake, she often dwelled on Cecerie. Asleep, she dreamt of Lucian, tortured by their final moments together.

On nights when Hale couldn't sleep at all, she and Esmeralda would sneak round the side of The Smuggler's Cottage and smoke the strangest strain of weed that burned amethyst and tasted of raspberries. Those nights were few and far between with the weed trade having dried up. Still, Esmeralda had been a welcome distraction amidst the chaos, never sleeping much herself. Hale wondered if she wasn't the only one who had nightmares.

She got off the bed and buttoned her fly, then strapped her dagger around her waist. She hadn't had the heart to use it yet, but the more she carried it, the closer that moment was coming. Her fresh top clung to her toned abdomen, shaping around her breasts which had finally returned to their normal size. Thankfully, Foric's cooking rivalled her mother's, for Aveline had no urge to feed her firstborn.

She'd sooner stab me with a fork.

Taking her faded olive trench coat from where it hung on the bedpost, Hale slipped her arms in. She tied a black bandana around her neck and flicked her collar up, leaving the suite and descending the staircase back to the bar. When she had finished dinner, she rounded up Esmeralda and Walter, and they exited the tavern.

"Foric had Pontfedil's address, but it's still a little bright for burgling," Walter said.

"*Vamos*," Esmeralda said, gesturing the opposite direction of High District. "I have something important I must do first. We can kill some time."

She led the way past the square. Hale gave a thumbs up to the dirty-faced boy from earlier, who was sitting cross-legged on the ground, wolfing down a huge bowl of stew. *At least he spent his payment on something sensible.* He saluted her and she returned the gesture. *Goddess, he reminds me of Lucian.*

"Ya paying more debts again, Es?" Walter asked as they strolled side by side.

"I told Ximo I would collect something for him. Just bringing it to him, *viejo*. That's all."

"Good. I don't want to have to pick ya up from another bloodbath."

They rounded the next corner. Esmeralda glared at Walter as if he had said too much.

"It was nothing," she told Hale hurriedly before she could voice her concern. "Just some people wanting me dead."

"Right. Nothing," Hale drawled, amused. "So why didn't you tell me?"

"What are we, pen pals?" She laughed.

"D-Doesn't mean I want you getting hurt."

Esmeralda glanced over her shoulder. "You hear that, Walter? She cares. Guess I know who's picking me up from my next beating."

Walter wheezed a laugh. "Fine by me. It will give my back a break."

They continued down the next street until Esmeralda directed them off the beaten path, down a tight alleyway. "Wait here." She disappeared round the next corner, following a group of scantily dressed male prostitutes who greeted her by name.

"Does she know them?" Hale asked.

"More like they know her," Walter said. "She and Ximo are old friends."

"Who is this Chee-mo?" Hale asked, sounding out the pronunciation.

"Ximo Palomino. He runs a brothel there called The Busted Cherry."

Hale snorted. "Charming name." From the crowds hanging around outside, she guessed it earned more than Maven's brothel in the basement of The Smuggler's Cottage.

Esmeralda returned a while later with lipstick on her cheek

and a bottle of port that she slipped into her side-satchel. "*Vamos.*"

Hale rushed to catch up as she strode past them both. "Well, how'd it go?"

"How did what go, sweetness?"

"Your little rendezvous. N-Nice shade of lipstick Ximo wears."

Esmeralda wiped it off as Walter laughed. "*Gilipollas.* Mind your own fucking business."

CLOSING IN

If prison had taught Hale anything, it was that time was a valuable thing. Losing track of it had been a nightmare, but the longer she stared at her battered pocket watch, the more nervous she became. The others waited beside her in a High District alleyway until it was dark enough to burgle; Walter resting against the wall, watching sludge drip onto the ground from an open drain above, Esmeralda swigging port like she hadn't a care in the world.

When it was time, they pulled up their hoods and pattered across High District's damp streets. At the end of the next alleyway, Hale checked both ways, making sure City Guard weren't patrolling. *They're not due for another ten minutes.* Their smoky breaths threatened to betray them the closer they got to their target. They passed the silhouette of the huge fountain in the centre of District Plaza from earlier that day. The water had been switched off now, but the breeze was swirling the contents of the shallow pool.

When they reached the back door of the Pontfedil Estate, Hale readied her lockpicks, slipping them out of the suede purse Esmeralda had gifted her during their first job together for Maven. She jiggled the rosary of the single cylinder deadbolt as Esmeralda and Walter kept watch. A beautiful *click!* caused a ripple of approval. She twisted the knob and ushered the other two inside.

An acrid, earthy scent greeted them in the estate's low-ceilinged hallway. Hale closed the door behind them. Esmeralda and Walter had already set off to inspect the giant humming tank to their right.

"Oil heating," Walter whispered to their unasked question.

"Some nobles still have it."

"*Una mierda.*" Esmeralda snorted. "I guarantee you it's running on sorcery. Oil died off centuries ago. This *puto* is likely draining Cecerie's power as we speak." Both Hale and Walter stared at her. "What? I'm just saying what everyone else thinking."

"We *weren't* thinking it," Hale said. She spotted a staircase lining the left wall that led upwards from the basement. "You two go search for some valuables we can sell to Maven's contact. I'll find something that connects Pontfedil to … Cecerie."

She had almost said Felix. Truthfully, she wasn't sure what to look for, or if Felix was really wrapped up in all this. She didn't want to believe it. She recalled Pontfedil mentioning some evidence in a safe. Whatever was in there, it could prove useful.

They ascended, careful so as not to creak the wooden stairs. At the summit, Hale paused, listening for movement on the other side of the freshly painted door. *Judging by the smell.* Hearing nothing, she picked her second lock of the evening.

Breaking into someone's home was a crime as old as time; bursting that protective bubble of self-preservation which fed one the belief that four walls and a locked door equalled safety. A burglar robbed not only someone's possessions, but their nerve. *And this isn't a world to be faced without one.*

When the door opened, they dispersed; Esmeralda and Walter searching the downstairs living rooms. Hale headed straight for the next staircase. She had broken into many estates in Ortivana, but something about being on the stairs always made her feel more exposed. *Especially after what happened with Lucian.* She shivered. *Stop picturing it.*

She followed the sound of snoring, entering a bedroom at the far side of the landing. The door was ajar, presenting enough room to slip inside. She crouched in the dark at the foot of a king-sized bed. A man and a woman lay snoring beneath the covers. Sweat stung Hale's vision as she inspected the couple, who tossed as if sensing her presence. She spotted shadowy silhouettes of a wardrobe, portraits, and a side table. *Too obvious. No one's hiding a safe in any of them.*

Feeling a fluffy rug on the floor, she flipped up the end and traced the floorboards, hoping to find a nook. It didn't take long. She pried away the fake floorboard to reveal the silvery outline of a safe. Smirking, she checked on the couple to make sure they were still asleep, then placed the wooden cover aside. She tried to jerk the safe open, using her lockpicks as leverage, but it wouldn't budge. Feeling the twisting tumbler, she discovered what kind of safe she was dealing with. *There must be a code nearby.*

Her knees cracked as she straightened. She froze as the man reacted to the sound.

One ... Two ... Three ...

He rolled over and fell back into snores.

Hale exhaled. She placed the wooden cover back and flipped down the rug, then tiptoed around the bed frame towards the man's side. Up close, she could smell remnants of Pontfedil's aftershave and alcohol mixed with soupy perspiration. The front of a triple-drawer nightstand caught her attention, and she spotted his holstered gun on top, next to an unlit candle. *Does that shoot, or is it there for show?* Guns were ceremonial at best, but she still didn't want to find out. She moved the strap away from the drawer and pulled the handle. *Locked.* It took only a second to pop it.

She cringed as she rifled through Pontfedil's underwear and withdrew a leather-bound folder hidden in the drawer's depths. Perching it on the corner of the cabinet, she searched through the parchment scraps inside, hoping the couple were stupid enough to write down the code to their lockbox. Realising she couldn't read in the dark, she decided to risk letting in some light. She crept to the casement window on the opposite side of the room, making a crack in the curtains. A speck of light from street lanterns outside crept through the double glazing. Hale squinted to read:

... account number: 2180

Deposited sum of twenty rubies on 2nd January. Didn't want him sending Escudero's goons to beat the crap out of me again. Why can't these Swashbucklers stay out at sea where they belong? I hate …

Hale swept the first page to the back of the pile. She scanned the second, a torn excerpt from some sort of logbook.

… missed a payment again. Wish someone would tell him that corundum has to be mined in Xeveria, cleaned, and transported to Anferan on a trustworthy ship. I swear, the slums spit out a newer, more impatient criminal annually. Just when I'm finally getting used to the last one. I can't keep up with the demands of this latest prick. How he ever found out that my family was in the corundum mining business is beyond me. I hope …

Knowing she was pushing her luck, Hale's curiosity won out against her instinct to call it a night. She was sure the others had left by now. She flicked to the second last page, hoping to find the name of the man who was blackmailing Pontfedil.

… told him that's it, I wasn't putting my family name at risk for him anymore. He didn't care about our reputation, and even less about my refusal. My defiance earned me a shiner and a broken rib. I couldn't even bear to tell Fontaine how it happened. Spun her some story about being mugged to gain her sympathy. She rode me pretty hard last night. When I went home to Hillary and spun her the same tune, she ran me a bath. I married such a prude, I swear. Tried to get her to join me in the tub but …

Hale glanced back through the gloom at Pontfedil cuddled up with the wife he was cheating on. *Oh, Hillary. If only you knew.* She refocused on the papers and flicked to the last one, praying to the Goddess that the man wouldn't go into more detail of sexual endeavours. This page was dated prior to the others.

… finally met him in person. His handshake was firm, like he was asserting his authority. I've encountered this many times, so it didn't faze me at all, and we got down to business. I'm interested in investing in his plans. He's the type I can count on to double my profits. His accent was strange, definitely not Anferanian. I couldn't place its origin though. I told him my name and he told me his. What kind of surname is Legat?

Hale jerked away from the curtains, casting the room back

into darkness. At the same time, the noblewoman sat up. Yawning, she got to her feet, bypassing where Hale had pressed against the wall in desperation, as if that would somehow make her invisible. She felt the woman's body heat go by. Still half asleep, Hillary left the room, totally oblivious to her presence. Her bare feet slapped down the hallway and a door closed. The sound of her tinkling told Hale she only had a minute to escape.

She streaked across the room, shoving the papers back into Pontfedil's journal and placed the folder into the drawer beneath his briefs. A flush of water sounded from the privy. Hale slipped behind the curtains again, opening the window latch. Wind whistled into the estate as she swung her legs onto the stylish balcony. She caught the double windowpanes and closed them as quietly as possible. Realising she couldn't lock them from here, she broke off a piece of branch from one of the many plant pots on the balcony and wedged it where the panes joined. Without wasting time admiring her work, she climbed onto the slender balcony rail, baffled that Pontfedil hadn't woken up amidst all the noise.

Balancing against the wind, she shimmied across the estate's external panelling, along skirting protruding from the outer wall. Reaching the external sewage pipe that was flushing out Hillary's business, Hale clung to it and slid two storeys, all the way to the ground. Her feet landed in the drainage, and she scanned the street for guards as her heart raced. Seeing none, she dashed around the estate's perimeter, back into the alleyway where Walter and Esmeralda were waiting. She'd never been more relieved to see them.

"What happened?" Esmeralda asked. "Did you cause a commotion?"

Hale mopped her forehead, shaking. "L-Let's get out of here." Pushing Felix to the back of her mind, she took one of Esmeralda's bags and slung it over her shoulder. They followed Walter, who was already at the end of the alley. Hale was glad the other two had managed to steal something. Maven's contact would be waiting.

On the way to Hilltown, Hale found it difficult to concentrate. When Esmeralda paused at Walter's signal to let a patrol pass, she almost collided with her. After ten minutes travelling through the city, she succeeded, unwittingly forcing Esmeralda into the open. Illuminated by street lanterns, Esmeralda darted back into cover. She shoved Hale into a dark nook in the alleyway wall, pressing herself against her.

"Es, what are you—"

"Sshh!"

Hale stayed quiet.

A dog barked in the distance and steel sounded on the cobblestones, stopping at the end of the alley. "Who's there?" a male voice called.

The flames of his lantern licked along the bricks, falling short of the inlet concealing them. Esmeralda smothered Hale's open mouth to shut her up as she hyperventilated. An agonising moment passed, and Hale resisted the urge to scream. All that existed were their simultaneous pulses, ticking down the seconds until they were found.

The guard sounded closer ... closer. Then, out of nowhere, an explosion.

"Goddess!"

He retreated as rallying cries sounded from the adjacent streets, with horns and whistles ringing in the night. Esmeralda dragged Hale from their hiding place, unaware that Hale was about to faint. They stared at the sky, wondering what had saved them. Thick smoke was billowing over Hilltown, where they were scheduled to meet Maven's contact. Walter ran across the road towards them.

"Did ya fucking see that?" he exclaimed. "What in the name of the Goddess?"

Hale was reminded of Ortivana. It was a strange coincidence that the same night she caught her first whiff of Felix, something in Anferan went up in smoke.

Esmeralda was the first to snap back to reality. "*Vamos*. There will be guards all over the place. We'll not be selling to anyone tonight."

*

Back in Maven's office, the boss sat clutching her hair. There was a plate of untouched meatloaf in front of her, attracting flies, and a huge stack of documents covered her desktop. They had finished telling her the tale.

Esmeralda was pacing, irritated, as was often the case in Maven's presence. Hale had her own habits too, staring up at the books behind Maven's desk while the woman spent ten minutes scolding them. Maven finally resurfaced.

"Look, forget the explosion," she said. "It was probably some renegade sorcery gone wrong. The immediate concern is why I have three sacks of trinkets holding none of the things I listed as essential. If I have to interrogate you all, I will."

"Interrogate?" Esmeralda rounded on her. "*¡Que te den!* You think we stole your goods?"

"Maybe I'll start with you, Admiral. You have a habit of sticking your fingers where they don't belong."

"Watch who you threaten, prig, or I won't hesitate to wedge another stick up that tight little ass." Esmeralda's words were rapid and sharp.

Maven bounded out of her chair and Hale retracted her gaze from the books, watching Walter wedging himself between both women. They continued snarling at each other over his head. Using his frail body as a barrier, he ushered Esmeralda to the furthest corner as Maven finally retook her seat.

"What happened?" she asked Hale, exasperated.

"It was my fault," Hale said, flinching as Esmeralda knocked over a lamp. "I f-found a floor safe but …" She rushed to come up with an excuse that didn't involve mentioning Felix's name. "I-I was almost caught. Once the nobles were awake, the job was too risky. Es and Walt did good stealing whatever they could, so if you're angry with anyone, it should be me."

Maven observed her like she knew Hale wasn't being truthful. She rifled through their trio of rucksacks, checking what valuables they had managed to gather. A chalice, necklaces, rare textbooks, rings, weapons, broaches; her anger deflated with the rising value of each.

"I suppose it's a decent haul, even if it's not what I asked for," she relented. "Shame you missed the buy I set up. We need all the corundum we can get. The brothel isn't making much at the minute."

"Maybe you should try employing gigolos under the ripe old age of seventy," Esmeralda said.

Maven ignored her.

"Rearrange the buy," Hale insisted. Her own funds were running dangerously low.

Maven stroked her chin, flicking the solitary hair. "Fine. Tomorrow evening. Same time, same place. I'll get word to the buyer." She departed the office, slamming the door, ending any further debate.

Hale withdrew the pack of Merta's cards. "I could use a drink. You got deep pockets, Walter?"

"Only for you, my dear."

*

If the last six months in Anferan had taught Hale anything, it was to always keep her guard up in the tavern, especially when it was full like tonight. As Esmeralda nabbed the last dribble of whiskey, Hale scooped her winnings into her purse, wary of Esmeralda's tendency to dip into the pot when no one was looking. Esmeralda laughed, gesturing her surrender.

"I'm not stealing from you, sweetness. I learned my lesson. My wrist still hurts from last time."

Two nights previous, Hale had spotted Esmeralda slipping into her meagre winnings after she'd cleaned out the entire table. She had slammed the pommel of her dagger into Esmeralda's knuckles and took great pleasure in seeing the bruise was still there. Those in the tavern at the time were stunned that someone confronted her, but it was possible that Esmeralda enjoyed their scuffles. Hale wondered why she was the exception, knowing Esmeralda would have shanked anyone else who had the gall. The admiral made a lot of exceptions where she was concerned.

I wonder why that is.

As usual, Esmeralda was fixated on her, leaning back in her chair, oblivious to the attention she attracted. Hale couldn't blame the surrounding men for staring. Every one of them was plotting how best to win Esmeralda's favour, something which happened often when they drank together. A group of younger lads in the corner were egging on their friend to make a move, but Hale was the only one who had her full attention.

As Walter struck up conversation with Jakson, Esmeralda leaned towards her, close enough that no one could earwig. "What's with you tonight, uh? You seem distracted."

Hale uncorked a fresh bottle of rum and topped up the empties at the table. Before she could respond, the tavern door flung open, letting in a gust of wind. Everyone fell silent and the music grinded to a stop. A soldier entered, shaking rain from his hair. Hale's chest caved. *That armour.* She would recognise it anywhere.

"No …" She shook her head, feeling the walls closing in.

The tavern picked up again, the musicians striking up fresh chords as the man approached the counter and ordered a drink. Hale shot to her feet. Shaking, she withdrew her dagger and headed for the bar, shoving people out of her way. The soldier had his back to her, waiting to be served. *This will be easy. So easy. So quick.* Her palm sweated on the hilt. Before she could slit his throat, someone restrained her.

"What are you doing?" Esmeralda spun her around.

Hale tried to push her off. "Let me go!"

Esmeralda hugged her despite her best attempts to escape. "Sshh," she whispered. "I've got you." She directed Hale's dagger back into its sheath, despite Hale's unrelenting grip. "*Tranquila,* sweetness. It's ok."

"No." Hale struggled, but she couldn't break free. "Let me go. Let me …" She convulsed into sobs, tugging to no avail as Esmeralda continued whispering in her ear words that she didn't understand. They could have been dancing for all anyone knew. The tavern was so crowded that the soldier remained oblivious to their presence. Esmeralda touched the nape of Hale's neck, guiding her head onto her shoulder. She tried easing the dagger from her but Hale wouldn't let go.

"Give it to me," Esmeralda muttered. Hale clutched it tighter. "You are not a killer. Let it go, Hale. Please, let it go."

The music changed from a lively jig to a gentle harp's refrain. Defeated, Hale released her grip. Esmeralda secured the dagger back in her belt and captured her in a tight hug. Lulled into submission, Hale swayed with her as the harp entered pianissimo, and the first real tears she had cried since Lucian's death soaked into Esmeralda's shoulder. Unable to stop them, she buried her face in Esmeralda's neck, heaving uncontrollably as the weight of what she had almost done crashed down upon her.

"Sshh." Esmeralda stroked her hair, and somewhere beneath the pain, there was comfort.

Hale put her arms around her waist, pressing the curve of her spine as she pulled her closer, making sure Esmeralda was real. In that moment, it didn't matter that Esmeralda was a Swashbuckler; one of the Tripartite. It didn't matter that she smelled of alcohol, mixed with the delicate tinge of perfume. Hale cried herself sober, allowing Esmeralda to guide her back from madness, gradually bringing her to her senses.

When the song finished, Hale raised her head. Through glassy vision, she saw Esmeralda's face lined in concern. Esmeralda made to brush her cheek, but Hale backed away, suddenly aware of their surroundings. *What am I doing?* She cast an anxious glance at the bar, but the Sovereign soldier was gone. Killing a soldier in a crowded tavern was an utterly foolish plan that would solve nothing. Unable to comprehend what she'd been about to do, she held Esmeralda off and raced up the stairs to her suite, taking the stairs two at a time.

Once inside, she slammed the door shut, blocking out Esmeralda and the world. Thankfully, the suite was devoid of Aveline. Panting, Hale clawed her way to the sofa by the fire, sinking onto it. Esmeralda's words echoed in her head. '*You're not a killer.*' An odd thing to say to a convicted murderer, but the way she had said it made it sound as if she didn't believe

Hale had killed Lucian in such cold blood like the rumours said. Only three people knew the truth about that day, but Lucian was gone, and she hadn't spoken to Felix since. With the Sovereigns this close to home, her time was limited. If Felix was in Anferan and connected to Pontfedil, she had to find him, however little she desired to face him.

BLACKMAIL

The next morning, the air was crisp, forcing Hale to hold the lapels of her coat closed, cursing its lack of buttons. At this early hour, the streets were eerily devoid of life. She turned right at the end of the road, dodging the corpse of a starved mutt. Maggots poured from its half-eaten stomach, and her own heaved. Early risers had begun construction on their stalls by the time she reached the market. She took a quick browse while the vendors sorted their products underneath coloured canopies.

Thinking she would buy something special to give Cecerie if she found her, she lingered near a jeweller, considering a necklace with a purple orb. Its contents swirled and it dangled from a thin black rope, locked together by a delicate silver clasp. The orb called out to her.

"How much?" she asked the shopkeeper, picking it up.

"Fifty sapphires."

"Three emeralds. That's all I have."

He stroked his greying stubble, inspecting her gear for anything he liked. "That dagger." Hale cursed her lack of buttons again. She pulled the lapels closed, covering her weapon. "Come on. It's an even trade. Decorate that pretty neck of yours." He ogled her cleavage as she reopened her coat.

"It's not worth just the n-necklace. What else do you have?"

He grumbled, having thought her easy prey. Making sure no one was watching, he retracted a mouldy cardboard box from under the table. "Take a look and be quick about it."

Hale rummaged for anything of value. *A small, religious hardback; a few ugly gold rings; a bronze bullet; a silver chalice; a diamond-encrusted letter opener ...*

"This," she said, taking out a battered obsidian compass that dangled from a small black chain.

"That?" Seeming to reconsider mocking her, he gestured for the dagger.

"And I'll take the little snow globe as well," she added, spotting it on the corner of his kiosk. It had a tiny cathedral inside that reminded her of *An Caisleán*. She detested the place, but her mother had always loved the architecture. *Maybe a gift will soften her up.*

"Bleeding me dry, you are. Now give it to me."

She was more than happy to let the weapon go. Last night had scared her to her core. If she couldn't be responsible for what she did with it, carrying it might not be the best idea. Esmeralda wouldn't be happy, of course, but violence was more her speed than Hale's.

Feeling lighter without it, Hale slipped the trinkets into her pocket and clipped her new compass onto the inside of her coat, alongside her pocket watch. She headed in the direction of High District, back towards Pontfedil's estate.

Today, the nobility were out in force, discussing the carnage from last night's explosion. Stuffed shirts carried themselves with the stench of self-importance, turning up their noses at her because she was uncoupled. Hale didn't care enough to let it bother her. *Traditionalists. Some things are better left in the past.* A few nobles voiced their disgust aloud, mocking her dirty boots and faux suede coat. Taller buildings in the next street acted as a more effective buffer against both the gossipers and the gales, and Hale quickened her pace. She soon found herself standing in the same lane from last night, staring up at the balcony she'd leapt from. It was much higher than she remembered. Passers-by watched her, and wary of attracting attention by loitering, she crossed the single-lane street. Ignoring her reservations at this insane plan, she knocked on the front door of the estate.

Footsteps sounded on the other side of the green double doors, and a hint of blond appeared in the frosted glass. Hale imagined, for a fleeting moment, that it was Felix. The doors opened inward, and a beautiful woman in her late twenties greeted her, wearing an innocent smile.

"May I help you?" She scanned Hale's tattered coat and undercut, in contrast to her pink corseted frock.

Ah, Hillary. We meet again.

Hale cleared her throat. "Excuse me for the in-interruption, Mrs Pontfedil." She spoke carefully, so as not to stutter. "My name is Ms Legat. Your husband and I have a meeting scheduled for this morning. I was given this address."

"Geoff?" Hillary said, confused. "He didn't mention it over breakfast."

"Is he here?" Hale asked. "Forgive me, I'm in a bit of a rush, and I'd like to get this deal finalised."

Hillary glanced over her shoulder. "Geoffrey? Can you come here for a moment?"

Her voice echoed down the hallway, into which Hale knew, post-break-in, was the downstairs sitting room, at the rear of the estate, adjacent the door that led down into the basement. She braced herself as an imposing man exited the estate to greet her.

Geoff Pontfedil was well over six feet, wearing a perfectly tailored suit.

That surely skinned him a few thousand corundum.

"What is it? What do you want?" He scowled at her. "I'll have no beggars at my door harassing my wife. You'd better have a good reason for interrupting my morning cigar." He admonished Hillary, and she cowered under his flying saliva.

"Oh, I'm not here for a donation, Mr Pontfedil," Hale interrupted, if only to save Hillary from his bullying. She wanted to give him another shiner to match the one he already sported. "The name's Legat. I believe you've met my brother." She figured using the name 'Hale' would scare him.

Colour drained from his face. "Legat?" He shielded Hillary behind him, more so that she couldn't see than for her safety. "Don't you mean Hale?"

She grimaced. *So much for that plan.* "Word travels fast."

"Why are you at my door, Ms Hale?" Pontfedil wasn't falling for her smoothness as easily as his wife.

"Unfortunately, Felix believes your business arrangement has come to that point where he has to, how do you say, clean house?" She took great pleasure in the droplet of sweat leaking down Pontfedil's brow. "I'm here to have one last chat, to see if we c-can't come to some arrangement that suits both parties. Can we step inside? This isn't a conversation I want overheard."

Pontfedil pondered the request while his wife questioned him from the hallway. "Hillary, dear," he interrupted. "Make yourself busy in the kitchen while I take care of this."

Hillary obeyed without disagreement, and Hale entered the estate past Pontfedil's welcoming arm. The home was more elegant than she'd thought, having been unable to appreciate its beauty in the dark. She followed him to what she assumed would be an upstairs sitting room, well out of Hillary's earshot. Hale examined the decor that she hadn't been privy to before. The Pontfedil Estate was beautifully furnished, with barely a speck of the scarlet wallpaper visible beneath the number of hanging oil paintings of bearded men. There wasn't a single woman. *Charming insight into the family tree.*

"You like art?" Pontfedil asked, as if trying to find some common ground.

They reached the first-floor landing and passed the tongue and groove panelling lining the long stretch of corridor.

"No. Just wondering which of these paintings you'll miss most if we can't come to some agreement."

Pontfedil mopped his forehead on his sleeve. "I find it strange that you're here, I must say. I have a meeting arranged with Felix later today. I figured we could iron all this out then."

Hale couldn't control her surprise. "Where are you planning to meet him?"

"The silo in Shanty Hilltown, of course." He gave her another suspicious glare, as if wondering if he should have revealed that. Making nothing of it, he twisted the knob of the sitting room door and ushered her inside, snapping it shut behind them.

Hale paced the rectangular room, scanning the stylish sideboard that held three huge aloe vera plants in pewter pots. She watched Pontfedil, who had seated himself upon one of the two black leather sofas with plush velvet cushions. Centred between them was a large golden coffee table, upon which he was stuffing the most ridiculous pipe.

"Don't mind if I smoke, do you?"

"By all means. Excuse me if I don't have time for pleasantries, but I'm a busy woman, as you can imagine."

Pontfedil scoffed. "I struggle to see what pressing business a woman could have, if I'm honest."

Oh, the usual. Burgling. Espionage. Attempted murder.

She sat on the corner of the table in front of him, and he rested back against the cushion to get some distance as she encroached on his personal space.

"Am I making you uncomfortable?"

Pontfedil swallowed, loosening his collar. "As a matter of fact, yes."

Hale flicked up her eyepatch, and he cringed at the disfigurement beneath. "You see this? My brother did it," she lied. "To his own sister. So, what will he do to you when he finds out you've been holding out on him?"

"Now wait a minute. I've paid Felix everything I …"

Hale leaned even closer, staring deep into his steely-grey irises. "I'd be careful about what you say next, Geoffrey. Or that black eye of yours might just …" She clicked her tongue, imitating popping it out.

His breathing stuttered. "I … I'm telling you the truth."

Hale stood and resumed pacing the room. She considered another angle to get him to open up. "Bad move, getting off on the wrong foot with me, considering what all I know about you."

"Meaning?"

"Meaning, I wonder what Mrs Fontaine would say about you funding the local riffraff she's dedicated her career to eradicating." The silence that followed her words told her she had his attention now. "Or better yet. I could s-slip into conversation with Hillary that you have broken the sanctity of your marriage, for the simple fact that she is, and I quote, 'a prude'." She smiled at him over her shoulder. "Can you guess where I'm going with this, little miner?"

At this, Pontfedil laughed. "Fine. How much do you want?"

"Just like that?"

"Corundum is what it always comes down to. Everybody wants a percentage, and I'm like the fucking bank of the Ancestors. Just name your price so we can end this."

Hale folded her arms. "I don't want your precious stones, Pontfedil. I want what's in the bedroom floor safe."

"How do you—"

"Doesn't matter. You want this harassment from Felix to end? Give me what I want, or we go downstairs, and I tell Hillary the truth over that tasty little breakfast she's preparing."

"She would never leave me," Pontfedil blustered, his face pinkening with rage.

"She will if I offer her the means. Which I'm seriously considering. Or maybe I'll just kill you outright. Then she won't have much of a choice. I gather she's used to such, what with being married to you."

Pontfedil wasn't eager to test her. He deflated under the layered threat. "Fine. Wait here." He got off the chair.

Hale laughed. "A-Actually, I'll be coming along. Wouldn't be the first strange woman in your bedroom, would it?"

Seeing there was no way out, Pontfedil led the way. Remembering the gun on his bedside table, Hale stayed alert. *Hope that thing isn't real.* She entered his bedroom for the second time in the space of twenty-four hours and watched Pontfedil pull aside the mat, revealing the safe.

"Do you mind?" he asked, hesitating to input the code while she watched.

Hale turned away, using the reflection in a picture frame on the wall to spy on him. Pontfedil flipped up the corner of the mat, revealing a six-digit code inked beneath it. If it wouldn't have blown her cover, she would have laughed.

So dumb it thwarted a pro like me. Not bad, Pontfedil. Not bad at all.

Hearing the clicks as he rolled the tumblers into place, Hale waited for the sixth. She turned in time to see the safe door open. He emptied the contents, producing a piece of old parchment and a small silk sack with a pull-string. He got up and shoved them at her.

"I hope this will please Felix. It's all there. All the evidence I have against him. I'm not meeting him anymore, so you can tell him from me that this is where we part ways. For good. I want nothing more to do with your wretched family."

"Understood."

She followed him back down the stairs, and Pontfedil opened the front door. Despite her desperation to leave, she couldn't help but glance down into the kitchen, smelling delicious bacon. *Good luck, Hillary.* Pontfedil cleared his throat, and Hale nodded goodbye. She exited the estate, hoping to the Goddess she never set foot in it again.

It was lashing rain. Surprised that had worked, she tucked the parchment and pouch into her pocket. As she did up her coat's mismatched buttons, her skin prickled. *I'm being watched.* She stared up at the three-storey estates that lined the length of the roadside. *No one leering out the window. Balconies are clear. Roof is too high to track from.* Not wanting to draw more attention, she merged with the umbrella-clutching couples going about their business.

She flittered between them, hoping whoever was following her would lose track. Seeing the entry to the sewer, Hale quickened her pace. She darted off the beaten path, and the immediate smell of this morning's shit made her gag. Panicked, she retraced her route from the previous night, trudging through the flowing excrement of High District. After a few seconds, she glanced over her shoulder. Seeing no one behind her, she stopped.

Digging in her pocket, she withdrew the piece of parchment, unfolding it. It appeared to be a hastily drawn map of Na'Revas. *Walter might know who made it.* A lump formed in her throat as she spotted Ortivana, a dark shadow making up one quarter of the Cuatro Isles continent. Then there was Anferan, east of Ortivana. It was closer on the map than the journey here suggested. Hale traced from Anferan back past Ortivana and down through the Neverending Ocean, where it curved around the huge, mountainous country of Stonawal, the Sovereign homeland. It was here that Sovereign Altus ruled the Tripartite. She brought the map closer, reading the name beside an X someone had marked there in ink on top of an island she had never heard of before.

"Sailor's Creek?" She slipped the strange map back into her pocket, withdrawing the silk pouch next. For a second she thought it was empty. Spreading the drawstring opening, she dug inside, receiving an unexpected prick. "Ah!"

She felt around its depths more carefully. Her index finger slipped into the circumference of a ring; the only thing the bag contained. She lifted it out, admiring the entwining black vines. The ring had a purple stone that pulsed unnaturally, like the pendant she'd bought earlier for Cecerie. The vines on either side of the stone broke off into the shape of a snake's tongue; the very thing that had pricked her.

Her skin tingled again, and she put the ring in the bag, sliding it back into her pocket. Someone was behind her, trying but failing to be silent. Wishing she hadn't sold her dagger, she turned to confront her tail. As she did, something hard struck her face.

She was only on the ground for a second; long enough to fall victim to the sewage. The overpowering scent wafted up her nostrils as she massaged her cheek. Grey clouds drifted into the corners of her vision, revealing an orange sun straight ahead. *No. Not the sun.* She squinted through the dizzying effects of the punch, and finally, her attacker came into view.

"Maven? Ow! What the fuck!"

"You're a hard person to sneak up on."

"Why the hell are you jumping me?" She spotted the map and pouch in Maven's possession, along with her recently

Everlasting Rain

purchased gifts and unread evidence against Felix. "And ... robbing me?"

Maven stared down at the trinkets. Hale watched her withdraw the elegant ring from its pouch and slide it onto the tip of her chubby thumb. "Did you think you could get away with double-crossing me?"

"Double-crossing? What are you talking about?"

"No one plans a heist without a contract from me. Surely Esmeralda told you that?"

"I wouldn't say it was a plan. M-More of an impulse really. Besides, what do you want with an old map?"

Maven tiptoed through the sewage to get closer to her. "You mustn't tell Esmeralda about this."

"Why?" Hale asked. "What is it?"

Maven turned away, as if testing how much she could trust her by offering Hale a free shot. "I've been planning something for a while. A voyage to the most hidden location in Na'Revas, said to possess the greatest wealth known to both human and sorcerer-kind."

"Sailor's Creek?"

Maven circled her, pacing the sewer. "Once upon a time I had planned for Esmeralda to lead my expedition, but sadly, she and I will never get along." She paused. "I've been impressed with *your* work since you've arrived, however. We could do great things together, you and I."

"I don't agree with your methods." Hale pointed to the lump forming on her temple. "Have you freed Mrs Fontaine yet?"

"She was disposed of."

Hale was sickened by more than just the sewage now. "You shouldn't have done that. Her disappearance will trigger an investigation." She stared at Maven, for the first time seeing the evil in her.

"Fontaine was a leech. But I digress. It might interest you to know that I've recently come into possession of a ship and crew that could rival Esmeralda's. Sailor's Creek is the destination. How would you like the opportunity to lead the expedition?"

Her request caught Hale unawares, who'd gone from thinking she was about to be murdered, to being offered the most high-profile job in Anferan's underworld. "I-I don't know a thing about sailing, save for what I learned on the way here."

"But you *do* understand loyalty, something Esmeralda doesn't. I can't give *her* the location. She would swipe the treasure right out from under me."

"And I wouldn't?"

Maven scowled. "You owe me a debt for breaking you out of that prison."

"Esmeralda saved me. Not you."

"And who passed the contract onto her in the first place?" She pointed to herself. "Your mother came to me, and *I* hired Esmeralda, the only person capable of pulling it off. She jumped at the chance to get back to Anferan. Her crew was wilting in exile. Pathetic."

Hale wasn't sure what to say. She shook her arms, trying to shimmy some of the faeces off her clothes. Maven patted the only clean part of her she could find: a shoulder that wasn't entirely stained.

"Don't pass up this opportunity, Hale, out of some misguided loyalty. She may have drafted you into her crew, but Esmeralda doesn't care about you. You think, if the situation was reversed, that she would pass it up?"

Hale bit her lip. "No. I suppose she wouldn't."

"Excellent. Then I'll make preparations. For now, keep this information to yourself. Uttering a word about Sailor's Creek to anyone would jeopardise both of our livelihoods."

She walked off, her subtle threat hanging in the air.

"Maven?" Hale called. "I'll take my loot back."

Laughing, Maven tossed the necklace and snow globe over her head, keeping Pontfedil's possessions. Hale caught the globe before it smashed and picked up the necklace, watching her depart, wondering what new shit she had slipped in.

EL OTRO LADO

You can't ignore me forever, Esmeralda.

"I can try," Esmeralda replied, arguing with the voice in her head.

Her skull was caving in, or her brain was swelling. Somehow, she had made it upstairs to her suite, hiding her distress from Walter. Talking to herself was a sure sign of madness. She pounded another sip of Ximo's 'special' port, but all the alcohol in the world couldn't block out this latest episode.

Why won't you listen to me? The internal voice persisted.

"*Porque eres un fantasma,*" Esmeralda said aloud.

I'm not a ghost. I'm alive. You must listen. You are the only one who can save her.

"*¡Déjame en paz!*"

I can't leave you alone, Esme. I have to show you something important. Maybe then you'll finally believe I'm real.

Esmeralda squeezed her head, struggling to block the voice out. Her vision was glitching; the image of her suite flickering as the force invading her brain tried to show her something she didn't want to see. Undoubtedly a cruel trick to unhinge her. She hoped Walter wasn't following to check if she was as ok as she had promised. It wouldn't be the first time he had found her in a pool of her own blood, and she'd be forced to tell him another lie about how it happened.

She wiped away a trickle of blood that had skirted down her neck, dripping from her inner ear. This latest bottle of Ximo's port was supposed to break magical transmissions. She attempted another sip, but the bottle slipped, smashing between her feet. Staggering, she rammed into her vanity table, bringing half its contents onto the floor. Drowning in darkness, she lay on her back staring up at the ceiling, falling into the abyss the voice in her head was sucking her into ...

... Why must sound always travel in waves? It made it harder for her to hear the men speak, for their words to penetrate the silver liquid she was submerged in. The egg was the only home she could remember, yet her desire to relive the outside world was growing stronger. Remnants of sorcery in her veins had almost left her, suctioned through vine-like tubes that penetrated the gel she was cocooned in. The liquid surrounding her had once been purple, back when she first remembered being stripped and encased in the transparent shell. Now, it was a pearly white, meaning she was close to the end of her lifespan, but this wasn't about saving her.

She wasn't sure why this particular conversation had piqued her interest. She had listened to the robed man speak in the past but could only ever make out a few words. The whiter the liquid around her became, the more acquainted she grew with the laboratory's secrets. She pushed through, using what little power she had left to project her image through the egg, dragging Esmeralda's reluctant subconscious along with her.

Ah! Solid ground!

She stared out at her spectral on the other side, amused that her consciousness had the decency of clothing her, even though she no longer recalled the touch of fabric on her skin. Her spectral stared back, observing her truer, naked version still floating in the liquidised containment field. Her long black hair spiralled, giving the impression of a mermaid (minus the tail). Mermaids had always been her favourite fictional creatures.

Her spectral departed, crossing the concrete squares, weightless and soundless, completely invisible to the two men standing by the window, deep in conversation.

"... told me you had her under control," the robed man was saying.

The long-haired blond man standing in front of him was disgruntled. "I did what you asked, Trevus. I captured her."

"You didn't tell me she was this unstable."

"It's the stress of the abduction."

Trevus paused at the vertical slit for a window. The spectral peered over his shoulder and got tunnel vision as she stared down at the traffic dotting the sea around Anferan's docks, a long way beneath the top floor of Oblivion Tower. It was a far way to fall down the mountainside.

"You better not be messing me about," Trevus said.

"I wouldn't dream of it, Commandant. You will have Cecerie once she is safe to be moved, but she tore half of Hilltown apart last night. Wrangling sorcerers is dangerous, but my sister even more so. I must keep her hidden until City Guard crawl back into their hole. It would be foolish to try moving her again so soon."

Trevus turned back. "Fine. But I want regular updates on her progress."

The blond man gave a curt nod. "We have a bigger problem. If we hope to use Cecerie's powers without fearing repercussion, Lana must be incapacitated."

"You tried that in Ortivana and she survived, sprang by the very admiral in your employ."

The blond man tensed. "Esmeralda double-crossed me, but she will get her comeuppance. For now, it's Lana we must worry about. She loves Cecerie. She'd kill anyone who comes within arm's length of her."

"So, what do you suggest?"

"I recently hired Maven to steal some evidence that Pontfedil had, connecting me to a string of high-profile murders in Ortivana during the war. With the Sovereigns landing in Anferan, I couldn't afford to have it crop up."

"No. It would complicate matters."

"Exactly." He nodded in agreement. "But in dealing with Maven, I discovered she has planned an expedition to Sailor's Creek, with Lana captaining her ship. If this is true, maybe we could use her."

"The Sovereigns are here," Trevus reminded him. "Why not let them arrest her again?"

The blond man folded his arms and exhaled. "You said yourself how terribly that worked in Ortivana. If Lana's on our tail, let's spin it to our advantage. If we can control her, we don't need to kill her."

Trevus peered at him from under his hood, like he was trying to read his mind. The spectral found she wanted to recoil from his purple glare, even though she couldn't be harmed in her current form.

"If all these dots you've drawn connect, we'll be wealthy men, Felix. See to it that they do, won't you?"

The man named Felix bowed and took his leave. His footsteps echoed as he removed himself from the open-plan office, walking between the eggs in the adjoined laboratory. The spectral watched him admire her naked form in the egg. She'd been in there far too long to have retained any dignity. He left, closing the door behind him, and she watched Trevus.

The Scour commandant was staring back out the window. "You're getting more adventurous."

The spectral froze.

Trevus stared directly at her, as if aware she had been there the whole time.

"I assume," he continued, "if you have finally mastered the art of spectralisis, that telekinesis is child's play to you?"

The spectral nodded, casting a terrified glance back at her egg, wishing she had never left it.

"Good," Trevus said, smiling. "Then I would like you to deliver a message to whomever you have been conversing with all this time, for I believe our interests may be aligned."

*

Esmeralda jerked back to life. Blood was leaking from her eyes and nose. She sat up, using the hem of her vest to clean her face.

"Who hit ya this time, *amiga*?" Walter was sitting by the circular table in the centre of the room, watching her.

She massaged her head where she had whacked it off the ground. "I don't remember, *viejo*."

How could she tell him the truth? That no one had ever attacked her over debts. That all the times he had found her bloodied and unconscious like this were because of her visions. Or were they premonitions? She wasn't quite sure. All she was certain of was that each time that voice infiltrated her mind, it was to send her information she could use to stay ahead of the game. Or stay safe.

Sitting up, she rested back against the wall beside her bed, watching the room drift in and out of focus. The tavern bustle one floor below was a low rumble. She reached for Ximo's port then remembered it had smashed. The liquid had dried into the floor, crested where she had lain.

"I can't keep doing this," Walter said, moving to sit on the edge of her bed. He gave her a handkerchief to wipe her nose. "Tell me what's been going on." She got to her feet and headed for the door. "I'm serious, Es," he called down the hallway. "Ya keep up like this, then I'm gone. I know there's something ya ain't telling me."

She paused at the top of the tavern's staircase. "Just leave it alone, Walt. For your own good."

She descended back into the tavern and pushed through the crowds. Taking up her usual spot at the bar, she gestured to Foric for a drink. Walter bypassed her, stony-faced. He left the tavern, slamming the door a little harder than usual. Esmeralda wished she could talk to him. She leaned on the counter, head bowed, recalling snippets of her latest vision and the message Commandant Trevus had sent.

Sailor's Creek …

It seemed Trevus wasn't content in keeping all his eggs in Felix's basket. She hadn't heard mention of the Creek in years; odd, considering it used to consume every waking moment. Only one man in the world knew where Sailor's Creek was and how to get there and back safely. She would pay him another visit later. For now, she dwelled on the treasure said to reside there; a treasure that had once destroyed her life.

Don't do this, the voice in her head said.

"Why can't you leave me alone, uh?"

"You asked me for a drink," Foric snapped, thinking Esmeralda was talking to him. He slammed the bottle on the counter and she cursed, tossing him a few extra corundum in apology. She tipped some port down her throat, but as she was enjoying the renewed buzz, someone slapped her ass.

"Lugsy, want to lose a limb?"

A middle-aged scoundrel with massive ears slipped onto the stool beside her, smelling like an infection. "Come on, Admiral, that ain't nice. How about you dish me out a freebie?"

"The brothel's downstairs, *hijo de puta*. Don't dare touch me again."

Lugsy slid his arm around her, blowing down her neck. The last breath to rest there had been Hale's. Esmeralda reacted so speedily she could have fooled anyone she was sober. She twisted Lugsy's arm up his back and smashed his face on the countertop, watching him collapse at her feet.

His friends howled, rushing to his aid, and soon the entire tavern was brawling despite Foric's yells. Laughing, Esmeralda fought them all, toying with the unskilled riffraff. With each one she struck, the voice in her head dimmed, eventually leaving her in peace.

TRUTH SETS YOU FREE

Fuming that Maven had stolen Pontfedil's loot and the evidence against Felix, Hale was thankful she hadn't come away with nothing. Maven was recruiting her to spite Esmeralda, but the possibility of leading an expedition meant if Cecerie's trail went cold, she could make enough corundum to kick-start another search. Wanting nothing more than to slide into the establishment to bathe, she continued onward, ignoring the jeers of passers-by at her messy attire. *I can only imagine the ridicule if Walter and Esmeralda see me like this.*

No sooner had their collective laughter sounded in her head when Esmeralda was thrust headfirst through the entrance to The Smuggler's Cottage.

"Ey! Get off me, Foric."

Foric released her when they were far enough from the door. "You're barred! At least for tonight."

"This is bullshit!"

Foric mopped his forehead with the dirty dish rag, bringing his voice to a regular decibel. "Look, I saw what happened, alright? He went too far. Any other day I would have let you away with it, but you're a bastarding menace, Es. Need I remind you of the brawl a few nights ago?"

"Jakson caused that, not me."

"*You* finished it."

"So? We're pirates! It's a bit of fun."

"The two women and three men with broken bones didn't agree," Foric snapped.

Esmeralda pursed her lips. "Can I at least finish the drink I paid for?"

He glanced up at the sky as if on his last nerve and, noticing

Hale, said, "You deal with this. I've had enough for one day."

Foric entered the tavern and returned moments later, chucking Esmeralda's coat over her head. Esmeralda tore it off, but bit her tongue. Hale leaned against the tavern's exterior, smirking.

"Oh, don't look at me like that," Esmeralda told her.

"Are all pirates this much trouble?"

"Only the very good ones, sweetness."

Hale chuckled, leaping back as Foric threw out another brawler with massive ears and a broken nose. He glared at Esmeralda and staggered to the opposite side of the street, clutching his face. Esmeralda twisted her arm to check the deep cut on her elbow and hissed as she prised a piece of glass from it.

"*Cabrón*. He'll think twice before touching me again. Hale, could you …" She held her nose, retreating from her. "Oof, what *is* that smell?"

"Oh, I … fell," Hale mumbled. Just as she had imagined, Esmeralda laughed. "Alright, alright. I'm getting a bath."

Esmeralda intercepted her at the door. "*Espérate*. You are not cleaning off that amount of *mierda* in a tub the entire tavern shares."

"Then where?"

She paused for a second. "*Vamos*. There's a place nearby."

Confused, Hale followed her, hoping it was close.

As they traversed through the slums, Esmeralda chatted about what had set both Foric and Walter on the warpath. Hale was only pretending to listen. She was thinking about Maven's offer, wondering if she should tell Esmeralda about the boss' double-cross. If she told her the truth, maybe Esmeralda wouldn't help her with Felix. Deciding that wasn't a risk she could afford, she kept quiet.

"You ok?" Esmeralda said, when Hale hadn't done much more than react at the correct moments of her story. "You're not still thinking about that Sovereign, are you?"

Hale latched onto the other topic plaguing her. "No, but now that you mention it, th-thank you for … well … you know." She stared into the distance, suffering a fresh wave of embarrassment. "I guess p-prison messed me up worse than I realised."

"Sounds like you need a drink."

"Is that your answer to everything?"

"Not everything. Alcohol doesn't have any answers, sweetness. It just helps you forget the bloody questions."

Hale laughed despite herself. *She's got me there.*

They headed towards the docks, taking their usual, mud-filled route. Hale tensed as they passed Scours standing guard by the city perimeter hassling villagers. She wondered how many innocents would be hauled off to Oblivion, under the pretence of having sorcery in their veins. According to the rumour mill around town, no one who visited Oblivion ever came back. Seeing the Scours reminded her too much of her childhood. Only when she and Esmeralda were beneath an arching tree tunnel a safe distance away, could she relax.

Well, as well as one can relax when covered in shit.

Esmeralda led the way, instructing Hale to stand downwind. The harbour loomed on the horizon as they descended the steep, slippery path. A salty breeze wafted inland, greeting them as they entered the eclectic market, and they stopped at a stall.

"What have you today, Hedge?" Esmeralda asked the vendor, popping off the cork and sniffing the bronze liquid sloshing inside.

"Anferanian mead," Hedge replied, stroking his magnificent auburn beard. "Or I have some limoncello in the back."

"*Está bien.*" She tossed him an emerald before he hunted through his crates. "This will do."

"You sure? May as well have a wee browse while you're here."

Hale lingered a short distance away, paying little attention to their conversation as Esmeralda rattled through Hedge's dusty bottles. A light breeze tickled her face as she gazed at the ocean, spotting a ship so far away it was a dot. *Maven really thinks I can captain one?* She knew was blackmail, but the offer was still incredible. *Enough to stop me telling Esmeralda about Sailor's Creek? Enough to make me leave her crew and become her competitor?*

She withdrew from the ocean, watching the end of the admiral's exchange with the bootlegger. Esmeralda knew almost everyone on the island. She bid Hedge goodbye and took off her coat to conceal the litre of mead she had purchased at a discount. The sun had disappeared behind the clouds, but today's humidity was at an all time high. Hale followed a layer of perspiration dripping down Esmeralda's neck. She cleared her throat, surprised by the longing it stirred in her.

"Where are we heading?" she asked, hurrying alongside Esmeralda back in the direction they'd just travelled.

Esmeralda made a break in the bushes to their left, taking them off the beaten path. "You'll see."

Making sure they weren't being watched, she ushered Hale between the trees. Hale squeezed through the opening beneath her arm, and Esmeralda clambered in behind her. The branches sprang back into place concealing them, and the chaos of the docks was drowned out by thick shrubbery.

Daylight was extinguished by a multitude of leaves and flies. The scent of moss and wet tree trunks clogged Hale's nostrils, giving her relief from her current predicament. She was as amazed at Anferan's beauty as the first day she arrived. The Goddess' creativity had gone wild here, with trees jutting at angles unimaginable. Gnarled roots threatened to trip the unworthy as they trekked through the traitorous dimness. Vines clung to the fabric of Hale's trousers, forcing her to rip free. She sweated as they entered so deep into the forest that Esmeralda drew one of her daggers to carve a path. Hale followed as she slashed away obstructions. What they found on the other side left her speechless.

At first it appeared to be more greenery. Upon closer inspection, Hale realised the solid ground in the centre of the clearing was an illusion, a reflection of the cavernous trees overhead. As she neared the invisible edge, her foot slipped in, soaking all the way up to her thigh.

"*Cuidado.* The water is deep," Esmeralda warned. She circled the edge of the lough as if familiar with where the pool began and dropped her coat on the ground beside a moss-free rock. Twisting the cap off her purchase, she sat on the stone, taking a healthy swig.

Hale sank another inch into the surprisingly clear depths. *There must be some kind of sorcery involved here.* She watched particles of shit simmer off the floating lapels of her coat and disappear. It was almost a shame to spoil something so beautifully pure, but she was relieved to finally get clean and the water remained unaffected by her contamination. "Is this safe?"

"Safe if you can swim," Esmeralda called.

Hale paused, half submerged. She frowned up at her. "You can't *swim*?"

Esmeralda cursed. "I'm, er, afraid of water."

"What?" Hale couldn't help giggling. "How is that possible? You're a S-Swashbuckler, for crying out loud. You spend most of your life at *sea!*"

"And any good Swashbuckler will tell you that once you're in the water, you're pretty much done for," Esmeralda snapped, angrier with herself than Hale. "Just hurry up and wash so we can go, uh? I cannot believe I told you that."

Hale stopped laughing, not wanting Esmeralda to think she was laughing *at* her. *So Somateria mollissima can't swim, huh? Wonder if her crew know that.*

Sparing Esmeralda further blushes, she swan-dived deep into the lough, her pores screaming in protest. She stared through the depths, scouring the sandy bottom. It was made up of supple beige soil, without a pebble or sign of life. She had never seen anything so unpolluted.

Resurfacing a few metres from her entry point, she swam back to the bank where Esmeralda was swinging her leg from a rock, a metre from the edge.

"Don't even think about dragging me in," Esmeralda warned, thumbing her mossy dagger. "*O te mato.*"

Hale didn't require a translator to understand the death threat. She accepted the bottle of mead from Esmeralda's cautious reach, taking a swig. *Ugh, that's strong!* "You must have an iron gut," she said, setting it on the grass.

She took off her coat and empty weapons belt and propped them up on the bank. Esmeralda tossed a bushel of red berries that she tore from the nearby shrubbery.

"Saldrasines. They're good for scrubbing dirt off."

Hale caught the floating Saldrasine berries and crushed them between her palms. She lathered herself, head to toe, in their purply-red juices. "Oo, they smell good!"

"Eat them if you like. They're great for making wine. Something the Ortivanian in you might appreciate."

Hale bit into a clean berry and winced. "Eugh, a bit tart, but the aftertaste is kind of sweet. I doubt you could make much more than country wine with these though. Ortivanian wine is made with grapes."

Esmeralda rolled her eyes. "You and your Ortivanian wine."

Hale finished washing her hair and scrubbed her clothes, rinsing, and ringing them out. Esmeralda took them, one by one, spreading them across some nearby rocks to dry. Before passing her the denims, Hale double-checked the snow globe and pendant were still safe inside her pocket. Wearing just her underwear, she helped herself to another drink, gagging again on the foul cocktail. "Oh, that really is potent."

Esmeralda laughed and snatched the bottle before she floated too far away. "You have such an unrefined palate, sweetness. This is honey mead. Hedge brews it himself. Granted, he brews it a bit strong, but I was addicted to this stuff in prison."

Hale starfished on her back, enjoying the magical water carrying her overworked muscles. "You must have been in the luxury wing. I don't remember the S-Sovereigns having such fancy hooch."

Esmeralda giggled. "What did you even do to get locked up there?"

"You already know my story."

"I know a version. Why don't you indulge me? You just don't strike me as the cold-blooded killer the Sovereigns paint you as."

Hale pushed off the bank until she was far enough away to avoid answering. The water carried her into the centre of the lough, putting distance between them. She didn't want to spoil this tranquil moment with a miserable recollection of the past.

"Finished yet?" Esmeralda called a while later. "I'm bored. I thought you would bathe naked, at least."

Hale laughed, ever amused by Esmeralda's cheek. She flopped upright from her sprawl and swam back to the water's edge. "Pass me the mead again, will you?"

"Got a taste for it now?" Esmeralda teased, offering it to her.

As Hale drank, she watched over the top of the bottle as the admiral kicked off her boots, rolling her stretchy leathers above her knees. Esmeralda sat on the verdant bank, hesitating before dipping her toes in the lough. She winced and shut her eyes, as if it made it easier not to look. The discomfort it caused her was immediately apparent.

How did I not notice it before?

Esmeralda squeezed fistfuls of grass, resisting whatever internal trauma was taking hold until her body acclimatised. When the torment was under control, Esmeralda stared out at the lough, as if she was now able to appreciate its beauty.

"How do you do it?" Hale asked.

"Some days are better than others. I am never comfortable near water, but aquaphobia does not dictate my life. I'd be a pretty poor Swashbuckler if it did."

Hale watched her tickle the water's surface, and stared down at her own hands, wondering what would happen if she tried to take Esmeralda's. "You make it look so easy, f-facing your fears."

"I've just had a lot of practice. And not much choice." A muscle in her jaw twitched, and she glowered at the lough. "Piracy was the only way to escape Xevería."

"Why did you have to escape?"

Esmeralda shuddered. Her grip on the bank tightened.

Hale wanted to comfort her, but the message didn't transmit from her brain to her limbs. It was like trying to convince someone to jump into fire; they could do it in theory, but why would they? She closed her fist, staring up at Esmeralda, defeated. "Maybe I'm not quite there yet."

"Or maybe you just need some incentive."

Without warning, Esmeralda lunged into the pool.

"Es!"

She disappeared in the disturbed water. Before Hale could dive under to save her, Esmeralda resurfaced a short way off. Trying and failing to stay afloat, she left Hale with no choice but to grab hold of her.

"What the hell are you doing?" Hale yelled, pinning her against the bank. "Are you mad?"

Esmeralda's coughing became mixed with laughter. Her swarthy face was a pasty shade despite riding some unknown high. Hale's anxiety turned to bewilderment, and eventually she started laughing too.

"Looks like I'm not the only one living my worst fear," Esmeralda said, glancing down at Hale's arms locked around her waist to keep her afloat. The water level gradually settled around them.

Hale was exasperated. Her skin was on fire, but she couldn't let Esmeralda go however much she wanted to. "A-Anyone ever t-t-told you you're …?"

Her bottom lip was trembling so much she couldn't speak. Esmeralda glanced down at it. She played with loose hair at the nape of Hale's neck, driving her insane. Up close, Hale saw flecks of ochre in her eyes. How could she go behind Esmeralda's back, setting sail on Maven's ship without her?

"What are you thinking about?" Esmeralda whispered, reading the expression on her face.

Hale groaned as she brushed a wet strand of hair behind her ear. It was difficult to think with such unexpected intimacy. "I …" She swallowed. Esmeralda was getting closer. "I h-have to tell you something. T-Two things," she corrected, remembering the secrets of the day.

"I'm listening."

"My brother, Felix. He's in Anferan."

"Where?"

"A s-silo in Hilltown."

"I know the place."

"Can we go then? Later, around midnight?"

She nodded. "And the second thing?"

"Maven's going to—"

Esmeralda kissed her.

The air in Hale's lungs dissipated. She felt like she was back under water again. Every nerve in her body tingled, and it took her brain a second to catch up with reality. Unsure of what was driving her, she eventually kissed her back, slowly at first; uncertain.

Her body burned differently now. A brief moan escaped her, from distress or desire she wasn't sure. She could taste the mead on Esmeralda's tongue. Esmeralda pulled her closer in the water, leaving nothing between them, running her fingers through Hale's hair, sending shivers down her spine. Hale's mind was swirling. Something awoke inside her that had been dormant for so many years. The deeper the kiss got, the less anxious she became, and she remembered how this was supposed to go.

*

Later that evening, Hale lounged in bed with another one of Maven's books propped open. She normally read well, but tonight she couldn't focus, and was using the paperback as a deterrent. She stared at the faint text, having lingered on the same word for the past ten minutes.

'Consuming.'

Every inch of her was consumed by thoughts of Esmeralda. *How did one kiss spiral into sex?* Flashes of what had transpired between them in the lough replayed, over and over, in her mind. Her underwear being slid aside. The sodden grass in her clutches as she pinned Esmeralda's body against the bank. The rushing water. Their combined moans. The taste of Esmeralda's skin ...

She flung the book across the bed. The distraction wasn't working.

Distraction.

She wondered again why Esmeralda had silenced her before she could reveal Maven's plan. *Although the way she did, I have no complaints.* Since prison, she doubted she would ever be able to be so intimate with someone again. She wasn't even sure she wanted to until now. Maybe it was the even ground Esmeralda had created. That had clearly been her intention, and there was something to be said for levelling the playing field, putting herself in a compromised position just to make Hale feel more at ease.

Hale pined, reliving it again, and buried her face in her pillow. She ruffled her hair and got up. Rolling her shoulders, she ambled to the sitting area, and plunked herself on the sofa beside her mother. Aveline continued knitting a thick, half-finished maroon scarf. Its stitches were tight and precise. She repeated the knit and purl as Hale chose a different book from the pile underneath the coffee table, hoping another story would keep her mind off Esmeralda. She forced herself to read an entire chapter of the book about a superhuman named Loup. As she flicked to the next chapter, her mother spoke.

"I got the gift you left me."

Aveline had stopped knitting. Hale watched her shake the little snow globe and sit it on the coffee table. "Oh yeah. I b-bought it in the market."

They observed it snowing together.

"Bought it? You didn't steal it?"

"Of course not." She paused. "Do you like it?"

"I do." Aveline surveyed her for the first time in weeks. Her stare was searching, and Hale sensed she was building up to ask her something. "Tell me what happened."

"N-Nothing," Hale stammered, thinking she meant Esmeralda.

"Tell me what happened to my son."

Oh. Shit. Not again.

Most conversations they had landed on it. Hale returned to her book, but the words stared back at her with even less meaning than before. Her heartrate climbed, pulsating so hard it pressed against her back. "You already know what happened."

"Not according to you," Aveline said. She picked up her knitting again, needles clicking faster, and more intense. "I'm ready to listen to your side."

Hale dog-eared the page, tossing the book onto the table. She got up. Aveline gave up knitting and followed her to the bunk bed. She paused at the headboard, as Hale sat on the end, removing her socks.

"This is not something that can be fixed overnight, Lana. I want you to tell me how it happened. If you're really not to blame then maybe I can learn to forgive you."

Hale unbuttoned her shirt. It was still damp from the lough. She removed her eyepatch, placing it in the lone jewellery box on the vanity table. Rummaging in a drawer for a nightshirt, she glimpsed her mother's reflection in the dresser mirror. Aveline gaped at the scars criss-crossed along her back; burn marks from Sovereign branding; slices from their whips; a ribcage that still jutted at an abnormal angle. It was the first time Hale had revealed evidence of the torture she had gone through, but this didn't deter her mother from the topic.

"Please," Aveline begged. Her words were muffled behind her hand as she tried to hide her revulsion.

Hale quickly pulled on a clean nightshirt. She leaned on the dresser, watching her mother in the mirror. "Do you remember when Father took me to that execution?" she asked, struggling to stay composed.

Aveline nodded. "I never thought I would witness the day when you pushed him away. He always regretted the wedge it forced between you."

"I never told anyone, but I reckon he knew her," Hale said, steering the conversation away from Lucian. "The woman the Scours burnt to death."

"He did. That's why he attended."

Hale spun around. "What? Who was she?"

"The leader of the Freebooters. Nyra. Your father gave up the names of her and her closest generals and usurped her. He outed his own sorcery to the Tripartite in the process. I'm not sure if it was the Sovereigns or Scours who eventually killed him, but either way, he wrote his own death warrant the day he sold Nyra down the river."

An image of Nyra's face staring over the heads of hundreds of nobles was still clear as day in Hale's mind. *She stared directly at us. She must have known what he had done.*

She found her way to the bed, and Aveline sat down beside her. Hale jerked away as she made to comfort her.

"All this time," Hale muttered. "You knew he was a traitor?"

"Your father had many secrets, some of which he told me, and some I wish he didn't. I'm sorry." Aveline's apology was barely a whisper. "Tell me what happened, Lana. I didn't even get to bury his body."

Hale's irritation increased as they landed on Lucian again. "P-Please don't make me." The image burned a hole in her gut. She was sweating, wrestling back the acid threatening to shoot up her throat. Aveline tried to touch her again, but she lashed out, swinging aimlessly in blind panic.

"Ah!" Aveline recoiled.

"Mother!"

Blood dripped on the floor, and Aveline backed away. "What did you do? What did you *do?*" She retreated to the sitting room, using the scarf she had been knitting to blot her face. Her knitting needles fell loose, clattering across the floor.

Hale rushed towards her. "I'm sorry. It was an accident—"

"It's always an accident with you!" Aveline screamed, spattering Hale with saliva and blood. "It's never your fault, is it? Me? Lucian? Cecerie? It's never your fucking *fault*, Lana!"

"Mother—"

"You don't *get* to call me mother anymore!" She picked up the tiny snow globe on the table and threw it at Hale, who ducked, cowering as it shattered against the wall.

Silence followed; each of them glaring at the other. Hale wasn't sure who was more in disbelief. Her for the sudden change of pace, or Aveline for the accidental nosebleed. She stood, dumbstruck, drenched in broken glass and fake snow.

"Get out!" Aveline screamed. "Get out! Get out!"

She repeated the words, battering Hale towards the door. Forcing her into the hallway, she slammed the door in Hale's face. Hale smacked it with her fist then rested her forehead against it, catching her breath. Turning away, she gaped down the stairs at the nosy drunkards interested in who was yelling. She darted out of view and leaned back on the nearest wall, sinking to the floor, staring at her palms, ruing what they'd done. Suddenly The Smuggler's Cottage disappeared.

Blood continued seeping through her fingers regardless of how well she plugged the hole. His blood. Not the assailant's. Lucian lay sprawled on his back, a pool of scarlet gushing from his head despite Hale's attempts to put pressure on it. It saturated her dress as she knelt beside his lifeless body.

"No ... No, no, no. Luce, no."

"I can't believe you did it!" Felix was standing over her, yelling. He sounded almost gleeful.

"It was an accident!" The floor was swallowed up by the endless river. How many pints did the human body have? "It won't stop! Goddess, why won't it stop!"

"You killed him! You fucking killed him, Lana."

"It-It was an accident. I didn't mean ..." She frowned up at Felix. "I sent him home! Why didn't he go? Why didn't he listen to me?"

"Guards!" Felix screamed. "Guards!"

At first, Hale thought he was warning her. Then, the ugly truth hit. Felix sneered as he beckoned the guards towards her, and at last, Hale finally understood.

She scrambled to her feet, wielding the same rock that had killed Lucian. "You? You set this up!"

She swung for Felix, who knocked the rock loose. Her other fist collided with his face and he stumbled backwards against the wall, holding his broken nose. He ran away, avoiding her next punch.

Their footsteps resonated down the corridor as she gave chase, but his silvery-blond locks disappeared as he rounded a corner. Suddenly, she was pummelled into the wall by a golden battering ram. Winded, she scowled up at the platoon of Sovereigns surrounding her.

"We have you now, General Hale," the nearest soldier said. "There's no getting out of this one. You're under arrest for murder."

She scuttled as far as she could, but there was no escape. Felix had made it so. The Sovereigns didn't draw their weapons. They didn't have to. Instead, their boots stamped down on her in an endless flurry, until she could no longer raise her head.

ADMIRAL RIVERA

"Hale? Are you ok?"

Esmeralda's voice sounded miles away. Hale jerked awake. She had collapsed on the landing, slumped against the wall at the top of the stairs. Esmeralda helped her to her feet and ushered her into a suite at the end of the hallway, bypassing people who had left their rooms to enjoy the domestic.

Shutting them out, Esmeralda left Hale standing in the middle of the studio apartment in her bare feet and resumed what she'd been doing previous to the interruption.

"You're cooking?" Hale asked. Her ears were ringing. She crossed the room and leaned over Esmeralda's shoulder, watching her stir red wine into the mince. The pan's intense sizzle took a moment to die out.

"Just heating up some leftover beef from my *empanadillas de carne*. Have you ever tried them?" Esmeralda smiled back at her.

"No." She felt her face burn.

Esmeralda turned her attention back to the pan and Hale exhaled, remembering how to breathe.

"Well, I must invite you next time I make them. For now, we will make do with a chilli. You like beans, right?"

"S-Sure." Hale rubbed her head, shaking glass particles from it. "I don't understand. You're m-making me dinner?"

"I was making myself dinner, but there is enough for two. Get yourself a bowl from the cupboard, uh?"

Hale obliged; anything to put some distance between them. Trying to maintain her composure next to Esmeralda for an entire meal would be impossible. There was something so intimate about dinner. *And a homecooked dinner at that.*

Hale sat at the round table in the centre of the suite, surrounded by four stools. If the admiral hadn't invited her personally, she would never have guessed anyone lived here. It was a nondescript suite, apart from the made-up bed in the corner and boots kicked underneath. A vanity table's contents had been tipped on the floor, but Esmeralda was impervious to the mess.

"You don't have a lot of stuff," Hale said, searching for a topic.

"It's still on the ship."

Of course. She writhed with embarrassment.

She sat in silence, counting the various stains on the walls and floor until Esmeralda had finished cooking. Esmeralda brought the food to the table and filled them a bowl, dropping the empty pan into the pre-filled sink beneath the dirty window. "Wine?" she asked, opening a new bottle.

"What's wrong with the other bottle?" Hale held up the empty glass Esmeralda gave her.

"That was for cooking. This is an expensive burgundy. Shouldn't you know the difference? You're Ortivanian."

"Mm, but I'm also a d-dirty peasant. We'll drink whatever you put in front of us."

Esmeralda laughed. She took a seat across the table facing her. "*Salud.*"

"Cheers," Hale said, toasting her. She took a sip, and they tucked in.

The chilli was delicious, if a little spicy. Hale drank her wine quicker than she should have. Thankfully the generous helping of food meant her stomach had a bit of extra padding. It was difficult to say whether Esmeralda's cooking was as good as her mother's, but it was definitely better than Foric's. She concluded Esmeralda was a close second.

"I didn't think you cooked," Hale said between bites.

"Is that so odd?"

"You're just full of surprises, that's all."

An image of them pressed together in the lough appeared in Hale's mind, and she focused on her food, presuming

Esmeralda was thinking the same.

"So ..." Esmeralda breezed over it. "I take it things between you and your mother are not improving, uh?"

Hale grimaced. "Heard that, did you?"

"Half the tavern did." Esmeralda swallowed another sip of wine. "What's her issue with you? Is it still about your brother?"

"Can we talk about something else?" Hale cringed at her own bluntness. "Sorry, I don't mean to be rude."

Esmeralda laughed. "You are the farthest thing from rude."

"S-So these *empana*-things you make. Are they a Xeverían dish?"

Esmeralda seemed exasperated by the abrupt topic change. "Er, some say they were invented by the Ancestors, but as to which ancient country they originated from, I could not tell you."

"I imagine the Ancestors stopped writing most things on paper when they made those machines. Do you ever wonder if we could get their tech up and running again like Xeverían people want?"

"I don't want to think about that."

"Why not? I doubt it would be scarier than sorcery. My sister has this kind of sixth sense, like she can read e-emotions or something."

Esmeralda kept her eyes on her chilli.

"And my father?" Hale thundered on, buoyed by nerves. "He could make plants grow in a matter of seconds, from seedling to flower and back again. Our cottage was surrounded by the most beautiful forest where I used to ..." Esmeralda had stopped eating, and Hale wondered if it was maybe time to change the topic for *her* benefit. "Are you ok?"

When Esmeralda looked up, her eyes sparkled. "Of course," she said, a little too joyfully. "Would you like some more wine?" She filled Hale's empty glass without waiting for an answer, her pouring unsteady.

"Here, let me." Hale took the bottle before the glass overflowed.

Esmeralda relinquished it and got up, bringing their bowls to the sink.

When Hale had filled them another glass, she stared at Esmeralda, wondering what had just happened. Esmeralda stood with her back to her, a tight grip on the sink's edge as she daydreamed through the window at the mist settling outside. Hale picked up a stained tea towel from the counter, offering it to her. Esmeralda dried her hands. As she gave it back, their fingers brushed, sending shivers up Hale's arm. She tossed the rag on the counter, and made to retreat, but Esmeralda took her hand.

Hale resisted the urge to break free. She met the admiral's amber gaze, finding softness she hadn't anticipated beyond the usual intensity. "What is it?" she asked.

Esmeralda brushed a piece of glass off her head. "Your hair is wet," she muttered.

"I know."

"And your eye. It looks sore." She attempted to touch the scar that was devoid of its usual patch, but Hale pulled back.

Esmeralda's face fell. Releasing Hale, she walked back to the table to retrieve her wine. They took their seats again, and Hale continued to watch her, wondering what was wrong. Wondering why the topic of sorcerers had made her sad. Unable to witness her so agitated, she pulled out the pack of Merta's cards from her trouser pocket.

"Do you want to play a game?"

Esmeralda shook her head. She paused. "Tell me more about your sister."

"Why?"

"What other kinds of magic can she do?"

Hale put the cards away. "She healed people for the most part. During the civil war, F-Father would bring wounded rebels and civilians back to our cottage. Tiny Cecerie would float between their s-sick beds like a little fairy, patching them up and sending them on their way."

Esmeralda smiled. "She sounds like a sweet kid."

"She is. Was," Hale corrected. "She isn't a kid anymore. She was fourteen when I was arrested."

"Do you ever wonder why the Sovereigns arrested you for killing Lucian?"

Hale winced. Hearing his name aloud was always uncomfortable. "What do you mean?"

Esmeralda shrugged. "I mean, they could have arrested you for anything, couldn't they? Espionage, theft, betrayal. Why would they choose to label you 'The Child Killer' and arrest you for the death of a peasant boy so insignificant to them?"

Hale had never considered it until now. She had been too preoccupied with the actual murder. "I s-suppose murder meant they could sentence me to death."

"And yet they kept you alive for three whole years. Doesn't that seem odd to you?"

"They tortured and interrogated me, asking questions about my brother."

"Lucian?"

Hale shook her head. "Felix. He set me up."

"He betrayed you?"

"He had an accomplice." Hale really didn't want to talk about this. She hated Esmeralda for prying, but her mother's persistence seemed to have opened the floodgates. *Or maybe it's the wine.* "From what I gather, they put the pieces in place; set the wheels in motion for Lucian to … and for me to …" She shook her head, sighing. "I suspect Felix sold me out to the Sovereigns to save his own skin, then disappeared before their good graces ran out. Lucian was just in the wrong place at the wrong time. And … I killed him. I killed him, ok? Fuck."

Hale grabbed fistfuls of her hair and leaned her elbows on the table as the weight of her crime crashed down upon her. Telling Esmeralda wasn't anywhere near as difficult as telling Aveline, but it still broke her in half to talk about that night.

Esmeralda puffed, absorbing her story. "Any wonder you don't talk about it. It sounds very complicated." She said nothing for a moment, picking a loose splinter from the table. "Why would Felix set you up like that? Do that to his own family?"

At this, Hale resurfaced, throwing her a wry smile. "I'll let you know when I find him." Hoping Esmeralda was done with this line of questioning, she asked, "Do you have any siblings yourself?"

Esmeralda peeled the splinter away and ceased fiddling, swirling her glass of wine. "You know what I think?" She met Hale's eyes again. "That the Sovereigns marked you as a threat and didn't want to make you a martyr. They ruined your reputation instead of killing you so that the Freebooters would turn their backs on you, making them easy pickings. After all, who would associate themselves with a ruthless child killer?"

Hale was winded. "That's not what I am! It was an accident. Fuck! Why will no one believe me?" She sank the rest of her wine, slamming her goblet on the table. "If that's the way you see me, then w-why did you ... I-I mean, why did we ..."

Esmeralda stiffened. "I don't know."

Hale's heart sank. "Suppose I don't either. I'm sure it didn't mean anything to you."

"Why would you say that?"

Hale stared at the table. "Well, you are a pirate. Isn't that just what you do? A woman in every port, as they say."

She glanced up, seeing Esmeralda's expression change. Esmeralda got to her feet. "You should go."

"What?"

"Leave. Now."

"Es—"

Esmeralda stormed to the door, holding it open. A muscle in her jaw was twitching.

Reluctantly, Hale did as she was told. She hovered in the doorway, the groove cool on her bare feet. "Uhm. Well, th-thank you for dinner."

"Mm-hm."

Hale waited, but Esmeralda avoided looking at her. "Are you, um, still smuggling with us this evening for Maven?"

"No. I have somewhere else to be."

"Oh." Hale hovered a little longer, wiggling her toes. "Well. Goodbye then. I'll maybe see you later."

"*Adios.*"

Hale understood she was dismissed. She exited the suite and Esmeralda slammed the door, locking the deadbolt on other side.

EL TRABAJO IN TWOS

When she met Walter downstairs, he questioned Esmeralda's absence.

"She's sitting this one out," Hale replied, shoving her feet into a pair of boots that she had been brave enough to steal from her mother's suite. Thankfully, Aveline had gone to bed, meaning she could grab her coat and eyepatch too. She held open the tavern door, letting Walter exit first.

"Something up?" he asked.

"Nothing."

"Esmeralda is never up to 'nothing'."

"She said she was busy. Can you drop it?"

Walter arched his brow. "Little touchy, aren't ya?"

"Sorry." She exhaled. "I'm just nervous."

He led the way out of the slums, towards the steep mountain pass up to the outer walls of Hilltown. It was here that Anferan's skeletal home of defunct artificial intelligence resided. One could have mistaken it for a junkyard, if not for the fact it was heavily populated with those too poor to even live in the slums. Tonight, its people were sound asleep by the roadside. *On empty stomachs, no doubt.* Hale's own stomach squirmed, more so with how she had left things with Esmeralda than because of the chilli.

The ground was barely visible in the dark; piled with technology's corpses, stacked in the form of shanties along the hillside. A graveyard, some called it, sickened by the idea that these machines could have once been alive. The Ancestors dabbled in profanity. They considered the emergence of sorcery a blessing; thankful that magic had destroyed the old machines and sent the world back to zero. Others considered both to be a sin and believed the only way the world could be reset was by wiping sorcerers from existence like the machines. Hale wasn't sure where she stood on the matter but trod on the carcasses of AI as she would have never considered treading on human bones. They cracked under her feet all the same.

It was difficult to carry the bags of stolen trinkets while trying to keep her balance. Walter carried the other two bags, and they kept watch for any sign of City Guard, but it was difficult in the dark. A few times she almost lost her footing, her feet becoming tangled in wires connected to obsolete circuit boards. Hilltown was like something lifted straight out of history. *No one even remembers what half this shit is anymore.* She kicked aside a cube-like piece of plastic with a broken screen.

Together, they plodded through the tight streets that the locals had made trekking to and from the slums each day. When they reached the top, Walter placed his satchels on the ground, panting from the strenuous climb.

"The buyer should be down this next road." He pointed towards an opening called Tin-Hut Street, according to the spray-painted sign. Endless rows of corrugated steel cast ominous shadows. A rat popped up in the distance, making Hale jump.

Walter sniggered. "Afraid of a little rat?"

"Considering they used to treat my body like a buffet."

"Ha! At least ya can joke about it." He readjusted his bags of trinkets before they slipped off his shoulder. They travelled the rest of the way in silence.

Maven's buyer finally came into view at the far end of the makeshift lane. The lantern burning in his grip illuminated his shaggy brown hair and matted coat. Hale got a waft of mould. It was hard to make out his face beneath his greasy beard, but his skin was a similar shade to Esmeralda's; swarthy, but with none of her smoothness.

"Walter, you got the stuff?" he asked, skipping pointless pleasantries.

"That depends." The man gestured to the three crates

behind him, and Walter cracked one open, catching a glint of corundum inside. "All's in order."

Hale dropped the bags by the contact's feet. He ogled her. "Do I know you, lady?"

"No." She grabbed a crate of corundum, passing it into Walter's waiting arms.

"Nah, wait a sec." He grabbed her as she picked up another, and the crate smashed on the ground.

Hale shook him off. "T-Touch me again. I dare you."

Her reaction triggered something, and he grinned toothlessly. "I *do* know you. Hale. The Child Killer."

Walter slipped himself between them, preventing the man from getting a better view of her. "Ya've made a mistake, young blood. The deal's done, so why don't ya leave?"

"I ain't got no beef with you. Respect, respect, and all that. But she's a wanted woman. I recognise her from the posters those Sovereigns have been bandying about town. Huge bounty on her head."

Walter withdrew a revolver Hale never knew he possessed, cocking it in the man's face. "Don't make me blow yar head off, Skeevy. I can't afford to waste the bullet."

Skeevy faltered, staring down the barrel. He backed off, pointing at Hale. "You're lucky the old man was here. It won't take those Sovs long to find whatever hole you're hiding in." He collected the satchels of loot and disappeared into the shadows, his threat hanging in the air.

Hale exhaled. "Thanks, Walter." She picked up the broken crate, shaken from the encounter. Walter chased one of the tins that had escaped, scanning it in the faint rays of the moonlight. It was hard to tell whether the contents were purple or silver. "What is that?"

"Ya don't reckon this is some kind of sorcery, do ya?" He shuddered as he said the word.

Hale peered over his shoulder for a better look. "Raw sorcery, I think. I can feel it."

"Ya don't mean it could be alive?"

Hale frowned. "Hard to tell. Only Scours deal in stolen

glowy bits. Would Maven touch the stuff?"

"That woman would sell her left tit if it would make her some corundum."

Hale cursed. "Let's get out of here before there's another explosion. Raw sorcery is potent. If that's what it is, it's far too unstable to be carried around like this."

*

They carried a crate each back to The Smuggler's Cottage, where Maven protested her innocence. Hale observed her quietly from the corner. Maven touched her orange ringlets every few sentences. She blinked little. *No voice tremors. No hesitation. Seemingly genuine shock at finding out what she had acquired.* Nothing screamed out that she had known what was inside those crates. *Yet why am I so unsettled?*

After a few choice words with Walter, Maven stormed out, slamming the door behind her as was custom. Her short fuse wasn't out of the ordinary.

Walter flipped his revolver in the air then slid it back into its holster. "I'm away for a kip. My back's killing me." He grabbed his sack of corundum that Maven had left each of them in payment.

Hale did the same, and trudged upstairs. Aveline was still sound asleep, buried under a mountain of blankets. Hale rifled under her bed for the envelope Maven had given her when she first arrived, re-reading intel on Cecerie in case she had missed something. With raw sorcery now in the mix, she had to find Cecerie quicker than ever. Finding Felix would surely be the key.

*

23:34
The Busted Cherry

"Taking the night off, Rivera? I'll get your usual ready."

"No, don't," Esmeralda hurried, before the heavy-set hostess departed. "I'm not here to play, Jacinta."

"Now that I think about it, you haven't paid for any of our services in years. I hope—"

"I need to speak with Ximo. Is he here?" Esmeralda interrupted.

The elderly courtesan scanned the high-class brothel for the owner. The place was packed to the brim, meaning it took her a while to spot him over the action. "He's headed into the back room. I'd hurry if you want to talk. He didn't go in there alone."

Esmeralda thanked her. She squirrelled through a sea of half-naked bodies, all of whom were trying to seduce their way into her purse. As she passed the bar, the tender slid her usual shot of rum across the counter at her silent gesture. She sank it, knocking on the office door to the left of the server. Moments later, an attractive, swarthy man with a perfectly trimmed goatee and purple blazer opened the door to greet her.

"*Almirante*. Back so soon?" he asked, being careful not to stumble into her. "You'd better start buying more than drinks soon. Jacinta is convinced you're cheating on us."

His collar was loosened; his dicky bow hanging off. His red-rimmed eyes were unfocused, his sleek, side-parted hair slightly askew.

Esmeralda smirked. "I see you've cracked open the good stuff," she teased, admiring the bottle of cognac he was holding. "Got a sec, *cariño*? It's important."

"For you? Anything. *Entra. Entra.*" Ximo stood back, allowing her to slip inside. He closed the door behind them, blocking out the noisy establishment.

The office was thick with the stench of weed. Esmeralda ogled the three naked whores spread across both his sofas, one male and two female, all smoking fat joints. "Looks like I'm interrupting something wondrous. I won't take up too much of your time." She accepted his offer of a swig of cognac.

"I assume this is why you're here?" He shoved her the usual green bottle of magically enhanced rum that she was using to subdue the voice in her head. She slid it into her coat pocket. It was somehow better just knowing she had it. "The last time you looked this ill, we were kids making castles in a playpen and you had … *Ay, Diosa,* what did your *padre* call it?"

Esmeralda sniggered. "A digital virus."

They both laughed.

"Right," Ximo said. "*Eso es.* Your old man was so full of shit."

"Like the rest of Xevería," Esmeralda agreed. "That's why we ended up here, uh?"

"Speaking of." Ximo rummaged through the drawer nearest him. "It's good that you came by. Saves me the trouble of tracking you down."

"*¿Qué pasa?*"

"You're not going to like this." Finding what he was searching for, he slipped her the piece of parchment. "There's been a few rumblings around town about Maven."

Esmeralda frowned, remembering Hale trying to tell her something in the lough. Then there was the vision she had succumbed to. "I'm already aware."

Ximo stroked his goatee. "Then you know what she has, I presume?"

"The map!" Esmeralda exclaimed, suddenly putting it together. "*Cómo carajo* did she get her grubby claws on it?"

Ximo jerked his head for them to move out of earshot of the whores. He changed from the Sovereign tongue to Xeverían in case someone else was listening in. "I lost that map years ago, but I still remember where the Creek is, and there's no way I want Maven to be the person who uncovers the greatest fucking treasure of our time. We shed blood and bone for that loot, Esme. I still have the scars from those Sovereign bastards."

Esmeralda sighed. "Me too."

"Then we agree! You need to go after it. It's too powerful for Maven to have."

"No one even knows what it is, Ximo." She shook her head. "All this talk about a mythical treasure. At this point, I couldn't care less."

Ximo's face lined with concern. "Why? What's going on?"

Esmeralda made a face, hoping he could guess so she wouldn't have to say it aloud. He understood immediately. "Again?"

"I think she's alive."

"Ugh, we've been through this!" He realised his words had been harsh and readjusted his stance. "I know that's not what you want to hear, but I cannot watch you go down this road again. We watched her die, *nena*. We saw it happen. And nothing, not even magic, can bring her back."

Esmeralda wrestled back tears, angered by his dismissal. "There is only one way to know for sure."

Ximo's face lost its colour. "*Diosa mía.* That's why you're helping Hale? No! Tell me it isn't true." Esmeralda's silence confirmed it. "What are you thinking? This isn't you." He grabbed the lapels of her coat. "Esmeralda!"

"*Suéltame,*" she snapped, pulling herself free. "I am not asking for your approval, Ximo. But if I have to go to Sailor's Creek you're coming with me."

"I'm not a Swashbuckler anymore. I left that life a long time ago. You can have my corundum to fund the trip, but don't rope me into your shit again."

"You'll always be a member of my crew," Esmeralda said. She traced along the front of his blazer, taking a moment to admire the fabric. "I have to do this, Ximo."

"No, you don't."

He's right, said the voice in her head.

Esmeralda rested her face in his chest. She hadn't expected him to understand, but he was probably the only person who could. Ximo hugged her. It was his usual reply, knowing that when it came to this, there was nothing anyone could say to placate her.

Ok." He sighed. "I'll come. For a cut of the profits, of course."

She closed her eyes, inhaling his expensive cologne, thankful he hadn't made her beg.

*

"Ready to go?"

Midnight had passed, and Hale had assumed Esmeralda wasn't coming to find Felix as promised. She had just sunk her pint and was about to leave when Esmeralda appeared at the bottom of the stairs. The admiral beckoned her outside, barely looking at her.

So that's how we're playing this? Hale lamented.

They drew their collars against the gales and walked towards Hilltown together. Esmeralda stared dead ahead, and Hale couldn't believe how much things had changed from hot to cold in the space of a few hours. She followed in silence until she couldn't take it any longer.

"Are you alright?"

Esmeralda's movement was lethargic, like she was exhausted.

Or drunk.

"Just had a long night," she replied.

"You and me both." Hale told her what Maven might be up to. "And she claims she didn't know it was sorcery, but I don't trust her."

"She's a master at playing games."

"Says you."

Esmeralda finally regarded her with bloodshot eyes. "What does that mean?"

"N-Nothing." Hale wasn't sure what she preferred, not mentioning the sex, or having to talk about it. Realising she hadn't much to say on the matter herself, she latched onto Esmeralda's new-found sourness and neither of them spoke the rest of the way.

They made their way up the steep mountain pass which led to the ominous outer walls of Hilltown. Hale almost lost her footing several times as she climbed over huge chunks of metal. Visiting this place once was enough, never mind twice in one evening. Esmeralda took her a different route once they were halfway up and led her down a low slope along the opposite cliff-side. She slid the rest of the way on her bottom, through the only piece of mud visible amidst the debris.

"How much farther?" Hale asked, cascading down the bank as recklessly as Esmeralda.

Spikes sticking out of the ground ripped her coat, and she

touched the bottom in time to avoid two armoured thugs guarding the gates. Behind them stood a silo, ten stories high, sandwiched between mountainous peaks. Adrenaline surged through her. She clenched her fists. Felix was finally within reach.

THE SILO

Hale wondered if she should have told Walter where they were going. Each second spent in the company of this new Esmeralda put her on edge, like she was falling into a trap. She followed her across the gravel terrain until they found a small hole in the perimeter to the silo grounds. Hale bent down and pulled a loose sheet of metal free, poking her head through.

"It's clear," she whispered, straightening up.

"I'll go first." Esmeralda said.

She bent and squeezed her body through the tight space. Hale imitated her. She was skinnier than Esmeralda, but her bulkier clothes attracted every sharp edge imaginable. The edges of the rusted iron barrier scraped her sides, tearing the pocket off her coat. When she was halfway through the hole, heavy armour clinks echoed in the nearby courtyard.

Fuck!

She pulled against the fabric, unable to rip free. Esmeralda grabbed hold of her beneath the arms and dragged her out, and they both dived into the depths of a huge metal dish with an aerial protruding from its middle. Pressing into its deep curve, their bodies intertwined, and Hale bit her fist to stop from screaming. Her heart sounded loud enough to betray their presence, pounding in her ears. She couldn't ignore the smell of Esmeralda's honeyed fragrance and held her breath as footsteps drew near.

"What is it?" a man called.

Hale distinguished his Ortivanian accent from the usual Anferanian twang. *Refugees outrunning the war?* She curled up tighter, spooning Esmeralda, the puddle of stagnant water they were resting in soaking through her clothes. The men were right on the other side of the dish. It was a miracle they hadn't searched it, but their conversation told Hale they weren't very bright. The smell of rusted metal brought back memories of prison, and she grasped the dagger strapped to Esmeralda's thigh, threatened by the memory.

"Thought I saw something," a second man replied.

"Over there! We've been breached!"

Hale cursed inwardly. In their hastiness, they hadn't replaced the loose metal sheet they climbed through. She listened to more of the conversation.

"Maybe it was always like that? Hard to tell in this junkyard."

The other man snorted. "Are you as stupid as you look, Elgin? We do this patrol every night. Have you ever seen that hole?"

"Ain't seen a hole since I've got here." He sniggered. "I'll go sound the alarm."

"I'll go! You'll probably go via The Cuatro Isles. Just stay here and guard the entrance. The intruder could still be at large."

The sound of the leader's heavy boots became faint as he jogged away. Esmeralda, who hadn't moved throughout the conversation, suddenly closed her hand around Hale's, which was still resting on the dagger's hilt. Hale relinquished it, battling her overwhelming nausea as Esmeralda drew the blade herself. They crept to the edge of the dish, careful not to disturb the resting water, and peeked over the side from the shadows.

Their only way out was blocked by the remaining guard. Hale unravelled from Esmeralda as best she could, guessing what she was about to do. The thug was bent over, still examining the hole. As he straightened up, a sudden realisation came over Hale. She gestured for Esmeralda to wait, ignoring the admiral's questioning frown. Praying this less-lethal tactic would work, Hale jumped out of the dish.

The man spun around, weapon raised. "Who's there?"

"Elgin! It's been a long time," Hale said, shaking the water from her coat sleeves.

"Who is that?" He squinted through the semi-darkness from under his matted, curly bangs.

"Don't you recognise me, comrade?"

Elgin leaned forwards, lantern aloft. "Well, fuck me sideways. General Hale?"

"In the flesh," Hale said, smiling. She smelled alcohol as he grabbed her in a one-armed hug and tried her best not to knee him in the balls. *He always was the touchy-feely type.*

"Thought you were still in prison, girl!"

"E-Early release. You know how it is."

He finally let her go. "I see you didn't get out unscathed." He gestured to her patch. "Shame. You always did have pretty eyes."

Hale shrugged. "Comes with the job. What are you doing here, El?"

"You know, I always did like you." He seemed too drunk to listen to her. Hale backed off as he leaned in again, ducking beneath his arm.

"Just answer me," she said. "What is this place?"

Elgin snapped out of his sleaziness. "It's a hideout for what remains of the Freebooters. We've been here over a year now."

"The Freebooters?" Hale asked. "I heard the S-Sovereigns hunted down those remaining after I was arrested?"

Elgin wheezed. "Heard wrong then, didn't you, General?" He pulled her tighter towards him again, and Hale's skin crawled, thankful for his steel armour buffer as she pressed against it. "Always regretted not having my way with you. Out of respect for your father, I didn't ever try. But I won't make the same mistake twice. You're not my leader anymore."

Before his kiss connected, there was a *clunk!*

Elgin staggered into her, face-first, and she darted out of the way. Esmeralda was standing behind him, her expression thunderous.

"Take the hint, *cabrón*." She restrained him, twisting his neck. The ensuing crack echoed like a whip.

Hale baulked. "Es, what are you—You didn't have to kill him!"

Esmeralda scooped Elgin up and tossed his remains into the dish. They heard a *ding!* and *splash!* as he hit the bottom. "Don't tell me you'll miss him, 'General'." She sniggered. "General of what?"

"I *was* a General," Hale snarled, growing angrier with Esmeralda as the night went on. "I led the Freebooters in the war. You know this."

"Of course. I'm sure you were very formidable, uh?"

"Goddess, what's with you tonight?"

"Oh, nothing. Just didn't realise I was in the company of such greatness." She gave Hale a mocking salute.

Hale swallowed a few choice swear words. Loathing Esmeralda, she strode towards the silo entrance before Elgin's comrade returned.

They slid along the smooth, curved wall until they reached giant double doors, leading into a dark interior. The silo smelled of rotting flesh, something Hale was unfortunately accustomed to. Esmeralda pushed the cracked door open wider, checking it was devoid of guards. She squeezed inside and was swallowed in blackness.

"Wait," Hale whispered. "I'm losing you."

Esmeralda didn't reply.

Unable to see more than a metre ahead, Hale shuddered. She wasn't afraid of the dark, but the unknown was growing more unsettling. Her footsteps were light and cautious as she made her way towards what she assumed was the centre of the silo, wondering what she would find. *Where are the other Freebooters?* Her sinking sensation intensified as she reached a nondescript door, the only thing apparently on this floor. She envisioned someone watching her and stole a glance over her shoulder. The curved corridor behind her was deserted. Esmeralda was nowhere to be found.

Cringing at the door's squeaking hinge, Hale entered the room. It was brighter in here thanks to a lit candle on the desk, located in the centre of what appeared to be an office. She crossed the scantily furnished interior, pushing open the next door at the opposite wall. A rickety staircase behind it led downwards, back into darkness. The putrid smell was more intense here, wafting upwards. She recoiled. *Not going down there if I can help it.*

Voices echoed from below and she dashed behind an overturned cabinet as two men ascended the staircase into the office. Too curious to be scared, Hale lay on her belly, peeking out from behind the cabinet, watching them.

The men paused by the central desk.

"… didn't show," the blonder of the two said, pouring them both a drink. "So much for Pontfedil funding our trip. We'll never find Viperidae now."

"What about Trevus?" the other man asked. He rolled his 'r' like Esmeralda. Something about both men's voices were familiar. "Still suspicious, uh?"

"I can handle him. Told him he can have what's left of Cecerie when we're done with her, but it will be a lot harder to keep her from him, now we have no fucking ship." He kicked the leg of the table. "I swear, that bastard Pontfedil will get what's coming to him."

"Calm yourself, Felix. We will find another investor."

Felix?

Hale's breath caught. She would never have guessed it was him at first glance. If not for his silver hair, she would be dubious still, but when he removed his jacket, she recognised the numerous tribal tattoos snaking up his arms.

"What about your aunt Maven's new ship?" the other man asked after a moment's pause. Hale couldn't get a good look at him. She wished he would step into the candlelight.

Felix leaned on the desk, head bowed. "I've already considered it. She proved her worth when she stole back the evidence Pontfedil had on me, but I told you already. As long as she's working with Lana, we can't fully trust her."

The man snorted. "That sister of yours has a habit of mucking up our plans."

"All but one. At least we tricked her into taking out that little weasel Lucian. To think my adoptive *father* had actually left a will stating that *that* little bastard was to take over leadership of the Freebooters."

"Having the Sovereigns lock Hale up was the right idea."

"And it was working, right up until Esmeralda decided to meddle."

"Esmeralda—"

"Is right over here."

Hale gasped. Esmeralda sprung out of her own hiding place on the far side of the room. She exited the shadows, approaching the two men.

"You!" the foreign man boomed.

Felix restrained him. "Leave it, Escudero," he ordered. "Go. Make sure Cecerie's still tied up. I'll take care of this." He shoved the man towards the staircase.

Esmeralda chased him, buffeting Felix aside despite his best attempt at stopping her. Hale was impressed at how gracefully she evaded him. She watched Esmeralda sprint down the stairs after Escudero as Felix picked himself up off the floor. He cursed, dusting himself down, soaked in his own whiskey. Seeing her moment, Hale climbed out from behind the cabinet.

"I might have guessed you would be behind all this," she said.

Felix swivelled. His eyes widened. "Lana?"

She glanced around the office, noting the high ceiling. "Odd place for a f-family reunion, huh?"

Felix quickly regained his composure. "Yes. So glad you could join us."

Up close, he was exactly how she remembered, silvery-blond hair that fell past his shoulders, dishevelled, thanks to Esmeralda's dexterousness. His usual ensemble – a black vest and beige three-quarter length breeches – was as bedraggled as she could remember. He had the same scar on his left temple where he had once been glassed in a bar fight. The only difference to his face was his crooked nose, thanks to a punch she relished throwing to this day.

"You were foolish to break in here," Felix continued.

"Why don't you have me arrested?"

He laughed dryly.

Hale approached the central desk which held an old portrait of a blond-haired family. They beamed up at her through the golden frame, emanating happiness from another lifetime. Curious, she picked up the painting. The oil had cracked with age. She traced the face of the young boy sitting between his parents. He was no older than three or four, she guessed. The date on the bottom corner under the artist's initials read *4103*. The boy wouldn't be much older than she if he was still alive today. Placing the portrait down, she met Felix's glare.

"What are you doing here, Fe?" Her voice was barely a whisper. She hadn't expected to be so emotional upon seeing him again.

"I could ask you the same thing."

He scanned her from head to toe, searching her for a weapon, but that had never been her style. Seeing none, he unhooked his knife-belt, placing it on the desk beside the picture. The blade was shining with fresh blood. *Esmeralda,* she couldn't help but think. *Maybe she didn't escape unscathed.*

"I understand you're quite the businessman now," Hale said.

Felix flashed his golden teeth. "And I hear you're supposed to be rotting in Sovereign prison."

"After you set me up?"

"Well, you did murder our little brother."

"O-Only because you put him in harm's way!" Her voice reverberated off the walls. "Oh my …" She blanched, suddenly recalling why she recognised the other man's voice. "It was Escudero, wasn't it? The man you were fighting in that crypt in *An Caisleán*? Except you weren't fighting at all, were you?" Cursing her stupidity, she said aloud what she had known all these years. "It was a set-up. The fake intel on Viperidae to lure me there. Your encouragement of Lucian, goading him into helping me, knowing he would get caught in the crosshairs."

"Very good, Lana. Yes." He folded his tattooed arms, displaying some new muscle.

Hale wrestled back her fury. "How long have you been working for the Tripartite? Who is it now, Fe? Sovereigns?

Swashbucklers? Or have you sold out completely and sided with the damn Scours?"

Felix's laughter startled her. He picked up the portrait she had been looking at, tracing the paint. "Do you know who this is?"

"No."

He shoved it at her. "Look closely."

Cautious, Hale brought it towards the candlelight for a better view. The woman holding the little boy was around her thirties, with purple veins along her neck that Hale hadn't spotted at first glance. "Nyra?" she whispered in disbelief.

"Father never told you why he adopted me, did he? Figures. He was a lying sack of shit."

Hale was still struggling to piece it all together. "So, she was … Nyra was your mother?"

Felix pulled a bottle of brandy from the drawer and poured them both a shot. He raised his glass. "To your health."

Hale made sure he took the first sip. She swallowed the tiniest sip of her own. "Drinking was always my thing, not yours. Anyone would think you were trying to poison me."

He moved so fast that she barely had time to react. The drink had been a distraction, restricting her to give him the advantage. She tossed the glass in his face as he lunged over the desk towards her. Her reflexes were still too quick for him.

"Argh!" Felix howled. He stumbled, bundling his shirt to dry his face. "That wasn't very sisterly."

"Stay away from me! H-Haven't you done enough damage?"

"Says 'The Child Killer'."

He blocked her as she took a swipe at him and grabbed her throat. Hale's feet left the floor as he slammed her onto the desk, pinning her by the neck.

THE LEGEND OF HALE

"Stop!" someone yelled nearby.

Felix and Hale stared at the doorway.

The mood of a seventeen-year-old wasn't for one to predict, but a seventeen-year-old sorcerer even less so. Cecerie's shawls fluttered behind her in a non-existent wind; like a crow fluffing its feathers before flight. Her purple veins, like so many sorcerers, penetrated the darkness, streaking up her arms and neck. *And legs*, Hale knew, even though she was wearing thick tights.

"Let her go," Cecerie said.

"How did you get out?" Felix snapped.

He relinquished Hale, who coughed, massaging her throat. She straightened up off the desk, astonished. Cecerie had grown up so much, possessing only a hint of the fourteen-year-old she remembered. She had always been small for her age, but gone was the childish figure, replaced with that of a young woman. If not for the eyes, Hale might have questioned if it was her. *Hazel, like Lucian's*. Cecerie's long brunette curls had been twisted into a messy knot, with ringlets cascading down her face. A face that was ghostly pale.

"Ceci?" Hale croaked.

Cecerie welled up. "It's me."

"You look …"

"Yeah. You too." Reluctant to get closer, she fiddled with the hem of her shawl. "It's … good to see you."

Is it? A lump formed in Hale's throat that had nothing to do with being strangled now. She cast Felix a scathing look before rounding the desk towards her. Stalling in front of Cecerie, she was incapable of what Cecerie was expecting. A hug. Something so simple.

She gestured for the embrace, but her arms fell limp. Cecerie did what she could not, cautiously putting her arms around her. It was then that Hale noticed the heavy chains binding her wrists.

"It's ok," Cecerie said. Her voice was soft and timid. She threw Hale the tiniest of smiles as they parted.

Hale hadn't considered what she would do when they met again. All her attention had been focused on finding her. How did one pick up the threads of an old life? Was this how soldiers felt, coming home from war?

"Did you tell her yet?" Cecerie asked Felix.

"I was about to," he said, pouring himself another drink. "Perhaps you would prefer to do the honours?"

Cecerie looked at Hale. "Father betrayed us, Lana. He wasn't hiding me for my own protection."

"What? What do you mean?" Hale asked.

A shadow crossed Cecerie's face. "I was a baby when my powers materialised. But I wasn't born with them like other sorcerers."

Hale squinted at her.

"Felix found proof. Letters Father had written to Nyra Legat, begging for her help to create a sorcerer child. Illegal genetic engineering. He wanted to add a copy of her sorcerer genes into my genome, but she refused, calling him an abomination. Injecting Nyra, he stole some of her powers instead, and artificially infused me with magic that my body couldn't contain. I was only a month old." She placed the portrait down and stared back at Hale. "Haven't you always wondered why I have those fits?"

Hale cast her mind back to when Cecerie used to have tantrums as a child. She had accidentally torched the roof of their cottage once, when Father wouldn't take her to the market. From that day onwards, Hale had been allowed to take her on supervised visits, if she promised to keep her temper in check.

"So, Father *made* you a sorcerer?"

Cecerie nodded. "But Nyra laid claim to me when she

found out what he had done."

"And that's why Father had her executed," Hale finished. At last, some of this was making sense. "But what was he creating you for? And why wouldn't he use his own magic?"

"To be the key to Viperidae. The only key." She shook her head. "Nyra Legat created it, so only her powers could activate it. Goddess, I thought it was a myth. That he was insane. He taught me of Viperidae before he died, but I never believed it existed."

"Viperidae." Hale felt sick. *The weapon supposedly hidden in An Caisleán.* "It's real?" She turned to Felix.

"Yes," he confirmed. "It's an artefact said to possess the power to lead sorcerers out of oppression. '*Tar Amach.*' You've heard them say it. It means 'emerge' or 'come out', to encourage the sorcerers out of hiding. Viperidae is supposedly the way, and it's hidden in Sailor's Creek."

"Sailor's Creek?" Hale cursed. *So that's what Maven's targeting.* The sorcery she and Walter had smuggled for Maven was making more sense. Maven wasn't as innocent as she had protested. *I must be losing my touch.*

Felix nodded. "I've been playing the Tripartite against each other for years, but Viperidae is the only way to topple them for good."

"So, you sold me out to the Sovs and kidnapped your own sister for *this*?"

"You aren't a part of this," Felix snarled. "You're just in the way. You're *always* in the way."

"Because you're always wrong."

"Oh, here we go," Felix sang. "Saint Lana, telling me again how to do my fucking job. The only reason any of the Freebooters are still alive is because I took care of them."

"You threw them at the Sovereigns and watched them get slaughtered! You never stopped to plan or th-think of the consequences. A-All you ever wanted was power."

"Stop!" Cecerie said, before Hale and Felix clashed again. They were an inch apart, glaring at each other. Hale didn't back down.

Felix finally retreated, rustling through his desk drawer. "I have a plan this time," he said. "Commandant Trevus thinks I'm on his side, but I have no interest in giving Ceci to him."

"The Sovereigns are hunting you, Lana," Cecerie said. "The Scours are hunting me, and the Swashbucklers are pitting everyone against each other. Viperidae is the only thing that can calm the Tripartite. They'll never stop unless we have a better weapon than they do."

"I thought you were being held captive," Hale said, unable to understand why Cecerie would willingly participate in something this insane. "I thought you needed my help."

Cecerie shuffled her feet. "I am captured," she admitted, raising her arms to show the shackles. "But Felix showed me that Viperidae is the only way to save you. To save us!" She raised her voice at Hale's scoffing laughter and tried to take her hand. "Please, sister. I'm tired of hiding."

Her emotions spilled over, and she brushed away a tear. Hale remembered a time when she would have wiped them for her, but this wasn't the little sister of her memories. Cecerie had never been interested in adventures or ancient artefacts. *Or been this close to Felix.* She glanced from one to the other, wondering why Cecerie was on board with his crazy plan.

"You know he's only in this for himself, right? He doesn't care about you."

Felix smirked at Cecerie. "See? I told you she would try poisoning you against me."

"Be quiet. She has every right not to trust you," Cecerie snapped.

Hale had heard enough. She wasn't sure what they were angling for, but she didn't want to find out. "We're leaving, Ceci. Let's go." She held out her arm, gesturing for Cecerie to exit the silo, but Cecerie stayed put.

"Not until you agree to go on Maven's expedition," she said, with another glance at Felix. "And hand Viperidae over to us."

"What?" Hale couldn't understand it.

"He knew you'd come for me, so Escudero bound me to

him."

"Escudero? Oh shit." She wished she hadn't sold her dagger, for in that moment she'd have run Felix through. His face was full of glee.

"Little Ceci's free will is a thing of the past," he confirmed. "And you say I never plan anything."

"You're controlling her?" Hale couldn't fathom what had become of the brother she used to fight alongside. "Why are you doing this to us?"

"Because by enthralling Cecerie, I finally control you." His eyes narrowed. "It's genius really. If I'd planned this years ago, little Lucian might still be alive." She lunged for him again, but he evaded. His laughter deepened her disdain. "You have a habit of spoiling my plans. You did it with the Freebooters. You did it with Father. But never again. You want Ceci back? Then get me Viperidae."

"Fuck you!"

Felix clicked his fingers, and she watched in horror as Cecerie snatched up his dagger from the desk, holding the blade to her own throat.

"Ceci, no!" Hale tried to drag it from her grip. The blade halted before it broke the skin, unwavering no matter how hard she pulled.

Felix continued. "Your choice, Lana. Agree to find Viperidae for me and take Cecerie home today. Or watch her die like Lucian."

Hale didn't want to bow to his wickedness. Maven wasn't going to just let her walk away with Viperidae after the expedition. Then there was Esmeralda. Siding with Maven would be considered a betrayal, turning Esmeralda into an enemy, one she couldn't afford to have.

She froze with indecision, watching the solitary candle on the desk burning to the end of its wick. Seeing no other choice, she gave in. "Fine. I'll do it. Now, let her go."

Cecerie dropped the dagger at Felix's command. Her irises changed from purple back to their normal hazel, and Hale caught her as her legs wobbled, bearing the weight of the chains she was attached to. She steadied Cecerie, hoping she wouldn't collapse for she was incapable of carrying her.

Felix finished his drink, placing the empty glass on the table. "Glad you finally see sense. Have fun in Sailor's Creek, won't you?"

Hale glared up at him. "One of these days …"

Felix snorted. "Idle threat. I'll be waiting eagerly for your return. I must say, I'm disappointed, Lana, I really thought you'd put up more of a fight."

*

Early that morning in the tavern, Cecerie was captured in a lengthy hug by Aveline, who cried into her shoulder for several minutes then dragged her to the booth in the corner. Foric served them a hearty meal as Hale sat on a barstool alone. Seeing Felix again had rattled her. Her legs still jittered, nerves dangling on edge as she rued being blackmailed again. *Crossed and double-crossed. It's becoming difficult to track who's screwing who.*

"Vibrate much more and you will fall off that seat." Esmeralda said, taking up the vacant stool beside her. "Aren't you happy to have Cecerie back?"

"Where did you go?" Hale asked through gritted teeth.

"When?"

"You abandoned me in that silo! Where were you?"

"Chasing Escudero, *obviamente*. He escaped, but I found Cecerie chained up in the basement. How do you think she got free?"

Hale wasn't placated. She spotted blood dripping from a cut on Esmeralda's forearm. "Are you hurt?" she asked stiffly.

Esmeralda dabbed it. "Grazed it on your brother's knife. It's nothing." Hale sipped her drink. "Look," Esmeralda continued. "Whatever I may have done wrong, say it, sweetness, but the truth is I held up my end. You have your sister back, and you have your life. There wasn't much more that I promised you."

They stared across the tavern towards Cecerie and Aveline, who were finishing off their bowls of stew, dipping generous slices of fresh bread. Cecerie acted more like her usual innocent self, as if whatever influence Felix and Escudero had over her was wearing off. Distance didn't count when it came to sorcery, though, and, despite hating herself for doing it, Hale had kept Cecerie's chains upstairs. She despised the idea of tying her up again, but if it was between that and letting Felix control her, she didn't see much of a choice.

"She seems ok, all things considered," Esmeralda continued, oblivious to Hale's ongoing worries. "You may not have saved Lucian, but you saved her. Isn't that something worth celebrating?"

Hale swirled the whiskey around her glass. "I suppose."

"Ey, contain yourself," Esmeralda said, smirking. "Why so miserable, uh?"

Hale pulled herself together. "No, you're right. I got her back. I'll figure out the rest of it later."

"Good. Now, go. Spend time with your family." Esmeralda got to her feet. She leaned in, placing a kiss on Hale's cheek, lingering for longer than necessary. "Goodbye, sweetness," she whispered in her ear. "Take care of yourself."

Hale stared after her as she left the tavern. Sides were forming, and she wasn't sure which she was on. The knot in her stomach told her she was playing someone else's game, being controlled by invisible strings. Growing tired of the constant headache, she scooped up her drink and joined her family at the table. She immediately wished she hadn't, as she caught wind of their conversation.

"... never saw the body. The Sovereigns disposed of it."

"I wonder if they even buried him," Cecerie said. She wiped her nose on a tissue her mother passed her across the table.

"I hope so," Aveline said.

Cecerie turned to Hale. "What happened? How did Lucian die? You were there, weren't you?"

Hale caught Aveline's ire and avoided Cecerie's question.

"Hush, child," Aveline diverted, patting Cecerie's shoulder. "Finish your bread. I'll clear the bowls."

Hale focused on the papered ceiling, saying nothing as Aveline cleared the table. It was odd having her stick up for her. *Our fight is probably the last thing on her mind.* She closed her eyes, not realising she had fallen asleep until Cecerie shook her.

"Wow!" Cecerie exclaimed, shocked at how violently she jerked awake. "Are you ok?"

"F-Fine," Hale said. The tavern was quieter now, with most of the patrons cleared out.

"Are you coming upstairs? Mother's gone back to bed, but we can sit for a bit longer."

Hale raised her heavy head. Her neck was numb from the awkward angle she had dozed off at. She massaged it, allowing Cecerie to take over, sending a wave of sorcery from her palm into the trapezius. The ache disappeared unnaturally fast. She hung on as long as she could until her flesh burned, and she squirmed free.

"Goddess! Did I hurt you?" Cecerie asked. "My magic is more unstable these days."

"I'm fine. Just freezing. Let's go upstairs. We can talk in front of the fire."

They ascended to their suite and sat on the settee, lowering their conversation to a murmur so as not to wake their mother.

Hale smiled at Cecerie. "Can't believe how grown up you are."

Cecerie giggled. "It's my birthday next week."

"Eighteen, right? That reminds me." Hale dug in her pockets and gave her the necklace with the purple orb. It flooded with a strange consistency at her touch, casting an unnatural glow. "May as well give it to you now, considering I m-missed the last few."

"Wow." Cecerie's eyes lit up. "Do you know what this is?"

"Er, p-pretty sure it's a necklace."

"Well, yes. But I read in one of Father's old tomes that you can store sorcery in a pendant like this. It's not sick like how the Scours do it though. The sorcerer must give it willingly. It can't be extracted. It acts as a kind of protection over the wearer. I wonder where this one came from. Or who it came from." She held it gingerly, as though holding a precious piece of someone's soul.

"Whoever it was, I don't reckon it was given willingly," Hale said. "Otherwise, who would give up such a gift?"

"A scorned ex-lover?" Cecerie smirked. "It is said that when sorcerers take a mate, they often give one of these to their partner."

"Aaand now you've made it weird. Give it back." She tried to snatch it, but Cecerie's tightened her grip.

"No way! I love it. Help me put it on?" Hale squirmed in her seat, clutching the frayed leather. Cecerie sighed. "Can you just talk to me? You jump every time someone so much as scratches themselves." She slid closer to her across the settee. "Lana." She encouraged Hale to look at her. "Just say it, ok? Whatever it is. I won't think any less of you."

Hale wanted to tell her. There was no one in this world who would understand what had happened with Lucian as much as Cecerie, the most compassionate person she'd ever met.

Seeing it was no use, Cecerie let her be. She finished the last of the wine she had been drinking with breakfast and rested back into the sofa, balancing the stem of the glass delicately between her fingers. "You and Esmeralda seem close."

"In a way."

"She was kind to me when we sailed to Anferan," Cecerie continued. "Told me I reminded her of someone."

"Who?"

Cecerie shrugged. "Didn't ask. Didn't give the impression she wanted to talk about it." She scratched her neck, and her violet veins illuminated beneath her shawl. She covered them up, sensing Hale watching them. Trying not to spook her, she flicked up Hale's eyepatch and winced at the carnage underneath. "Goddess," she whispered, having to look away. "Did the Sovereigns do that to you?"

"I don't remember." Hale covered it again. Cecerie touched her hand but she jerked away.

"Don't recoil from me," Cecerie begged. "It's all anyone's done since I got here."

Despite her discomfort, Hale let Cecerie rest her head on

her shoulder. "Did Felix hurt you?"

"Escudero did. But not in any way you could understand," Cecerie muttered. "No non-sorcerer ever could. He injected me with something. I can hear necromancers, dark sorcerers from the beyond, whispering in my head."

She's right. I don't understand. Hale glanced at the pile of chains in the corner. "I don't want to chain you up again. I-I c-could never do that."

"You might have to."

"When?" Hale asked, doubting she would ever be able to make that decision in a vacuum.

"You'll know. I can sense the change coming even now. Won't be long until Escudero reaches out through the abyss, and I am once again bound to his and Felix's will."

"They're not controlling you right now?"

"Oh, they're there, idle in the back of my mind, listening to everything we say. I have free will right up until it conflicts with theirs."

"I'm s-sorry this has happened to you," Hale said. She couldn't keep up the closeness and shimmied an inch down the cushion into her own space.

Cecerie raised her head. "Don't you dare apologise to me. After what you've been through? And you still managed to spoil Felix's plans."

They both laughed.

"I suppose I *am* a permanent pain in his ass," Hale said.

"You are," Cecerie said, still giggling. "And mine. And all of ours. But you always fight, whether for us, or against us when we get out of line." Her expression became serious then. "Look, you don't have to tell me what happened between you and Lucian. Not if it's too hard. When the day comes that you do want to talk, I'll be here, but until then, we can sit in silence, as often or as little as you need to."

In that moment, Hale remembered why she had missed her. It was wonderful to have Cecerie back, even if she wasn't the child she remembered. She could never tell if it was the sorcery, or if Cecerie was so adept in reading people, but she always knew the right thing to say when someone around her wasn't themselves. They would have the next few days together before the expedition departed. Hale had experienced how dark the world could get without Cecerie in it and had no desire to go back. Stealing Viperidae for Felix seemed like the best of a bad lot of options, but she didn't trust what he would do with that power. *Then there's Escudero ...*

He was the bigger threat, even getting under Esmeralda's skin. If what Father said about Viperidae was true – that it could end the Tripartite – then it was worth keeping away from cretins like Escudero. Power in the wrong hands was a problem. Whether Escudero would be that problem remained to be seen.

DEPARTURE

As the expedition veered closer, Cecerie's sleeping pattern became more erratic. She woke up screaming like she used to when she was little, and it killed Hale not being able to comfort her.

"You're worrying me," Hale said, when the day of the expedition finally came.

They sat eating lunch by the harbour, dangling their feet over the edge of Dock S24, as they shared one last meal on dry land. It was a rare sunny day. They had finished packing up the ship, and Hale was losing the will to leave Anferan the closer the time came. She still hadn't told Esmeralda she was leaving, but she hadn't had the chance. Esmeralda had gone AWOL since the night Cecerie had returned – not even Walter knew where she was. Hale started to wonder if that last 'goodbye' had been final.

The sun disappeared behind the clouds, and Cecerie refrained from taking another bite of her sandwich. She placed the thick round of bread and corned beef onto the pewter plate between them, and as she stared out at the glittering ocean, Hale noticed a flicker of something behind Cecerie's eyes. Dark rings had persisted under them since the night terrors.

"Worrying you how?" Cecerie asked. Her voice sounded surprisingly monotone.

Hale chewed the crust of her own sandwich and dusted crumbs into the water. "This is the first thing you've eaten in two days." The bowl of stew Foric had made on the first night was the only thing Cecerie had kept down.

Cecerie pulled the black shawl back across her varicose veins as the coastal breeze threatened to uncover them.

"There's something you're not telling me, Lana."

Hale had been hoping to avoid the topic. If she said the words aloud, she'd be forced to admit she was afraid. She stared back out at the horizon. "I don't want to leave."

As she had predicted, her words deepened Cecerie's mood. Cecerie reached towards the plate like she was going to pick up her sandwich. The plate rattled as she pushed it towards the edge of the pier and before Hale could catch it, it splashed into the water.

"Cecerie!" She watched the floating bread, seeing the silhouette of the corned beef sinking underneath. "That meat was expensive."

Cecerie didn't care. "What's going on with you and Esmeralda?" she asked in an offhand way. Hale's stomach contracted in a manner which had nothing to do with food waste.

"W-Why would you ask that?"

"Escudero said she wasn't to be trusted. Did Esmeralda say something to put you off going?"

Hale shook her head. She had knocked on Esmeralda's room in The Smuggler's Cottage every chance she had the last two days, but Esmeralda either hadn't been present or hadn't answered.

Cecerie continued. "If you're putting this off because of her, then you're doing it for the wrong reasons. We don't owe Esmeralda anything."

"That's not true," Hale said. "You don't understand what she s-saved me from."

"She did it on Maven's orders," Cecerie reminded her. "Don't throw away this opportunity because of some misguided loyalty. Maven is the one letting us live rent-free in her tavern. She's the one giving us this opportunity, not Esmeralda." She paused, watching Hale closely. "Did something happen between you two?"

Hale didn't have the heart to lie. She nodded, hoping it would suffice. Cecerie didn't reply. Together, they watched a flock of gulls fly overhead. One of them was lagging behind the others, fighting, trying to keep up.

"Mother won't be happy."

"Ha! When is she ever?"

"Whatever happened, it can't lead to anything good. Swashbucklers are bad news, Lana."

Hale got up, struggling to keep her anger under control. "I don't need this." She walked away.

Cecerie chased her along the pier. She spun her around, her expression one of fury. "You swore to protect us. You swore to Father you'd protect *me,*" she reminded her, looking nothing like her innocuous self. "So, you'd better go on Maven's ship as planned, or I'll tell Mother everything."

"Ceci." Hale shook out of her grip. "This isn't you talking." She could see that this fury was being manipulated by Felix. The real Cecerie would have kept her secrets until her dying day, not held them over her as blackmail. Hale knew there was no reasoning with her now. She walked away, leaving Cecerie fuming after her all the way back to the tavern.

*

Back in The Smuggler's Cottage, Hale wrapped the maroon scarf around her neck her mother had gifted her. It was a different one than Aveline had used to blot her burst nose a few nights earlier. The fabric was soft under Hale's chin, and she buried her face in it, smelling a hint of perfume as Aveline stood waiting for her reaction. Hale caught Cecerie glaring at her over Mother's shoulder, and realised Aveline's staring wasn't because of the present.

"She told you?" Hale guessed.

Aveline nodded. "A Swashbuckler, Lana? Really? Just when I think about forgiving you, you go and …" Her voice trailed off as its increasing volume attracted attention from nearby drinkers. She waited until they stopped watching, continuing at a regular decibel. "After you saved Cecerie, I was willing to try putting this all behind us. I'm trying to forgive you."

"For what? The accidental nose-burst or the accidental murder?"

Aveline sighed. "Don't joke about either. I'll admit, I

pressed you too hard that night, and I shouldn't have. Admiral Rivera informed me that Lucian's death might not have been entirely your fault."

Hale was stunned. "I ... don't know what to say."

"Neither do I." Her eyes narrowed. "I wasn't sure why you confided in her and not me, but now it's all starting to make sense."

Hale sighed. "I didn't m-mean for you to find out this way."

"You didn't mean for me to find out at all," Aveline snapped. "How long have you kept this a secret?"

"My sexuality? Or the pirate I slept with?"

"Don't get smart with me. I hardly care that she's a woman. I do care that she's a thieving slave trader who'll sell you down the river the first chance she gets." As Hale bypassed her, she grabbed her arm. "Lana, I'm talking to you!" Hale jerked away. At this, her mother gave a humourless laugh. "So, you'll let that filth touch you, but not me?" She waited for Hale to argue but she did not. Aveline sighed and took a step back, allowing her to relax. "We'll talk about this when you get back. Just promise me you'll take care of Cecerie on this expedition. I've lost enough children as it is."

Hale flattened out her jacket, relieved she was off the hook. She gazed around the tavern she'd reluctantly come to call home. She'd been disoriented when she first arrived, but she had to admit, The Smuggler's Cottage had an undeniable charm despite its shady backdoor dealings. She watched the bard she'd long admired, plucking a delicate tune. The woman winked at her, and Hale grinned. She'd never gotten her name or commended her for her wonderful talent. *Now I might never get the chance.*

Deciding it was time, she downed the last of her pint, plucking up the courage to cross the room. As she opened her mouth to say hello, the musician's face changed from friendly to fearful. Her fingers slipped from the harp's strings and the music fell flat. Hale twirled in time to duck as a bottle came flying towards her head.

Reacting on instinct, she plunged a right uppercut into the attacker's ribs, yelling when it only connected with his golden armour. Her knuckles throbbed, but there was no time to wallow as three more Sovereigns closed in. A shot of adrenaline coursed through her. She sidestepped, kicking in the back of the next man's knees where his armour was weak. Before she could finish him, two others grabbed her, lifting her off her feet. She swung her boot at another's face, knocking him to the floor, and struggled with the overpowering arm around her neck.

Swinging as much of her weight forwards as she could, she flipped the strangler over her shoulder. She reached for his blade, but as she did, a bag was smothered over her head. Her wrists were clapped in irons. She struggled, and a flash of lightening sparked around her. She shook the bag off her head, managing to break free for enough time to charge the tavern's exit.

"Hale, what—" Walter caught her as she tried to push past him in the doorway.

"Sovs!" Hale yelled, fighting him off.

The Sovereigns reformed, closing in on her. The other patrons in the bar were cowering behind their tables. Foric had ducked behind the counter with Aveline, and Cecerie was nowhere to be found. No one wanted to get in the way of Sovereigns and their prey.

To Hale's surprise, Walter shielded her behind his frail body. He drew his weapon, pointing it at the soldier in the centre. "Stay the fuck back."

The Sovereign faltered, as did his henchmen. "You don't want to do this, old man. Hand her over and Sovereign Altus will reward you personally."

Walter swirled his rapier. "That ain't gonna happen." He backed out of the tavern, his aim never wavering, pushing Hale out behind him. As soon as the door shut, he encouraged her to run. She did, glancing over her shoulder. Walter held his aim on the door in case the soldiers followed, but the door to The Smuggler's Cottage remained closed. She stopped at the end of the street, waiting for him to catch up.

"Cecerie escaped out the back," he panted as soon as he was close enough. "She's up ahead. Get yaselves to the docks. If ya lucky, Esmeralda's still preparing to leave."

Hale did a double take. "Esmeralda?"

Walter nodded. "Kid, I hate to tell ya, but Maven's expedition is total bollocks. Ya can't get to Sailor's Creek without Es and Ximo, so do yaself a favour. Get on the right ship. It's time to choose a side."

Hale couldn't believe what he was saying. "Ceci would never go for it."

Walter gave her a sympathetic look. "She comes with chains for a reason."

He broke her out of her own shackles, and they ran downhill through the trees, towards the cliffs, staying off the beaten path in case there were more Sovereigns on the lookout. As they approached Dock S24, Hale crept onto Maven's ship and retrieved her possessions from the hold. Ill at the thought of using them, she picked up the pile of heavy chains inside, carrying them onto the deck where Cecerie was staring out at the water. Before she could turn around, Hale clamped them on her, sealing her magical hands by her sides.

Cecerie's scream curdled in her throat, and her veins pulsed, sending an electrical surge through her skin. Hale received a small shock. Sickened, she knocked Cecerie out with a quick elbow to the back of the head and dragged her off the ship before the crew could amass for departure.

"I can't believe I did that," Hale wheezed, reaching Walter's hiding place in the bushes.

"It's for her own good," he said, inspecting the welt on Cecerie's head. "Don't worry, kid. Just get ya ass aboard before Esmeralda departs. Hurry!"

"A-Aren't you coming?"

"Nah. I'm sitting this one out. Here, take this." He gestured to his pocket towards a mason jar with tiny, skeletal fairies floating inside.

"What is it?" she asked, holding up the jar to admire them.

They were grotesquely pretty, making her smile despite the situation.

"Messenger fairies," Walter said. "Very rare. They're not really alive. It's some kind of magically enhanced tech, but nothing on this planet moves faster. There are four in total; two in my jar, two in yours. When ya're on the expedition we can use these to keep in touch. Just whisper your message to it and let it fly. I have an inkling we'll be needing each other, kid."

"Thanks, Walt." She shoved the jar into her pack, touched. "Find my mother. Make sure she's safe."

"I will. Now let's move. I'll help ya aboard the ship." He picked up Cecerie and they both jogged towards the area Hale guessed The Eider's Cry was docked.

The ship's lanterns soon flickered in the distance, as those from Maven's ship lit up too. *The crew must have arrived.* She hoped leaving them leaderless would delay them. As she neared Anferan's edge, Hale stopped, staring back at them. *Have I made the right choice?*

The Eider's Cry was already near the cove by the time she caught up. Hearing Esmeralda issuing orders to her crew, she was consumed by both dread and excitement. She skipped over the rocks along the coastline, and, once she was close, whistled to attract attention. Jakson saluted from afar, and redirected the ship, lowering the plank onto a land bridge to let her board. The thin slab of wood sank under the combined weight of her, Walter and Cecerie. As soon as she reached the deck, she collapsed onto her knees, exhausted. As Walter lowered Cecerie down, Esmeralda squeezed into view between her men, all of whom had crowded around.

"Hale?" She eyed the heavy chains binding Cecerie and gestured to one of her companions. "*Ay,* Ximo. What did you do, uh? Where did he get to?"

A well-dressed man in a plum suit, whose tanned complexion and dark hair matched hers, squeezed into the clearing. *So this is the infamous Ximo?* Hale wondered if he and Esmeralda could have been related. He inspected her, nodding in approval.

"Good, you made it." He smirked at Esmeralda. "I can see why you like her. She's a mighty fine—"

"Don't finish that sentence," Esmeralda snapped. "Why are they here?"

"I sent Walter to get them," he said joyfully. "Surely you didn't want Maven to sail away with your flavour of the month." He chuckled, as did a few of the crew. Hale flushed but pressed on past the crew's whispers and wolf-whistling.

"I'm calling in my favour," she said to Esmeralda, who looked less than pleased.

"*Diosa mía*. You cannot be serious."

"You need us," Hale said. "Cecerie is the only way you are getting Viperidae, and you're the only way we find it. We can work together."

Walter disembarked, as if eager to avoid the negotiations. He swam back to shore like a man half his age, while the men still aboard shifted their feet, glancing at one another. Esmeralda didn't reply. She picked Cecerie up off the deck and carried her away like she weighed nothing. Hale got to her feet and followed. She expected them to stop when they were safely out of earshot, but Esmeralda opened the trapdoor and encouraged her down into the same hold Hale had once stayed in. The ship's berth still stank of sweat. Men shouted overhead like the first time she'd boarded.

The Eider's Cry drifted away from the shore, visible through the portholes as they bypassed the cots and swinging hammocks. It didn't strike Hale to be afraid, but the longer they walked, the more uneasy she grew. Esmeralda revealed another compartment that Hale had never seen, holding open the porthole to let her through. She faltered near one of the ship's rustic cannons as Esmeralda set Cecerie on the floor, sliding a small burlap sack filled with rice underneath her head to keep her comfortable. Hale stared around the dimly lit cabin. *This must be where the ship's old battery was located.* It smelled of sulphur and stale smoke, but the cannon she leaned on for balance was cold. It soothed her warm, sweaty skin.

"Tell me what happened," Esmeralda said.

As Hale told the story of Cecerie's peculiar behaviour and the Sovereign ambush, Esmeralda hunted in various tool bags in the hold. Hale imagined they were there should the cannons ever require tinkering. She had no idea how cannon-fire worked, or if it even still did. By the time she finished her tale, Esmeralda had plied the restraints off Cecerie, dumping them in the corner. She put on newer, different chains, heavier than the first, and slipped something down Cecerie's throat from a tiny brown bottle.

"What are you doing?" Hale asked, sickened by Cecerie suffering in this manner.

"It is a sedative that Ximo created. It will keep her unconscious for the trip."

"And the chains?"

"An extra precaution. This room will contain her, but if she is at the stage you say, then Felix's will is now hers. And by extension Escudero's. I am impressed she held out as long as she did. It's ... difficult, having someone invade your head." She paused. "We cannot afford to have her involved. Not until we are holding Viperidae in our hands." She straightened up.

Hale stared. "You knew all along, didn't you? That I was planning to side with Maven?"

Esmeralda turned to her. "*Sí.*"

Hale massaged her throbbing knuckles where she had punched the Sovereign's armour. *Of course she did.*

Silence passed between them as the ship wavered, signalling they had reached open waters. Hale imagined Anferan disappearing in the distance, becoming a dot like Ortivana. She was nauseated. The stale air in the hold wasn't helping.

"You d-didn't tell me you were leaving." She heard the accusation in her voice and cursed herself for being so transparent.

Esmeralda swept the bandana off her head. She raked her hair, ruffling it back to its true volume and mopped sweat from her brow, tucking the bandana into her coat pocket. "Why would I? You were planning on betraying me."

Guilt snaked through her. "I changed my mind. I wanted to tell you the truth. I tried."

"I know that too." Esmeralda studied her for a moment. "But I had to stop you. Maven has ears everywhere, even at the lough. She would have had you killed had you betrayed her."

Hale swallowed. "And what would have happened, had I betrayed *you?*"

Esmeralda folded her arms and rested against the nearest cannon. "I don't make a habit of killing people I ..." She faltered. A faint blush crept across her cheeks, and Hale realised she wasn't the only one struggling to find footing in their new dynamic.

Mustering up the courage, Hale approached her, and Esmeralda unravelled into a more inviting stance. Hesitant at first, Hale extended her swollen hand, ignoring the agonising urge to retreat that always bit deep. It shook as she made to touch Esmeralda's cheek, and she faltered, unable to commit. Esmeralda closed the distance she couldn't, sending a fresh bolt of nerves coursing through her as she took Hale's hand instead. She inspected her injured knuckles.

"You need something cold on those. Ximo might have a salve."

"Who is he exactly?"

"An old friend from Xevería. An expert on sorcery if there ever was one."

Hale counted the uncomfortable seconds, remembering how Esmeralda had coped at the lough. She glanced at Esmeralda's lips, wanting to kiss her, but such a thing seemed impossible now. Esmeralda, guessing that was her aim, cupped her face, guiding her into a soft kiss; cautious, afraid of hurting her. And it did hurt. It hurt like hell. Unlike in the lough, where both their phobias were tested, here, Hale's was the only one exposed.

Hale bowed to hide her agony, pulling back. "I can't."

Esmeralda exhaled. "It's ok." She gave Hale the distance she so obviously desired and rested back against the cannon. "I must admit, I'm relieved you are here."

"You are?"

Esmeralda smiled. "I did not, how do you say, *relish* the idea of leaving you behind."

"Why not?"

"Why, indeed." She bit her lip. "What happened between us was … unexpected."

Hale snorted. "Like you didn't initiate it."

Esmeralda laughed, flashing her that familiar crooked grin that had Hale hooked from the beginning. "I suppose I did." She became solemn then. "It didn't mean nothing, Hale. I want you to know that."

Hale didn't know what to say. Remembering the awkward dinner with Esmeralda, she cleared her throat. "My mother said you told her about Lucian."

"I did not tell her everything," Esmeralda replied. "Just enough for her to stop hating you."

"She has a right to hate me."

"Maybe so. But you don't deserve it."

"Thank you," Hale said. "I don't know why I told you. It just seemed e-easier than telling her, and I had to tell someone. It was eating me alive."

"I know."

Hale sighed. "So, where do we go from here?" she asked, dreading the answer.

"Simple," Esmeralda replied, straightening up. She tied her bandana back around her head. "We go find the so-called greatest treasure of our time, and hope that we live to tell the tale."

STORM TORMENTA

September, Year 4132
Two Months Later

The needle of the compass Hale held jittered between south and west. She flipped it shut as the reading became erratic, tucking it inside her coat. The wind slapped her face, lifting her hair, and she ducked out of the oncoming storm, nuzzling into the scarf her mother had made her. The last of Walter's first message from the messenger fairy he had sent had died out, leaving a small pile of ashes in her palm. She tipped them overboard, recalling echoes of Walter's voice that the fairy had whispered in her ear.

"Yar mother is safe, kid. The Sovereigns ransacked the tavern, but I got Aveline out in time. We can't trust Maven. That bounty on yar head is far too tempting. For safety reasons, I won't tell ya where we're staying. Just be careful. Watch Esmeralda."

Leaning over the ship's edge, Hale considered his words. Cecerie had been restrained below deck since their departure, being fed through injections by Ximo at Esmeralda's orders. *Watch Esmeralda.* Had Walter meant the words as concern or as a warning? As she watched the obsidian depths crack with white waves, Hale couldn't shake the guilt. Had she let Cecerie down? The last time she had been at sea, she often felt the urge to drown. Now, it was like she was already submerged. It had been too good to be true, finding Cecerie so easily, but it still made her happier than she'd been in years having Cecerie with her. What Hale knew about sorcery could fill a thimble – more than most commoners, but still leaving her unequipped to solve the issue of Felix's enthrallment. Her sister was in there somewhere. She had to find a way to coax her out. Ximo was trying, but even he agreed that finding Viperidae seemed key.

Thunder rumbled in the west, and Hale surveyed the ship's rear. Somewhere in that direction, through the gloom, was Ortivana. The sky transformed to amethyst as the ship entered the beginnings of the Ortivanian storm and the first droplets of rain on Hale's skin transported her home. She inhaled the familiar dryness in the air, hoping for pleasant memories, but it was all tainted with reality.

"Hale?" Jakson's voice caught her unawares. She hadn't seen him approach her blind spot and quickly pocketed her jar of fairies. "The boys need me to help them haul in the sails. Can you steer us through the oncoming storm?"

Hale's stomach dropped. "M-Me?"

She followed him past the Swashbucklers issuing orders to each other and rushing to get into position as the weather worsened. Those off duty were ushered into the hold to keep the deck clear of unnecessary obstacles. Hale watched a tattooed amputee scoop up his checkers board and playing pieces. His magical prosthetic leg glowed in the dark as he bunged the board into its battered box, passing the game to his comrade in the lower deck, and they descended through the trapdoor, pulling it closed to keep it airtight.

Hale ran to the helm and seized the revolving, unoccupied wheel, experiencing the immediate, powerful drag of the ocean. She battled for control while Ximo attached her to a harness, tethering her to the floor by her waist as a forceful wave splashed over the deck.

"Keep her steady!" Ximo yelled, running off.

Wind whistled through gaps in the sails, and she squinted up through the onslaught, watching the men tugging various ropes, reefing the sails while the storm tore them apart. She plotted a more southerly course away from Ortivana. Her coat sagged with the water's weight, and every muscle she had screamed in protest as her body was battered back and forth until she could no longer retain her bearings.

A freezing wave cut through her again. The storm caught the sails, forcing the ship sideward into a double-overhead swell. Hale yelled, taking another thrashing. The metal clips of her tethers clinked under the strain and she wondered how long they could hold her. In a desperate attempt to shield herself, she crouched against the ship's wheel, only straightening up when the latest swell had fallen. She checked on the men. One of the crew was dangling overhead, swinging from a flailing rope. Horrified, she watched as he smashed into the mast of the mainsail.

"He's trapped!" she called to Ximo. "Cut him free!"

Before anyone else could act, a figure darted through the rain, headfirst into the storm. The ship surged, throwing everyone off balance, but this figure rolled away with ease. Hale forced her tired body upright, desperate to keep the ship steady as she watched the unknown rescuer dodge the ship's debris, scaling the huge mast like it was nothing. Another wave sent the vessel off centre, and Hale's tethers clinked again. The scarf she wore unravelled and blew away. *We need to get out of this storm!*

The injured crew member was hanging upside down, his arm bent at an unnatural angle. The men on the deck were yelling, and Hale learned it wasn't for the hangman, but his would-be saviour, who was nowhere to be found. Her grip on the helm slipped and she knew then she was out of her depth. Before she could succumb to the storm, she was shoved aside by someone wrestling the helm from her.

Esmeralda commandeered The Eider's Cry, rotating it with the strength and expertise that Hale lacked, before the ship took another beating. She flexed against the storm without a safety harness as more of her men washed overboard. Seeing the admiral's boots slip on the river-like deck, Hale hugged her from behind, holding her upright against the hurricane. Esmeralda's body reverberated as she screamed orders to what remained of the crew, but Hale had no idea what she was saying. Closing her eyes tight, she pressed her cheek against Esmeralda's coat, clutching her as another wave crashed over them. The tethers were put under further strain, supporting their combined weight. Hale had never been so cold. She wasn't aware of much in that moment, but she did know one thing: she had to keep Esmeralda alive. Otherwise, they were all going to drown.

*

Diosa, ayúdame. Dame fuerza. No quiero morir.

Esmeralda stirred and jerked to the side, coughing up salt water. Pushing herself onto her sodden feet, she shook off the weight of her waterlogged coat, and scanned her surroundings. The sky was overcast. A damp sail flapped in a light breeze, hanging from the splintered remains of its mast. Red, yellow, black and green had somehow dimmed in brightness, but the battered remains of The Eider's Cry remained afloat.

Still spluttering, she strolled along her beloved ship, kicking aside the remains of the taffrail. Succumbing to her leadership training, she made mental notes of what had to be repaired and avoided where the ship's rail had broken off completely on the starboard side. One strong wave would be enough to sweep an unsuspecting victim into the depths. Shielding from a beam of sunlight fighting to get through the clouds, she gazed out at sea, succumbing to her usual nausea. Bodies littered the water's surface, flitting amongst the floating debris. She winced, unable to watch.

On the port side of the ship, she spotted Hale lying on her stomach with Ximo holding her by the ankles; his normally kempt hair curling back to its natural wildness. Wondering what they were doing and why it had attracted the attention of all survivors, Esmeralda went over.

"Lower!" Hale shouted. She leaned further into the ocean, hooking at the drowned remains of Jakson. The huge fishhook finally latched onto his soaking attire, allowing her to drag him within range. Together with Ximo, she hauled Jakson's massive body from the water, lying him flat on the deck. Esmeralda watched her kneel by his head. Hale adjusted his neck and attempted resuscitation with two rescue breaths and a set of thirty chest compressions. There was no response.

Joder, ¿está muerto?

Esmeralda sank to her knees as Hale tried again. Inwardly, she prayed to a deity she didn't believe in. On the third attempt, Jakson was revived, bringing up half the ocean. Esmeralda relaxed. Ximo slapped Jakson's back, while Hale punched the deck to rid herself of irritation from having touched him. Esmeralda wanted to calm her, but she couldn't move. Between herself and Hale, she wasn't sure who was living the bigger nightmare.

"You?" Jakson asked, surprised at who had saved him. As shocked as Hale that he was alive, he knocked her over, throwing his massive arms around her.

"Don't," Hale pled, squirming to detach herself. She elbowed him in the ribs to get him off, and he let her go.

"Shit. Sorry, I forgot." He flashed her a wonderfully white smile instead, and Hale managed one back.

"The admiral's not going to be happy you hugged her woman, Jak," Ximo said, loosening his dickie bow and top button. "Or that she gave you a little kiss."

The rest of the crew watching them tittered, and the stress of the last twenty-four hours siphoned off them.

"We're definitely getting drunk tonight, lads," Jakson said, heaving himself to his feet. His suggestion met raucous cheers. Jokes and teasing were thrown about as those who had survived the storm revelled in their luck. They fell silent as they noticed Esmeralda nearby, holding chunks of the ship's rubble. The cheering had triggered her. How dare they joke when the ship was falling to pieces around them! How dare they revel at being alive when fifty per cent of the crew were in the ocean! Esmeralda was so ready to explode that she wasn't sure any of it would come out in the common tongue. Her brain couldn't translate this particular brand of melancholy, but she had to find some words.

"No one is drinking a damn thing until we have made up the time we lost," she managed through gritted teeth. "Get back to work!"

She was shaking. She wished Walter was here. He was the

only one who could level her when the strain of leadership overwhelmed her. Still, it gave her some satisfaction to see a ripple of fear in the men. They kicked into action, grumbling in disapproval, but none dared challenge her.

Hale was the only one who stayed. She waited until the others were out of earshot. "Wasn't that a bit harsh? He almost drowned, Esmeralda. Is it so wrong that he'd want to celebrate?"

Raging, Esmeralda flung the pieces of her beloved ship into the ocean. She held her head, leaning against the broken railing. "Don't tell me how to run my ship, Hale."

"I wasn't."

"You should have woken me when that storm hit. *¡Me cago en tu puta fucking … argh!*" She squeezed the rail. She couldn't focus with the ocean rush pummelling her ears.

"I d-did the best I could," Hale said.

Esmeralda picked up another section of broken sail and threw it overboard. Some of the crew were watching her, but she didn't care. She wasn't sure how much of what she was feeling was to do with the ship, and how much of it was because she still felt like she was drowning.

"The damage isn't that bad," Hale offered kindly. "It w-won't take us long to fix."

Esmeralda spun around and Hale stepped back, wary of her wrath. "Go check on Cecerie."

"But—"

"Now, Hale. If we lose her, we have lost Viperidae."

Hale's fearful expression changed to anger. "I might have known you'd only be thinking about the treasure."

"I'm thinking about this crew, and what we've already lost. It's my job."

"Screw your job! Don't you care about anyone but yourself? We're not sacrificing my sister so you and Ximo can get your damn loot."

Esmeralda snapped. She grabbed Hale by the scruff of her shirt. "You think you know me so well, don't you?"

"No, but you make it *so* easy to guess." Hale yanked herself free, her emerald glare wide and furious.

Esmeralda sighed. She didn't want to argue. She had already hurt her, in more ways than Hale knew. Sooner or later, she would open that door, but not while there was still so much at stake. Taking her silence for victory, Hale retreated, and Esmeralda didn't see her the rest of the evening.

*

Lana! Save me!
Lucian? Where are you?
I'm here. Save me! I don't want to die!
You won't. I've got you.
"Lucian!"

Hale awoke in her cot with a sharp gasp. Her skin was a soupy mess, her white shirt plastered to her skin. Her mind prickled with remnants of her latest nightmare, and she sat up, placing her feet on the cold floor, clutching her head. *I have to get a grip on this.*

On the cot beside hers, Ximo was snoring, tufts of goatee fluttering with each exhalation. He was reaching under his pillow, clutching what Hale guessed to be his weapon. *It's like he's expecting something bad to happen.* She, too, had the same concerns. Her gut screamed out for them to turn back, but that was impossible now.

Her desire for fresh air outweighed her body's weakness. She zig-zagged between the crew's cots, and hammocks swinging in the open-plan cabin. The cabin stank of stale men, alcohol oozing through their pores as they slept. Tonight's drinks had been had after all, as Esmeralda had succumbed to the need herself and opened the first cask of ale.

Fighting with the lock at the top of the ladder, Hale finally managed to heave the door open, and she flopped out onto the deck. It took a moment for her ears to adjust, but as she lay staring up at the newly repaired sails, she picked up on the faintest hint of singing.

> "In a broken world,
> Beneath the stars,

With treasures I won,
There are many.

A bottle of rum,
And twenty-five women.
I pay them a gem,
Which is plenty.

Yet despite all the fun,
I feel I'm dishonest,
The feelings I feel,
They are empty.

I just want a person,
To have for my own,
But all the world does,
Is resent me."

Where is that coming from?

She got up. Her bare feet slapped along the slippery surface as she walked to the back of the half-repaired ship, following the delicate humming still audible over the ocean. The night was calm since the crew's earlier revelries had died out. As Hale approached the ship's stern, she spotted Esmeralda prancing around in the dark. A half-drunk bottle of rum dangled from her hand, and she held one of her daggers in the other, slashing at the air with well-trained combinations. Hale picked up the admiral's discarded coat, putting it on. It was still damp.

"So, this is what you do when everyone's asleep."

Esmeralda spun around at the sound of her voice, holding her dagger *en garde*. She swigged another mouthful of rum, then placed the glass bottle on the deck. "You just going to stand there, admiring?" She tossed Hale her spare dagger. "Come on, sweetness. Let's see what you've got."

Hale gave it a twirl. She chuckled as Esmeralda pranced again, slashing the air with her own blade. "H-How much have you had to drink?"

"Not enough, but I can still kick your *culo*." She lunged so fast that Hale just about ducked her swing. "Not bad, uh."

They circled each other, and adrenaline surged through Hale, washing away the weakness caused by her nightmare. She lunged, slicing a hole in Esmeralda's vest.

"Ey," Esmeralda complained, checking the damage along her abdomen. She touched the slight flesh wound, stunned. "After all the clothes I've shared with you." She tutted.

"Who taught *you* how to share?"

Esmeralda attacked in reply, and their daggers clashed thrice against the silence of the night. Hale ducked under a wild combination that would have been more precise had Esmeralda been sober. She caught the admiral's ankle, tripping her onto her back, and Esmeralda planted the deck.

"You know," she groaned, staring up at Hale. "That would've hurt a lot drunker, had I not been less sober."

Hale laughed. "Think you mixed your words there, Admiral."

"Help me up." She raised her arm in the air. When Hale didn't respond, she glared up at her. "We have sex, and this is where you draw the line? Come on. *Ayúdame*."

Hale rolled her eyes. Reluctantly, she took Esmeralda's hand. Esmeralda yanked her down on top of her, and rolled over, straddling her on the deck. She pinned both Hale's arms above her head, as Hale struggled beneath her, verging on panic.

"Tell me, how does it work, this touch phobia of yours?" Esmeralda's wicked smile widened. "Where did you even get it from, uh?"

Hale's yell tore from the back of her throat. "Get off me!"

Esmeralda let her go, seeing she was about to implode. Still laughing, she sidled off her, lying on the deck beside her. She snatched her bottle of rum, taking another drink, dribbling it down her face.

Hale sat up. "You're an a… a… asshole!"

"Of that, I am sure," Esmeralda said.

She stared up at the sky, humming the same tune. Hale stole the bottle from her, taking a sip to calm her nerves. It was sweet and smooth to taste. *Definitely not Hedge's finest again.* She lay back down beside the admiral, listening to the song that didn't have any more words. Words didn't matter much when it came to Esmeralda. If anything, they were nothing but a distraction, for it was times like this, when Esmeralda let her guard down, that Hale felt as if she truly knew her. Unfortunately, Esmeralda seemed to realise this. Her humming eventually died out, and the gentle rush of the ocean took precedence.

Hale turned, finding Esmeralda's face beside hers. "Why did you stop?"

Esmeralda's sullenness deepened. "Reminds me of someone I knew."

Even in the darkness, Hale saw a sparkle of tears. "Who?"

Esmeralda focused on the stars. "You remember I once told you that I, too, was tortured in Sovereign prison?"

Hale fiddled with strands of Esmeralda's damp hair stretched across the deck. "We d-don't have to talk about that."

Esmeralda continued, regardless, letting the alcohol fuel the conversation. "When I was suffering from what you are now, there was no one there to hold me still." She looked at her. "I know why you're up here, Hale. Why you're awake almost every night after everyone has gone to bed."

"It's not because of you, believe me."

Esmeralda breathed a laugh. "*Gilipollas.*" Her amusement vanished as quickly as it appeared. "The darkness brings it back, doesn't it? Makes it harder to ignore?"

Hale wasn't sure she liked this new forthcoming Esmeralda, peeling away her layers. She knew Esmeralda felt more exposed than she did, however. Maybe that alone is what made her answer honestly. "You won't t-tell anyone, will you?"

"I'm not about to go spreading it around."

"Good." Hale relaxed. "I have a reputation to protect." Esmeralda shook with silent laughter. "What?"

"You are starting to sound like me."

They both laughed. A few seconds of silence followed which only the waves interrupted. Hale plucked up the courage to break it.

"Esmeralda?" She raised her head; better to see the pain behind the admiral's eyes. This drunk Esmeralda was so vulnerable, that she almost didn't ask her next question, but a part of her believed Esmeralda wanted her to. "What happened to you?"

A question so simple, yet so invasive. It was the most personal thing she could have requested, yet Esmeralda seemed to be considering it. Hale continued to twirl a strand of her hair, and for a second, expected Esmeralda to clam up. She was surprised when she finally got a response.

"Eleven years ago," Esmeralda began. "I was twenty. I had just started making a name for myself in Swashbuckler circles. I left Xevería, became rich and infamous, with only my closest friends aboard." She glanced at the dilapidated sail. "This ship has been with me from day one."

Hale laid her head down and listened. She could listen to that voice all day.

"But that worked against me," Esmeralda continued. "I had this bright idea, you see, that I could infiltrate Stonawal. That I could sneak into Sovereign Altus' palace and rob him blind."

"What?" Hale laughed. Even she knew that was a death sentence, and she had infiltrated her fair share of palaces. She felt Esmeralda's fingers intertwine with hers, asking permission to hold them. Hale obliged, trying not to let it bother her. It was a rarity for Esmeralda to need support.

"*Fue un desastre,*" Esmeralda continued. "I underestimated the mountains on that Goddess-forsaken island. My original target was Sailor's Creek, but we had no idea of its exact location. We were hundreds of kilometres off course. I thought because of this ship's lack of magical tracers, I could slip into Sovereign waters unnoticed and make the trip worthwhile, but with sails as bright as mine, I had painted myself a pretty target. The legends of *Somateria mollissima* had already reached

Sovereign Altus' ears. I was a threat to all things Sovereign and Scour; the biggest taliswoman for Swashbuckler dominion over the Tripartite. Of course, I had no idea about any of this at the time." She allowed herself to chuckle at her naivety.

Hale shivered and pulled the lapels of Esmeralda's coat closed around her as it started to drizzle. Goosebumps had risen on Esmeralda's skin, but she didn't seem bothered. *Or maybe she's too drunk to feel cold.* Hale huddled closer to her for warmth and refocused on keeping Esmeralda's hand in hers despite every fibre of her being screaming for her to let go.

"Myself and my first mate at that time, Ximo—"

"Ximo?" Hale hadn't taken the well-dressed businessman for a Swashbuckler. She supposed it made sense. *Explains how Esmeralda knows him so well.* She'd thought it was maybe because Esmeralda was a regular at The Busted Cherry. *Maybe she hasn't been buying hookers as much as I imagined.*

"Joaquín and I go way back."

"Joaquín?"

"That's Ximo's real name. He is a cartographer like Walter. He had drawn me a map of the main vault's location, stealing some old blueprints of the palace. We declared ourselves royals on the spot, but before we could escape the vault with the loot, an entire golden army had us surrounded. I couldn't tell you how much those *cabrones* beat us." She paused as the topic overwhelmed her. Her fingers tightened around Hale's. "They eventually tossed us in cells."

Hale pictured her own version of Sovereign prison. The cells she remembered vividly, even though *An Caisleán's* were likely different to what Esmeralda experienced in Stonawal. "H-How did you escape?"

"I didn't," Esmeralda said. "Not exactly. What I neglected to tell you was that another member of my crew was captured as well. Gabriella. She was the youngest I had ever recruited. There was only two years between us. She was … special to me."

"You mean you were sleeping with her?"

Esmeralda snorted. "Ximo and I were both sleeping with

her actually. Gabriella fairly got around. Anyway, she was thrown in the cell next to ours, not long after Ximo and I were captured. She had tried to save us but gotten herself caught. We listened to her being tortured, over and over and ... over." Hale sensed that Esmeralda was getting to the worst part of her story. "While Ximo was off being interrogated one day, the Sovereigns made me watch Gabriella's punishments. I heard every scream. Saw every foul, disgusting thing they did to her."

Hale cringed. "Did they kill her?"

"Worse. They made me do it."

Esmeralda cleared her throat but didn't continue. Hale brought her back with a squeeze, seeing no tears in Esmeralda's eyes this time. Instead, she recognised her own trauma mirrored in them; a bottomless hole that couldn't be plugged. Esmeralda's soul was as scarred as her own.

"*La maté yo*," Esmeralda finished. "Killed one of my own. The sadistic *cerdos* gave me a knife, dangled my freedom in front of me, and I ran her through with it. More than once."

Hale struggled to comprehend the callous way in which she spoke. "They were t-torturing you too, Esmeralda. You are not responsible for her death."

"I didn't feel remorse. Truthfully, I still don't." She swallowed audibly. "I had killed many people before that day. I have killed a hell of a lot more since. Sooner or later, Gabriella would have cracked and given us all up. She'd have told them about our plans for Sailor's Creek, then none of us would have made it out alive. I had no problem taking her life, no matter how much she may have meant. I chose myself and Joaquín over her, and I'd do it all again if I must."

Hale was stunned. "What are you expecting me to take from this story?"

"Nothing. But you asked me what happened, sweetness, and that's the only part of my story I am comfortable explaining." She pulled away and held her palms in front of her, staring up at them as if remembering what they'd done.

"I'm s-sorry for asking," Hale muttered, wondering how many lives those hands had claimed.

"*Está bien.*" She let her hands rest on her chest. "I understand why you did. You want to know that it gets better. Right now, your body has cracked under so much strain, but give it time, sweetness. Unlike me, you don't have to go through it alone. Not if you don't want to."

The pain in Hale's heart lessened at her words, but Esmeralda's warmth felt tainted now. It was strange to have someone claim to understand what she was experiencing. Hale couldn't help but compare Esmeralda's story to her own. *Is this why we are drawn to each other? Shared trauma?* She wasn't sure.

Esmeralda seemed just as indecisive over whether to push her away or draw her close. Hale guessed she had more than one thing to atone for, but how pitilessly Esmeralda spoke of Gabriella made her unsure if atonement was what Esmeralda was searching for. She could have easily been cleansing her palette to make room for more paint. The way this expedition was shaping up, there was sure to be a few more drops of red.

DEPTHS

The expedition sailed on for the next few weeks until they lost themselves in fog. Thick in the brume, they could only see a few feet ahead, as if all life beyond the ship had ceased. The sole interruption to their purgatorial existence was the constant shushing of the ship splitting the ocean. The Eider's Cry drifted through silvery unknowns, ushered by a non-existent breeze, as Esmeralda guided blindly from the helm. *Or was she blind?* Hale imagined her to have some sort of sixth sense, an ability to see what the rest of them could not.

The crew had come to a standstill, unsure what was required of them. *Unsure if we're approaching danger.* Hale was licked by perspiration. Her muscles were weak and heavy. *Are we deep within the eye of another storm?* At any moment she expected chaos would once again be thrust upon them. She had no idea how to protect herself against an invisible enemy. She huddled as close to Ximo as she could without inadvertently brushing against him.

"Shit running down your leg?" Ximo muttered in her ear.

"Is that joke to make me feel better, or you?"

"Bit of both," he admitted. "I think we will all need clean drawers when this is over, no?" His laughter broke through the tension, and Hale chuckled. Ximo was the oddest of fellows.

The fog became thicker and denser the further onwards they travelled. A ghostly touch traced her spine from bottom to top, and she flicked up the frayed collar of her coat, holding the points closed underneath her chin. She missed her mother's scarf. Her last nerve had been triggered as an unnatural sweat broke out under her clothes that she feared had nothing to do with the weather. Whispers sounded in her ear that didn't belong to the crew.

She read the damp map Ximo was holding. "You made this?"

He nodded and pointed to their estimated position: half a mile from the X marking Sailor's Creek. Hale leaned in. This map's ink was fresher than the one Maven had stolen from her, despite its sagging under the current conditions. She recognised Ximo's handiwork. His artistry was different than Walter's. The map Walter had made her of Anferan was simple, easy to read, without unnecessary details. Ximo's map was stylish and flamboyant, possessing an artistic flair, detailing forests and mountains upon the landscape, each labelled with a name and estimated square miles. The landmarks had river veins flowing through them, leading to miniscule sketches of waterfalls and rock pools.

It's almost overkill. Like he's worried we'll miss something important. Or perilous.

Hale wasn't reassured. She cast the admiral a glance over her shoulder. Esmeralda wore a black tricorne over the top of her red bandana. Hale had never seen it before. It did little to keep the ends of her hair dry, forming puddles of moisture that leaked off its curved edges. The collar of Esmeralda's coat was pulled up like Hale's. *Does she feel the same icy chill I do?* Her eyes were fixed firmly ahead, navigating a safe path on instinct alone.

"How does she do it?" Hale asked Ximo, jerking her head at the occupied helm.

Ximo cast Esmeralda a glance. "Sailing isn't always about what you can see, *amiga*. Sometimes you have to feel your way around."

"I imagine Esmeralda's feeling quite a few things right about now."

Ximo smirked. "Worried we'll crash?"

Worried we'll … something.

They were only travelling around ten knots, or so some outdated dials on the binnacle had told her earlier. Her gut was telling her they were about to graze a cliff, or something else huge and hull-damaging. Then something happened. She clutched her head, succumbing to pressure she couldn't explain.

Go back. You must go back!

"You alright?" Ximo touched her arm in concern. His voice sounded miles away.

Hale groaned. It was as if her head had been carved in two. She left Ximo and stumbled away, crouching amongst piles of water barrels stacked on the other side of the deck. A migraine, so severe, electrocuted her. She hunched, trying to claw out her skull. She pressed her face into the deck, slamming against the dew. Nothing would work to defeat the throbbing.

The pain vanished as quickly as it had consumed her. Hale regained her sight, shocked at the sudden sense of relief. She sat up onto her knees, waiting for her vision to recover. She touched her forehead, confused. *What in the name of all the Ancestors ...?* Shaking, she got to her feet, thankful no one else had noticed. She patted the stack of barrels in silent thanks and re-joined the rest of the crew who had kicked into action.

"What's happening?" she asked Ximo, leaning back on the starboard rail beside him. The Swashbucklers around them were discussing orders, preparing the ship to drop anchor at Esmeralda's instruction.

"Sailor's Creek is two hundred metres that way." Ximo pointed again into the mist. "We can't get the ship any closer without running aground."

"So how are we getting there?"

"We have to take Cecerie with us, aboard the life raft."

"L-Life raft?" Hale's question was answered as two crew members hauled ropes on the rear sector of the port side. She and Ximo joined them, helping them reel something up the side of the ship. A small wooden boat with two ores inside finally came into view through the mist. It emptied its seawater, ready and waiting to escort them. "You've got to be kidding me."

"What's the matter, sweetness, afraid of a little water?"

Esmeralda appeared behind them, casting a smirk in Hale's direction.

Hale snorted at the inside joke. "I take it you're staying here?"

"Why?" She ignored the surrounding crew who were watching her closely and took off her tricorne, flinging it at the man closest to her. Slithering between Hale and Ximo, they watched her climb over the ship's edge into the tiny life raft. "Well?" she said, startling them all. "You coming?"

Ximo helped pass unconscious Cecerie into the raft, with Hale in tow, cradling Cecerie's lolling head so she wouldn't get injured. The longer their trip went on, the more she deteriorated. Hale was terrified of what this expedition would mean for her. The raft swayed under their combined weight, creaking in complaint, and she nestled into the thwart at the boat's rear, facing Esmeralda in the centre. Once Ximo had settled in the front with Cecerie in his arms, Jakson and Fidel began to lower the raft.

Hale tensed with each uncomfortable drop, feeling a sickening churn. She clutched the low sides of the raft and cast a dizzying view into the water. The tide offering to catch them seemed calm. Fighting the urge to puke, she stared at Esmeralda, knowing she was likely faring worse. Esmeralda's breathing was shallow, her face white amongst the haze. The further they dropped, the more ghostly she appeared. Hale was suddenly jealous of Ximo who, seated behind Esmeralda, didn't have to witness her torment. The rush of the ocean became louder with every gut-wrenching inch of descension. Hale wondered if she should say something; do something to help her. Like their day at the lough, Esmeralda was throwing herself headfirst into a phobia that always seemed to hold her in a stranglehold.

As their raft was released, Hale finally understood Esmeralda's fear of water. The waves were choppier than expected, rushing up over the sides, drenching them in ice. Deaf from the gales, Hale clutched the wooden boat tighter. Esmeralda was no longer frozen, rowing them away from The

Eider's Cry's suction. They soon lost sight of the ship in the mist. Nestled deep in the eerie calmness, the waves finally settled, and Esmeralda's intense rowing gave way to a gentler paddle, allowing Hale to relax her grip.

"You alright?" Esmeralda asked her, rowing in accordance with Ximo's navigation.

The closer they got to Sailor's Creek, the less Hale desired it. "H-How long until we get there?" she asked, wishing she was on dry land.

"Approaching any second," Ximo called over his shoulder. The lapels of his grey duster rippled in the wind. "Esme, take us in. *Despacito*. Something is not right."

Esmeralda did as instructed. The open ocean soon gave way to a small stream, with silhouettes of land breaking through the fog on either side of them. Hale was claustrophobic. The voices in her head resumed, but they were an unintelligible whisper now.

"Can I row for a bit?" she asked, desperate for something to do.

Esmeralda's brow rose. "You know how?"

Hale shrugged. She must have looked desperate because Esmeralda didn't object. She offered the oars for her to hold, and they swapped thwarts, careful not to tip the raft on its side. Esmeralda gave Hale a few instructions, and their expedition meandered upstream, against the water's natural flow. Glad for something to concentrate on, Hale relished the burn as she dragged the oars through the cloudy current.

"Pull us towards that inlay," Ximo said minutes later. "We are here."

She did as she was told, directing the boat to shore. When it ran aground, the three of them climbed out onto soggy earth, Ximo scooping Cecerie into his arms. Hale arched her back, relieving the discomfort of being cramped up. They stared up at a huge clump of trees bearing over them, hiding them in the outskirts of a sparse forest.

"F-Feels like we're back in Anferan," Hale said.

Dew dripped from a leaf and landed in the centre of her

forehead. She wiped it off, taking in the forest's obstacles. Thin tree barks bent upwards at awkward angles, like broken bones healed without a splint. The woods were strangely devoid of wildlife, like their calls had been silenced somehow. Yet life surely existed of a different kind, and true enough, Hale shook away a leech before it sucked through her leather boot. She writhed, sickened by the realisation that the mud they were standing in was squirming with other, worm-like creatures.

Ximo checked his map. "I don't understand. It says we are—"

Esmeralda dragged them onto the infested ground.

"What—?"

"Sssh!"

They lay on their stomachs, concealed behind a small bush on the forest perimeter. Hale tried to ignore the sensation of insects crawling beneath her clothing. They foraged under the open seams and she clamped her mouth in case something entered uninvited.

Goddess. Stop. Please stop.

A few seconds after Esmeralda's tackle, the sound of male voices carried within the forest.

"… something's wrong? Maybe we should check it out. Definitely heard someone."

A second man replied. "The entire Creek has ghosts, idiot. We've been here ten years. Surely you know that by now."

Esmeralda made to get up but both Hale and Ximo held her back. She reluctantly squelched into the mud again between them and Cecerie.

"There could be a whole squadron of them," Ximo whispered. "We have to sneak past."

"They've gone," Hale said, moments later, jerking her head up to peer into the bleak forest. "Let's go. Nice and easy. I'll take point."

Sneaking was what she did best. She sank into the mud and pushed herself up into a hunkered pose, shaking out what she could of her infestation. Ximo picked up Cecerie and filed in behind her, with Esmeralda taking up the rear.

The forest was small and nondescript, possessing none of Anferan's striking greenery. It smelled less overpowering, for which Hale was thankful. This enabled her to get a whiff of the cigarillos the strange men were smoking. She tracked the invisible clue to their location, leading the way, deeper into the forest, pausing every so often to make sure there were no more mercenaries littered amongst the trees. Searching the forest floor, she noticed two distinct sets of footprints. Taking up the centre, Hale stalked the tracks, signalling for the other two to flank on either side.

After around ten minutes of sweating in the darkness, they finally came to a clearing. Hale concealed herself between the thickest bushes at the forest's edge, shielding from attacking midges. A waterfall sounded nearby. Breathing shallowly, she spotted a cliff of unimaginable heights. Its peak was cut off by the fog. At the base, two men stood guard by the entrance to an open cave.

This is surely the entrance to Sailor's Creek.

Spotting Esmeralda and Ximo, who had faltered a few metres from her location, the three of them nodded, acknowledging the unspoken plan. Esmeralda scurried to the right, skirting the natural edges of the clearing, while Ximo held his position with Cecerie, allowing Hale to overtake on the left.

"What was that?" one of the men asked, startled by Ximo's birdcall.

The guard tossed his cigarillo and laid an arrow along his bow, pointing it at the bush where Ximo was hiding.

"I heard it this time," said the other man, nearest Hale, sinking the last of his canteen. She got the faintest hint of whiskey as she flanked him. "Who's—Argh!"

Hale knocked the man unconscious with her elbow, while Esmeralda slit the throat of the other. They caught the bodies and dragged them out of sight. Hale felt her way around in the dark, removing the man's bow and quiver of arrows. She searched his ragged hunter jacket, taking what little corundum he had and shoving it into her pocket, along with his case of cigarillos. *My tobacco cravings are greater than yours.*

"You know how to use that?" Ximo gestured to her new bow as they rendezvoused in the clearing. It was a short bow, easy to hook around her until she needed it. The arrows were made of duck feathers and cheap wood, as if the former owner had made them himself.

She took one out and spun it. "Just point me at a target."

Esmeralda looked over at Hale's victim. "You didn't kill him."

Hale ignored her sceptical exchange with Ximo and did a quick search of the cave's opening. "All clear. This looks like our way in."

"Ximo, stay here in case more savages show up. I think they are former Armada," Esmeralda said. They listened to her bleeding victim choke to death. "Goddess knows how long they have been stranded here. Hale, we should go on ahead with Cecerie." She flicked a match behind Hale's ear to light the lantern she'd obtained from the guard.

Hale rubbed the friction burn, scowling. "I hate when you do that."

"It was the only dry part of you I could find."

She took the lamp from her, freeing up Esmeralda's arms to carry Cecerie as Ximo passed her over. He cracked open the barrel of his revolver to double-check his ammo.

"Meet me back here in two hours," he said. "If you are not here by then, I'm heading back to the ship."

"Without us?" Hale asked. "What do you—"

"He's right," Esmeralda insisted. "This island is unnatural. It keeps you prisoner the longer you stay."

"We are well-versed in Sailor's Creek, *amiga,*" Ximo told Hale. "We know what we are up against. Trust us."

Hale puffed. "Fine. It's your funeral pyre."

Ximo laughed. He kissed Esmeralda's cheeks then sat on the nearest rock, producing the most ludicrous pipe.

Esmeralda prodded Hale towards the entrance. "*Vamos,* sweetness. We don't have much time. This sedative won't last forever."

They stared at Cecerie. She bore violently purple veins across her cheeks and forehead, signalling her powers were fighting off the heavy sedation. Whatever sorcery Father had injected her with was spreading, in what Hale could only assume was a reaction to Viperidae's presence. She threw a concerned glance back at Ximo's outline, wondering if she should have insisted he come along.

"We shouldn't be splitting up. Ximo has more knowledge of sorcery than I do."

Esmeralda sighed. "He promised me he'd get us here, and he did. I won't ask anymore of him, Hale."

"But what happen if Ceci wakes up?"

"Just keep moving. She'll be fine."

Hale held the lantern aloft and led the way further underground. It did little to penetrate the blackness, and navigation became harder the deeper they got. The gravel beneath them became loose and uneven the further the cave sloped, and she slipped a few times, catching the wall to steady herself.

"You know," Hale said, hoping that talking would distract her from her growing unease. "They say the air is thinner where sorcery dwells." Esmeralda lost her footing, and she instinctively caught her, steadying her before she collapsed under Cecerie's weight.

"*Gracias*," Esmeralda said, straightening up. She heaved Cecerie, getting a better grip on her. "What makes you say that? The air isn't thin here. In fact, it's almost as if there is too much of it."

"That's the problem." Hale took smaller steps now, anxious as to what lay further in. The walls became so tight that they had to go single file. "It's seeping into my lungs without me asking. Like a soul slipping down my throat, searching for a host."

She stopped dead, and Esmeralda collided with her. Their path abruptly ended, giving way to a huge opening filled with—

"Water." Esmeralda breathed the word like a curse.

The dislodged limestone caused a disturbance in the pool but disappeared beneath the depths. The water appeared magically pure, much like the Anferanian lough. It was brighter in the pool's centre where the cenote widened, taking in both natural and supernatural light. Inexplicable floating balls of purple flames illuminated the darkness, showing how far it stretched. The surface ended about a hundred metres across to the opposite wall. A small waterfall trickled into it from another alcove like theirs on the far left, but the water levels didn't seem to be rising.

"You see that?" Hale said, pointing to the right. "That little hole where the water's escaping. I'm guessing that's got to be our only way through." Esmeralda sank onto her backside as Cecerie's weight became too much for her. Hale hunkered down beside her, realising it was actually nerves that had made her collapse. "You can do this," she reassured her.

Esmeralda shook her head. "It's too deep. I don't think I can."

"I'll go first with Cecerie, ok? You only have to be under for a s-second, then I'll help you stay afloat like … before." An image of the two of them pressed together in the lough crossed her mind, and she knew Esmeralda hadn't missed the reference.

"Ok," she relented.

Hale took Cecerie from her. Feeling lightheaded, she squeezed towards the alcove's edge, shimmying herself and Cecerie between the tight walls. As she stared into the depths she got tunnel vision, almost sucked in before she was ready. She leapt from the nook, cradling Cecerie so they both fell feet first, shooting into the pool like a joint torpedo.

Every fibre of her body screamed as they were submerged. Trillions of tiny bubbles rumbled around her and she opened her eye, following them to the surface. Their combined weight had taken them deeper than planned. Battling against her fatiguing muscles and haphephobia, Hale kicked, propelling them upwards, inhaling sharply as she broke the surface. Panting, she searched their surroundings for immediate danger.

Seeing none, she stared up at Esmeralda.

Esmeralda was dangling her legs over the edge, staring at the arrows which had floated from Hale's quiver, bobbing on the surface. Hale scooped them clear of the drop zone, popping them back in. Cecerie was like a dead weight in her arms; it took all her kicking power to keep them both afloat. Hale watched Esmeralda get to her feet, legs trembling.

"Jump, Esmeralda! You can do it!"

Ashen-faced, Esmeralda stared into the circling ripples that Hale had made. Hale listened to her cursing and wondered if she had made a mistake going first, but Esmeralda hesitated for only a second. Persistent in her fearlessness, she leapt, feet first, dropping for an age before she splashed.

Hale waited, unable to see what was happening through the water's disturbance. Unwilling to let Esmeralda suffer for long, she ducked under, spotting her flailing a few metres deep. Abandoning Cecerie for a split second so she could grab a hold of Esmeralda's jacket, she pulled them both to the top, expelling the last of her air in a bubbling scream as exhaustion ravaged her. She gasped as they surfaced, and Esmeralda did the same. Hale encouraged her to wrap her arms around her neck.

"Agh, not so tight."

"Sorry!" Esmeralda loosened her grip and rested her forehead against Hale's wet hair.

"Kick, Es. I can't hold us all up."

"I know. I know." Esmeralda kissed her head as if it wasn't counterproductive. "Let's go. We can kill each other later."

Needing no further encouragement, Hale swam them to the hole in the rocks. She touched the outline, noticing the amethyst substance leak onto her skin. *Signs of magic. Unstable magic at that.* She peered through, trying not to let it suction her in prematurely. The pool gave the illusion it was emptying, but the water level remained constant, magically preserved.

She composed herself. "You ready?"

Esmeralda tightened her grip. Not waiting for a reply, Hale ducked under the rock wall, and they were swept downwards with the current.

Their simultaneous yells echoed as they picked up speed, too fast for Hale to control. She clutched Cecerie as they scraped against pointed rocks, speeding away from Esmeralda.

The water finally thinned, and their momentum propelled them towards what she hoped was safety. Crushing pain surged through her left shoulder as it took the brunt of the fall, with Cecerie landing on top of her. Esmeralda then flattened them both.

As the water dripped around them, Esmeralda rolled onto the ground beside her. They lay catching their breaths, unable to speak, staring up into the cavity they'd fallen through. Winded, Hale pushed Cecerie off. Curling onto her side, she touched the bow and arrows, amazed they were still intact after the impact they'd had on her spine. Esmeralda got up first, bending to inspect Cecerie, who was remarkably still unconscious. Hale reached for her sister. A trickle of blood seeped down Cecerie's temple but otherwise she had survived the fall.

Three loud cracks overhead made them gasp.

Hale froze. "Was that—"

"Ximo," Esmeralda finished.

Hale had never heard gunshots before. Each pop ricocheted through her body as though she was the one who had been riddled with them. Was it fear or shock that held her? She couldn't remember how to move, like her mind had lost command of her muscles. *Or are my muscles simply ignoring the commands?* She stared up through the hole, hoping Ximo was alright.

Esmeralda's voice roused her. "Come on, Hale. We are almost there."

"How do you know?"

Esmeralda pointed behind Hale and smiled. "Should we knock, or just let ourselves in?"

THRALLS AND REMNANTS

It was impossible to tell where the collapsed building ended, and the tunnelling cave began. Rocks changed from natural granite to dried remnants of cement, mixed over several millennia. The double doors Esmeralda gestured to were golden and bronze, adorned with eight panels, each depicting some long-lost ritual. Hale recognised the bearded face in the designs; resembling a statue that had once stood outside her cell in *An Caisleán*.

We are standing on the grounds of a former God.

It reminded her of a pilgrimage held every thirteenth day of the month in Ortiva City honouring the Goddess. Esmeralda hunkered to investigate the architecture as Hale squinted to make out the faded engravings over her shoulder. She watched Esmeralda wipe dust from a section of the massive door that hung diagonally on broken hinges, still attached to the dilapidated frame. The rest of the building had caved inwards, under the land that was burying it. She glimpsed a clearing through the thick debris field, lit by the same unnatural orbs from above. It was some kind of marble hall.

Hale leaned over Esmeralda's shoulder to inspect the writings above the heads of the unknown characters. In one of the panels, a human male was spreadeagled, with two other males spread likewise on his flanks. "What does it say?" she asked, unable to comprehend the scripture.

"I.N.R.I.," Esmeralda sounded aloud, tracing the miniscule lettering over the central man's head.

"What does that mean?"

"You tell me. You're the historian."

"Reading doesn't make me a historian. Besides, Maven's

books spoke nothing of Ancestral Gods." She scanned a huge plaque that had fallen off the crumbled outer wall. Its marble was chipped, but well kept. A corner of the plaque had broken off entirely, but the foreign script was clearer here than the door. Unfortunately, Hale was only versed in the common tongue. "Can you make this out?" she asked, pointing to a section on the top right corner.

Esmeralda moved closer and Hale became distracted by her faint perfume. She watched Esmeralda's eyes flicker from left to right, absorbing the foreign script. A trickle of water streamed from a strand of her hair. Hale should have been more interested in their surroundings, but she couldn't concentrate on anything else. Esmeralda dabbed her forehead absentmindedly, unaware that Hale was entranced by the water sliding down her face.

"*Itervam portam sanctam.*" She traced the new lettering, leaning in to read the line below that was harder to make out. "*Apervit et clasvit.*"

Hale came back to her senses. "And that means?"

Esmeralda stroked her chin, scanning the words again. "Well, if it is anything like Xeverían, '*portam sanctam*' could be close to *puerta santa,* meaning … holy door?" She got to her feet. "Who cares? Let us see what is behind this holy threshold. There's a sentence I never thought I'd say."

She returned to Cecerie and picked her up, then squeezed through the doorway, climbing through the building's collapse. Hale followed, careful not to catch her wet coat on the various nails mixed in the debris. The academic in her would have loved Esmeralda to attempt translating the rest, but she sensed this place held no interest for her beyond the sordid. Esmeralda was here for treasure, not a half-broken archway with no significance other than to hold up the ceiling.

Hale climbed over iron rods protruding from the ancient foundations. She cast the uneven ceiling a precarious glance, afraid it might give way any second. The pressure on her head intensified the further underground they travelled. This mysterious building was surely home to the cave's secrets. *Or it is the secret itself.*

She darted between untidy lines of broken pews to examine what she could of the stone floor. *This is not the work of nature.* Each stone was mapped with hardened grit, a different colour than the last. It was as though they had all deteriorated unevenly due to generations of footprints walking over them. A chill crept through her as a breeze blew from an unknown location. She looked up, spotting Esmeralda ahead, crouched in front of a broken marble column.

"Did you find something?"

Esmeralda didn't reply.

Hale hopped the broken seats and climbed over toppled, faceless statues, approaching an altar of sorts. The marble corpse of a woman holding a dead man caught her attention. The woman's face reminded her of a stained glass window in an interrogation room; one she used to stare through regularly. This statue held a similar tenderness. She looked around for more, but most of it was lost to time, leaving only scarred remains.

Hale approached the altar, casting an anxious glance at the twin columns on either side, blackened and curled with golden vines. One had been carved completely in half, still boasting an approximate six-metre stature, compared to the other's twelve. She ascended a three-set staircase, absentmindedly touching her bow, thinking she might need it soon. *It's much too quiet in here.*

Esmeralda was still hunched on one knee, adjacent a huge mosaic towards which all the broken seating was fixated. Clutching her head, she rocked back and forth, muttering under her breath. Cecerie lay on the ground beside her.

"Are you praying?" Hale asked in disbelief.

Esmeralda's laughter was muffled. She raised her head. "As if. I just wacked my head off the altar when I bent over." She showed Hale the small gash that she was blotting with her bandana.

Hale snorted. "Aw, you'll live."

"Oh, thanks for the sympathy."

"Call me when it breaks the skin."

Esmeralda pointed to where she had been investigating. "Check it. I think there's something there."

Hale was busy inspecting the massive mosaic overlooking the altar's golden table. Many of the pieces had fallen loose, but the colour had been mostly preserved thanks to lack of sunlight and human intervention. Again, the same man's face was at the forefront of a golden backdrop. She found him unsettling. Focusing on the table instead, she spotted an outline of dust as though something had recently been removed.

"Someone's been here," Hale said. She bent down beside Esmeralda and fidgeted with the marble plinth that had piqued Esmeralda's interest.

"What are you doing?" Esmeralda asked.

Hale pressed against a loose piece of marble, and the centre section of the plinth pushed out, scraping against its counterpart. She eased it onto the floor, tensing to master the unexpected weight, considering it was only the size of a book. A small snake was engraved on top.

"Goddess above. This is it," Hale whispered, wide-eyed.

"How did you know how to open that?" Esmeralda asked. "It wouldn't budge for me."

"Throughout y-years of sorcerer persecution, old altars like this were used as secret compartments. It's called a slab safe, activated by a pressure point. Father said that during the time when sorcerers shifted Earth's tectonic plates, most of them disappeared into hiding in ruins like this one. On holy ground, the veil was thin enough for them to illegally enact help from necromancers, making them more formidable."

Esmeralda snorted. "You and Ximo have more in common than I thought." She touched the marble cuboid, only to have Hale slap her away. "Ey!"

"I had a sorcerer father," Hale explained. "Doesn't mean I'm interested in sorcery. I s-studied his manuscripts when he died, hoping to protect Cecerie from, well, herself."

"Any idea why she would turn on you like this?"

"She didn't turn on me." Even saying it aloud, Hale wasn't sure it was true, but she had to believe Cecerie was the same person beneath the madness. "Every sorcerer has some kind of varicose veins, but Ceci's are different. No sorcerer I've met ever had them. I n-never noticed how odd it was."

"Not even your *padre* had them?"

"My father was an Elemental. He could manipulate the seasons," she added when Esmeralda was confused. "It was likely an Elemental who caused a quake big enough for this building to become buried so deep underground." She withdrew one of Esmeralda's bronze daggers and wedged it along the marble slab, hoping to find an opening.

"Are you saying Cecerie could do this?"

"Not intentionally," Hale replied. "Cecerie is afraid of her powers. M-Magic explodes out of her when she's most vulnerable. She can't control it as well as other sorcerers can. That's why she stayed in hiding most of her life."

Esmeralda took the slab from her as her attempts to open it became rough and impatient. "So, is this Viperidae or not?"

Hale traced the faded engraving. *"Tar Amach,"* she read aloud. "Yes, I am certain this is it. There is no safer place to hide such power."

"Hmf. I expected it to be bigger."

Hale returned to where Cecerie was lying, feeling guilty for having let her down. She had no idea that Father had tortured her. Even sedated, every muscle in Cecerie's body was taut, like she was still being tortured internally. "How do we get her to open it?"

"The snake in the centre?" Esmeralda suggested. "Looks like something could be inserted there. *No lo sé.* Ximo might know more. Let's get back to the ship."

"We should check if there's anything else of value here. I doubt we'll be m-making a second trip."

Hale left Cecerie's vigil and searched the rest of the ruins. If Viperidae was something powerful enough to overthrow the Tripartite, it could mean upending the world again; only this time it wouldn't be continents splitting, but islands too small to survive.

She crossed the cracked floor, towards a hidden vestibule to the left of the altar. The preserved furniture inside indicated it was from a more recent decade. Something about the patterned armchair was familiar. She traced the frame of the doorway before sitting at a dainty desk; so delicate she was surprised it could hold the weight of the golden tabernacle upon it.

Don't open it. Don't let it out. You mustn't!

The voice she'd heard on the ship whispered louder in her head as she touched it.

"Why?" Hale whispered.

You're wasting time. Leave this place before he finds her.

"Be quiet!" She couldn't concentrate.

"I didn't say anything," Esmeralda's angry reply echoed from the main hall.

Ignoring the icy breath on her neck, Hale split the tabernacle's doors. Loud pitter-patters startled her as corundum overflowed onto the desk. Esmeralda rushed into the vestibule, weapon wielded, and together, they stared at the small fortune, multiplying, spilling onto the floor.

"*¡Hostia!*" Esmeralda picked one up, inspecting it. "Pure gems?"

Hale picked up an emerald, the clearest she had ever found, like royal jewels prised from a Queen's crown. Esmeralda thrust the slab safe at her, disinterested now. She shovelled the corundum back into the tabernacle, a hungry glint in her eye. Hale squeezed the slab safe into her pocket and helped her repack the treasure. They closed the delicate doors, laying the tabernacle flat to keep it closed.

"Ximo will be sick when we show him this," Esmeralda said, beaming. "Here, help me lift—"

Her words were drowned out by the sound of falling rocks. Hale dragged her to the floor as a fireball smashed off the vestibule's archway, vaporising it. They crawled beneath the desk for cover, and only when the rocks had settled, did Hale hear voices. She peered back into the hall, squinting through the settling dust.

"She is here." The voice was Cecerie's.

I told you to run, the internal voice whispered in Hale's head. She wished she had of listened to it now.

A man's voice spoke. "Viperidae's casing has been removed from the altar. I was told only you could touch it."

Hale peeked from under the desk on her belly, spotting Cecerie crouched at the altar, inspecting the rectangular hole where the slab safe had been hidden. A man with swarthy, weather-beaten skin stood over her. His attire was that of a Swashbuckler, patched with skull and bones that she recognised as the Saristca Armada. A machete was dangling from his waistband.

"It's Escudero," Hale whispered to Esmeralda. She withdrew her bow, prepping an arrow. She straightened up to her full height, aiming it at the altar. "Let her go!"

Escudero didn't react.

Cautious, Hale moved into the open, taking steady aim at his head. Stepping over the debris, she positioned herself in the centre of the hall, unprepared for what she saw.

Cecerie's body rose from the floor, rotating as wisps of amethyst smoke billowed beneath her. Gone were the familiar hazel eyes, replaced with luminous amaranthine hue. Vapour leaked from the sockets as if her insides were aflame.

Hale's aim faltered. "Goddess. What did he do to you?"

Sparks shot from Cecerie's nails. "The necromancers offer that which no mere mortal can understand." Her voice echoed with multiple speakers, like she was no longer an individual, but a collective.

"Necromancers?" Hale tightened her bowstring, aiming at the back of Escudero's bald head. "Turn and face me, coward."

He obliged, flexing his chiselled biceps as he swivelled, folding his arms across his tattooed body. He was smaller than Jakson, but somehow more intimidating. "Lana Hale," he grumbled. "I am glad we finally have a chance to speak."

"Save it," she said. "Let her go."

"First, tell me, where is Viperidae?"

"I-It isn't here."

Esmeralda moved behind her, using the rubble as cover.

Escudero gave a low, dangerous chuckle. "Oh, don't waste your time lying. Where is your accomplice, *señorita*? Admiral Rivera and I have some unfinished business."

"I came alone."

His face was lined with scars too numerous to count, wrinkling further in his frustration. "You could not have made it this far without her ship. It is the only ship in the Armada untainted by sorcery. Any other ship, the Creek destroys."

"Then how did *you* get here?"

"With Cecerie's help. Once you were inside, I ordered her to summon me. An old sorcerer trick to ensure that only the master of this lair could invite others if she so wished."

Hale glanced at Cecerie then back at him. "And the other men on the island?"

"Shipwrecked. Long ago, like many others, hunting for the treasure you now possess." He glanced behind her, and Hale wondered for a second if he had noticed Esmeralda, but his eyes bore back into hers. "Admiral Rivera has a knack for gaining people's trust. Tell me, how did she gain yours?"

"What do you mean?"

He smiled. "Ask Felix. He is the latest person she stabbed in the back."

Hale shot an arrow over his shoulder in warning, quickly taking aim with another. "Bullshit! They didn't know each other."

Escudero straightened to his full height. All trace of playfulness disappeared, and Hale sensed she had pushed him to his limit of niceties. From her peripheral, she saw Esmeralda had made it to the hole in the far wall, dragging the tabernacle with her.

Of course, she prioritises the bloody treasure.

"You are not as tame as Felix proclaimed," Escudero said, sounding invigorated. "But you are no killer, either. I was hoping we could come to some arrangement. I have no interest in your sister beyond selling her to Trevus. I am here for Admiral Rivera."

"And like I said, I came here alone."

He laughed. "Your deception could use some work. I can smell her perfume. That bitch always leaves a stench behind. What do you say, Hale? Cecerie's life for Esmeralda's? An uneven trade, I'll admit, but she won't live long, I assure you."

Hale took a few steps to her right, nearing the hole. Esmeralda seemed to be struggling with the tabernacle's bulk. *I need to keep him talking a while longer.* "What is this about, Escudero? Why do you want Viperidae?"

"That safe holds the answers you seek. Give it to me, and I will tell you everything."

There was no hiding the bulge of the slab safe in her coat pocket. 'Everything' sounded appealing. She was tired of having her head in the sand; tired of walking into everyone's traps, unsure of who to trust. She touched her pocket, wondering if giving him it was the only way to open it. To find out what it was, and why everyone seemed eager to kill each other over it.

At that moment, Cecerie became animated. Hale took cover as she cast a wave of electricity across the hall. It cracked off the wall behind Hale's head, and she barrel-rolled out of the way of falling rocks. Escudero shoulder tackled Cecerie out of the air, and she crumpled under his weight.

"Run!" she screamed at Hale from beneath his clutches. "Run, Lana! I'll hold him off." Her purple irises flashed hazel, as if she was fighting Escudero's possession.

Hale scrambled over the rubble to save her but was buffeted out of the way by Esmeralda as the ceiling caved in directly above. Avoiding another rockslide, Hale watched Esmeralda spring onto Escudero's back. Cecerie ripped free from his weakened clutches as both pirates wrestled amidst the debris. Seeing Escudero withdraw his machete, Hale made to intervene again, as more of the building fell. She dragged Cecerie out of harm's way instead, shoving her towards the hole in the wall.

"Leave her! We have to get out of here," Cecerie said, as Hale doubled back.

The floor shifted beneath her. She watched Escudero and Esmeralda tumble clear as another piece of the ancient ceiling caved in. They got back to their feet, their weapons clashing as they duelled. Esmeralda dual-wielded her daggers, swinging them in a skilful pattern that took Escudero unawares. Using speed to combat his brute strength, she ducked his wild swing, cutting open one of his arms.

Hale was blind to what happened next as she dived aside, sucking up her legs before a falling stone column crushed them. Cecerie screamed and became rigid as magic was forced out of her. Esmeralda's scream joined hers and, thinking the worst, Hale searched for her in the wreckage. She finally located her, barely recognisable beneath the dust, staring at a patch on the ground shaped like Escudero, who was nowhere to be found.

Esmeralda slashed at the ground, over and over until Hale restrained her. She ushered Esmeralda to what they hoped was the exit, and they sprinted after Cecerie, who was a few yards ahead. Esmeralda stooped to pick up the tabernacle.

"Just leave it," Hale said.

"No way!"

Knowing it was a two-person job, Hale shoved Cecerie onwards and ran back to help. Together, she and Esmeralda jogged awkwardly through the tunnel, sharing the weight of the treasure. The tunnel closed behind them, and they were forced to stop running as the path split into three.

Hale panicked. "Which is the exit?"

"You're asking me?"

Rumbling increased in volume and water started leaking through the ceiling at an alarming pace. Wind was whistling down the tunnel to their right, making Hale's mind up. She ran that way, encouraging Esmeralda to follow. They didn't make it more than a few metres before getting swept off their feet in a surge of water. The tabernacle slipped from Hale's arms as more water burst through the surrounding earth, flushing them out of the cave at inescapable velocity.

TWISTED

Hale's stomach lurched as she was spat out the end of the tunnel. Her split-second scream was hampered as she splashed into a rock pool below, her momentum carrying her all the way to the bottom. She caught glimpses of trees overhead as the muddy waterfall continued to batter her. Using her last gasp of air, she dragged herself to the surface with tired arms, inhaling at the first opportunity.

The continuous downpour forced her back under, and water flooded her ears. Stones continued plummeting like hailstones and she swam through the pool with heavy strokes, resurfacing when she was far enough away from the plunge. Exhausted, she sank under again, unable to pull herself out.

Someone grabbed her, hauling her onto the bank, and she flopped onto her back upon the grass.

"You ok?" Cecerie's face appeared above hers. "Goddess above! How did we escape that one?"

Hale coughed up a lungful of water, and Cecerie assisted her, tilting her on her side so she didn't choke. Disoriented, Hale spotted the dented tabernacle through blurry vision. A few metres away, its doors had cracked, leaving a scattered trail of corundum in the valley. Spluttering, she crawled around the water's edge, seeing no movement in the depths. *Where are you? Esmeralda, where are you?*

A faint moan sounded from the surrounding forest.

"Ceci, over here!" Hale yelled.

Cecerie helped her to her feet, and they staggered through the mud into the clearing.

"There!" Cecerie pointed to a flattened section of tall grass.

They rounded a large rock to find Esmeralda's body nestled between the greenery. Esmeralda's arm was twisted up her back. Her left ankle was bent at an unnatural angle. She wasn't moving. Hale sank to her knees beside her.

"Es?" She turned her over. "Es, t-talk to me."

Esmeralda remained unconscious.

"No," Hale whimpered. "No. Don't be dead." She stroked Esmeralda's hair. "Open your eyes!"

Cecerie checked her pulse. She shook her head.

Hale's gasp became dry heaves, too overcome to shed tears. She buried her face in Esmeralda's lifeless body, clutching the lapels of the admiral's coat. *This can't be real.* She was vaguely aware of Cecerie's hand squeezing her shoulder as she tried and failed to breathe, her chest tightening with each attempt. *No. You're not dead. We're fine.* She whacked Esmeralda's body with her fist.

Esmeralda suddenly came to, coughing up blood. Stunned, Hale withdrew. She quickly assisted Esmeralda into the recovery position as Esmeralda started retching, sweeping away stringy remnants from her mouth and nose. Cecerie raised her into a seated position, and Esmeralda keeled sidewards into Hale.

"You're ok," Hale reassured, hugging her. "You're ok." She kissed the top of her head and breathed a sigh of relief, staring up at the heavens. "Ceci?"

Cecerie took over comforting her while Hale repositioned herself to better inspect Esmeralda's injuries. She focused on the ankle dislocation, sickened to find the broken bone had pierced the skin. Luckily, she had set bones in the past, patching up Freebooters during the war. Cecerie started channelling magic in her palm to seal the open wound on Esmeralda's temple, but Hale stopped her.

"No. It's too risky."

"But—"

"You're not yourself," Hale said. "After that cave-in I don't want you using anymore sorcery until you know you are able to control it."

Cecerie let the magic burn out. She cradled Esmeralda's head and kissed her hair, compassionate even amidst her own torture. It killed Hale not being able to trust her own sister, but there would be time for apologies later. She refocused on Esmeralda's mangled foot that was twisted one-hundred-and-eighty degrees the wrong way. Clasping it in both hands, she counted. "One, two—"

"No count," Esmeralda moaned.

"It was more for me to prepare, than you."

"*Ay*, just do it already!"

Without further delay, Hale twisted her foot back into place, with Esmeralda's screams echoing long after she passed out.

A flock of birds left the surrounding trees. Hale exhaled, taking in the scenery. This forest had more life than the previous one. On another day, she might have found it peaceful.

She placed Esmeralda's leg back on the ground and left her in Cecerie's care, taking long strides through the hip-height grass, entering a thicket of trees. It took several minutes for her to find dry wood to use as splints and a potential crutch. By the time she carried them back, Esmeralda had woken, still resting in Cecerie's embrace.

"Show me your arm," Hale said.

Esmeralda shook her head, cradling it, trembling from head to toe. Hale prised the injured arm free to better inspect it. Realising she wouldn't be able to undress Esmeralda without causing her further agony, Hale took off her own coat and removed her shirt, wearing only her drenched bralette. She ripped the hem of the shirt into shreds and used the fabric to tie a stick to either side of Esmeralda's forearm, where she assumed the break had occurred. Esmeralda let out a trail of curse words as she yanked the restraints to tighten them. Using the remains of her shirt, Hale created a sling, wrapping it around Esmeralda's neck. Cecerie assisted her arm into it then raised Esmeralda to her feet. Hale picked up the third, much longer stick she'd found and gave it to her for support.

Through her pain, Esmeralda smirked. "You're good at that."

Hale laughed, relieved that she could speak even if her voice was weak. "N-Next time you dive, don't miss the pool."

"Next time you strip, don't stop halfway."

The three of them laughed, releasing some of the tension. Hale put her coat back on, checking Viperidae was still safe in her pocket. How many more sacrifices would they have to make to get it home?

As Esmeralda and Cecerie talked, she located the broken tabernacle, picking up any loose corundum scattered along the ground. She lifted it into her arms, shivering as its coldness touched her bare abdomen.

"Holy shit." She clenched her teeth and carried it back to the others. "We need to find the ship fast. I d-don't know how long I can carry this."

Esmeralda scanned their surroundings. She gestured for Cecerie to check her pockets, producing the map of Sailor's Creek that was miraculously still folded there. Hugging her crutch so it didn't fall, Esmeralda shook out the damp parchment, and Cecerie helped her unfold it, holding it for her to see.

"I think we are here at the X," Esmeralda said. "This is the real entrance to Sailor's Creek. The one we should have taken."

"Then why didn't we?" Hale asked.

Esmeralda made a face. "You try sailing through thick fog."

So, she didn't know where she was going. Hale wasn't surprised. "Can we get back to the ship from here?"

Esmeralda stared at the horizon but she could barely hold her head up. "It shouldn't be too far to the shore. Let's get moving, uh?"

"Wh-What about Escudero?"

Cecerie met Hale's eyes. "He's back in Anferan. He forced me to send him back before we escaped the cave. I couldn't stop it." She looked close to tears.

"It's alright," Hale said. "At least we know he isn't chasing us." She smiled, hoping to reassure her. "We got what we came for. Viperidae's safe. Let's just focus on getting home."

As Cecerie and Esmeralda began the trip to the shore, Hale

glanced back up at the hole in the mountainside, triggered by something Escudero had said. *He's the latest person she stabbed in the back.* Watching Esmeralda limping ahead of her, she wondered. *Could Esmeralda really have known Felix?* Deciding to bury it for now, Hale readjusted her weight to get a better grip on the loot. She fell into step behind Esmeralda and Cecerie, not taking her eyes off either of them until they reached the shore.

*

When they finally reached the archipelago's edge, Hale's pocket watch told her it had only been an hour. *Must have stopped working in the water.* Exhausted, she sat on the cliff beside Esmeralda and Cecerie, who dangled her feet over the edge. Her back ached. Esmeralda waved her crutch to attract the attention of The Eider's Cry which was floating nearby.

"They can't see you through the fog," Hale said, surprised that she had to point it out. "We need something to draw their attention. Got any matches?"

"Not any dry ones."

Hale remembered the case of cigarillos she'd stolen from her victim earlier. She withdrew the small leather case, taking out one of the thin cigarillos lined on one side, and the loose matches wedged in the other. She struck a match behind Esmeralda's ear.

"Ey!" Esmeralda complained.

"Annoying, isn't it?" Hale said, lighting the cigarillo, taking a puff. She put it between Esmeralda's lips and lit herself another, striking behind Cecerie's ear this time.

"Ah!"

"You're drier," Hale said, taking a puff. "Got any alcohol, Es?"

"Now is not the time for a tipple, sweetness."

"I need something to help burn the crutch."

"Forget it," Esmeralda said, the cigarillo dangling from her mouth. She continued waving at The Eider's Cry in desperation. Knowing she was holding out on her, Hale slid her hand up the inside of Esmeralda's leg. "Ey!" Esmeralda jerked away, but not before Hale felt the canteen strapped to her inner thigh.

"Don't think I won't go in there for it," she warned her.

Esmeralda gave in. After a second of rustling down her slacks, she withdrew the tiniest of canteens.

Hale grinned. "Any more surprises down there?"

"Why don't you see for yourself?"

Cecerie groaned. "Can you two not? I'm sitting right here."

Hale laughed. "Don't worry, sis. It's probably just more of Hedge's finest."

Ignoring Esmeralda's protests, she doused the crutch in whatever potent beverage Esmeralda had smuggled all this way. When she stubbed out her lit cigarillo on it, the end of the stick ignited. The fire finally sparked to life, and she waved it until they had attracted the ship's attention.

When The Eider's Cry rotated towards them, Hale shoved the lit crutch into the grass and relaxed. She took one of the fairies from her tiny jar and whispered a message.

"Where did you get those?" Esmeralda asked.

Hale freed her fairy into the sky, watching it disappear. "Walter. He's been keeping me updated on Anferan since we left. Just telling him we're on our way back. He told me Maven is out for our heads and the Sovereigns are still hunting for me around town."

"I wasn't aware you two were keeping in touch."

Hale raised an eyebrow. "That a problem?"

Esmeralda didn't reply. She smoked the last of her cigarillo and flicked it over the cliff's edge.

With nothing to do but wait, Hale tore up some blades of grass, sprinkling them into the sea, still wondering how to confront Esmeralda about Felix. Recognising the grass from sketched images in one of Maven's books, she pocketed some of it, realising it was sphagnum moss, a plant found in swampy areas with numerous healing qualities. She glanced at Esmeralda's leg, noting the dark bloodstain around her ankle. Without asking, she squeezed some of the moss to expend its water and stacked the wound's makeshift dressing with as much of it as she could. The fact that Esmeralda didn't react was worrying. She tried to rouse her but Esmeralda lay semi-conscious, babbling incoherently. *We have to get her back before infection sets in.*

The Eider's Cry loomed closer, coming into focus through the fog. Hale recognised Ximo's silhouette climbing into the raft. *So, he made it.* Although she didn't know him well, Ximo had grown on her. He seemed to be the only person besides her who was interested in Cecerie as a person, speaking about her like she was human rather than some dangerous weapon ready to implode. With his sorcery expertise, he could be a valuable ally, the difference between Cecerie fearing her magic and using it for good.

Mentioning they needed to get to lower ground, Cecerie roused Esmeralda, and helped her up. They began a three-legged descent down the sandy bank, while Hale picked up the tabernacle, following them to a small beach below. She slowed to a dander as they walked across the sand, watching Cecerie toss stones into the water at Esmeralda's insistence. It was hard not to smile, watching them stumble every time they leaned down to pick up another. Cecerie's laughter was like music to Hale's ears. It was rare to see her so carefree. Something about Esmeralda drew out the mischief in people, despite whatever cruelness life had dealt them. Not wanting to miss out on a fleeting moment of joy, Hale quickened her pace to catch up.

"You know …" Esmeralda panted, having difficulty navigating her way across the uneven terrain. "The first thing I'm doing … when I get back … on the ship?"

"Drinking?" Hale guessed.

Cecerie laughed.

"You think you know me so well," Esmeralda said, smirking.

"Am I wrong?"

"Well, no. But that's not the point."

They halted where the shallow tide trickled over their toes, watching Ximo row the tiny boat aground. Hale placed the tabernacle down onto the sand, giving her arms some respite.

"Alright. What *are* you g-going to do?"

Esmeralda sat down on the sand, pulling Cecerie down with her. "Sleep," she whispered, resting her head on Cecerie's shoulder.

Hale chuckled. "I was expecting something a bit more exciting."

"Well, if you join me … it might be." She winked at her.

Hale flushed. The idea of being afraid of such a thing was laughable, but she wasn't sure she was capable of lying next to Esmeralda for an entire night, especially since discovering her potential secret. She tried to enjoy the last few moments of peace until Ximo got them. *There will be time for disagreements later.*

He splashed into the shallow water, striding towards them. "Well, don't you three look like shit?" He ruffled Cecerie's hair with a huge smile. "*Hola,* Little Sparkler! Good to see you finally awake."

"Er, who are you?" Cecerie asked, frowning up at him. The others laughed, remembering she had been unconscious, and they hadn't been officially introduced. As Cecerie and Ximo got acquainted, Esmeralda coaxed Hale into helping her up. Reluctantly, Hale obliged, and they limped towards the raft.

"Are you testing my haphephobia again?" she asked, as Esmeralda put her arm around her shoulder.

Esmeralda hummed softly. "Maybe. Or perhaps I am just using you as a crutch."

Hale chuckled. "People warned me you were a self-serving pirate. I never learn," she teased, feigning offence. She slid her arm around Esmeralda's waist, guiding her into the raft as best she could. Esmeralda winced, and Hale climbed in beside her as they waited for the others to catch up. Breathless, Esmeralda nestled into her.

"Is this ok?" she whispered.

Knowing Esmeralda was in more pain than she was, Hale nodded, resting her chin on Esmeralda's head, hugging her tighter. She was surprisingly clammy. As much as it was uncomfortable being this close, she couldn't deny it was nice having someone to hold. Hale was glad when the others caught up, eager to get back on the ship.

Ximo dropped the tabernacle into the raft and helped Cecerie in. He climbed in after her, and rowed them out to sea, where The Eider's Cry was swaying majestically in wait. As soon as they were close, Jakson tossed a hawser over the side that Ximo scooped out of the water. He tethered it to the raft, knotting it around a small metallic loop. Hale did the same with another cable, tying it to the back to keep it steady. The ocean was calm as Jakson lowered a rope ladder down the side of the ship for them to climb. Cecerie went first, ignoring the rope entirely and projecting herself and Esmeralda upwards in a flash of amethyst smoke. Ximo marvelled at her magic, but Hale was unimpressed. *If she was determined to use it, could she not have transported Esmeralda earlier?* It worried her how cavalier Cecerie was acting with something so unpredictable and volatile.

"After you," Ximo said, gesturing to the rope.

By the time Hale reached the top, her energy was spent. She cringed as the men pulled her aboard, and she rolled onto the deck, lying there until she was able to catch her breath. She spotted Cecerie sitting far from the crew, all of whom were wary of her lack of shackles. Her veins had shrunk back beyond the neckline of her shawl, and her eyes had returned to their usual hazel. By all intents and purposes, she was healthy. It was this alone that made Hale quash her disapproval and hug her, hoping the gesture said what she could not.

"I'm fine," Cecerie promised, pleasantly surprised by her affection.

Hale hunkered in front of her. She teared up as she stared up into Cecerie's face. "Are you sure?" She was gaunt, with eyes ringed worse than before.

Cecerie nodded. "I'm just tired. Ximo promised to give me another sedative so I can get some rest."

Hale caressed her cheek. "I love you, you know."

"Maybe you're the one who needs a sedative," Cecerie said. Hale laughed. "You should go help Esmeralda. I'm fine."

Esmeralda was busy bickering with Ximo, beating him away

as he tried to help her. The crew cheered as she invited them to split the treasure, and she limped over to where Hale and Cecerie were sitting. She placed a kiss on either of Cecerie's cheeks. "You ok, sweetness?"

"You both need to stop your fussing," she joked. "I can't remember much, but ... thank you. If Ximo hadn't sedated me, I doubt I'd have had the strength to fight off Escudero in that cave."

Esmeralda winked at her. "That's my girl. Why don't you head downstairs for some rest, uh? I need to take your sister somewhere private."

Hale blushed and Cecerie giggled. She set off towards the hold. "No more magic," Hale warned her. Cecerie merely waved in response.

"Cute kid," Esmeralda said, staring after her.

When she was sure they couldn't be overheard, Hale confronted her. "You have some explaining to do."

Esmeralda sighed. "Not here."

She gestured for her to follow, and Hale got up, allowing Esmeralda to lean on her. They bypassed Ximo who was guarding the tabernacle from Fidel and Figaro. Hale opened the latch to Esmeralda's cabin, and Esmeralda descended first with difficulty. As Hale descended behind her, she recalled the first time she had entered Esmeralda's cabin, suffering a wave of shame. *I hope this time doesn't end in bloodshed.*

She lit the lantern on the wall at Esmeralda's instruction and stared around the cabin. The piles of scrolls on the desk had gotten bigger. She wondered where Esmeralda got her intel. As they reached the bed, Hale took pity on Esmeralda, untying her sling, helping her pry off the wet coat. Esmeralda sank onto the foot of the bed, cradling her swollen arm.

Hale hunkered to her level. "C-Can I see?" She gestured to her arm, but Esmeralda ignored her.

"Just ask me whatever it is that you need to," she replied.

Hale shook her head. She hadn't yet found the words, and she wasn't sure Esmeralda was up for it. At her silent insistence, Esmeralda lay back on the bed, allowing her to remove the rest of her clothes. She covered her face with her good arm as if not wanting Hale to see how much pain she was in.

"There's a first aid kit in the top drawer," she said, voice muffled in the crook of her elbow.

Hale retrieved it. She took off her coat, hanging both hers and Esmeralda's on a hook on the back of the door. When she got back to the bed, Esmeralda was shining with sweat. Hale unbuttoned the tiny pouch of medical supplies. Clearing away the makeshift bandages and moss around Esmeralda's ankle, she cleaned the compound fracture, surprised Esmeralda had made it this far in such high spirits. *The adrenaline must be wearing off now.* She dressed the ankle as delicately as she could with some fresh bandaging, manoeuvring Esmeralda up the bed, resting her back against the headboard.

"Nightcap?" Hale suggested, knowing it was the only thing that would give her some relief. She grabbed the decanter and two glasses and brought them to the nightstand. Sitting on the bed, she poured them both a generous helping and rested back against the headboard beside her.

"*Salud.*" Esmeralda toasted weakly, clinking her glass off Hale's. She necked it, holding it out for another, and Hale topped the next one to the brim. Shivering, Esmeralda rested her head on Hale's shoulder, causing Hale's skin to burn hotter than the whiskey. In that moment, Hale was very aware that her upper half was only covered by a damp bralette.

"You've been lying to me," Hale finally said, eager to distract them both with conversation. Unfortunately, this was the only topic she could think of.

"Yes," Esmeralda whispered.

It was the answer Hale had been expecting, but it still kicked her in the teeth. "You knew Felix, didn't you? Before you met me?"

Esmeralda took another sip. "I met him during exile in Ortivana. Did some odd jobs for him, here and there."

"H-How come I never met you?"

"It wasn't Freebooter work. Assassinations, mainly.

Assaults. He was determined I never cross your path, in fact, and that was the best way to do it."

Hale drank more whiskey. "There's more to it."

"There is always more to everything if you look hard enough."

"But you *are* hiding something else from me." She tamed her anger. "Aren't you?"

Esmeralda raised her head. "I am," she admitted, drawing closer. She stretched over Hale and put her empty glass on the nightstand. Her face hovered inches from Hale's, whose heart hammered in anticipation, waiting for an answer. "*Te quiero,*" Esmeralda finally whispered, staring deep into her eye. "*Me odio por quererte, pero no sé cómo parar antes de hacerte daño.*"

Hale was stunned. "I ... d-don't know what that means."

"Don't you?" Esmeralda asked softly.

Hale swallowed. She could practically taste her, so close that their breaths merged. This time, Esmeralda didn't help her. She waited, tempting Hale to manage it on her own. It was an internal battle, one Hale desperately wanted to win. She inched towards her. Struggling for a moment, their lips finally touched, and every question or doubt she had ever had about Esmeralda, shot right out of her mind.

LA VERDAD AT LAST

Diosa mía ...

Esmeralda had never waited that long for a kiss, but when it came, it was better than she could have hoped. She touched Hale's cheek, giving her some gentle encouragement, surprised she was able to overcome her haphephobia. When Hale didn't pull away, she grew optimistic, tracing down along her neck, brushing across the strap of her bralette, sliding it aside. Before she could slip it off, Hale broke away.

"Stop."

"Ok," Esmeralda whispered, refraining from going any further. Their faces lingered together, as if Hale didn't want to retreat fully; so close, yet so far, clinging to any form of intimacy that didn't involve triggering her phobia. Esmeralda swept a loose lock of hair that was still damp behind her ear. "Is this alright?" Hale nodded, and Esmeralda stroked her cheek, careful not to startle her. "Are you ever going to tell me why you're like this?"

Hale's sigh tickled her face. "Why are *you* afraid of water?"

Esmeralda traced her scarred jawline. "I almost drowned once. Well, someone tried to drown me." She had never wanted to talk about it, but she could give Hale some truths to make up for the one she couldn't tell her. The one that would change everything. She was losing her regardless, so what was the difference? Why spoil this wondrous moment with more lies?

"Who?" Hale asked.

"Escudero." Esmeralda fought the urge to be sick at saying his name. She rued that he had escaped her again, after waiting so long to find him. "He took a shine to me, many years ago. I had something he wanted."

"What was it?"

Esmeralda ignored the question. If she answered, then she would have to tell her how she lost it, and that story was why she over-drank, over-smoked, and overdid everything.

"He chased me across Na'Revas," she continued. "The third time he caught up with me, on the docks in Coutoreál, I was ambushed, and we fought on the beach." She rested her forehead against Hale's, the weight of her past taking its toll. "The scars on my back are from his blades. He dragged me into the water and," she swallowed, "held me under."

Recalling the taste of saline, her tongue became dry. "Next thing I remember was waking up in the sand. Escudero was gone and so was what he stole from me. I had not heard from him in many years; not until I started working for Felix and found out they were in bed together." She cringed even thinking about it, how Felix had played her; made her kill in Escudero's name. She wished Hale hadn't asked her to relive the horror, but she had asked her to do the same. "That is my story. Your turn."

Rather than encourage her, Hale grew more reluctant. She withdrew from Esmeralda entirely, lying on her side, turning away. "I don't remember what happened to me."

"Hale, it is nothing to be ashamed of."

"It wasn't like that," Hale replied quickly, as if not wanting her to get the wrong idea. "I know that's what everyone always presumes but I'm certain of that at least. The Sovereigns would never touch an Ortivanian peasant in that manner. I just … just …"

Esmeralda stroked her arm. "Hale, it's ok."

"I don't remember. It's like my memory has been erased somehow."

"You don't remember anything at all?"

She exhaled, hugging her body's shakes. "I r-remember waking in my cell after torture one day. I could tell it was morning as the amethyst sun sh-shone through a crack in the ceiling. There were deep lashes across my back. Blood gushing down. Merta, the old lady in the next cell, had made a habit of checking on me. This particular time, she stroked my cheek, and ..." Hale tensed. "It burned, like pouring scalding water into an open wound. She touched my arm, and I screamed. She touched my leg, and I kicked. From then on, after every torture session, we would play card games instead. If I responded, she knew I was ok. When I won a game, she would leave me to rest."

Esmeralda wished there was something she could do to help; wished Hale would look at her. Suddenly, she understood Hale's reluctance to talk about it aloud. "You don't want to remember, do you?"

"What difference will it make?"

"All the difference. To you. Not to me." When Hale remained silent, Esmeralda tried a different approach, tracing the burn marks along her side, wondering if sustaining them was what had triggered Hale's phobia. "You want to know why I always touch you? Take your hand. Brush your arm. Even when I know it hurts?"

At this, Hale leaned back. She seemed to want to know everything but give nothing away herself. To anyone else it might have been infuriating, but Esmeralda understood such reluctance. She knew Hale had often wondered the answer to this particular question, to the point where Esmeralda's constant triggering of her phobia would one day annoy her enough to ask it.

"You were a mess when I found you in Ortivana. You had shut the world out. I worried that if no one pushed you to feel something other than pain that you would never learn to cope." She stroked Hale's hair. "You would revert, further and further, into yourself, shutting out everyone who cares about you. But shutting out the world is never an answer, sweetness, however easier that may seem at the time."

She watched Hale's tears fill and, unable to help herself, leaned down to kiss her again. This time, Hale didn't pull away. Their bodies met as Esmeralda leaned her weight upon her, unable to rest on her broken arm. She sank into Hale's warmth and, for the first time since she had met her, didn't feel like she was causing her harm.

*

December, Year 4132
Three Months Later

Anferan's shores finally teased on the horizon, exciting Hale. They were a day or so away, and she couldn't wait to show Mother her share of the tabernacle treasure, wondering where they would choose to buy a home. *Betraying Maven surely means we are no longer welcome guests in her tavern.*

She glanced back at the helm towards Esmeralda, hoping that would mean they spent less time drinking. Esmeralda's alcohol intake had increased since her injuries, and Hale wondered what was in that special bottle that Ximo always brewed specifically for her. Noticing her staring, Esmeralda smiled at her. Hale mirrored it before turning back towards the sea.

Every time Esmeralda looked at her, she felt apprehensive, as if the first good thing to happen to her since as long as she could remember was about to disappear. They spent most nights together, patrolling the deck while everyone was asleep. Esmeralda's injuries meant she was incapable of doing a shift alone like she preferred. In the morning, Hale would sometimes accompany her back to her cabin, but she always left before Esmeralda woke, fearing that her recurring nightmares would be a topic for conversation. Yet for all the times she had screamed Lucian's name aloud, Esmeralda hadn't mentioned it. It was comforting sharing a warm bed with her, instead of sleeping in the hold with the rest of the crew.

On nights that she didn't spend with Esmeralda, Hale visited the private cabin that had been set up for Cecerie in the cannon room. It was a prison, but a voluntary one which Cecerie had insisted upon for everyone's protection. If she ever felt like she was losing control, she could chain herself to the bed. Only Esmeralda had the key, ensuring her safety from the rest of the crew. Despite this, Cecerie was the happiest Hale remembered. They talked often, reminiscing about their childhood and hilarious times with Lucian. They both missed Ortivana's black market. Cecerie regretted never tasting Ortivanian wine, having been too young at the time. Hale promised to find a bottle for her someday, wondering if Esmeralda's friend, Hedge, could procure some. It had finally started to feel like everything was falling into place for the first time since leaving Ortivana.

Thinking of her last visit to Cecerie, Hale touched where Viperidae was still safely nestled in her pocket. It refused to budge no matter what Cecerie tried. If a magical bloodline was key, then it must be some kind of ritual they hadn't learnt. This didn't stop Cecerie from cutting herself and watching droplets of her blood splash off the snake engraving. To her dismay, it remained an old slab; pretty and smooth, if nothing else. Throwing it at the wall hadn't helped either.

Retracting her view from the horizon, Hale climbed up the mast to the crow's nest, taking over watch from Figaro. She twisted the bronze spyglass he passed her, focusing on the immediate vicinity, hooking her elbows over the edge of the giant bucket she sat in. The ship's sway was impossible to ignore up here, and the first few times she had taken the job, she'd thrown up over the side. Fidel hadn't been too impressed, considering it landed on him. *And laughing at him didn't exactly help my cause.* She was convinced the old man would get her back in some way, so staying out of his way seemed smart.

The gentle sway of this morning's calmer waters made it easier to enjoy the view. She zoomed in on the amethyst patch of sky that veered off to the left, apparent even though Ortivana was many miles to the west. She couldn't see it from here, thanks to the haze of Everlasting Rain, and wondered if this was why Ortivana didn't get many visitors to its shores. It was hard to anticipate an island with such unpredictable weather. Most ships ended up wreckages along the shore. *Unless they were The Eider's Cry, of course.*

She glanced back at the aft, towards the helm. Steering one-armed and bow-legged hadn't deterred Esmeralda from sailing. Using the wheel as a crutch, she directed the ship through open waters, still skilled, if a little off balance. It was nearly the end of her shift. She seemed exhausted. She had gotten more tan during their months at sea, but leaner despite their impressive food supply after raiding a merchant ship a few weeks back. Despite a healthy complexion, Hale suspected Esmeralda was anxious about something. She often referred back to their conversation, that first night after Sailor's Creek, wondering why Esmeralda had been so open and honest.

There had been no further talk of Felix. Hale was sure that Esmeralda regretted not telling her the truth. Things would never be simple between them, but Hale couldn't keep her distance anymore. Whatever Esmeralda was, she felt something for her that couldn't be explained. Frankly, she didn't want an explanation. It was comforting to discover that she could feel this way about someone again. *Good to know that my desire to be close to someone hasn't been totally beaten out of me.*

She loved Esmeralda for coaxing her out of her shell, even if it didn't always work in the way she hoped. Although Esmeralda's wildness still scared her, having someone committed enough to break down every wall she put up, to find the person she was underneath the trauma, made Hale eager to push through the ache. Being forthcoming wasn't in either of their natures. It was sure to be the reason they'd implode. For Hale, this would be nothing new, for nothing in her world ever lasted.

"*Hola, cariño.*"

She jumped, retracting the spyglass. Esmeralda had finished her shift and climbed into the crow's nest. "You shouldn't be up here."

Esmeralda snorted, sitting beside her. "*Tranquila,* I'm fine." She extended her arms. "May I?" Hale nodded, allowing her to cuddle her to combat the breeze. Touching her was becoming more familiar; easier to deal with. She rested her head on Esmeralda's shoulder, and they elevated their legs over the edge of the crow's nest. "I was about to go to bed, but Figaro told me your shift had started, so I thought I would pay you a visit before turning in."

"And scare me half to death, as usual," Hale said. "You really shouldn't be climbing on those injuries." She felt Esmeralda's silent chuckle. "I mean it, Es."

"Ah, you worry too much."

Hale bit back a retort, concentrating on Esmeralda's breaths to counteract the urge to break free. Her head was spinning the opposite way the ship was wavering, disorientating her further. She raised her head, staring up into the wind, begging it to cool her skin. Esmeralda touched her cheek, tilting it to face her, and placed a gentle kiss on her lips. "I just wanted to do that before going to sleep," she said. "I can see you are uncomfortable. I will leave you be."

Hale stopped her from getting up. "M-Maybe stay a minute."

Esmeralda settled back down, sitting side by side, instead of embracing this time. Together, they stared up at the sky, watching the first sign of clouds come into view. "You still find it strange? The blueness?"

"No," Hale said lightly, crossing her arms. "This is what Ortivana should be like. Her purple skies are just scarred by magic."

"Maybe she will again, one day."

"I like to think so," Hale said, smiling.

"Ooh, is that a speck of optimism?"

Hale laughed. "It's been known to happen. I used to be a 'look on the bright side' kind of person."

"I believe you. It's just nice, seeing some of the darkness lift."

"Well, you might be to blame."

Esmeralda chuckled. "I'll take the credit."

Their conversation died out as the wind continued to whistle around them. Hale peeked out over the side with her spyglass, taking a quick scan for any danger. Seeing none, she rested back in the nest. "We're almost home," she said, breaking the peaceful silence.

"Mm." Esmeralda sounded half asleep. "What will you do about Maven?"

Hale folded her arms again, watching a flock of birds overhead flying in triangular formation. "I guess that all depends on you." Esmeralda didn't ask what she meant. Hale decided to speak about something else that had been bothering her since Sailor's Creek. "I heard a voice, Esmeralda. The closer we got to Viperidae. It was telling me to go back before Escudero arrived, like some kind of warning." Esmeralda stiffened beside her. "Did you h-hear anything like that?"

"What did it sound like?"

"A woman. Her accent was similar to yours."

Esmeralda cleared her throat. "Probably a spirit," she said, focusing on the birds. "Sailor's Creek is haunted by unimaginable things. I wouldn't worry about it too much."

Hale was unsettled by her simple reasoning.

After several minutes, a gentle snore told her Esmeralda was fast asleep. Her beautiful features wore none of the stress of the day, softer in slumber, deceptively innocent. Tired rings had materialised beneath her fluttering eyelids, and her mouth was slightly agape.

Feeling a little braver, Hale put an arm around her, allowing Esmeralda's head to loll onto her shoulder. She moaned in response but didn't wake. It was easier holding her like this. Hale was tempted to kiss the top of her head, but refrained, already pushed to her limits. The crow's nest wasn't meant for two people, but if this was to be the final moment of peace, like always, she would endure.

BEST LAID PLANS

Remembering the first time she had set eyes on Anferan, Hale was impressed with the progress she had made. She had travelled a long road in a short space of time, but that didn't make the road any less meaningful. She accepted a joint from Ximo as they rested against the ship's rail, watching the docks come into view. Little blotches of orange gradually came into focus: the native redheads darting through the marketplace.

"It is not half bad, I suppose." Ximo had been complaining about the quality of weed for the past ten minutes. "You should come to Xevería, *amiga*. We have all kinds of herb imaginable."

"For the last time, Ximo, Ortivana has the best weed. *And* we have the best wine."

His barking laugh let out a plume of smoke. "*Ay,* give me that back. You must be high as fuck." He snatched the joint after her second puff.

Hale chuckled, exhaling smoke out her nose. "Can we unlock Cecerie yet? She would love this view."

The slick greenery to the left of the marketplace was sparkling in the sunlight. Again, like at the lough she now knew was buried within the forest, Hale wondered if there truly was sorcery at play when it came to the island's wildlife. She was eager to get Cecerie's opinion.

"I don't see why not," Ximo said. "Ask Esmeralda for the key to her cabin."

Thinking Esmeralda would be asleep, Hale started to say as much, when Esmeralda called Jakson to take over the helm as they neared the docks. Surprised to find her awake, Hale made her way to the rear of the ship towards her.

"Here, Hale. Take these down into the hold." Esmeralda dumped a huge pile of cargo into Hale's arms. "Then go get Cecerie. I want her restrained, but she can come up on deck." She placed the key to Cecerie's cabin on top of the boxes. Before Hale could respond, Esmeralda had walked away, having not made eye-contact.

What was that about?

Deciding not to dwell on it, Hale rushed down into the hold, eager to free Cecerie before they got too close to the docks to be able to revel in the magnificent scenery. She dumped the cargo outside the cabin and let herself inside with the key. Cecerie was reading a battered book Walter had left behind.

"Are we there yet?" She dog-eared the page and sat up.

"Almost." Hale unhooked the chains from Cecerie's bed and Cecerie held out her hands, guessing that was where she had planned on clamping them next. "Admiral's orders. Just to make the others feel safe when you come upstairs."

"I understand," Cecerie said. Her arms sagged as the weight of the chains restrained them. "Honestly, it will be good to get out of this cabin."

"Come on. There's s-something I want to show you."

Hale took the weight off the chains so Cecerie could stand, and they made their way to the upper deck. By now, the crew were stacking cargo along it, waiting to offload once they docked. The tabernacle shone more golden than ever, reflecting the sunlight from where it was stacked atop the loot.

"Wow!" Cecerie exclaimed, watching the last of the evergreen forest on the horizon.

Hale smiled. "Knew you would like it." They leaned on the rail, watching the last of Anferan's wildness come into focus, along with the docks.

"It's so peaceful watching it from afar," Cecerie said. She rested her head on Hale's shoulder.

As they got closer to the docks, Hale stiffened. "Shit. S-Something's wrong."

Cecerie straightened. "No. Lana, it can't be." Her face

drained the last of its colour.

Hale sprinted back to the aft, bounding up the staircase. "Stop!" She told Esmeralda. "You must stop! It's an ambush!"

Esmeralda stared straight ahead. "It's the Scours," she said calmly.

"I know," Hale said, glancing at the shining silver platoon lined along the harbour in wait. "We must go back."

"I can't."

"What? Wh-What do you mean you can't? Why?"

"Fidel," Esmeralda said. "Now."

Something hard smacked the back of Hale's head, and she fell onto her knees. The second whack was harder, sending her face first into the deck, and the last sign of daylight was extinguished.

*

Wheels crushed over gravel, and Hale opened her eye, watching the ground pass beneath her. Her head was aching. Armoured footsteps plodded along on either side of her, becoming sloppy as they ascended a muddy hillside. She listened to villagers gasping as she passed, gossiping about what crime she may have committed. Feeling like she was floating a few inches from the ground, she tried to break free of her restraints, but her arms and legs were tied to the corners of some kind of torture rack. Her face was spattered with mud, and she fell limp as blood rush from her limbs, giving her pins and needles.

Eventually, the ground levelled out and became smoother, lessening the jostle on her splayed limbs. The wooden wheels of her mobile prison rolled over marble flooring, and she flinched as heavy doors slammed behind her, bringing forth a chill that reminded her of *An Caisleán*. Incense clogged her nostrils, and her vision became unfocused, mesmerized by the intricate marble floor patterns.

"*Commandante* Trevus," Esmeralda's voice sounded nearby.

Hale tried to raise her head, but her neck muscles had gone to sleep. A new set of footsteps echoed in the entrance hall.

"Admiral Rivera. We meet at last. I am pleased to find that

Escudero's descriptions of your beauty were not unjust."

"Save the pleasantries, *cabrón*. I have what you asked for. Now give me what I want so I can leave."

Trevus gave a low chuckle. "Not so fast, my dear." He neared Hale's left side, inspecting something in the wheel-rack beside hers. "Ah, Cecerie. My white whale. I have waited a long time for you."

"D-Don't touch her!" Hale snarled, struggling to see anything but the floor.

Trevus let Cecerie's chains fall. He approached the next rack, bending to Hale's level. "Ah, you have brought me a spare. Two Hale sisters for the price of one."

"No," Esmeralda replied. "You asked for Cecerie and Viperidae, that's it. Let Lana go."

"I don't think so."

Esmeralda dashed towards him, but the armoured Scours surrounded her, blocking her path. "She holds no value to you!"

Trevus got up. "On the contrary. The Sovereigns have put a huge bounty on her head, and now I plan to collect."

Esmeralda lunged again. "*¡Hijo de puta!*"

"Calm yourself, Admiral. You have done well. Let us continue this meeting in my office. Guards!" He clicked his fingers. "Bring Cecerie Hale to the lab. Lock the Child Killer in a cell and send word to Sovereign Altus in Stonawal that she has been detained. That fat bastard will drool at the mouth."

Hale moaned as they separated her from Cecerie. She listened to Esmeralda's escort fading away but could do nothing to resist her captors. They wheeled her out of the entrance hall, taking her down towards what she imagined would be dungeons. True enough, the stench of dampness greeted them below ground-level; the kind of mould that only thrived in darkness.

She face-planted the moist concrete as the Scours unhooked her from the rack, and her nose burst. She couldn't raise her arms to wipe it. When the cell door locked, panic set in. *Goddess, not this shit again.* A stone floor, anchored against her neck. Something nibbled at her toes as she lay on her side. *Rats!* This time she had the strength to kick out at them. Her tormentors squeaked as they scurried away.

Her limbs gradually rushed with warmth as her nervous system and circulation rebooted, and finally, she was able to sit up. She massaged the welt on the back of her head. *I'll kill that bastard Fidel.* It was easier to be angrier at him than Esmeralda. The latter didn't bear thinking about.

A high-pitched scream scorched her ears, and she looked for the source. *I have to get out of here.* Stemming her running nose with her sleeve, she grabbed the rusted bars of her cell, hauling herself onto unsteady legs. She staggered to the door, rattling its hinges.

"It's no use," someone said, after her third attempt.

Hale pressed her face between the bars, staring into the cell opposite hers, on the other side of the dank corridor. "Felix?"

His blond hair came into view, then his pointed face. "Well, don't you look like shit."

"No thanks to you and your lackey!" She kicked the door when it wouldn't budge. "How long has Esmeralda been in your pocket?"

"Esmeralda?" Felix started laughing.

"What's so funny?"

He shook his head, clapping in lazy applause. "Goddess above, she is relentless."

"What do you mean?" Hale asked. "Aren't you working with her?"

"If I were, do you think I would be in here?" His amusement soured, and he glared at her through the bars. He had a purple shiner ringing his left eye.

"Who gave you that? I should send them flowers."

Felix scowled. "You would be better served finding us a way out of here. Escudero and Trevus used me before I could use them. I know you don't believe me, but I was trying to keep Cecerie safe from them."

"It's not your job to keep her safe. You lost that right when you sent Lucian to his death."

"My mother's magic and blood runs through her veins. She is as much *my* sister as she is yours." He paused. "That battle currently raging for control inside Cecerie is because I insisted on enthralling her as well as Escudero, to ensure that he couldn't recklessly discard her for his own gain. We were fighting over her, but Trevus broke my connection, and now she's in danger."

"She's always in danger!" Hale snapped. She shook her head, deflating against the bars. "I don't know why Esmeralda would do this to her."

"Esmeralda is probably on Trevus' payroll. He has something she wants, you see."

"What is it?"

Felix shrugged. "She worked for Escudero in the Saristca Armada years ago, back when she was just starting out with the Swashbucklers. Their business went sour and Escudero stole something from her."

"What?"

Again, Felix shrugged. "No idea. And we're never going to find out unless we get out of here."

"We?"

"I know where Trevus' office is. If you have any hope of saving Cecerie before he gets here, then you're going to need my help."

Hale laughed. *Oh, the gall.* "You think for a s-second that I am going to trust you again?"

"You don't know Esmeralda like I do, Lana. She's made a deal with Trevus, I'm sure of it. Cecerie's life is in danger. Don't you care?"

"Don't talk to me about caring." She balled her fists, desiring nothing more than to pummel his face. "Weren't you and Escudero planning the same thing? You were all using her as a bargaining chip."

"I didn't want this! I only made them think that so that I could get close enough to protect her. I was going to take Ceci away. Like I got her away from Father's madness."

"What do you mean?"

"I killed him. Didn't Ceci tell you?"

Hale slid down the bars. She was fighting a never-ending battle. "Why?" she whimpered.

"That bastard killed my mother, then stole me and raised me as his own. He did experiments on Cecerie, his own child. When I found out what he did to her I made sure he never lived to see another day. Why do you think Aveline never liked me?"

"Because you're a treacherous leech?"

He slammed the bars. "Listen to yourself!" His frustration finally matched hers. "You have fought for peace your whole life, but for the Tripartite to end, something has to take its place. Viperidae is the only thing powerful enough to do that. It is what your father wanted. It's what my mother wanted. It is what all this has ever been about."

"Then you are no better than they were," Hale said, getting up so she could say it to his face. "Suckling at the teat of power while you sell your comrades down the river. You make me sick. I will *never* help your cause."

Their conversation was interrupted as the basement door opened. Two Scours entered and unlocked Hale's cell. She backed against the far wall, ready for a fight. There was no time to plan a perfect escape. Whoever had screamed wasn't Cecerie, but surely the real Cecerie wasn't faring much better. She pounced at the first guard, clawing away his purple hood.

"Ximo?"

Ximo gave her a sheepish grin. "Don't kill me, *amiga*. I come in peace." He eased out of her clutches and held up his hands in surrender. The other guard removed his hood too.

"Walter?" Hale exclaimed. "What are you doing here?"

"Saving ya, 'course. Esmeralda's orders."

"Esmeralda's?" Hale didn't understand.

Ximo brushed his goatee. "She owes me big time for this. Prison breaks are expensive."

Hale had no idea what he was talking about, but she didn't care for questions anymore. She pushed past them both, exiting the cell, scanning the hallway for an escape. "We need to find Cecerie."

"Wait!" Felix stretched through the bars. "Let me out. I can help you! You can't leave me here. You need me to get to Trevus' lab."

There was desperation in his eyes. Hale faltered. *Do I?* He was the only brother she had left. Without understanding why, she took his tattooed hand. He smiled, appearing much like the brother she once knew. He squeezed, and she squeezed back; tight ... tighter, enough for his smile to turn to a grimace when he realised his mistake. With a jerk, she twisted harder.

Crack!

"Aaahh! My arm! You broke my arm!"

"Did I?" She tugged him forward as hard as she could, and his forehead collided with the bars, knocking him unconscious. "Good luck, brother. I hear prison can be a bitch."

She ran down the hallway, allowing herself a laugh that surprised even her. On the inside, she was torn to shreds. *Felix murdered Father. I can't believe it.* Scour prison was far too good for him.

"You're letting him live?" Ximo asked, as he and Walter caught up.

"I am *not* a killer," she insisted.

"But you killed—"

"I know what I did, ok? I know what people think of me." She saw the accusations, even now, on both of their faces. "I didn't mean to kill him ... L-Lucian. I didn't mean it." Her voice broke, and she shook her head, ruing it for the millionth time. "I don't care if Felix deserves death. I'm not doing that twice in a lifetime."

Walter sighed. "Maybe ya're right, kid. That bastard can rot in here. Don't become a murderer just for him."

Hale was glad at least one person understood. In the basement doorway she spotted two naked, unconscious Scours. "How did you manage that?"

Ximo held up a tiny device that was still sparking an electrical current. "A taser. Silver armour is highly conductive."

"Full of magical gadgets this one," Walter said. "But my

need is greater." He took the taser from Ximo and unhooked his armour. "Here, Hale, put this on. Ximo will help ya find Ceci."

She did as she was told, allowing him to hook the silver plate armour across her body. "What are you going to do?"

He pulled up her new purple hood. "I'm taking care of yar mother. We're commandeering The Eider's Cry and getting outta here."

"You're leaving?"

"Maven's on the warpath, kid. More Sovereign platoons have landed than I've ever seen. It ain't safe here anymore. I'm done with Es. The crew ain't taking her back after this, so I'm taking command of the ship. Yar mother will be safe with me, I promise. I'll send ya a message when its safe. Now go, save yar sister. I'll wait at the docks 'til midnight, but if ya're not there by then, we ain't waiting."

The idea of abandoning another home didn't sit right, but if it meant keeping their freedom, Hale would take it. She nodded and watched Walter shuffle off. She wasn't sure she could trust him, but what choice did she have?

Her knees almost buckled with the weight of the cuirass; an odd way of reminding her they were running out of time. She had never worn heavy armour. She retrieved one of the staffs beside the unconscious guards, aware the weapon was a threat only to sorcerers, whose powers could be drained by the crystals on the end and recast back at the source. She remembered watching the Scours do it to Nyra Legat all those years ago. *Yet nothing stopped her from splitting open the sky.*

Despite her anxiety, Hale tried to focus, but her energy was at an all-time low. Escaping Oblivion Tower wouldn't be easy. Seeing Ximo already at the end of the corridor, she set off in the same direction, hoping they weren't already too late.

*

It was sweltering, as if fires raged within the tower's walls. Hale traced one as she passed, experiencing the powerful surge behind it. The stone reminded her of *An Caisleán,* only without the Ancestor's religious ornamentation. Instead, someone had carved statues of former commandants, each with their own labelled plaque. Both males and females lined the hall, all the way around the circular bend at the end, leading to a carved architrave. A staircase led upwards to the unknown.

She paused, glancing over her shoulder. "Do you know where we're going?"

Ximo nodded. Seeing no other option, Hale followed him, upwards and onwards, until her legs burned, threatening to give out.

It smells different up here.

She gagged, covering her nose, rounding another curved, nondescript hallway ahead as the stairs levelled out. The smell reminded her of her old cellmate's decomposing body. When she rounded the next bend, she froze.

Two Scours were on patrol, wandering towards them. They were larger, more rotund than the others.

"Act normal," Ximo whispered, reducing his pace.

Hale walked alongside him. The guards were twenty feet away, then ten. *This isn't going to work.* Panic took over. Noticing a door to her right, she decided to risk it and redirected Ximo inside, like this was where they were headed all along. She closed the door and pressed her back against it, listening as the patrollers continued chatting. Their voices died as they got further down the corridor.

Able to breathe again, Hale paid attention to her immediate surroundings, wondering what they had interrupted. Her stomach contracted. Rows upon rows of mysterious human-sized ... eggs? *There is no other word for it.* They were lined as far as she could see, giving off a peculiar hum. Curious, she touched one, watching the silvery substance swirl inside, the surface of which settled halfway. The eggs appeared to be plugged into various tubes that all met up at some kind of mainframe attached to the internal wall. The equipment reminded her of junk littered around Hilltown, and she wondered if Trevus had repurposed some of the Ancestor's tech for his experiments.

"This must be the lab Felix mentioned," she whispered.

"Looks like it." Ximo sounded wary, and this bothered Hale more than it should have. If he didn't know what these things were, they must have been more advanced than anything he had studied.

Stealthily, so her clumsy footsteps didn't echo, Hale traipsed along the girdled floor, peering into each egg as she passed. They were all empty. The scent of decomposition was stronger here, mixed with an overpowering chemical that Hale recalled smelling when Foric washed his glasses in the tavern. She could taste it in the back of her throat. There were windows in the lab, unlike in the hallways, as if whatever was being grown required light to thrive. Hale thought wildly of plants. *Why would someone go to all this trouble to cultivate things that grew on their own in the wild?* Plant life certainly had no problems growing in Anferan. *No. This is something more sinister.*

Turning left at the end of her row, she came face to face with Ximo, who had walked parallel on the other side. His face was shimmering eerily in the silver light. They passed ten to fifteen more sections and finally heard muffled voices, arguing from the next room.

A door at the end of the laboratory beckoned, and Hale stepped lighter, sneaking up to it. She cracked it open a centimetre, enough to see through, but found she was staring at a wall. *We have to get inside.* Knowing her heavy armour wouldn't slide through unscathed, she unclasped the cuirass, shivering as her damp clothes met the cold air. Leaving their armour in the corner but keeping their staves, she and Ximo slipped through the open door.

Hale was surprised to find more eggs on the other side. They were fewer and farther between, meaning she could listen to the ongoing argument clearly.

"This changes nothing," Escudero was saying. Hale darted around one egg and in behind another, trying to get close enough to see. It smelled different here, as if someone had tried to cover the rotting odour with a sweeter scent. She recognised the smell as Saldrasine berry. "You and I still have unfinished business."

Esmeralda's sarcastic laughter carried. "Our business ended the moment Trevus offered me this deal," she said in a sepulchral tone. "You never had what I wanted."

Hale had never heard Esmeralda so unhinged. She couldn't see what Esmeralda was gesturing to. Cursing inwardly, she rounded the second last egg and cowered behind the final one, closest to the open-plan office. With Ximo hot on her tail, they peeked out from behind it and immediately ducked. Whatever Escudero was looking at was inside the very thing they were hiding behind.

"I can't believe this is where he's been keeping her." Esmeralda sounded disgusted, analysing the contents of the egg. "I thought you wanted her for yourself, Escudero, but like most Swashbucklers, you just wanted to sell her to the highest bidder."

"After he had his way with her, of course." The third voice belonged to Trevus.

Hale heard a slap and imagined Escudero was rubbing his cheek right about now. Her fingers were sweating on the staff; a staff she so desperately wanted to beat him over the head with. She peeked out again and noticed this time that someone was lying stationary on the ground between Escudero and Esmeralda. The black shawl was instantly recognisable.

Cecerie!

Hale grasped the staff harder, struggling to be patient now. As she was about to exit her hiding place, Commandant Trevus spoke again.

"Enough. Admiral Rivera, you have proven your worth. As have you, Escudero."

"And what about what I want?" Esmeralda said. "Like I said, I couldn't care less about your pathetic grab for power."

Trevus gestured to the egg. "As you wish. She is all yours, as promised."

There was movement within the egg's mechanics. Something was suctioning through the tubes. Hale backed away, and Ximo darted behind another, predicting they were about to be discovered. Before Hale could find another hiding place, the egg dropped from its holder, smashing on the slated steel floor. As the remainder of the transparent liquid leaked through the grates, Esmeralda dashed to the aid of whatever had spilled out of it. Exposed, Hale looked up to see Escudero and Trevus.

"Ah," Trevus said, sounding displeased. "I should have known you would worm your way free. It seems no prison can contain you."

Wanting to keep Ximo's presence hidden, Hale straightened to her full height. Shaking, she clutched the staff tighter and rounded the egg's obsidian mechanics. She stepped over various tubes into the centre of the office. Curious, despite her fear, she stared down at what had been inside. Esmeralda was cradling a naked girl in her arms. She had a pale but youthful face, resembling someone who had recently drowned. The veins streaking across her body were chrome rather than purple. Esmeralda patted her cheeks, trying to wake her, but the young woman remained unresponsive; dead as dead could be.

Hale turned to Trevus. "I'm h-here for Cecerie," she said, fighting to keep her voice even. Her legs were shaking, betraying how frightened she was. The scent of rot had escaped the egg along with the dying girl. Hale was struggling to ignore it. She wished she was more confident, but it had been a long time since she had faced down a Tripartite leader, and she wasn't anywhere near as equipped as she should be. *I just need to get Cecerie out alive.*

Trevus grinned. "I am afraid that is not possible, Ms Hale. You see, Esmeralda has agreed to trade Cecerie for—"

"Stop!" Esmeralda interjected. "Don't you dare say her name." She hugged the unconscious girl tighter, rocking her back and forth. "You tricked me." She traced the girl's hair. "Come ... Come on, sweetness, wake up. *¡Despierta!* It's over." Hale didn't understand the rest as she switched languages completely.

Seeing she was distracted, Trevus clicked his fingers, and Escudero pounced. He wrestled the staff from Hale's grip, and she shrivelled as he beat her with it repeatedly. He had Viperidae in his other hand. Esmeralda was shouting over her own cries, and Hale counted the whacks in her head, just like she had in prison. When she was down and unable to resist, Escudero ceased.

Paralysed, her body pulsed where each of his blows had connected. Escudero stood guard, acting as a buffer between her and Trevus. A free shot at any Tripartite leader was worth dying for, but she couldn't tempt herself to try. Trevus hauled Cecerie along the floor towards one of the other eggs that still contained the substance. Hale tried to get up, but Escudero's knee collided with her jaw. Her body finally gave up. She had no more fight left in her. One last cry from Esmeralda sounded in her ears, before her mind shut down and she blacked out.

Wait ...

She wasn't unconscious. The office had succumbed to sudden darkness with thick smoke rising towards the ceiling. Escudero was screaming on the ground beside her and another cry she could only assume was Trevus echoed nearby. Where Cecerie had lain was now a patch of purple fire, emanating incredible energy.

Hale followed the upwards trail as the flames licked the toes of a floating body. Cecerie was perched in the air, her skin covered in ruptures, showing shockingly hollow insides.

EVERLASTING RAIN

Hale had never envisioned the true extent of her sister's powers, but watching Cecerie manipulating the elements brought back memories of when she was a child. She felt like she was eleven years old again, standing in Ortiva City with Father. *Only this time I'm not watching the sorcerer burn.*

Despite her injuries, Hale staggered to her feet, hurtling straight at Cecerie. She tackled her out of the air as purple flames singed the dangling ends of Cecerie's shawl. Cecerie wailed as she hit the floor, deafeningly, like she was possessed. Hale cowered over her, protecting her from the Everlasting Rain which she knew from her childhood was a silent killer.

"A day will come." Cecerie's multi-voice words failed as she wrestled with her, sparking with amethyst lightning. *"Tar Amach."*

Escudero and Trevus were howling, burning in a pit of their own flames. Esmeralda was still crying over the unknown dead girl, with Ximo trying to pry her away. Cecerie continued to struggle, and Hale was thankful for the gaps in the grates so that the permanent downpour wouldn't pool around them. It was already hard enough trying to pin Cecerie's arms above her head.

"Ceci, it's me," she panted. "Stop. P-Please. Stop!" Fire scorched her arms, and it was all she could do to hold on. Her skin was cooking from the inside out. "Ceci, please. Calm down. *Tar Amach.*"

She had no idea what made her say it, but Cecerie ceased fighting at the words. Her necromancer voices evolved into a cursed whisper, continuing long after she had stopped.

Oblivion Tower imploded, showering them in glass as the windows shattered simultaneously. Wind swept into the lab as chunks of the outer wall broke away, and the foundations moved beneath them, releasing each of the empty eggs. The Everlasting Rain continued to ooze between the cracks, requiring no clouds to hold it. Breathless and drenched, Hale stared down at Cecerie pinned beneath her. The fire had extinguished. She wasn't struggling anymore.

"Ceci?" She patted her cheeks. "Wake up."

Cecerie was still.

No. You can't be dead.

She begged for someone, anyone, to help her. Escudero was dead. Trevus was a few metres away, shrivelled into a pugilistic charcoal horror. Esmeralda was still kneeling a short distance away, oblivious to the world's end. Ximo's attempts to pry her from the dead girl were falling on deaf ears.

"Switch," Hale ordered, leaving Cecerie and dragging Ximo away. She shoved him towards her sister, then sank onto her knees beside Esmeralda. "Es? Es! Look at me."

Esmeralda's gut-wrenching sobs continued to tear from the back of her throat, and up close, Hale finally understood why. No word was powerful enough. No mere sentence could explain. Tears funnelled down her own face as she stared, open-mouthed, at what Esmeralda was hugging.

The young girl's body was deteriorating rapidly; sinew slipping off bone, like chunks of suspect meat that attracted flies on market stalls at day's end. Her ribs jutted through her necrotic skin. As Esmeralda hugged her tighter, more of her organs splayed onto the floor. Hale had never seen anything so repulsive. She couldn't look away no matter how hard she tried.

The tower continued to collapse around them. Knowing they didn't have much time to escape, Hale kicked into survival mode. Hating herself, she forcefully detached Esmeralda from the girl, but Esmeralda refused to let go. Hale cradled Esmeralda's sodden face. "We have to go," she said calmly. "Now, Es. Come on. I've got you."

Something behind Esmeralda's eyes told her she had gotten through at last. Her bloodied hand slipped into Hale's burnt one, and Hale was able to guide her to her feet, just as a huge piece of the ceiling caved in above. She pushed Esmeralda out of harm's way and dived on top of her. When the dust settled, she helped them back to their feet.

By now, Ximo had scooped Cecerie into his arms. "I've got her," he told Hale. "Follow me. I know the way out."

Another piece of the ceiling fell, and they darted for the exit, back through the open doorway that no longer existed. Their boots rattled along the metal floor as they rushed back towards the staircase, thankful it was still intact.

With each level they descended, Hale's body waned. *I have to make it. Can't stop now.* Her burns were superficial and limited to her hands and wrists. *Nothing a salve won't fix.* She tried not to worry about Cecerie. She tried not to think about Escudero, or the dead girl Esmeralda had been grieving over. Trevus' death was the only thing she couldn't block out. *One dead Tripartite leader,* she couldn't help thinking. It shouldn't have satisfied her this much, but it did. *How many people has that cretin drained in those eggs?* She tried not to picture what he had been planning for Cecerie as they passed frantic Scours on every staircase. It wasn't until they reached the collapsed entrance hall that the guards became aware of who they were.

"Stop them!" one of the uninjured ordered.

Those who could rally gave chase. Hale barged Esmeralda through a door to her left, much like the one on the upper levels. The room it led to was cloaked in choking debris, reminding her of the day Lucian had died. *Not now. Not now.* There were too many parallels for her to avoid. The explosions. The tailing guards. The screaming. *Goddess, the screaming!* She shook herself back to the present. This was not the time to get lost in memories. Cecerie's life depended on her being sane. *That's if she's even still alive.*

Hale tripped over an overturned chair as the exit appeared through the smoke. Falling, she lost sense of where she was, until Esmeralda pulled her from the rubble. She watched

Esmeralda kick open the locked, heavy double doors. They ran outside, immediately stilted as they faltered on the edge of a collapsing cliff. Overlooking the docks, they could see various lit lanterns and golden ships offloading platoons.

"Sovereigns!" Hale shrieked.

They scanned the Everlasting Rain for signs of Ximo, who was already carrying Cecerie down the forest lane leading towards the slums. Esmeralda dragged Hale down the hill, and they ran as fast as they could, trying to outrun the invading soldiers.

Nearing The Busted Cherry, every street was full of people watching Oblivion Tower collapse in the distance. Some people cheered, while others were disturbed, wondering aloud about the number of deaths. What remained of the Scours and the Sovereign investigators stood guard on each street corner, but thanks to Esmeralda they were able to remain incognito. Hale hadn't realised how many alleyways the slums held, but Esmeralda knew damn near every one of them. When they finally set eyes on the brothel, Ximo was waiting for them in the doorway.

"Quickly!" He ushered them inside, locking the door with a deadbolt. He and Esmeralda argued in Xeverían as he carried Cecerie upstairs.

Hale leaned against the door and slid down it, unable to stay upright any longer. She sat there for Goddess knew how long, listening to her heartbeat. Although her burns weren't serious, they still stung. An elderly courtesan took pity on her. Helping her up, she led her upstairs to a room at the far end of the scarlet hallway. Any other night Hale would have been amused by the suggestive portraits in thick golden frames, but right now she only had thoughts for Cecerie. Before she knew it, she was sitting on a sofa in a fancy suite, staring at a table filled with various baggies of weed. She looked to her left, to where Cecerie was being tended to on the four-poster bed by Ximo.

"H-How's she doing?" Hale asked, getting to her feet, wondering when she had even sat down. Someone had removed Cecerie's shawl and replaced it with a pale pink, silk nightdress. It was harrowing to look inside her severed skin and see nothing, neither purple nor crimson.

"She is comatose," Ximo said. "I cannot wake her."

"But she's alive?"

"I think so. Yes." His hands were shaking as he began pipetting strange liquid from a small brown vial, squeezing droplets onto her open wounds. He then rubbed a salve across to create the illusion of skin. Hale watched in amazement as he rubbed the same salve on her own burns, and the roaring red skin turn pale and cool.

"Thanks," she said, relieved. Her body still hurt from where Escudero had hit her, but the ache had been dulled by adrenaline.

"I have heard of magic like this, but never treated it." Ximo sat on the corner of the bed and, using some kind of pliers, snipped away the flaps of Cecerie's skin which had ruptured beyond repair. "Magnificent!"

"What? Get away from her!"

Ximo held up his tools as Hale grabbed the scruff of his collar. "Ey, I am helping her." He untangled from her grip. "This can be hard to watch, but I have to finish trimming the burnt flesh. Trust me. She is in the best possible care." When Hale didn't appear placated, he glanced across the suite towards the open balcony, where the light curtains were floating in the breeze. "Go speak with Es, uh? Let me work on her alone. It is better this way. Trust me, *amiga*."

Hale didn't much feel like leaving Cecerie's side to interact with someone who had just betrayed her. Then she remembered the rotting corpse Esmeralda had been crying over, and curiosity temporarily outweighed her anger. With one last lamenting look at Cecerie, she left Ximo to finish and hobbled out onto the balcony.

Esmeralda was standing with her back to her. The sound of the sliding door closing made her glance over her shoulder. Seeing Hale, she turned back towards the night, watching the ruins of Oblivion still aflame in the distance. Horns sounded around them, and numerous soldiers trampled through the streets below.

"Should you really be out here?" Hale asked, leaning on the low wall beside her. The pitter-patter of Everlasting Rain on the overhead canopy was oddly relaxing, reminding Hale of home.

Esmeralda cupped a glass of wine in her trembling, blood-soaked hands. She was covered in a thick layer of dust like Hale and Ximo, but she somehow looked even more worse for wear. She took a healthy sip, with an audible swallow.

"It's too dark for them to spot us up here," she replied. "We will hide until morning so that Cecerie can be treated. Ximo has a plan to smuggle us onto a ship."

"With Walter?"

Esmeralda shook her head. "That ship has sailed. Literally." She snorted softly. "Cannot say I blame him. He never condoned my plan."

"He knew?" Hale watched as another piece of the tower collapsed. It was oddly beautiful, fire. From a safe distance, she could admire it, despite the destruction. Seeing the Scour capital collapse should have brought her great joy, but all she felt was a dull, sickening ache. "Why?" she whispered, struggling to put her pain into words. "Why did you do it, Esmeralda?"

"Desperation."

Hale knew she deserved more than a one-word answer. "D-Don't give me that," she whispered. "Just ... don't." The full magnitude of Esmeralda's betrayal overcame her, and she took a deep breath, willing herself not to break down. "You s-sold ..." She could barely utter the words. "You sold my sister to the Scours! How could you?"

Esmeralda riled from her state of subdued shock. "Do you think I wanted this?" she snapped. "To do to you what I had done to me, all those years ago? They stole my sister from me!"

"Your sister?" Hale repeated, taken aback.

The wine glass slid from Esmeralda's grip, falling over the balcony. She clamped her mouth, backing away from the edge, and slid onto the wooden chair in the corner. Her body convulsed, and Hale realised she was sobbing, shocked to see it twice in one evening.

Unsure of what to do, she sat down on the vacant chair beside her. She considered comforting her, then remembered what she had done, and the urge to help dissipated. She glanced into the suite to where Cecerie lay, broken, thanks to Esmeralda's selfishness.

"You could have told me," Hale said, grasping the chair handles in lieu of wringing Esmeralda's neck. "You should have."

"I know. But I was scared."

"Don't give me that!"

"What do you want me to say?" Esmeralda asked. Her face was shining with tears, making fresh streamlines down her dirty face. "That I failed her? That I failed you? The Scours harvested her, Hale. They drained her to the end of her …" Esmeralda's words ran out of steam.

It was agonising listening to the distress in her voice, so much so that Hale wasn't sure how to respond. Part of her wanted to hit Esmeralda; the other part wanted to relate. She wasn't sure which part she wanted to listen to. Unable to form a response, and unwilling to watch Esmeralda fall apart, she got up and walked back inside.

Ximo was gone. She sank to her knees by Cecerie's bedside, taking her hand, startled by how cold she was. *Come on, Ceci. Wake up!* She buried her face in the blankets, blotting her tears before they fell. Esmeralda sniffled as she entered the suite behind her, sliding the balcony door shut to block out the wind.

Neither of them spoke for a time. Hale listened to Esmeralda's attempts to light a fire in the grate. When she finally let Cecerie rest, she found Esmeralda sitting in front of the fireplace in a trance. Her back was to her, but Hale could tell Esmeralda's tears hadn't ceased. Knowing she had to hear her out, Hale filled them both a glass of wine from the drinks trolley, bringing it to her on the settee.

Esmeralda accepted without looking at it, clasping it like she had the other. Her gaze didn't break from the flames. Hale watched them flicker in her eyes. "You have questions."

"Of course, I do," Hale said softly. She took a sip, surprised to discover the wine was Ortivanian. "But n-nothing you could say right now will ever make up for what you did."

A fresh tear leaked from the corner of Esmeralda's eye and her jaw trembled. She met Hale's glare. "You got your sister back, Hale. You got her back, and I have *nothing*. So don't sit there, accusing me of being another two-bit slave trader, when you would have done the same damn thing in my position."

Hale clenched her fist, but couldn't hit her, no matter how much she may have deserved it. Esmeralda's face was already contorted with more agony than any punch could ever inflict. Hale imagined if the situation was reversed. Would she trade someone's life for Cecerie's? *Is Esmeralda right? Would I do the same?* She had always protected Cecerie, but it never seemed to be enough. What she saw when she looked at Esmeralda wasn't hatred, but a mirror of her own failures. It was that same regret she felt when Cecerie suffered at the cruelty of others, when she had failed her, over and over.

"I didn't plan on betraying you," Esmeralda continued, as if desperate to make her understand. "But once the voice started talking to me again, I knew I didn't have much time."

"The voice? What are you talking about?"

"The voice in my head," Esmeralda explained. "Her voice. Elena."

Ximo poked his head through the door to the adjoining suite. "Sorry for interrupting," he said as they both jumped. "I just wanted to let you know before I go to bed, Hale. Ceci is stable. I have stemmed any blood and fluid leaking from the wounds, and she's no longer hypovolemic. Honestly, I am pretty optimistic."

"Thanks," Hale said, relieved. *Finally, something resembling good news.*

"I left a first aid kit on the fireplace for you. Get those wounds treated then get some sleep. The Swashbucklers are departing Anferan after the arrival of the Sovereigns. I have arranged a deal with the Blue Shield Souzas. A ship will take us from here in the morning." He left the suite, snapping the door shut.

The sound of Everlasting Rain had lessened to a gentle storm, and the night became unexpectedly tranquil. Hale watched Esmeralda refill the wine glass, resuming her staring contest with the fire. Her eyes gave the impression they were melting. The image of her squeezing the dark-haired girl into a bloody mess was a powerful enough image for Hale to feel an unexpected pang of sympathy. She guessed Esmeralda was still in shock. After some hesitation, she stretched across the settee and touched Esmeralda's arm, stopping her from drinking anymore. The glass paused, halfway to her lips. Finally, she put it down. It was the first time Hale had seen her refuse a drink.

Esmeralda turned away. "I shouldn't have done it," she said, sounding ashamed.

"What drove you to?"

It was a simple question, but Esmeralda didn't reply. Predicting what was about to happen, Hale caught her as heaving sobs ravaged her again. The more Esmeralda tried to hold her grief in, the more it fought its way out. She resisted Hale's comforting arm, but Hale knew she wasn't used to being consoled. Gradually Esmeralda settled, burying her face in Hale's chest, and Hale leaned back against the cushion as a wave of exhaustion overcame her. Her skin should have been burning, but it wasn't. There was no urge to withdraw. No urge to push Esmeralda away in revulsion; to flinch or escape from her as usual. Like their day in the lough, the two of them were exposed, both facing their phobias together. *Only this time we're afraid of the same thing.*

"W-Why didn't you tell me you had a sister?" The cruel punch of using the past tense hurt Esmeralda anew.

"I don't talk about her," Esmeralda said. "She was gentle and kind. Nothing like me." Talking about who Elena was seemed to be giving her strength. "You remember I told you Escudero drowned me? Well, that was the day he found her.

He had been chasing us for years. I thought he wanted Elena for himself, but he sold her to Trevus like all the rest."

"To fuel Oblivion," Hale said. She remembered the eggs, disgusted. "And she ... Elena ... still speaks with you? Spoke," she corrected, cringing again.

Esmeralda picked dried blood from her nails. "She has been in my head since the day I lost her. I always thought it was because I blamed myself, you know?" Hale nodded, understanding that guilt. "That is how Trevus eventually offered me the deal. He discovered Elena had been communicating with me. He wanted Cecerie, and he knew you would stop Felix from getting Viperidae, so he convinced me to steal both from under you in ..."

"In exchange for Elena's freedom," Hale finished for her, finally piecing it together. "It was Elena who spoke to me in Sailor's Creek, wasn't it?"

"Yes." Esmeralda raised her head. "She was unhappy that I had taken the deal."

"She kept telling me to turn back." Hale shook her head. "Damn, I sh-should have listened."

She glanced back at Cecerie. Trevus must have been planning to replace Elena's waning powers with hers. *Where will it end for the sorcerers?* The Scours had once burned them at the stake, just like the Ancestors witch-hunts. Hale could never understand it. *Why is humankind so afraid of a figment of birth? Why must they kill or abuse what they cannot understand?* An endless parade of questions tormented her, and a sickness squirmed in her stomach that always did when violence came before understanding.

By now, Esmeralda had straightened up and was rubbing her skin raw to no avail. *I could have been doing the same with Cecerie's blood.* The sick thought prompted Hale to hug Esmeralda, really hug her, despite everything she had done. They may have fought the world differently, but their struggles were parallel. Their roles could be so easily reversed. Hale wondered if this is what lay in her future as she clutched Esmeralda's broken frame.

The fire was reduced to cinders by the time either of them spoke again.

"*Lo siento.*" Esmeralda's voice was thick with emotion.

"I know," Hale whispered, guessing she was sorry. She kissed the top of Esmeralda's head, lingering in her hair. That familiar scent wafted up her nostrils, mixed with dust from the debris.

"I am sorry," Esmeralda whispered again, as if saying it in one language wasn't enough.

Hale wasn't sure what else to say. She glanced towards a steaming bath at the far end of the suite that she hadn't noticed before now. *Ximo must have arranged it before he left.* Her own fingernails were caked in Elena's blood, and she couldn't help but think if it had been Cecerie's, would she really want to soak in it all night?

She got up, leading Esmeralda over to the tub. As soon as Esmeralda understood, she resisted.

"It will help," Hale promised. "Look at me. L-Look at what I am doing."

Esmeralda stared down at their interlocked hands. "Water is the last thing I want to be around."

"I understand." Hale saw the turmoil in her eyes. "But a bath won't hurt, even if it runs a little red. Escudero is dead, Es. He died a painful death."

"That's not going to undo what he did."

"No, but it will allow you sleep a little easier. And so will cleaning off Elena's blood. I'm sure she wouldn't want to be remembered this way." Esmeralda's reluctance waned, but she still didn't move. Hale imagined she was waiting for Elena's voice in her head to say it was ok, but it never came. "Trust me," Hale whispered.

Finally, she gave in. Hale helped her undress, peeling the stained vest over her head, and Esmeralda shivered, leaning on her as she bent over to help her out of her slacks. When she stood, they locked eyes. The storm brewing outside was nothing to the one thundering in Hale's chest. Esmeralda's betrayal had cut deep. As much as she understood why she felt trading Cecerie for Elena was her only option, it wasn't an easy thing to forgive. Some might have left her to fend for herself, but that wouldn't help either of them now. She assisted Esmeralda into the tub, and they froze, watching the water run red.

Blood seeped off Esmeralda's legs, circling, contaminating the tub. She clutched Hale tighter as renewed reluctance took over. Hale encouraged her to sit, and she sank onto her bottom, curling her knees up under her chin. Shock was etched across her face as Hale picked up a floating sponge, rubbing it along her shoulder blades, watching trickles of scarlet streak down her back. There were two large scars running the length of Esmeralda' spine, alongside the one she had once noticed peeking over the top of her dress in the Council of Commissioners. There was so much of Esmeralda she hadn't yet explored, having been afraid to do so before.

As she washed the remains of Elena away, Hale realised Esmeralda had suffered enough. They both had. They needed relief. Whether that would be in the morning, when they left Anferan for good, or in a year's time on another island, she wasn't sure. She wasn't sure of much anymore, except the road to forgiveness was long.

When the water had turned cold, Esmeralda looked at her, breaking out of her reverie. Hale tucked a lock of hair behind her ear, her hand lingering on her cheek. In that moment she was certain of one thing; trauma wasn't the only thing bringing them together.

Unsure of what to do next, she kissed Esmeralda, reassuring her. Escudero was dead, as was Trevus, with Felix likely buried along with Viperidae. He was slippery enough to survive such a disaster, but tonight Hale would take small comforts. Tonight, she would dig deep for Esmeralda's sake. Tonight, she had no urge to leave her side.

EPILOGUE

The pirate island of Puerto Libre was an odd place to hide, but it had proven more peaceful than Hale could have imagined. With clean beaches and golden sand, she dreamt she was back home in Ortivana, only here the sky was blue, and it never Rained. The sun had finally given her skin some colour, meaning she no longer resembled a walking corpse. She lay splayed on the sand in nothing but her smalls, face tilted towards the sky, listening to seagulls fighting overhead. It was hard to believe that only a few weeks ago, she was fearing for her life in Anferan.

"I brought you some watermelon," Ximo said, rousing her from her daze.

She sat up, taking a slice. Its juices ooze down her chin at the first bite. Ximo sat down beside her, and together they gazed out at the sparkling sea. In the distance, Esmeralda was walking barefoot around the tide's edge, wearing a red sundress, her long black hair fluttering in the breeze. She looked less like a pirate than Hale had ever seen; a natural beauty unsullied by Swashbuckler grime and no longer armed for war.

"How is she doing?" she asked Ximo.

"Hard to tell." He wiped his mouth before helping himself to another slice of watermelon. "She's still not awake but she's muttering in her sleep, so I guess that's progress. Still hasn't said anything coherent."

"I meant Esmeralda, not Cecerie."

"Oh." Ximo chuckled. "*No lo sé.* I was going to ask you the same thing."

Hale sighed, watching the end of Esmeralda's dress get soaked in the incoming tide. She noticed Esmeralda tense and release when the tide went back out. "It's like she's l-lost all the fight she had in her. I don't think I've ever seen her so subdued."

"She's lost everything," Ximo said. "Elena. Walter. Her ship ... You."

Hale stared at him. "She hasn't lost me."

"Does *she* know that?"

Hale groaned. "It's complicated." She threw the rind of her watermelon to the birds, watching the gulls swoop down upon it. "I don't know how to forgive her, Ximo."

"*Amiga,* she never meant to hurt you."

"And yet she gave it her best try anyway."

Ximo puffed. "I've known Esmeralda longer than anyone. She's impulsive and reckless, and unfortunately her friends and family are usually collateral. She grew up a lot after Elena was taken from her, but she's not perfect. There's no reasoning with her when it comes to Elena. That guilt of having lost her, it ate her alive for so many years, so when Trevus dangled Elena's freedom in front of her, she did what she always does; dived in headfirst and people got hurt."

"But you're saying I should forgive her anyway?"

"Not right away," Ximo said. "But the two of you have barely spoken the last few weeks. It's New Year's Eve. At least let her know that she has a chance at forgiveness, uh? If not for her sake, then for mine. I cannot watch my dearest friend punish herself again for hurting someone else she truly loves."

He got to his feet and squeezed Hale's shoulder, leaving her to her thoughts. Hale watched him retreat to their chalet. She turned back to the sea, taking in Esmeralda's silhouette. The admiral was shielding from the sun, staring out at the horizon. Before Hale got up to join her, a small fairy hovered in front of her.

"Walter!" She allowed the fairy to whisper Walter's latest message in her ear and watched its ashes fall onto the sand. Getting to her feet, she followed the lone footprints leading out to where Esmeralda stood.

The warm water was comforting as it trickled along Hale's ankles and her feet sank a few centimetres into the sand. Hearing her disturb the water, Esmeralda turned around, flashing her a familiar crooked grin.

"Ey," she greeted her.

"Hey," Hale replied. Esmeralda's eyes were soft and ringed red. "I'm s-surprised to find you out here of all places."

They stood side by side, staring out at the ocean.

Esmeralda exhaled. "It's too quiet back there. I keep reliving it all."

Blindly, Hale reached for Esmeralda's hand, squeezing it. "Well, I may have some news to take your mind off it." Esmeralda looked at her. "I just received a message from Walter. He and my mother are fine, sailing to the Cuatro Isles with the rest of the crew. They're not docking in Ortivana, obviously, but Walter has a friend in Milagros, the next island over. They'll stay there for a while."

Esmeralda exhaled. "That's good to hear. I am glad they are alright." She hesitated a moment. "Did he mention me at all?"

Hale nodded, smiling. "He said 'Tell that bastarding admiral she owes me a pint next time I see her, and I'll give her back the keys to her blasted ship'."

Esmeralda chuckled. "*Cabrón.*" Her amber eyes sparkled with tears as she stared back out at the horizon. The happiness on her face didn't last long. "To tell you the truth, Hale, I'm not sure I want the ship back."

"What? Why?"

"I only became a pirate to escape Xevería and provide for my sister." She grimaced, reliving Elena's demise. "It was the only option at the time. A way to not just survive, but really live. To see the world. To make something of ourselves. But Elena never liked what it turned me into. Truthfully, I don't either."

Hale touched Esmeralda's cheek, prompting her to look at her. "If that's what you want, then that's ok, but before you decide, you might want to hear the rest of Walter's message."

She paused, hoping this wouldn't add to Esmeralda's woes. "He still has contacts in Anferan. They've reported that F-Felix is still alive, and he and Maven have somehow managed to find Viperidae amidst the rubble."

Esmeralda's fingers tightened around Hale's. "*Mierda.* What are we going to do?"

"Nothing yet," Hale said. "As long as we have Cecerie, they can't use it. We need to find out what it is, but with the Scours and Sovereigns hunting us …" She shivered. "We're safe for now, but we may have to leave Puerto Libre soon. We must keep Cecerie hidden."

Esmeralda leaned her forehead against Hale's. "I promise I won't let them take her."

"Hey," Hale soothed, shocked by the intensity in her voice. She touched Esmeralda's waist, stroking the soft fabric of her dress. "I know you won't."

"Do you trust me?"

Hale leaned in to kiss her but hesitated before their lips met. She shook her head. Remembering what Ximo had said, she tried to put her emotions into words. "I still can't forgive you for what you did, Esmeralda," she whispered. "But I'm not s-saying that I never will."

She felt tears leaking down Esmeralda's cheek. After a sigh of relief, Esmeralda's lips found hers, kissing her as if it would be the last time. *It very well might be.* Hale's head went light. She wished she could kiss her back with the same vigour, but her heart still ached with betrayal, despite what Esmeralda awakened inside her. She leaned into the kiss, nonetheless, finding it impossible to ignore her feelings in that moment. The last few weeks of not speaking to Esmeralda had been hell. The next few weeks would be worse.

When they parted, Esmeralda smiled, and Hale was glad to see that some of the pain etched across her face had lifted. Truthfully, her own woes had temporarily been swept aside.

"You taste like watermelon," Esmeralda muttered, holding her close.

Hale sniggered. "Blame Ximo."

They broke apart as Ximo's yelling from the top of the beach interrupted the first private moment they'd shared in weeks. He was running towards them, punching the air like a madman. Unable to hear him over the rush of the ocean, Hale and Esmeralda ran towards him, worried something else had gone wrong. When they got close enough, they deciphered his screams.

"She's awake! She's awake!"

When he reached them, he grabbed them in a bear hug, knocking both of them senseless.

"Ximo, calm down," Esmeralda said, laughing.

"I cannot believe it! *Eureka!* She's awake! Talking and smiling and … *Ay! Madre mía.* All my hard work!" He held his head. "I thought it was hopeless." He swept back his curly hair, staring at them wide-eyed. "Come on, Hale! Esme! You've got to see her!"

Together, they ran up the beach towards the chalet. Hale had never been so excited, but her legs became heavier the closer they got. She faltered, coming to a halt. Realising she had stopped, Esmeralda stopped too.

"What's the matter?" she asked, walking back towards her. She caught her as Hale sank onto the sand. "Ey," Esmeralda soothed, hugging her. "It's ok. You did it."

"S-She's alive?"

Esmeralda laughed, withdrawing so that she could take Hale's face in her hands. "She's alive, *cariño*. You did it. You saved her." She kissed Hale and helped her to her feet, taking her hand. "Come on. Your sister is waiting."

Everlasting Rain

Everlasting Rain

BOOK CLUB QUESTIONS

1. What are some of the book's main themes? Did they resonate with you?
2. How do you think Esmeralda felt about Cecerie?
3. Do you think Esmeralda's ends justified her means?
4. What was the most difficult thing Hale had to face in the book? Why?
5. Who is your favourite character and why?
6. What do you think Viperidae is?
7. Why do you think Esmeralda and Maven clash?
8. What is your opinion of Hale's mother? Was she too harsh on Hale or not harsh enough?
9. What do you think motivates Felix?
10. Where do you see the characters a year from now?

Everlasting Rain